"GET AWAY FROM ME, MY LORD, ELSE I SHALL KILL YE!"

As the blade flashed in Isabella's hand, the Earl's yellow eyes narrowed. "So the rose *does* have thorns," he purred, his voice silky and low, "and wouldst see me murdered before surrendering her virtue." He stalked toward her. "Are ye so sure I would have to take ye by force, my lady?"

He laughed again as she blushed hotly, confused at his nearness and at the violent pounding of her heart. Her fingers, which now held the dagger at his throat, trembled. With a swift movement he knocked the knife from her grasp and pinioned her arms behind her back roughly so that she was pressed against his chest. He caught her hair painfully with one hand, twisting her face up to his.

"My lord, please," Isabella gasped, "ye are my warden. Surely the King did not give ye leave to trifle with an innocent maid."

The Earl's eyes glinted oddly at that, filling with cold amusement, anger, and yet a sudden, hot desire as well. He found the girl's nearness aroused him, and the sense of power he felt at knowing she was helpless against him filled him with a strange thrill of triumph besides. He tightened his steely hold upon her possessively.

"Where ye are concerned," he told her, "Edward has given me every liberty. His Grace has decided ye would make me an excellent wife."

"Rebecca Brandewyne, with the pen of a quality writer, has once again given readers a book they will long remember...a dynamite plot, a sizzling love story, an excellent read." —*Affaire de Coeur*

Also by
<small>REBECCA BRANDEWYNE</small>

No Gentle Love

Forever My Love

Love, Cherish Me

And Gold Was Ours

Published by
WARNER BOOKS

Rebecca Brandewyne

Rose of Rapture

WARNER BOOKS

A Warner Communications Company

For my photographer, Howard Eastwood,
and his wife, Donna,
who always make me look so good in pictures;
and
For Barbra Wren and Barbara Keenan,
dear friends and special ladies.

WARNER BOOKS EDITION

Copyright © 1984 by Rebecca Brandewyne
All rights reserved.

Warner Books, Inc.
666 Fifth Avenue
New York, N.Y. 10103

 A Warner Communications Company

Printed in the United States of America

First Printing, Mass Market Edition: May, 1985

10 9 8 7 6 5 4 3 2 1

The Players

AT RUSHDEN

Lady Isabella Ashley of Rushden, a noblewoman

Lord Giles Ashley, Earl of Rushden; brother to Lady Isabella

Lord Perceival Renfred, Earl of Oadby; warden to Lady Isabella and Lord Rushden

Lady Beatrice Biggs, Countess of Shrewton; mistress to Lord Oadby

Maude, a villager

Jocelyn, daughter of Maude

AT HAWKHURST

Lord Warrick (Waerwic) ap Tremayne, Earl of Hawkhurst; bastard son of Lord James Tremayne (deceased)

His Half Brothers:

Lord Madog ap Bryn-Dyfed of Gwendraeth, legitimate son of Lord Bryn-Dyfed of Gwendraeth (deceased)

Sir Caerllywel ap Powys, bastard son of Lord Powys

Sir Emrys ap Newyddllyn, bastard son of Lord Newyddllyn

Lady Hwyelis uerch Owein, their mother

AT ST. SAVIOUR-ON-THE-LAKE

Lord Lionel Valeureux, heir of St. Saviour-on-the-Lake; later, Earl of St. Saviour-on-the-Lake

Lady Gilliane Beaumaris of Devizes, bethrothed to Lord Lionel

AT COURT

King Edward IV (by usurpation) of England

Queen Elizabeth (née Woodville), widow of Sir John Grey; wife to King Edward IV

Princess Elizabeth, eldest daughter of King Edward IV and Queen Elizabeth; later, wife to King Henry VII

His Grace the Duke of Gloucester, Richard Plantagenet; brother to King Edward IV; later, King Richard III (by usurpation) of England

Her Grace the Duchess of Gloucester, Anne (née Neville); wife to His Grace the Duke of Gloucester, Richard Plantagenet; later, Queen Anne

Lord Harry Tewdwr (Henry Tudor), called the Tydder; wrongfully known as the Earl of Richmond; son of Lady Margaret Stanley by her first husband, Lord Edmund Tewdwr (deceased); later, King Henry VII (by usurpation) of England

Lady Margaret Stanley, Baroness Stanley; wrongfully known as Lady Margaret Beaufort, Countess of Richmond; mother of Lord Harry Tewdwr; wife to Lord Thomas Stanley; later, Countess of Derby

Lord Thomas Stanley, Baron Stanley, called the Fox; third husband to Lady Margaret Stanley; later, Earl of Derby

His Grace the Duke of Buckingham, Henry (Harry) Stafford; nephew, by marriage, of Lady Margaret Stanley through her second husband, Sir Henry Stafford (deceased)

Lord Dante da Forenza, *Conte di Montecatini*; Italian ambassador to England

Contents

Rose of Rapture

The weathered granite stones stood up
Like obelisks
Against the summer sky.
The names of those
Who slept beneath the windswept moors
Were faded now
With time.

Still, sometimes, she fancied
She could hear their voices yet.

It was not the gently stirring breeze
That sent the tall grass rippling,
But the plaintive sighs of those she'd known—
And loved—
Whispering faintly in her ear.
It was not the rain that fell,
But the tears of those long dead.

She did not seek them out,
But still, sometimes, they haunted her.

The villagers watched her lonely sojourns
And thought her fey,
That solitary figure
With the hawk upon her shoulder.
They shook their heads silently when she passed
And crossed themselves,
Murmuring a quiet prayer for her soul.

And she—she walked on with her ghosts,
Remembering the days of roses and rapture.

BOOK ONE

*Against
the
Summer
Sky*

Chapter One

The Moors, England, 1490

SOMETIMES, IF ISABELLA CLOSED HER EYES AND TRIED very hard, she could still see the solid, grey stone towers of Grasmere etched against the pale blue curtain of a summer sky. High above the gossamer wisps that were the serene white clouds, the sun would be shining with yellow warmth; and like prisms, the diamond-shaped, lead-glass windows of the house, struck just so by the bright rays, would be reflecting a thousand dancing rainbows upon the gently sloping lawn. Trellises of roses, the white roses that climbed the manor walls, would be in full bloom; and Isabella would be running, breathless with laughter, across the sweet, newly mown green grass.

That was how she wished to remember it, as it had been during her youth, when the winds of war—and love—had not yet touched her. But always, the sight of Grasmere burned and blackened, an empty shell of its former splendor, crept in to spoil the cherished memory.

She too had changed. Bittersweet wounds had left her heart and soul forever scarred.

There were dark doors in her past that would remain closed, though the footsteps of her thoughts sometimes led her to stand before them. There were places to which she would never return, though she'd once held a fondness for them in her heart: Rushden, her brother's keep, and Grasmere especially. Ghosts haunted her in those places: careless, laughing faces and dark, brooding ones; faces she had loved. For her, they did not lie buried in the graveyards, though she could see the names and dates of some chiseled into the weathered granite stones, fading even now. Nor were the others gone, though she knew some lay in unmarked ditches, hastily dug, then filled again.

No, those who had lived and loved so passionately were with her always: but especially, they lingered in those places of her past.

There were other places, of course, where the memories haunted her; and these Isabella could not escape. Westminster was one. There, like faded tapestries, shadowed figures of old moved before her eyes and played out their lives as though they were real and lived and breathed once more. In the pageantry of her mind, she knelt again at Court before the feet of kings and queens: Edward, of the three suns, who had outshone them all until his rich indulgence had taken its toll on him, exacting a price that had cost England dearly. But Ned had not known that. He had been cold in his grave by then, leaving only the memory of his handsome but dissipated face, filled with drunken laughter at some merry jest told by his raucous mistress Jane Shore—and disdainfully ignored by his queen, Elizabeth. Beautiful, mysterious Bess Woodville, who had schemed her way to the Crown. The King's Grey Mare, they'd called her, she, who had moved with the haughty grace of Mélusine and whose cold laughter had rippled like the silver strands of a mountain stream. It was said she was mad now, shut up in a convent with naught but Edward's bastard daughter Grace to attend her. Isabella shuddered at the thought, knowing even the highest could be dragged down to the depths of hell. Aye, Bess had reaped the harvest she had sown with her plots and her ambition, her hatred of Richard.

Richard. Dear Richard, whom Isabella had loved so fiercely and fought for with such unwavering devotion, understanding the man and believing in him, though others had not. Even now, historians dipped their pens into their inkwells to forever blot his character. She had read their words and longed to cry out fervently against them.

Nay! A thousand times nay! He was no hunchback, as their ill-drawn caricatures portrayed, no ugly dwarf, no deformed monster. Such tales were false and cruel! True, he was no golden god, like most of the Plantagenets, but a dark, somber youth, who paid for his passions with his life. Aye, one shoulder was slightly more developed than the other from swinging his heavy battle-ax, but except for that, he would have looked like any other man. He was the best of men—and kings. He should have lived.

But Richard had been slain in battle at Market Bosworth, and Henry had taken his place. Cold, calculating Henry, who ought to have died instead—

Nay, 'twas treason to think such thoughts, Isabella reminded herself sharply.

God would punish her, as some said that God had punished Richard, taking from him the beloved shadow at his side, sweet Anne, cut off in the bloom of her youth. Isabella had sat by the Queen's sickbed, had held Anne's trembling hand in hers, and—so that Richard might be spared the knowledge—had concealed the handkerchiefs that had come away spotted with blood from the Queen's lips and lungs. At Anne's death, the light of Richard's life had forever darkened. Aye, Richard had been dead long before Market Bosworth, long before Henry had come to wrest the Crown from his grasp.

Henry, the upstart Tydder, who had married Edward's daughter Elizabeth; gentle Bess, so different from her mother, who had also borne that name. Together, they had founded a dynasty built on the blood shed by those who had ruled before them.

Aye, so many lay dead now—those who had changed the course of history forever—and their memories were now blurred and distorted by time. The powerful Earl of Warwick, the Kingmaker, some had called him, had been slain in the Battle of Barnet. Marguerite, who had been a queen once too, had wasted away in abject poverty, forgotten, in some broken-down château in France; and her husband, another Henry who had been King, had been murdered, some whispered, in the Tower. His Grace the Duke of Clarence, George Plantagenet, imprisoned in the Tower too, had drowned in a butt of malmsey wine. Bonnie Lord Anthony Woodville, Earl Rivers, who'd had the Royal favor once, had been condemned as a traitor to the Crown. Sir Richard Grey, whose brother Lord Thomas Grey, the gay

Marquis of Dorset, ought to have been the one hanged for treason instead, had died with Earl Rivers. And His Grace the Duke of Buckingham, Harry Stafford, laughing-eyed Buckingham, had forfeited his head to the executioner's ax, a coward to the end.

Aye, most all were dead now, like so many others whom Isabella had loved—and hated; those who had been the victims of the ruthless schemes and machinations plotted by the powerful and the ambitious.

Only Henry, the Tydder, had survived; wary, watchful Henry, who now reigned from the throne where Isabella's beloved Richard had once sat. The civil war that would someday be known as the Wars of the Roses was ended: the white rose of York and the red rose of Lancaster intertwined, had become as one under the Tydder. Peace had come to England at last.

But for how long? Isabella wondered, looking out over the endless horizon. Men still dared to plot and plan, and the shadows of the Tower were still ever long and far reaching. She shivered at the thought, remembering.

She was safe, for a time, within the grey stone walls of which she was now lady, with the mighty sword of her lord to defend her. Many times, she had seen that blade glitter in battle, had seen its steel flash like lightning as it had plunged deep and true. And yet, Isabella had lain in the strong arms that had wielded that sword, and she had found them tender and loving. She had felt her lord's carnal mouth, which could curl jeeringly, kiss her lips gently in the darkness as he'd sought to drive the ghosts that haunted her from her soul. Even now, after all these years, her flesh still burned when he touched her, took possession of her, his hard body shielding her from everything save him.

She turned her gaze to the keep in the distance. He would be there, waiting for her, as he was always. Even now, she could see his tall, handsome figure searching for her. He spied her, at last, and ceased his stride. He would not intrude on her privacy if she did not wish it. He knew there were moments of solitude that must belong to her alone, and he respected that. Isabella glanced out once more over the windswept moors. The voices of the ghosts had grown fainter, as though perhaps this were the last time she would ever hear them. She hoped it was so; she had borne so much—only her lord would ever know how much: for it had been his shoulder she had leaned on, his love that had been her strength. . . . Her heart pounding slowly in her breast, Isabella lifted her skirts and began to run toward her husband's outstretched arms.

"Look, Ma." The child of a villein pointed. "'Tis the Lady of the castle. Oh, is she not lovely?"—this a trifle awed.

"Aye, there be no denying that, daughter. But she be a fey one nevertheless. Make the sign, Moll, and say a prayer fer the poor woman's soul."

"Don't ye do any sech a thing, Moll," another crofter chided. "And ye hesh yer mouth, Nellie Sims!"—this to the child's mother. "The Lady be no more fey than yerself!"

"Nay? Then how do ye explain that hawk, Sarah Plunkett? 'Tis always there, perched up on her shoulder, glaring at ye—the wicked bird! 'Tain't natural, a wild thing like that behaving so odd. 'Tis her familiar, most like; that's what I say."

"Nay, 'tain't, and if'n ye had more sense and less envy, ye'd know the Lady's had it fer many a year. She told me about it once, when I asked her. Its wing was broke, and she mended it, taming the beast whilst it healed. There ain't a kinder woman alive than the Lady. Why, didn't she come to yer house and sit up all night with yer Danny boy when he were ill with the fever, never giving a thought to whether she'd catch it herself, though she were scarcely up from her own sickbed? Saved his life; that's what, and ye telling yer Moll to cross herself as if the Lady was a witch. Fer shame, Nellie Sims!"

The other had the grace to flush guiltily.

"Well, if'n she ain't fey," Nellie offered grudgingly, "then why does she roam the moors like a little lost waif? Answer me that, then, Sarah Plunkett."

Sarah sniffed primly, as though she were privy to information that was none of the other's business.

"It be a tragic tale, Nellie Sims, and not fer the likes of ye to be hearing and making mock of. But the Lady's got her reasons." Sarah's voice lowered, and she shook her head pityingly. "She's got more than her share of reasons, poor soul."

Nellie snorted, still disbelieving.

"Well, if'n I had a man like the Lord," she announced, as though she could indeed get such a man if she wanted, "I wouldn't waste my time daydreaming about the past and wandering all over the countryside; that's fer sure."

"But, Ma, Pa says ye don't stay home now," Moll put in artlessly.

"Ye hesh yer mouth, Moll Sims!" The child's mother rounded on her angrily. "Ye're too young to be speaking up so bold to yer elders. 'Tis brassy, ye are; that's what. I'll smack ye where it counts if'n ye don't mind yer manners, and I'll pinch off yer ears too fer listening when they ain't supposed to be."

"I'll tell ye what, Nellie Sims," Sarah stated bluntly as Moll began first to sniffle, then wail at her mother's sharp reprimand, "ye're jest miffed 'cause the Lord ain't interested in yer sly tricks. Trying to make up to him, ye have been. Nay, don't deny it, fer I'm not the only one who's seen ye. Godamercy, woman! Ye oughta stop making sech a fool of yerself. Everybody knows the Lord ain't got eyes fer anyone but the Lady. Look at 'em." The villein nodded to where Isabella was now standing in the circle of her husband's strong arms. Her face was lit up radiantly with joy as she gazed up into his, and he was smiling down at her lovingly. "A body'd swear they was newlyweds, even after all these long years," Sarah marveled, then sighed wistfully, wiping a tear from her eye with the corner of her apron.

"Which jest goes to show ye the Lady *is* fey." Nellie smirked triumphantly with mean satisfaction. "Ain't nobody but a witch could've kept the Lord faithful all this time. Ah, he was a man fer the ladies once—before her. She's bewitched him; that's what."

Nellie Sims would have been very surprised to know that at that exact moment, her thoughts were the Lord's own. Softly, half-mockingly, he voiced them aloud to Isabella.

"The crofters think ye fey, my love. Is it true? Have ye indeed cast some spell upon me or laced my ale with some potion? I swear ye grow more beautiful with every passing day, and I—I love ye more dearly each time I see your winsome face. 'Tis hard to believe so many years have come and gone. Ah, sweet *Jesù*. What did I ever do to deserve ye, my love?"

"'Tis I who should be asking that question, my lord," Isabella replied, her eyes suddenly shadowed and far from the hill upon which they stood.

The Lord understood, as he always did, for he knew her every mood, her every thought, as well as he did his own.

"They are only ghosts, 'Sabelle," he reminded her gently. "Their images will fade with time."

"I know. Even now, they flicker and grow dim, my lord, like candles guttering in the darkness. I try so hard to hold on fast, but still, they are slipping from my grasp. . . ."

"Then let them go, my love. 'Tis time. Ye have grieved a lifetime for them already. They would not have wanted that."

"I know." Suddenly, she clung to him tightly, crying out in anguish, "So many, my lord . . . if only there were not so many! And still, I wouldst not give one moment of my life with ye to lessen their number! Oh, I am wicked— *wicked*!"

"Nay, 'Sabelle, only honest. Life is precious to us all and never more so than when we are in love." He took her hand. "Come—let me chase away those shadows in your eyes. Ye were not meant for sorrow."

He led her away to a sheltered grove nestled in a hollow of the land and there pressed her down upon the wild summer grass. The hawk upon her shoulder ruffled its feathers irritably at being disturbed and flitted to a nearby tree, where it perched watchfully over its lady. It would kill for her if need be, but it knew the Lord meant Isabella no harm. The expression on his countenance was tender as he gazed down at her. So pale, so lovely, she was. Her eyes, like the still waters of a sea, seemed almost too large for the delicately boned oval of her face, for she had been ill for a long time. Though her body was now healed, there was still a certain sad wistfulness about her spirit that touched him deeply.

She will always be too sensitive, too vulnerable, he thought. That is the price of her fierce passions.

The Lord studied her hand, lying in his, marveling at how small and graceful it was, its wrist so very slender. *Fragile*. That was how he thought of Isabella: fragile and needing so to be protected, though ofttimes, in the past, she had defended herself as well as any man. He kissed her palm lingeringly, then pressed her hand to his cheek.

"'Sabelle," he whispered.

He did not have to say more. She was already loosing the lacings of her gown, slipping eagerly, if a trifle shyly, from her garments. Though he was her husband, there was still a part of Isabella that blushed becomingly at knowing he desired her: for though, in her quiet way, she was a strong woman, the Lord was stronger; and she never felt it more than when he took her in his arms, and she cried out her surrender. She was so vulnerable to him. It was as though she were helpless against him, wanting him so and finding the words so very difficult to say. In the past, she had been hurt so terribly that, even now, it was hard for her to believe the Lord loved her, and only her, with a deep, lasting passion that time would never dim.

The Lord cast away his clothes, then smiled gently and joined her again beneath the shade of the old, gnarled oaks and spreading yews.

"'Sabelle, my love."

His words reassured her. She needed so to hear them. Then his lips found hers, kissing one quivering corner lightly, tracing, with his tongue, the outline of her mouth before claiming the whole of her lips softly, tentatively, at first, as though she were a young maiden, needing to be coaxed and wooed with gentleness and restraint. Tenderly, he kissed her mouth, then parted her lips to taste her. His tongue darted forth to explore the honey within, making her shudder with sudden desire as an electric shock of anticipation jolted through her body, causing her loins to quicken sharply. Low in her throat, Isabella moaned a little. She reached up to fasten her arms around the Lord's back, laid one hand against the nape of his neck, where his hair curled in thick rich waves. She pulled him closer, clung to him with her mouth, wanting him, needing him so desperately. It was from him she drew her strength. He was her guiding light, her port in every storm. There were no ghosts when he was with her.

Her tongue met his own, entwined about it with an intimacy that made her heart begin to thud wildly in her breast. Swirl for swirl, she followed where his tongue led, his lips sucked, his teeth nibbled, until she felt as though she were drowning in a molten sea—and she did not care. Feverishly, she kissed him back until they were both gasping for breath, and she could feel the hard evidence of his desire pressed against her as his body half-covered her own, and his hands began to move upon her flesh. Blindly, he tore his mouth from hers, his lips burning their way across her smooth countenance, seeming to scorch her face like a brand. He kissed her eyes, where her incredibly long black lashes made dark, crescent smudges upon her cheeks. He murmured love words in her ear, his breath warm where he blew faintly, his tongue just brushing the small, curved shell, making her shiver with delight and wanting. He wrapped his fingers in her hair, buried his face in the long, silky strands, inhaling deeply the sweet rose fragrance of her. Roses. Always roses. White roses.

Only white roses for Isabella.

They had named her for them. The Rose of Rapture, the courtiers had called her and sought to claim her hand. A thousand white bouquets had strewn her path, had been flung at her feet in homage, but the Lord alone had won her in the end.

The triumph of that knowledge spurred him on. Hotly, his mouth traveled to the pulse beating rapidly at the hollow of her slender throat, that sensitive place upon the curve of her shoulder, and then her breasts, which swelled softly, round and full, at his touch. Possessively, he cupped them, fondled them, taunted them until they ached with passion. Their tiny pink buds flushed and hardened, begging to be touched, tasted, taken. His lips closed over first one, and then the other, sucking gently before his teeth nipped lightly the rosy little buttons, held them in place for the flicking of his tongue as it tormented them to even greater heights. Isabella inhaled sharply as she felt the heat of her flesh begin to emanate from her body in waves of excitement. Once more, a broken moan escaped from her throat.

"My lord, my love," she breathed.

"'Sabelle," he muttered hoarsely in response.

The Lord lingered over her breasts, as always, for they enchanted him. He thought they were the most beautiful spheres he'd ever seen. They were so pale, he could see the barest shadows of the blue veins through which her life's blood flowed. They filled the palms of his hands as he caressed them; the hollow between them sloped like a gentle valley as his mouth crept down it tantalizingly, then enveloped her nipples once more. Again, his tongue titillated the small, rigid peaks, swirling around them deliciously in a way that sent sparks of fire radiating from them in all directions. Isabella felt the ripples of pleasure that coursed through her flesh, and she strained against him, hungry for more.

The Lord's lips began to sear their way down the length of her lithe body. There was no part of her he did not already know but want to discover yet anew: the sides he often tickled mischievously in the mornings, the slender waist, the thighs that trembled and opened for him of their own accord, the backs of her knees and the swell of her calves . . . her ankles . . . her feet.

He raised one dainty foot to his mouth and kissed her instep. He sucked her toes, which tasted of the tall sweet grass and wildflowers upon which she had trodden earlier. For a moment, his gaze rested eagerly, intrusively, on her face. Her head was flung back; her eyes were closed; her mouth was parted slightly in exultation. For the barest instant, the Lord's heart stopped beating, then started to thump rapidly in his breast. The sight of her countenance, naked in its expression of desire, aroused him fiercely, possessively. That look was for his eyes alone. No other man would ever see it. The Lord would kill any man who even dared to try. Isabella belonged to him—and him alone.

She sensed his searching stare; her eyelids fluttered open. Their eyes met, locked. Time was caught, held suspended.

Their breathing ceased, then continued raggedly as she turned away, made vulnerable again by his prying.

She is so shy, he thought. *She would hide her innermost thoughts from me, but she cannot. Even the very essence of her being is mine....*

The Lord reveled in that victory as his hands swept up to part her flanks. Slowly, slowly, he trailed his fingers along the insides of her thighs, then, with a low groan, bent his head to the downy curls that twined between her legs. He pressed his lips to the honeyed moisture of her womanhood, his tongue seeking, probing. Isabella gasped at the intimate contact. A burning ache seized her, where his tongue darted hotly, and began to build, spreading through her body like wildfire. The need to have him inside her was overwhelming, blinding her to everything but him.

Sensing her need, his fingers slipped inside her, easing her desire momentarily with their languid, fluttering motion. Again and again, he stroked her, filled her, tongued her until he could feel the tiny tremors that started deep within her, then burst forth uncontrollably as she suddenly arched against him, her hands wrapped in his hair to draw him even closer as she stiffened slightly, inhaling sharply once more, then gave a soft sweet whimper of ecstasy that held him spellbound until she relaxed beneath him. Then lingeringly, he kissed his way back up to her mouth and drew her near, breathless with expectation, as tentatively she began to explore his body as he had hers.

Isabella worshiped the Lord, as he had her, for he had suffered too in the past. Aye, once, they had been halves, searching blindly for that which would make them whole. They had found it in their love, and they cherished it more deeply for that, taking their time with each other, giving as much as they received—and more.

Caressingly, half-marveling, her hands moved slowly over her husband. She was filled with wonder and awe that this handsome man belonged to her and her alone. Her palms brushed lightly across the mat of hair that covered his sunbronzed chest. She loved the feel of it, soft and silky as it rippled through her fingers, in sharp contrast to the hardness of his firm flat belly, scored here and there with battle scars that shone whitely against his flesh. Deliberately, tauntingly, her hands slipped lower still, to his thick, muscular thighs and his manhood. The Lord shivered with pleasure as Isabella teased him tormentingly, her fingers trailing up and down his flanks before, at last, she grasped his shaft and began the motion slowly. After an eternity, it seemed, her lips closed over him, and her deliciously swirling tongue made him gasp aloud with joy. And then there was nothing for him but her and the things she was doing to him.

Finally, he could bear no more. He caught her tangled mass of tresses, and as she lifted her head to look at him, he moaned,

"My love..."

She smiled at the words as he drew her up, rolled her over on her back, and parted her thighs. Urgently, his maleness probed between her legs, found her, entered her, penetrating her slowly, plunging down into the warm, inviting pool of her with a sudden assault that made her catch her breath, then cry out with delight. Just as languidly, he withdrew, then spiraled down into her once more. Then, without warning, the Lord grabbed great bunches of Isabella's cascading satin mane, twisting her mouth up to meet his own. Forcefully, demandingly, ravishing her now, he drove into her. The violence of his passion exhilarated her. Isabella thrust her hips upward to receive him again and again, faster and faster, until his hands caught hold of her buttocks, lifting her, crushing her against him as he took her savagely, bringing her rapidly to climax. His own release followed swiftly. He shuddered and was still.

Their bodies throbbed against each other, gliding slowly back to earth as their rasps for breath mingled and filled the air. The Lord brushed a strand of hair from Isabella's face, then kissed her.

"'Sabelle, my love," he said.

It was enough. She sighed with happiness, snuggling within the cradle of his arms and laying her head upon his shoulder as he moved from her. The ghosts that had haunted her earlier were gone. There was only the Lord, her husband, now.

She nestled quietly in his embrace, listening to the gentle

sounds of his breathing as he slept, one arm about her to
hold her close. The intimacy of the moment filled Isabella
with as much contentment as the Lord's lovemaking had
done. There was something so warm and comforting about
lying next to him while he lay sleeping, vulnerable to her
now as she had been to him earlier.

Gently, Isabella kissed the Lord's mouth, then rose quietly so as not to disturb him. As she looked down tenderly
at his sleeping figure, she smiled softly to herself. How she
loved him. He was her fate, her destiny for all time. She
had known it from the very first moment she had ever looked
into his eyes.

Her mind drifted back . . . back to the beginning.

How many years had come and gone since then? she
wondered. How many years had passed since that day the
Lord had come riding up to Rushden, and she had first
beheld his handsome face?

The sky was growing grey, as though it would soon rain;
but Isabella paid no heed as she made her way to the moors
that once more beckoned to her. The breeze soughed plaintively, rippling across the tall grass and rustling the leaves
of the old oaks and yews; but Isabella did not hear the wind's
faint whisper. She was lost in thought, far from the heaths
upon which she walked, remembering.

In her mind, it was springtime at her brother's keep, and
she was just five years old. . . .

Chapter Two

Rushden Castle, England, 1470

THE TWO SMALL OCCUPANTS OF RUSHDEN CASTLE, WHICH
had been the home of the powerful Ashley family for centuries, huddled anxiously upon high stools and peered intently through the peep that looked out over the great hall
of the fortress. The younger of the children, Isabella, had
her tiny hand tucked securely within her brother Giles's for

comfort, the only measure of solace she was brave enough to seek. She longed to cling closely to him to lessen the apprehension she felt this day, but she dared not risk crushing the stiff brocade folds of her newly pressed gown. She had been strictly warned of the consequences that would follow the wrinkling of her attire, and she had no wish to discover whether or not Alice, her nanna, had meant the dire threats uttered so tartly earlier that morn.

Despite her attention to the peep, which she took turns sharing with her brother, the girl occasionally glanced fearfully over her shoulder to see if anyone had spied their presence, for the children had been ordered to remain in their chambers until sent for. But no one came. Everyone was too busy preparing for the arrival of Lord Perceival Renfred, Earl of Oadby.

Isabella choked down a ragged sob of panic at the thought and, with one tightly clenched fist, rubbed her eyes fiercely to brush away the stinging tears of grief that had suddenly filled them. Oh, if only her father and mother had not died! But Lord and Lady Rushden had succumbed to the dreaded sweating sickness that had swept the countryside, leaving Isabella and Giles alone in the world. As the sole heirs to the very rich Ashley estate, the two youngsters had subsequently become wards of the King; and their fates, from this day on, would rest in the hands of the nervously awaited Lord Oadby, the man appointed by His Grace to serve as their warden and whom Isabella was certain would be horrid and mean.

Why she felt this, she could not have said. She was a fanciful creature, and her imagination was vivid; and as no one had taken the trouble to inform her of anything about her shortly expected warden except his name, she had wildly drawn the most frightening conclusions about him. He was such an ogre, she had determined, that all were too scared to speak of him. The nervous flutter of activity of the servants below only served to confirm the girl's fears. Her stomach churned so badly, she was afraid she would be ill. That would be disastrous, for she would surely spoil her gown.

Her parents had been laid in their graves scarcely a few

months past, and this new and alarming twist of destiny
was more than Isabella's aching young heart could bear.
Her whole world seemed to be crumbling down about her,
and she was helpless to prevent it. She understood nothing
of the customs and politics involved in the appointment of
their warden. She knew only that a horrifying stranger was
coming to take charge of their lives.

"Oh, Giles, what is to become of us?" she asked plaintively, gently squeezing his hand to reassure herself that he
was real, that he had not been taken from her too.

The boy, though he wanted to offer his sister the words
of comfort she so desperately craved, was as apprehensive
as she and did not know how to answer her.

He shifted slightly on his hard stool, taking care to be
certain his silk doublet, neatly belted at the waist, looked
as crisp and clean as it had when he'd donned it. Giles also
had been sternly warned against disarranging his garments,
and, being a lad well versed in his duties, mindfully heeded
his tutor Master Jaksone's counsel.

"I do not know, 'Sabelle," the boy replied at last, his
face as grave as her own.

"'Tis awful . . . this waiting," Isabella said with a sigh.

"Aye, but it cannot go on much longer, dear sister. Do
ye not hear the sentries heralding Lord Oadby's arrival even
now?"

"Aye, but I wish I did not," she told him, her lovely
little countenance rapt once more with dread. "Oh, Giles,
why must he come here? Why can we not go on as before?"

"Because we are wards of the King."

"But I do not understand why. There are other children
at Rushden whose parents died from the sickness. His Grace
has sent no stranger to care for them."

"They are crofters, 'Sabelle," Giles reminded her gently,
"and of no importance. We are nobles, dear sister," he
stated, as though this would explain everything, as indeed
it would have, had Isabella been older. "I am the Lord of
Rushden now, and ye are its mistress."

It seemed odd to think of herself in her beloved mother's
place, and the girl cried out against it fervently, with all the
conviction of youth.

"Well, I wish I were poor and common!"

There was no time to say more, for just then, the stout oak doors of the keep were flung open wide, and Lord Oadby entered amid the servants' bows and curtsies. On his arm was the most startling woman that Isabella had ever glimpsed, and for a moment, her earlier misgivings were forgotten as she stared with shock and suspicion at the gaudy creature whom her mother would never have allowed to set foot inside the fortress.

The woman, Lady Beatrice Biggs, Countess of Shrewton, was clothed in the most appalling dress that Isabella had ever seen. A brilliant pink in color, it was cut so low across the bodice that not only did the Countess's small high breasts threaten to spill from the décolletage, but the crests of her dark brown nipples could definitely be observed. She wore a vibrant green surcoat, edged with gold lace, and a gold mesh girdle adorned with a vulgar display of emeralds. Around her throat and wrists were a necklace and numerous bracelets set with the same jewels, which also sparkled in the earrings that dangled heavily from her ears. Atop her elaborately coiffed black curls perched a high, steepled pink cap from which trailed yards of billowing wisps of pink-and-green material. Closer inspection revealed that Lady Shrewton's face was not extremely pretty but had been carefully painted to give the appearance of being mysteriously attractive. Her flashing dark eyes seemed to slant seductively, being expertly outlined with black kohl and shadowed with pale green powder. Her thin, pink rosebud lips pouted at the corners, and her nose lifted haughtily as she tossed her head and gazed about to be certain her entrance had been accorded the proper amount of attention. Upon perceiving that it had, she glanced down at Lord Oadby (for she was a head taller than he) and, with just a slight hint of a smile, struck him playfully with her fan.

"Lud, Percy," she trilled, "the place is as dark and gloomy as a dungeon."

Both Isabella and Giles gasped and stiffened at hearing their ancient home referred to in such terms. Why, Rushden Castle had stood since the time of William the Conqueror and was one of the finest keeps in all of England!

"Begging your pardon, my lady"—Sir Lindael, the master-at-arms, spoke up, deliberately misunderstanding the woman's meaning—"but we are still in mourning for the late Earl and Countess of Rushden."

The woman looked surprised for an instant, then, recovering, eyed the grizzled old knight with disfavor and replied, "Oh, aye, of course," before turning away coldly, as though guessing that Sir Lindael found her charms lacking, which indeed he did.

The master-at-arms was not at all pleased with the warden appointed by the King and thought Lord Oadby's mistress, Lady Shrewton, even less enchanting. Not for the first time since the deaths of the late Earl and Countess of Rushden did Sir Lindael wonder what was to become of Isabella and Giles. The minute the master-at-arms had entered the great hall, he had spied the two youngsters peering through the peep, and he knew they were filled with dismay at the sight of their warden.

Lord Oadby was so different from the children's father, they could not help but compare uncharitably the former to the latter. The late Earl had been a big, handsome man, whose generosity toward his family and his tenants had known few bounds. He had ruled his domain and all in it with the greatest of kindness and understanding, and though he had been stern, he had also been just. He had treated his yeomen fairly and their women with respect. No woman at Rushden had had to fear rape or abuse while the old Lord had been alive. He had loved his wife dearly and had never strayed from or struck her, even in anger; and those who had not accorded their own wives the same measure had soon found themselves unwelcome at the fortress.

By contrast, Lord Oadby was short and portly, with a balding head, small, lascivious eyes, and a big red nose, the color of which, Sir Lindael was sure, stemmed from an overindulgence in drink. Decked out like a garish Yule, Lord Oadby was garbed in a crimson silk cloak lined with green and an equally crimson satin doublet slashed with silver. His trunklike calves were encased in green hose, and he wore a pair of crimson shoes that curled up at the toes and from which hung tiny silver bells that tinkled as he, for all his bulk, minced along, a liberally scented, white lace handkerchief waving in one hand. The master-at-arms had no doubt that Lord Oadby was very wealthy and well placed at Court, for he could hardly have purchased the children's wardship otherwise; but nevertheless, the faithful knight was not impressed. He sighed to himself and shook his head. Hard times lay ahead, he feared, for he did not think that Lord Oadby would prove to be the equitable master the late Earl of Rushden had been. Already, Lord Oadby's leering, piglike eyes were roaming over the serving wenches appraisingly as he strutted and preened like a fat peacock before them; and for the first time in his long life at the castle, Sir Lindael saw fear on the maids' faces. He sent a silent prayer of thanks to God that Isabella was only five years old.

Upstairs, the two youngsters clasped hands even more tightly and gazed at each other with solicitude.

"Oh, Giles, he's even more horrid than I imagined," Isabella breathed, for she had not missed the way the usually friendly serving wenches had shrunk from Lord Oadby's rapacious assessment. "And that dreadful woman with him! Oh, Giles, do ye suppose that's his wife?"

"Nay," rejoined Giles, who was bright and had gleaned much from listening to the knights of the keep. "She's but his whore, 'Sabelle. God's wounds! He has brought his *whore* here to take our mother's place!"

In the children's eyes, this was an insult far worse than the one that had been delivered about their home: for their mother had been the most beautiful and gracious of ladies, and they had loved her dearly.

"Oh, Giles," Isabella whimpered again pitifully, her eyes filled with shame and fury at her helplessness to prevent this disgrace to their mother's memory. "What are we to do?"

"Nothing, 'Sabelle," her brother answered, his voice quivering with anger, his jaw suddenly hard and set, his face shadowed with hate. "We can do nothing, dear sister. But someday, I promise ye, I shall make that bastard pay for the insult he has delivered to us and ours; I swear it!"

"Not alone, dear brother, for I am with ye always in all

things. We must pledge our oath together, Giles," Isabella vowed, her fingers entwining even more firmly with his own. "We must make a pact to stand strong against this evil that has come into our lives and never forget this day."

"Agreed. Our blood on it, 'Sabelle," the boy demanded, drawing his jeweled dinner knife from his belt.

Solemnly, Isabella took her own blade from her girdle and slashed the palm of her hand, then pressed it against her brother's.

"*Fiat!*" they said as one. "Let it be done."

And in that moment was born a bond between them they were to share for as long as they lived.

Later, when Isabella and Giles were summoned to the great hall below to meet their warden and his mistress, the defiance that had so strongly gripped the children earlier was carefully concealed behind masklike faces. When they were presented, Isabella dropped a small curtsy, and Giles gave a slight bow—both politely but without deference.

"Here, now. What's this?" the Countess drawled, lifting one wickedly arched black brow at the youngsters' greeting, which she considered lacking in courtesy. "Do ye understand to whom ye are being introduced? This is Lord Perceival Renfred, Earl of Oadby."

"Aye." Giles nodded coolly to the woman. "And I am Lord Giles Ashley, Earl of Rushden."

"It seems ye are well versed as to your status in society," Lord Oadby interjected sourly upon being reminded that Giles's rank was as great as his own.

"My father was a man who knew his worth, my lord," Giles replied softly, "and I am my father's son."

"Aye, I can see ye are indeed," the Earl observed, his eyes narrowing speculatively as he recalled the lad's renowned and mighty sire.

The boy was his father's spawn all right: Rushden—and all it stood for—to the core. Frowning, Lord Oadby continued his unfavorable perusal of Giles. The Earl heartily despised children, though he had been the warden of many. He had found the role worthwhile, as he had reaped a vast harvest from very little seed. As with his past positions, he had purchased the Ashleys' wardship primarily because Rushden was a rich estate, and he fully intended to cram his purse with as much of its gold as he could steal without the King's knowledge. That the lad before him would doubtless someday discover his perfidy and seek to right the injustice did not trouble Lord Oadby. He had already murdered one ward who had proven a nuisance. The Earl would not hesitate to contrive such an accident for Giles, should it become necessary to do so. Arrogantly, Lord Oadby dismissed the boy from his mind and turned to study Isabella.

A tempting little morsel, the Earl decided, though 'twould be some time yet before she was ripe for the picking. He licked his lips at the thought. There was nothing like the sweet taste of a budding maiden's innocence, and Lord Oadby, who had quickly found this one of the more pleasurable aspects of being a warden, had had his share of unspoiled fruit. The young boys given into his care might grow to manhood and call him to account for his misdeeds if he had not managed them cleverly, but the young girls were helpless against him. Ashamed and horrified, the maids whom the Earl had forcibly dishonored had not dared to cry out against his wicked treatment of them, lest their disgrace at his hands be revealed. Afterward, Lord Oadby had always been kind enough to arrange suitable matches for them, and he had even taken the time to instruct the ungrateful wenches on the art of deception that might be practiced on their wedding nights to fool their unsuspecting husbands. Only one maid had ever been brave enough to threaten him with exposure, and the Earl had quietly sold her to a Moorish whorehouse. He had made a tidy profit and had informed the King that the girl had died in Spain of some lingering complaint. Lord Oadby had shrugged. A pity the climate had not, after all, as the physician had suggested, proven beneficial to her health.

Now, he spoke to Isabella.

"And ye, my lady, are ye as well versed as your brother?" the Earl queried.

"I am my father's daughter, my lord," Isabella answered, parroting Giles's earlier response.

Lady Shrewton sniggered at the reply, and Lord Oadby smiled blandly.

"And your brother's sister, 'twould seem," he remarked thoughtfully, then waved his handkerchief in dismissal. "Well, be off now, the both of ye. I fear the journey here has tired me more than I'd thought," he explained, glancing slyly at the Countess, who winked in return, "and I must refresh myself with a little nap."

Isabella and Giles said no more, glad to escape from his unwelcome presence.

At first, life at Rushden Castle went on much as it had before, and Sir Lindael breathed a sigh of relief, thinking he had been wrong about Lord Oadby and Lady Shrewton after all. Although the faithful knight continued to dislike the two, the old master-at-arms, not having access to the records of the keep and not being able to read in any event, could not see that the new warden intended the children or the estate any harm. Indeed, it seemed the Earl and his mistress went out of their way to be pleasant to all. They always had a flattering word for even the lowest of servants, none of whom realized that Lord Oadby and Lady Shrewton were cleverly gleaning every bit of information they could about Rushden and the weaknesses of its inhabitants. The Earl and Countess had played this game before, and they knew their moves well. Those whom they could not win through cajolery, they would intimidate through fear, but first, they must know enough about all to be able to gain the upper hand in any situation. Thus, it was only later, when Lord Oadby and Lady Shrewton were certain the household was firmly under their control, that things slowly but surely began to change.

In the beginning, the occurrences were such small ones, they might easily have gone unnoticed, had not the children's suspicions of their warden and his mistress already been aroused. Not adept at intrigue, Isabella and Giles complained about the incidents, and when the matters were easily explained as trivial oversights, the youngsters were

made to look foolish and unappreciative of their warden's
and his mistress's efforts on their behalf.

Lady Shrewton did not know that Isabella craved cinnamon sticks; they would have been ordered, despite the
cost of the precious treat, if the Countess had only been
told. Why, hadn't Lady Shrewton purchased the girl a very
expensive doll just last week? (It had actually been only a
straw baby won by the Countess at a fair, which the children
had not been allowed to attend. Isabella had thrown the
tacky thing down a garderobe into the cesspit below.) Lord
Oadby was not aware the dead tree by the stables was Giles's
imaginary ship. The Earl would never have had it chopped
down for kindling wood to warm the cool nights in his
chamber otherwise. (Though informed by the blacksmith
that it was Lord Rushden's favorite place to play, Lord
Oadby had said it was an eyesore and must be removed.)
How silly of Lady Shrewton to have given Isabella that
bolt of puce material. Of course, the color was all wrong
for the girl. (The cloth had been moth-eaten besides.)
How absentminded Lord Oadby was. It was he who had
borrowed Giles's solid gold-and-silver chess set and had
forgotten to return it. (The boy had found it buried beneath
a pile of clothes in the Earl's coffer.)

As time went on, and such happenings became bolder
and more frequent, there were those at Rushden who began
to realize how they had been duped by Lord Oadby and
Lady Shrewton, but by then, it was too late. Those who
dared to protest were informed they were no longer welcome
at the castle and were turned out without so much as a
tuppence. Those who stayed saw the futility of dissent and,
though they loved Isabella and Giles, could do little to help
them.

The youngsters themselves learned to remain silent about
the treatment they suffered, bitterly swallowing their pride
and hiding their burning desire for vengeance behind the
still, expressionless faces they showed to their warden and
his mistress. Eventually, the Earl and the Countess carved
a secure little niche for themselves at Rushden and, having
gained confidence in their ability to outwit any who ques-

tioned their actions, grew almost brazen in their pilfering of the estate. Together, they greedily lined their pockets with Rushden's gold, paying less and less heed to Isabella and Giles until the children were almost forgotten.

And like wraiths, the youngsters were content to remain in the shadows, watching and waiting as they pressed their palms together and whispered fiercely, *"Fiat."*

Chapter Three

The Coast, England, 1470

IT WAS DARK THAT SEPTEMBER WHEN THE SHIP THAT HAD lately sailed from France slipped up the coast of England to deposit her passengers upon the soil of their homeland. The men glanced about warily as they disembarked, for they were traitors to their King, Edward IV, though one among them had helped to put him on the throne. The lord they called the Kingmaker, Richard Neville, Earl of Warwick, stood silently for a time as he surveyed the country he had loved—and betrayed. Briefly, his heart ached as he remembered how gloriously, so many years ago, he and his cousin Edward had once marched into battle together to wrest the Crown from King Henry VI and claim it as Ned's own. Then the image of Bess Woodville filled Neville's mind, spoiling the picture recalled from the past, and his lip curled. Bess Woodville, a commoner, widow of Sir John Grey, a mere knight—and Ned had secretly taken her to wife! The King's Grey Mare, the courtiers had dubbed her upon learning of the marriage. But Neville had not laughed. He had been made to look a fool when the betrothal with France's princess, which he had been arranging for Ned, had had to be abruptly broken off. By God, the ignominy of it all. It was not to be borne, and Neville had not borne it. He had turned his back on the man whom he'd made a king and had fled to France to plot and plan Ned's downfall. Henry still lived, imprisoned in the Tower, and his wife,

Marguerite of Anjou, was now Neville's ally. He had made one sovereign. He could make another. Aye, Neville would go into battle with Ned again, but this time, they would not fight side by side.

Isabella understood little of the war that continued to rage between the Yorkists and the Lancastrians for control of the throne, though had she known then how it would someday affect her life, she might have paid more attention to the sober discussions she sometimes overheard. As it was, who wore the Crown meant nothing to her. She was too beset by her own problems to worry over worldly ones.

Glancing about cautiously to be certain she was unobserved, she slipped into the stables, which served as her place of refuge now, and, sighing with relief at finding herself alone, sank down upon a pile of hay. There, she hugged her shins tightly and laid her head on her knees as tears welled up in her eyes and ragged whimpers rose in her throat. Earlier, she had stifled her grief and misery born of Lady Shrewton's cruel remarks and sharp slaps. Now, Isabella let the great, racking sobs come. Oh, why had she ever been so foolish as to take one of the apple tarts that Cook had made for the Countess's dessert this evening? Oh, if only it had not been so long since the girl and Giles had eaten anything but plain meat, bread, and cheese, Lord Oadby having deemed these staples good enough for his wards. Oh, if only the treat had not been so tempting.

Isabella's mouth watered even now as she recalled how the fresh sweet aroma of the baking pastries had wafted into the courtyard, enticing her to the kitchen. There, Cook had taken one look at the girl's face, filled with longing, and, pitying her, had brusquely pressed one of the steaming tarts into Isabella's hands.

"Go on, m'lady. Take it!" Cook had snapped abruptly to cover her true emotions, then had muttered, "What the Countess don't know won't hurt her, and there's some of us at Rushden what's still got eyes in our heads, even if we pretends we don't. We got our own selves and families to think of, m'lady, and the rest are a pack of fools what lets a little cheap flattery blind 'em to what's going on beneath their very noses." Cook's lips had clamped together sternly, and, shaking her head, she had rattled her pots and pans with a great deal more violence than had been necessary. "Now get on with ye, m'lady. Can't ye see I've got work to do?"

Deeply touched, Isabella had given the astounded Cook a grateful hug of understanding before turning and racing blindly from the kitchen.

It had been the girl's misfortune to run directly into Lady Shrewton.

"Ye stupid brat!" the Countess had shrieked. "Why don't ye watch where you're going? Here. I'm talking to ye, wench." She had grabbed Isabella and shaken her roughly when, after mumbling her apologies, the girl had attempted to slip away. "What have ye got there . . . behind your back? What are ye trying to hide from me?"

"Noth—nothing, my lady."

"Let me see. Why, 'tis an apple tart." Lady Shrewton's eyes had narrowed with suspicion. "Where did ye get this? Well, speak up, wench! I asked ye a question."

And Isabella, remembering Cook's kindness to her and realizing that Cook would suffer too if the truth became known, had said, "I—I stole it, my lady, from the kitchen, when Cook wasn't looking."

The Countess had boxed the girl's ears smartly, then, meanly, had snatched the as-yet-uneaten treat from Isabella's hands. Smiling spitefully, Lady Shrewton had deliberately dropped the pastry onto the ground and crushed it into the cobblestones with her foot.

No one had ever laid a hand on Isabella in her life. Dazed and shocked beyond belief by the Countess's hateful blows, too hurt to even care about the loss of the tart, the girl had fled to the stables, Lady Shrewton's shrill laughter echoing jeeringly in her ears.

Now, the scrape of hinges made Isabella glance up quickly and hastily brush the tears from her eyes. A sudden shaft of sunlight flooded the stables as the door swung open wide, then the ray was blocked by the large bulk that soon filled the entrance. 'Twas Sir Eadric, one of her brother's knights. He had always treated the girl with the utmost gentleness and respect, so she had no fear of him and crept from her hiding place to see what he was about.

Carefully, the knight reached into his hunting jacket and withdrew a small rabbit. Though the animal quivered slightly in Sir Eadric's grasp, it made no attempt to escape.

Why, it's hurt, Isabella thought, realizing one of the creature's legs was twisted so it dangled at an odd angle. Hurt and suffering—like me.

The knight crooned softly to the injured beast but was apparently at a loss as to what to do, so the girl made her presence known and asked shyly if she could be of assistance. She had often accompanied her mother when Lady Rushden had made her rounds to care for the ailing crofters. Sir Eadric did not miss the tearstains, which streaked Isabella's cheeks, or the dirt from the straw, upon which she'd huddled, that now soiled her gown. Something had upset the child and sent her scurrying for a refuge, no matter how unfitting; and he did not have to look far to guess the cause.

"Here, my lady." The kindly knight knelt down and handed her the downy, trembling rabbit, which seemed to so enchant her, then took a handkerchief from his pocket. "You've mussed your face and dress." He wet the square of linen in a nearby barrel of water, then washed her up a bit, talking quietly to her all the while. Finally, he asked, "What brought ye here to the stables, my lady? 'Tis no proper place for a lass of your breeding."

"Lady—Lady Shrewton spoke harshly to me for a small misdeed," Isabella said as she stroked the frightened creature in her hands, marveling at the softness of its fur.

"Oh, she did, did she? Well, mayhap the Countess be having a bad day, my lady. Lord Oadby rode out early this morn and has yet to return," Sir Eadric offered by way of explanation.

"Perhaps," the girl dismissed the subject, wanting to put it from her mind and having become far more interested in the tiny rabbit. "How came ye by this poor animal, sir?" she queried.

The knight smiled a trifle sheepishly.

"I was hunting, my lady, and found the dumb beast just sitting at the edge of the woods. When it made no attempt to run from me, I was curious and approached it. I saw 'twas wounded, and—begging your pardon, my lady— 'twas so small a creature, I just couldn't bring myself to slay it. I brought it here, thinking to somehow mend the injury, but I confess I am at a loss as to how to proceed. I'm not much of a hand at treating wounds and the like."

"I will help ye, sir," Isabella told him gravely. "The rabbit's leg is broken, I fear. If we could but fashion a little splint of some sort..."

"Aye, 'twas what I had in mind too, but how can we keep the poor animal still long enough for the break to heal? It cannot be hopping about in this condition."

"We—we might build a cage for it here in the stables, sir," the girl suggested timidly, not knowing whether or not this would be allowed.

"Aye, my lady." Sir Eadric nodded thoughtfully. "But then, who is to care for the beast? I've chores enough as 'tis, my lady."

"I—I could see to its needs, sir," Isabella offered. "I've little enough to do and will scarcely be missed."

The knight was silent for a moment, then stated firmly, "Young though ye be, ye are mistress here at Rushden, my lady. Ye have but to order a thing, ye know, and it shall be done."

Isabella cocked her head at this, considering.

"I—I do not think so, sir," she replied at last. "Else Lord Oadby and Lady Shrewton would be gone from Rushden, for I do not wish them here. All is so changed since they have come."

"Aye, but 'tis a matter that will be righted in time, my lady. When ye and the young Lord are older, we shall see to it. Still, for now, 'tis best to be patient and proceed with caution. 'Tis a wise hunter who stalks his prey carefully and waits for the right time to strike."

Isabella gazed at him steadily at that, but Sir Eadric had begun to whittle a splint from a piece of wood and was not looking at her. Nevertheless, she understood quite well what he was saying to her, and her heart gave a little lurch of gladness.

"I will remember ye are my friend, sir," she declared softly.

"Ye have many friends here at Rushden, my lady. Never think ye do not."

She thought of Cook, and suddenly, the girl realized she and Giles were not so alone after all. There were others who also had their suspicions about Lord Oadby and Lady Shrewton and were simply biding their time, watching and waiting, as Isabella and her brother were. A lump rose in her throat at knowing she was still beloved by those at Rushden.

"Thank ye, Sir Eadric," she said simply.

He cleared his throat gruffly.

"Fetch Thegn and Beowulf, my lady," he instructed. "They can build a cage whilst we set this young rabbit's leg."

Thus was what later came to be called the Lady Isabella's menagerie born and with it a love the girl was to know for the rest of her life.

As he had planned, the Earl of Warwick caught King Edward IV by surprise, and His Grace, unprepared for battle, fled to the dukedom of Burgundy, where he hoped to obtain aid from its duchess, his sister Margaret, in regaining his throne. Neville, swelling with the thrill of triumph, marched into London and there released a much-befuddled Henry from the Tower and restored him to the Crown. All of England reeled under this shifting of monarchs, for they loved Edward, their golden god, under whose reign they had prospered; and King Henry VI, son of Katherine of Valois, was quite insane, being tainted with the Valois madness. A saintly, simpleminded man, he spent more time on his knees than on his throne, allowing whatever power he might have wielded to fall into his wife's grasping hands. As Queen Marguerite was despised by the English people, they clamored for their beloved Ned's return, preferring even his common Woodville witch to the royal French bitch of Anjou whom Henry had wed.

That year of 1471, Edward sailed for home and at Barnet, just north of London, met his cousin Neville in battle for the last time. The traitorous Earl of Warwick, seeing his cause was lost, cowardly attempted to flee the battlefield. Edward's men caught Neville at the edge of a forest, and in moments, the mighty Kingmaker lay dead. 'Twas a glorious victory, and none reveled in it more than Edward's brother Richard, Duke of Gloucester, who, at eighteen and fighting his first major battle, had brilliantly commanded one entire wing of Edward's army.

From Barnet, the men marched northeast to Tewkesbury and there soundly defeated Marguerite, slaying her young son (who, some said, was not Henry's true heir anyway, but the product of Marguerite's illicit affair with Edmund Beaufort, the old Duke of Somerset). Marguerite herself was sent home to France in disgrace, and Henry was taken captive to be imprisoned once more in the Tower.

Far away, at Rushden, Isabella heard only secondhand accounts of the fighting, excitedly reported to her by her brother, Giles, who brandished his dagger wildly, as though it were a sword, and vividly described the battles as though he had been present when they had occurred.

"Just think, 'Sabelle," he marveled, "Gloucester is only eighteen and already one of the finest military commanders in all of England! Oh, can ye not imagine what a sight he must have been . . . swinging his mighty battle-ax; his voice ringing out over the field, urging his men on; his banner, with its white boar, rippling splendidly against the sky? God's wounds, but I wouldst give my life to serve such a man as he!"

"Oh, Giles," Isabella sighed, "how can ye joy in the thought of war? When I think of those men who must be senselessly wounded or slain, it sickens me; and my heart aches for the women in their lives."

Her brother leaped down from where he had been standing upon a pile of hay, as though it had been a hill from which to survey a battlefield below.

"Ye do not understand, 'Sabelle. 'Tis the way of a man to fight and die. 'Tis only cowards like fat old Oadby who cower in their keeps. Why, I doubt if he has ever even entered a tourney!" Giles sneered with disgust and contempt.

"Probably not," Isabella agreed, reaching for another

handful of nuts to feed to the small, bushy-tailed squirrel that sat before her, its dark eyes sparkling as it stretched out its little paws eagerly to receive the treats. "What do ye say, Jasper?" the girl asked, holding up one of the nuts. The animal chattered brightly, and Isabella laughed. "Aye, thank ye." She nodded, delivering the earned reward.

As the creature greedily bit into the nut, the girl examined the tiny wound on its body, where it had been viciously bitten during a fray with another squirrel. The injury was healing nicely, and after satisfying herself that it required no more attention, Isabella turned back to her brother.

"The morning grows late," she noted. "We must hurry if we are not to be tardy for our lessons with Master Jaksone."

As Lady Shrewton had made it quite plain that Isabella was unwelcome in the sollar, where the women of Rushden gathered to engage in such feminine pursuits as embroidery and spinning, it had become the girl's custom to haunt the schoolroom with her brother. Master Jaksone, the tutor, would, in any event, have taught her how to read, write, and cipher; and though he found it odd that she was interested in other areas of study as well, he had no objection to her learning and instructed Isabella competently, just as he did Giles.

Other than her menagerie, which had now grown to a sizable collection of assorted beasts, her lessons with her brother were the only bright spots in the girl's life. Except for Cook and old Alice, her nanna, Isabella had no female companions and learned nothing of the womanly virtues and duties of a chatelaine that would have been taught her, had her mother lived; but if she realized she was lacking in the training that ought to have been bestowed upon her, the girl no longer cared. Though still unhappy, she had grown accustomed to her strange life; and in many ways, it suited her fey nature far better than another would have done.

Chapter Four

Rushden Castle, England, 1473

"ISABELLA! ISABELLA, WHERE ARE YE?"

The girl crouched down in the grain bin into which she had climbed earlier and did not answer. She would not come out! she told herself fiercely. Never! Not even if Lord Oadby and Lady Shrewton beat her would she ever leave this hiding place, this safe refuge she had found in which to lick her wounds. They were even more cruel than she had ever imagined, the Earl and the Countess. They were sending Giles away from her this very day! Isabella brushed angrily at the hot tears that streaked her cheeks, her grubby little fists drawn up tightly into clenched balls. How could they do this to her? Didn't they understand that her dear, beloved brother was all she had in this world? The girl wished she were dead. She would never come out, not as long as she lived!

"Isabella!"—the shouting continued, then the voice called again, much lower, "'Sabelle, please come out."

She lifted the lid of the grain bin slightly so she could see. 'Twas Giles, and he looked as though he'd been crying as well. The sight of him tore at her young heart. He was so fair. She might never see him again!

At last, certain he had come alone, she clambered out of her hiding place and brushed herself off. Her brother did not see her, at first, and started to walk away, his shoulders hunched forward dejectedly.

"Giles!"

He turned then and, as she ran to him, lifted her up in his arms, swinging her high into the air. For a moment, they clung to each other tightly. This was the worst day of their lives.

"Ye naughty wench! How dare ye hide from me?" her brother scolded through the tears he dashed away savagely

as being unmanly. "Especially with the Duke here and waiting? Christ's son, 'Sabelle! Do ye not realize he's the second
most important man in all of England! Lord Oadby is fit to
be tied."

"I don't care! I don't care! Oh, Giles, I cannot bear for
ye to be sent away!" Isabella wailed woefully in response.
"I shall be all alone here, and I shall miss ye so very much. . . ."

"And I, ye, dear sister." Gently, he set her down, releasing her hold on him, although he kept her hands in his.
He kissed them tenderly, then chucked her under the chin.
"Ye know I wouldst not leave ye, 'Sabelle, had I any choice
in the matter; but 'tis the way of things. I am of an age now
to be fostered, and only think, dear sister, what it means
to escape from this place and to be with Gloucester! Oh,
'Sabelle, 'tis my wildest dream come true!"

His voice had risen, and his eyes now shone with excitement at the prospect. Isabella was hurt. Why, it was
almost as though her brother were glad to be going away
from her!

"Try to understand, dear sister," Giles pleaded, seeing
her face and knowing he had wounded her with his last
words. "There is a whole world out there, beyond Rushden,
waiting for me. I want to see it. God's blood, 'Sabelle! I
cannot go on here! Each year does but grow worse, and I
cannot bear it!"

"Then take me with ye!" she begged. "Oh, please. Do
not leave me behind! We shall explore the world together,
as we have always done. Do ye remember the time we
found the badger with the blind eye? And the hedgehog
with the crippled paw? Oh, take me with ye! Please, dear
brother."

"Oh, would that I could, dear sister, but I cannot."

"Is it—is it because ye love me no longer, Giles?"—
her lower lip trembled pitifully. "Has this Duke of Gloucester taken my place in your heart then?"

"Oh, nay, 'Sabelle!" he reassured her fervently. "How
couldst ye even think such a thing? There is no one I love
more than ye. But to escape from Rushden. And to follow
the brother of the King! Oh, dear sister. 'Tis indeed a rare
honor, beyond all my wildest imaginings. Oh, 'Sabelle, ye

should see him! He is all that I dreamt—and more. If I do
well under his tutelage, I shall become a knight of the first
order. Do ye not wish to be proud of me?" he demanded.

"I have always been proud of ye, Giles," the girl answered softly. "'Tis only that this parting from ye saddens
me beyond measure. Ye are all I have left. Whatever shall
I do without ye?"

"Ye will manage, 'Sabelle. Somehow, ye will manage.
Ye are strong inside, mayhap, in your quiet way, even
stronger than I. Ye have borne more bravely our life here
at Rushden than I ever have."

"Nay—"

"Aye, dear sister, for your heart is still filled with love,
in spite of the hardships we have suffered, and mine holds
naught but hate. I wouldst be free of Rushden so I might
seek solace someplace as ye have done here in your menagerie. Oh, 'Sabelle, do not despise me for that!" He
suddenly crushed her to him fervently.

"Nay, I do not. How could I?" She hugged him tightly
in response, choking down, with difficulty, the lump that
rose in her throat.

"Look at me, dear sister," the boy ordered gently, sensing
her distress. "I want to engrave your beloved face into my
memory, as ye must mine, for I do not know when we shall
meet again. I expect, when I return, ye will be all grown
up, 'Sabelle, a beautiful young chatelaine with dozens of
courtiers at your feet," he jested lightly, trying to cheer her.

"Grown up, perhaps, for ye will be gone a long time, I
fear," Isabella said gravely. "Years, Alice told me. Oh,
Giles, 'twill seem like forever! But there will never be
anyone for me but ye," she claimed ardently.

"Ye say that now, dear sister, because ye are unhappy.
But someday, a fine lord will come riding up to Rushden
to seek your hand and your heart, and ye will run eagerly
to his arms, swept away by love. He will be your world
then, 'Sabelle, not me. That is how it should be."

"Nay!" she cried out in protest.

"Aye, dear sister. Wait, and see."

"'Tis true then? Ye do not jest?" the girl queried anxiously, her little countenance crestfallen with pain and disappointment.

"Aye, 'tis true. Why, surely, ye thought to be wed someday, 'Sabelle, just as I shall be."

"Nay, I had not thought it."

"Ye are young yet. That is why."

"Well, if someone must take your place then, Giles, I want ye to choose him for me. I'll have no man ye do not favor, and I—I do not trust Lord Oadby to judge wisely and well, with thought to my happiness in the matter."

Her brother's nostrils flared with anger, for he knew she spoke the truth, and the idea of his sister being made miserable in her marriage roused him to fury.

"'Tis a bargain, then, I promise ye," the boy vowed. "When I return, I shall bring with me the most handsome courtier in all of England. He will pay homage to your loveliness and strew roses at your feet!"

"Oh, Giles." Isabella smiled with pleasure at the thought, then sobered once more as the moment passed. "Ye—ye will write to me, will ye not?" Her voice broke. "Promise me," she whispered.

"Aye, of course, I shall."

"And—and perhaps ye will come home at Christmas?"

"If Gloucester gives me leave to do so, why, then, nothing could keep me away, dear sister. Mayhap I shall even have a husband for ye then," he teased. "Come. I dare not risk keeping the Duke waiting any longer. He is doubtless already wroth with me as 'tis, and I've no desire to start off my fosterage on the wrong foot. Please, weep no more, 'Sabelle. This parting from ye is hard enough as 'tis, and I wouldst not have your sweet face filled with sorrow at bidding me good-bye. Canst thou not give me one smile, dear sister? I have kept the second most important man in all of England waiting in order that I might see ye one last time before my leaving."

Isabella made an attempt at brightness, but her heart ached heavily in her breast all the same as she and her brother walked out into the courtyard together. There, Lord Oadby and Lady Shrewton were standing impatiently, along with a huge entourage of men. The Earl's porcine visage was red with anger and embarrassment at having been unable to control either of his wards before His Grace the Duke of Gloucester, Richard Plantagenet, brother of the King. What on earth must his grace be thinking? Lord Oadby glanced surreptitiously at the Duke's face, but nothing of Gloucester's thoughts showed upon his dark countenance.

"I am indeed sorry for the delay, your grace," the Earl apologized for the hundredth time, wringing his pudgy hands together worriedly. "'Tis just that since the deaths of their parents, the children have been unnaturally close and—"

"I quite understand, my lord," Richard said coldly, his deep slate-blue eyes flicking with contempt over the Earl's fat figure.

A toady, the Duke thought. How could Ned have given such important wards into the care of a man like Lord Oadby? Why, the Ashleys are one of the most powerful families in all of England and have served the Yorkist cause honorably and well. 'Tis an insult for a man such as this groveling pig to even set foot on Rushden. 'Tis just as well I am taking the boy away. The lad's late father would turn over in his grave if he knew his son was being reared by this unfit churl.

Gloucester's dark orbs flashed at the thought, and the Earl felt a shiver of fright chase up his spine. He loathed the King's brother, the supreme military commander who was said to be without mercy, and for a moment, Lord Oadby was invaded by a small sense of panic. What if Giles revealed his harsh treatment at the Earl's hands? Lord Oadby might have satisfied the questions of a lesser man, but the Duke stood second only to the King. God's blood! If only the Earl had known the boy was to be fostered to Gloucester. Lord Oadby would have dealt more kindly with the whoreson brat. But the Earl had not been informed of the King's decision to foster the lad to Richard until the Duke had arrived, unannounced, with the writ this morn, throwing the entire household into an uproar. Why, the castle had not even had a decent meal to offer Gloucester, the larder, except for Lord Oadby's and Lady Shrewton's private hoards, being nigh well empty. While the Countess had scurried to the cellars to discover what refreshment might be offered, the Earl had hurried upstairs to snatch Giles from the school-room and hastily bundle the boy into his best garments (which were none too fine, Lord Oadby having purchased the cheapest cloth available for his wards' accoutrements) in order that the lad might be presented to Richard. A highly flustered Master Jaksone had been curtly commanded to pack Giles's possessions at once; and Isabella, at last grasping the reason behind the household's frenzy, had burst into tears and fled—the stupid little bitch!

In all the confusion, it had not been until they were ready to depart that the boy had noticed his sister's absence and begged leave from the Duke to find her and bid her good-bye. And though Gloucester had been eager to be on his way to Middleham Castle to see his wife, Her Grace Anne, and their new firstborn, Edward, something in Giles's face had made Richard give the lad permission to seek out Isabella.

Now, as the children slowly approached, the Duke was glad he had done so. He too had known the bittersweet pain of parting.

"Ah, here they come, your grace." The Earl observed the youngsters' arrival with relief.

"I do hope your grace will forgive them." The Countess tittered nervously. "I'm sure that Lord Oadby and I have done our best, but—"

"Quite so," Gloucester stated dryly, gazing hard at Lady Shrewton.

Unfortunately for the Countess, she reminded Richard of his brother Ned's latest mistress, whom the Duke could not abide the sight of.

"Your grace." Though shaking inside, Giles stepped up manfully in the little silence that had fallen and swept Gloucester a deep bow. "I do apologize for having kept ye and your men waiting so long. I did not realize how quickly time had passed. Please, allow me to present my sister, Lady Isabella."

The girl bit her lip, distraught, and once more, tears stung her eyes as, at last, she recognized the full import of what she had done. In her overwhelming sorrow at Giles's leaving, she had behaved unforgivably before the King's brother. Isabella sank into a low curtsy and waited, eyes downcast, for the Duke's displeasure to fall upon her. To her surprise, for she had feared both she and her brother would have their ears boxed for their impertinence, Richard only took her hand and gently raised her to her feet.

"So ye are the young maid who is the cause of our delay," he said, but his eyes were kind.

"Aye, your grace. I'm sorry, your grace," Isabella mumbled, still not daring to look upon Gloucester's face.

"Well, what shall we do with ye, I wonder?" The Duke studied the girl thoughtfully, noting the raggedness of her garments and the way they hung on her small thin frame.

"I—I suppose I must be punished, your grace."

"Are ye often punished, child?" Richard questioned softly and did not miss the frightened, covert glance that Isabella threw Lady Shrewton.

"Only when I am bad, your grace." The girl's tone was so low, he almost didn't hear her.

"Well, I'm certain that isn't very often," the Duke declared, raising his voice slightly and fixing the Earl and the Countess with an unflinching stare. "Ye wouldst not be one of my wife's favorite little maids otherwise."

"Your—your wife, your grace?"

"The Duchess of Gloucester, child."

"I—I am one of her favorites, your grace?" Isabella queried with puzzlement, thinking she had misunderstood, for she did not know the Duchess.

"Aye, in fact"—Gloucester reached into his doublet and drew forth a shiny gold sovereign—"she sent ye a present and begged me to ask ye to remember her in your prayers." He pressed the coin into the girl's hand. "Will ye do that, my lady?"

"Oh, aye, aye, your grace," Isabella cried, looking up, for the first time, and gazing at him marvelingly, much startled and deeply touched.

This was the man said to have murdered the old King, Henry, who had died suddenly last year in the Tower; but in that moment, the girl knew the rumors were not true.

Richard was not tall, and his body was slender, but

Isabella, with her deep sensitivity, saw in the Duke the same quiet, inner strength that was her own, and she recognized a kindred spirit. Here too was a man who had suffered greatly in his past, for Gloucester had spent much of his childhood alone, in solitary confusion and upheaval; and the grief and bewilderment of those years was to shape his character for the rest of his life. Torn from his mother and sisters at an early age; his father dead on a battlefield and one brother, Edmund, murdered while Richard was yet a child; his brother Edward so suddenly crowned King; he himself knighted when he was but nine; the bestowal of his dukedom shortly thereafter; the betrayal by his cousin the Earl of Warwick; the hurried flight into Burgundy; the treasonous acts by his brother George, Duke of Clarence; the Battles of Barnet and Tewkesbury, which had left the King-maker dead—all these events had left their mark upon Richard, Duke of Gloucester, for all time. The pain that was always with him radiated from his somber slate-blue eyes. The slight crease between them told Isabella more eloquently than words just how often he brooded late into the evenings; and her heart went out to him.

She knew then, somehow, that she would love this man for as long as she lived.

"I shall inform her grace Anne of your kindness, child," Richard continued. "And ye must write to her and tell her how ye are doing. She would be most displeased to learn ye were unhappy and that all at Rushden was not well."

The Duke saw Lord Oadby and Lady Shrewton blanch at this and knew his point had been taken.

"Oh, aye, your grace. I shall write her this very day," Isabella promised fervently.

"And now, my lady, I must bid ye farewell. Kiss your brother good-bye, and wish us well on our journey."

The girl clung tightly to her brother for a moment, then reluctantly drew away and said, "Godspeed, your grace. I shall remember ye always. May God keep ye and Giles until we meet again."

Gloucester and her brother turned and swung up into their saddles, clapping their heels hard to their horses' sides. Isabella waited until they had galloped beneath the iron portcullis and clattered over the drawbridge to the hard road beyond. Then, hurriedly, she ran inside the keep, up the stairs to her chamber, and through the French doors that opened onto her balcony. Unmindful of the danger, she hoisted herself up onto the stone coping so she might watch the entourage until it was out of sight. As though he sensed her eyes upon him, Giles glanced back at the castle and waved. Her tiny countenance lighting up with joy, the girl waved furiously in return, nearly losing her precarious balance in the process.

Her brother was gone.

Her shoulders drooping with dejection at the realization, Isabella slid from the coping and went back inside, where she flung herself upon her bed, weeping bitterly.

"There now, my lady"—Alice, her nanna, had come to comfort her. "'Tis not as though the young Lord will be gone forever."

The old nurse stroked the girl's hair soothingly, for she treasured her charge and hated to see Isabella hurt.

"Oh, Alice, why did Giles have to go away?"

"La, 'tis the custom, my lady, as well ye know," Alice reminded her. "Lord Rushden will learn well under the tutelage of the Duke of Gloucester. 'Twas silly and most ill-behaved of ye to run away and delay their departure. They lost two good hours of daylight because of it, and mayhap now they will not be able to find adequate lodging for the night. And look! You've torn your gown besides with this nonsense of hiding from us all. 'Tis like as not you'll be severely punished for your disobedience, my lady." Alice's mouth was set grimly in a thin line of worry and disapproval.

"What does it matter?" Isabella inquired wearily, then buried her face in her pillow to muffle her racking sobs.

But the girl was not punished after all; and thereafter, when her life at Rushden improved considerably, Isabella clasped the gold sovereign to her breast and, each night, said a quiet prayer for Richard, Duke of Gloucester, and his wife, Anne.

Chapter Five

Rushden Castle, England, 1478

THE AFTERNOON SUN SLANTED DOWN IN FIERY RAYS UPON the land, touching the lush, sweeping green heaths and golden fields with brilliant warmth. In the distance, the contentedly grazing forms of cattle, sheep, and goats dotted the hillsides that sloped down into the moors ridged here and there with pale white stone. Along the spurs of rock themselves, gently laughing brooks sometimes babbled their ways to quiet pools that lay in the whispering hush of small forest glades dappled with the sunlight that streamed through the branches of the trees. A breeze stirred faintly, soughing plaintively to the great old oaks and pines, the ashes and poplars, wherein birds twittered melodically, and squirrels chattered gaily. Closer to the keep were the sounds of the crofters as they went about their chores and, now and then, the rattle of a lumbering cart upon the road, followed by the shouts of children and the barking of dogs as they chased the vehicle until it disappeared. From the outer ward of the fortress itself came the heavy, rhythmic clang of the blacksmith's hammer, but between the blows, all was still.

Isabella Ashley shifted impatiently from one foot to the other as she gazed out over Rushden's vast domain from her balcony—as she had done every day since receiving Giles's last letter.

Much had happened in the intervening years since last she'd seen her brother. In 1475, Giles had written that the Duke of Gloucester and his men were to take part in King Edward IV's campaign against the French King, Louis XI. But there had been no great battle after all, because cowardly Louis had bribed Edward, with a pension, to leave France. The Duke had been against his brother's acceptance of the monies and the signing of the Treaty of Picquigny as well,

which had caused the French King to take an extreme dislike
to Gloucester. Afterward, the untrustworthy Louis had subsequently entered into a plot with Richard and Edward's
brother George, the traitorous Duke of Clarence, to overthrow the English throne. Edward had arrested George for
treason and had imprisoned him in the Tower. As he had
done so many times before, Richard had pleaded for his
vain and foolish brother's life, but this time, Edward had
remained firm. Brother or not, the Duke of Clarence must
be executed. Upon learning of his fate, George, with some
macabre sense of humor, had demanded he be sealed in a
butt of malmsey wine, therein to drown. This perverted
wish had been granted, and only Richard mourned his brother's death.

  Sick at heart, the Duke of Gloucester was going home
to Middleham. As Rushden Castle was on the way, Giles
had written, Richard had decided to break his journey there.
Now, Isabella waited eagerly for the men's arrival.

"Oh, Alice. Surely, they will come today!" she cried.

The nanna smiled indulgently at the girl, whose enchanting face was filled with anticipation and longing.

"So ye have said for more than a fortnight now, my
lady—and without result," Alice teased.

"Today will be different. I feel it in my bones," Isabella
countered brightly.

Alive with joy, she hugged herself, danced a few lightly
skipping steps across the balcony, then pirouetted with a
flourish that made her skirts swirl high, showing a flash of
shapely legs that shocked the nurse.

"My lady!" Alice reprimanded with horror. "The watch-
men will see ye from the towers! Come inside at once!"

Disregarding the nanna's order, Isabella laughed breathlessly as she whirled to a stop, her cheeks flushed, her eyes
sparkling.

"Today is special," she stated firmly, excitedly searching
the wide expanse of terrain again.

Alice shook her head with silent resignation. The nurse
had done her best, but there had been no taming the girl.
The years of being allowed to run wild and forgotten had

left their mark upon her for all time. Isabella was as fey as the animals she found in the woods and upon the moors and brought home to the castle to tend. Hers was not the classical beauty sought by most women, but a strange, haunting loveliness as uncapturable as evening mist. Indeed, sometimes, Alice believed the girl was a changeling child, a forest nymph or a water sprite swaddled and left in the ornately carved crib that had once stood in the nursery. It might have been true after all, for Isabella moved like a fairy queen, with a shy grace reminiscent of gossamer wings fluttering gently on some soft and magical wind; and she could vanish quietly from a place in a manner that often made one wonder if she had simply disappeared to return to that land of elfin creatures whence she had sprung.

At thirteen years of age, her silky silver-blond hair streamed down to her narrow hips like a shimmering haze of moonbeams shot through with streaks of winter frost. Her velvet skin was fair, its sheen almost silvery too in certain light. Below her finely chiseled nose was a soft, full pink mouth, which could tremble vulnerably on occasion. Her jaw met her swanlike neck in a faintly shadowed hollow that curved down into gracefully sloped shoulders. The budding breasts that swelled above her slender waist were gently rounded, promising a ripeness at maturity; and though she was not tall, her lithe limbs were delicately proportioned.

But all this, as oddly alluring as it was, seemed to blur, to fade elusively, when one looked into her eyes—for it was Isabella's eyes one always remembered. Framed with silver-blond brows, and fringed with thick, striking black lashes, they were wide, fathomless, and deep grey-green in color, like a sea before a storm. Often distant, almost unworldly, those eyes appeared as though, without effort, they could gaze into a man's soul and discover his innermost secrets. Sometimes, if the truth they found was too painful to endure, the eyes would shutter against the knowledge; still, one would know that Isabella had glimpsed one's darkest thoughts.

It was startling in the girl; it would be spellbinding in the woman.

Someday, my lady will suffer for those eyes, Alice thought sadly, for despite all the harshness she has endured in her life, she knows little of the cruelties of the world.

And it was true. Those at the castle who, over the years, had come to know and love her thought of Isabella as a fragile child, needing to be protected from the unkindnesses that would have wounded even those made of sterner stuff. In a tacit, well-meaning agreement born of pity for her unhappy existence, they had done their best, within the limits of their abilities, to shield the often lonely girl from those things they had realized instinctively would hurt her.

For the most part, after Giles's leaving, she had lived a solitary life, wrapped up in her lessons and her menagerie; and because of this, the sweet and caring disposition that had been hers since birth had somehow managed to survive. But for all her gentleness of character, Isabella was not without strength and temper. It was simply that her strength was the quiet kind, which stems from within, like a candle glowing in the darkness or a willow bending in the wind. And her temper arose rarely for herself but rather in answer to the injustices perpetrated by others against all of God's creatures. Having known suffering, the girl could not bear to see it in others, and she would battle like a small fury against it.

But no thought of life's heavy burdens weighed upon her soul this day, and so Isabella was as bright and carefree as the fey nymphs and sprites to which others often likened her. Her laughter gurgled forth in a melody that might have belonged to the pipes of Pan; and old Alice roused herself from her silent musing, at last, at the girl's sudden cry of joy.

"He comes, Alice! Giles comes!"

The men were tired and dirtied with the stains of travel, but there was not one among them who would have complained to the Duke who rode at the head of their cavalcade. Their silence arose not from fear, however, but from love. The Duke grieved inside for his dead brother George, and none who followed him would have added to his pain by voicing discomfort. So they pressed on and said naught.

Presently, ahead in the distance, they spied their destination. Stern and tall, Rushden Castle loomed before them. With its thick, grey stone walls, machicolated battlements, circular watchtowers, and deep moat, it was much like any other stout, inland keep. But it was a fortress that had served the Yorkist cause—and served it well—and for that alone it was a welcome haven to the eyes of the men.

There, they would be greeted warmly and be served the best the castle had to offer—and without the thinly veiled rudeness that often characterized those keeps whose sympathies lay secretly with the Lancastrians. At Rushden, no eyes would watch the men covertly with sly resentment, grudging each mouthful of the intentionally poorly cooked food they consumed. There too, the bathwater would be warm, the soap soft, and the maids pretty. The men would lie upon clean rush pallets in the great hall and sleep soundly, with no fear of stealthy intrigues or the itch of hordes of lice and bedbugs to disturb their slumber.

Perhaps, after supper, Lionel could be coaxed to sing, and some of the ache in the Duke's heart for his dead brother would lessen with the ballads. There would be dancing, and mayhap acrobats and jugglers would perform and the fool tell a merry jest that would bring a smile to the Duke's lips and lighten his dark eyes, which were now haunted with sorrow.

As the men neared the keep, they saw the Duke's oblique words of warning to Lord Oadby and Lady Shrewton had been wisely heeded, for the vast acres of land were well kept, the crops, well tended. The crude, thatched cottages of the crofters were plain but built sturdily, and each boasted a small vegetable patch. The villeins themselves were, for the most part, clean and healthy; the garments upon their backs, although neatly mended in places, bore few signs of ragged neglect. When the retinue passed, the men hoeing the fields halted their work, bowed, and doffed their caps with respect; several beamed cheerfully and called happy greetings to the young Lord of Rushden.

"Welcome home, my lord! Welcome home!"

The women laid aside their baskets to drop pretty curtsies and smile shyly at the party on horseback while children scampered gaily alongside the road.

At the sight of them, the Duke of Gloucester roused himself, smiled, and tossed the bolder brats a scattering of silver coins. The youngsters whooped with excitement as they dashed to collect the shillings that glittered brightly in the dirt.

Aye, the men were glad the Duke had thought to sojourn at Rushden Castle. Even the most weary spirits lifted as the cavalcade quickened the pace of its steeds and hastened onward in orderly progression.

Like a flash of quicksilver, Isabella fairly flew out of her chamber, dashed down the long corridors and curved stone staircase to the great hall below, and shot through the massive oak doors to the inner bailey that barricaded her brother's keep.

It seemed forever before the entourage she had glimpsed in the distance drew near, at last, and called their lord's name to the sentries.

Faster, faster! the girl chanted silently as the iron portcullis was slowly cranked up on creaking chains. Never before had it taken so long to raise! Next came the barrier at the inner gatehouse, then there were perhaps a hundred men or more massing in the courtyard, their armor flashing brilliantly in the sun, their horses' hooves ringing out sharply over the cobblestones. But Isabella had eyes only for one.

"Giles!"

How tall he had grown and how fair. He was no longer the boy she remembered but a young man now. His silver-blond hair gleamed almost white in the summer sun, and his hazel eyes sparkled in his tanned face as they caught sight of her. His lips curved into an answering smile of delight before he shouted "'Sabelle!" in reply and dismounted with a single leap, tossing aside the reins of his steed carelessly as he ran toward her.

"Dear brother, art well? Have ye won your pennon? Art really a squire? Didst truly bring me a present?"

She bubbled over with questions as she flung herself into his outstretched arms and felt them close around her tightly; and he laughed and said, "Aye, and aye, and aye, and aye." And all was once more right in the world.

After a time, they drew apart, and her brother studied her in a way that made Isabella blush faintly with shyness and expectation, aware of the changes in her own body as well as in Giles's.

"You're beautiful, 'Sabelle, as beautiful as I knew ye wouldst be," he told her finally, and her lovely little countenance shone with pleasure and adoration at his praise.

"I quite agree, Giles."

Isabella glanced up at the rich timbre of the voice that had spoken and immediately sank into a deep curtsy as she extended one hand.

"Your grace. Rushden Castle is again honored by your presence."

"The little maid I recall is all grown up," the Duke of Gloucester noted as he raised her to her feet. "Hast remembered your prayers, my lady?"

"Aye, indeed, your grace. How could I have forgotten?"

"I am glad," Richard stated, then turned to greet Lord Oadby and Lady Shrewton, who were standing apprehensively to one side.

The years had not been kind to the greedy Earl and Countess. Lord Oadby's gluttonous figure had grown to monstrous proportions, and he suffered from gout. Lady Shrewton's once seemingly attractive face now sagged with wrinkles she attempted to disguise beneath layers of paint, and the flirtatious moue she made as she swept the Duke her curtsy appeared only grotesque.

"Welcome to Rushden Castle, your grace," the Earl greeted Gloucester nervously. "All is in readiness for your grace."

"Ye and Lady Shrewton having been given ample warning of my arrival this time, no doubt," Richard responded dryly. "Well, we shall see."

Then he strode inside, pointedly ignoring the Countess. She shot the Earl a quick, frightening glance, her face looking as though it were going to crumble beneath its thick

mask of powder; then she stared over at Isabella to be certain
the girl did not appear to be lacking in any respect to which
the Duke might have taken exception. Lord Oadby's pig
eyes followed those of his mistress, and he licked his lips
slightly at the sight, for he seldom saw Isabella. She took
care to keep out of his way. Well, well. The fey little bitch
had grown up to be quite an enchanting maid. The Earl
filed the thought away for future reference, then took Lady
Shrewton's arm, hustling her inside after Gloucester and
whispering orders curtly in her ear.

Isabella never even noticed them. She was still gazing
raptly up at Giles, who was smiling down at her teasingly.

"Well?" the girl asked breathlessly, scarcely able to contain her anticipation. "What is this present of yours, dear
brother? Ye have sent me so many already—the fan, the
carillon, the bolt of silk—that I cannot imagine what I am
still lacking. In truth, ye have been far too generous, Giles."

"Nay, those were but trifles. Think back, dear sister, to
the day of our parting. Was there not a promise given then?"

Isabella thought hard for a moment but could not recall—

"Wait! Aye, I remember now!" she cried. "Ye promised
to bring me the most handsome courtier in all of England
and said he would strew roses at my feet!"

"And I have found, *demoiselle*, that Giles is a man of
his word." Lord Lionel Valeureux, heir to the earldom of
St. Saviour-on-the-Lake and Giles's foster brother, bowed
low and laid a bouquet of white roses at Isabella's feet.

For the first time in her life, the girl was struck dumb.
No mere mortal, this, but a young god, descended from the
sun, surely! Even her brother, who was all things in Isabella's eyes, dimmed a little before the blinding brilliance
of the man before her. He was tall and well built; his muscles
were hard yet supple from the past six years of training for
knighthood. He wore the Gloucester livery, but the royal-
blue satin cloak lined with gold, which swirled down from
his shoulders, bore rosettes upon which were the badges of
lions—the St. Saviour coat of arms—instead of Richard's
white boars. His doublet too was of rich material, also royal-
blue in color and slashed with gold. A sword hung at his
narrow waist. Gold hose of the finest weave and high, black

leather boots adorned the strong legs he had planted in a cocky, self-assured stance.

His skin was as dark as honey; already, his handsome visage showed the shadow of a beard. His windswept blond hair was the gold of captured sunlight, and Isabella found she longed to reach up and touch it—just once—to see if it was as soft and silky as it seemed. His nose was straight; his lips were full and sensual; his jaw was square, determined. And his eyes—oh, *Jesù*—his eyes! Wide set beneath thick blond brows and lined with blond lashes, they were as blue as the summer sky—like his hair, a legacy of his Norman ancestors' centuries of intermarriage with the Saxons.

Isabella looked into those eyes—and was lost.

She felt as though she were soaring on the wings of the wind, for she discovered she was breathless with exhilaration. Her heart raced too frantically in her breast, and her mouth was so dry, she could scarcely swallow. Giles had chosen well indeed!

Lord Lionel continued to gaze down at her, inhaling sharply as he felt his loins quicken with hot desire. Giles had not told him how strangely haunting the girl's beauty was. In that moment, Lionel wanted her and determined to have her, never dreaming it was to become an obsession that would last as long as he lived.

Isabella managed to recover her manners and her tongue at last, bringing him to his senses as she spoke.

"My lord." She swept him a slight, graceful curtsy and retrieved the flowers he had laid at her feet.

Once again, he bowed low, this time over her hand, his lips just brushing her fingers, in the fashion of the Court.

"*Enchanté, demoiselle,*" he drawled, his blue eyes glittering with appreciation and desire.

Isabella blushed prettily.

"*Je suis aussi, seigneur.*" Her voice was so low, he almost didn't hear her words.

And so simply did Isabella's love for Lord Lionel Valeureux begin.

* * *

Ah, what a feast there was that evening! Rushden's servants had outdone themselves. Proud of their lord—if not his warden—they would not see Giles shamed again before one of such importance as the Duke of Gloucester by setting a niggardly table or being slow to carry out their duties. They hurried swiftly to and from the cookhouse, their arms heavily laden with platters and pitchers. No less than five courses were laid before the guest of honor (though Lord Oadby and Lady Shrewton groaned secretly at the expense).

Ten fat suckling pigs had been slain and roasted in their dripping juices, each mouth stuffed with a single shiny red apple that gleamed softly in the brightly blazing candlelight. Twenty plump, freshly killed chickens and twenty geese apiece had been baked and glazed with special sauces. There were trenchers piled high with beef, mutton, venison, goat, and rabbit that had been brought from the cool larder. Grilled fish—pike and carp and perch—lay upon skillfully arranged beds of lettuce garnished with large chunks of moist lemons, smaller cherries and berries, raisins and nuts, and slices of hardboiled plover eggs. Great tureens of lamprey eels and all manner of vegetables steamed alongside hot bowls of thick cream gravy, which waited to be ladled upon slabs of good rich bread. Meat and fruit pies and a selection of tarts to tempt even the most jaded palate were wheeled in on carts laden with other assorted pastries and sweetmeats, as well as red currant jelly and quince preserve. All this was washed down with tankards of cold ale and chalices of the best wine chosen from Rushden's dark cellars. There were, in addition, three subtleties presented to win the Duke's favor, each of which signified some aspect of the Yorkist battle for the Crown.

The first was an artfully crafted cheese display called Three Suns, which represented the three suns that Edward had seen in the sky before winning the throne. All cheered as they saw the three huge rounds of yellow cheese that depicted the suns. Then there was a crystallized fruit dish announced as The Crowning, which showed Edward being crowned King and that was met with appropriate shouts of *"Fiat! Fiat!"* And finally, there was brought forth a tow-

ering white confection, shaped like a rose and flowing with
honey, which was heralded as York Forever and to which
all raised their cups in toast.

Once the three subtleties had been carried around for all
to see, they were given places of honor on the sideboard,
and the meal continued.

The great hall rang with the raucous babble of voices
and laughter. Isabella, seated between Giles and Lionel at
the high table, was so excited, she could scarcely swallow
a mouthful from the many plates arrayed before her. Never
before had she seen such a display at Rushden! It was as
though they dined with the King himself, for the girl was
convinced nothing could have been finer. Her eyes sparkled
as she listened raptly to the conversations going on about
her—tales of Court and battles and faraway places—and
she felt very ignorant for knowing so little of such matters,
despite her lessons and her brother's letters. She worried
that Lionel would think her stupid and dull, though he flattered her expertly, outrageously, bringing blushes to her
cheeks, while Giles laughed and looked on with loving
approval. She felt so awkward and nervous and most unlike
herself that whenever a little silence fell, she bubbled over
with talk to fill it, then abruptly broke off, realizing she
was chattering like one of the squirrels in her menagerie.
She knew she had drunk too much wine, for her head was
spinning, and she felt hot and flushed. Her pulse raced as
she stole covert glances at Lionel beside her and wondered
if he had guessed she had fallen madly in love with him at
first sight.

It wasn't possible; surely, such things didn't happen.

But they do, she thought. I had only to look into his eyes
to know. . . . Oh, surely, he felt it too! 'Twas as though
suddenly an arrow pierced my heart—and I thought the
bards' songs of Cupid were only a myth!

Isabella blushed again and tried to concentrate on the
entertainment: the pretty maids in colorful costumes, who
danced on light feet; the acrobats and jugglers, who performed wondrous tricks of tumbling and sent bright balls
spinning with a whirl of flashing hands; and the fool, who
told bawdy jests and, with sly maliciousness, imitated those

who sought to make sport of him. Isabella prayed the nasty
dwarf would not see into her heart and expose her girlish
dreams to ridicule.

After supper, the long trestle tables were dismantled and
pushed back against the walls; and the gay lilt of the flute,
the thrum of the lute, and the echo of the harp filled the air
with music designed to lure those present into dancing. To
Isabella's surprise and astonishment, Richard rose and solemnly bowed low before her, ignoring the red flush of rage
and embarrassment that stained Lady Shrewton's cheeks at
being pointedly insulted. Honored, thrilled beyond belief,
the girl sank into a deep curtsy and extended her hand. She,
Lady Isabella Jane Ashley of Rushden, was to dance with
the second most important man in all of England! She would
never, not as long as she lived, forget this night or the
Duke's dark, sober eyes fixed kindly upon her face as he
guided her through the intricate maze of steps, then gently
laid her palm in Giles's outstretched hand when the music
changed.

"So, dear sister," her brother said, his eyes twinkling at
Isabella's highly apparent happiness. "Need I ask what ye
think of my choice for ye?"

"Oh, Giles, is it so obvious?" she queried anxiously.
"Have I made a fool of myself?"

"Nay." He laughed. "Ye have made Lionel the envy of
every man present."

Indeed, it was true: for none could help but mark the
favor that Isabella showed to the heir of St. Saviour, and
there were many who would have given much to be in his
shoes. Lord Oadby, especially, was most displeased with
the manner in which his ward was displaying her charms
and fawning over Lionel as though he were a prince. How
on earth had the tacky little caterpillar metamorphosed into
such a beautiful butterfly without the Earl having realized
it? Lord Oadby made a mental note to pay more attention
to the progress of his wards in the future—especially the
female ones.

Isabella did not see the lasciviously narrowed gaze of
her warden as he watched her closely, lustfully contemplating the possibilities of being the first to taste of her

innocence. She had eyes only for Lionel, who had claimed her hand for the third dance.

My Lord Lionel, now and for always, she vowed passionately to herself as she smiled up at him with the blind trust of youth.

Never had the days seemed so endless and yet passed so swiftly—too swiftly: for Isabella was young and in love in a way only the young can be—when love is new and shining like a beckoning star, and one rushes toward it without hesitation. It had come in a fleeting moment of breathlessness, a blinding flash of glory; and she reveled in it. First love is like that, clean and fresh, unmarred by the remembrance of pain that tarnishes later loves, no matter how hard one tries to polish it away, never realizing that sometimes, the dim patina, like that of old pewter, is more valuable for its scars.

The Duke of Gloucester had gone, taking his men. But, seeing the girl's crestfallen face and perhaps recalling his own sad, solitary youth, Richard had given Giles and Lionel leave to stay as long as the summer sun shone in the pale blue sky.

Every morning, Isabella rose, flung open her balcony doors, and begged the trees to keep their leaves just a little while longer; and perhaps because she was a child of nature, they seemed to hear her pleas and understand. Every day, she and Giles and Lionel rode beneath the shade of the spreading oaks and yews, the ashes and pines; and life was good. Never had the girl felt so alive, so filled with joy that she brimmed over with laughter and exhilaration. She galloped recklessly through the woods; she danced wildly in the meadows; she hugged herself with secret delight at night, when she lay in bed and thought of Lionel. She would mourn Giles's departure, but Lionel's leaving . . . ah, Lionel's leaving would be the death of her; she was sure. And so each day with him was like a treasure, to be held close and cherished.

It was as though some strange madness possessed her, for she was giddy with love. She could not wait to become Lionel's wife. Isabella had seen the way his eyes raked her budding young body and smoldered like embers with desire. She had felt the electric touch of his fingers and his lips upon her hands. She was certain it was only a matter of time before he gained permission for their marriage.

Oh, Lionel. *Lionel!*

The girl did not know she had cried the words aloud until she heard the echo of their refrain. She was soaring high above the ground; the swing that hung from a massive oak was her wings, and Lionel's arms were the arms that pushed her. He laughed.

"Higher, 'Sabelle!" he called. "I shall make ye go even higher!"

"Nay! Nay, already I grow faint."

"Then jump." He was suddenly there before her, his arms spread wide. "Jump! I shall catch ye."

She never doubted for a moment that he would. She let go of the swing, flying through the air into Lionel's outstretched arms. They closed about her tightly, and then she and he were falling, falling . . . tumbling upon the wild summer grass, their laughter ringing out over the small, hushed clearing wherein the swing hung. They stopped at last. Lionel looked down at her, his eyes darkening in a way that sent shivers up Isabella's spine.

He wanted her, wanted her with the hot passion that had come upon him like a fever the first time he'd seen her. It was all he could do to keep from ravishing her then and there. But he held back, for Isabella was no bored Court lady seeking a little amusement during her husband's absence, nor was she some yeoman's daughter who could not cry out against his rape of her. Isabella was a young maid of noble birth, Giles's sister, and, most important, the King's ward. Like the rest of His Grace's property, one damaged Edward's wards at the risk of one's life. Isabella would expect Lionel to marry her—and rightfully so. He swore silently at the thought, for much as he might have wished it, he was in no position to wed the girl. He was already betrothed—to Lady Gilliane Beaumaris of Devizes.

Lionel's eyes narrowed, glittering with anger and disgust as Gilliane's plain brunette image filled his mind. He had no desire to marry that timid brown mouse who squeaked and scurried from his presence; but she was the daughter of his father's best friend, and the betrothal had been arranged while Lionel and Gilliane had been in their cradles. There was nothing he could do about it, and his impotence in the matter galled him. Why should he be forced to marry Gilliane when a woman like Isabella lay within his grasp?

He was a Valeureux, damn it! Descended from the Normans who had conquered all of England. His bride ought to be the *crème de la crème* of women, not some colorless little mouse who would give him a parcel of brats as puny as she. He gazed down at Isabella raptly, his eyes still dark and hungry in a manner that almost frightened her. She was a prize worth having, this slender, silvery forest nymph whom Lionel held in his arms. Ah, what sons *she* would breed him: fine strong sons a man would be proud to call his own.

The thought of filling Isabella with such sons made Lionel's loins race with excitement. Never had he seen a maid who intrigued him so. Half-woman, half-child, she had bewitched him with her haunting grey-green eyes, her fey, wraithlike grace. He could almost fancy himself in love with the wench, as he knew she was fervently enamored of him.

Aye, Lionel wanted her. He must find a way to have her—Gilliane Beaumaris be damned!

"Ye wouldst drive a man mad, 'Sabelle," he muttered, then brushed a strand of silky hair from her face.

He's going to kiss me, the girl thought, her heart beating crazily in her breast. He's going to kiss me!

Oh, if only the blood would stop rushing through her veins at such a pace! She was so nervous, she couldn't even think. Her hands trembled slightly on his shoulders; her palms were as cold as ice and yet sweating somehow too. It seemed she had waited all her life for this moment, and now that it had come, she didn't know what to do. She swallowed hard, tilting her face up and parting her lips in what she prayed was the right manner.

Oh, how soft his mouth was, and how it thrilled her, moving against her own gently until she was accustomed to the feel of his lips and had begun to kiss Lionel back

with eager shyness, wanting to learn, wanting to please him.
Hesitantly, Isabella caressed his golden hair as he wrapped
his hands in her own silver cascade, his tongue finding its
way inside her mouth to explore the sweetness that awaited
therein. A warm glow filled her body at the intimate contact,
and she pressed herself against him, wanting to make this
moment last forever. A low moan emanated from her throat
as his hands slid down her back, crushing her to him, and
his lips grew more demanding. Suddenly, Isabella was
breathless with the wakening of her womanhood. Time
stopped and yet flew by on wings, it seemed; and then,
without warning, Lionel was drawing away from her, his
eyes lowered against her searching, love-filled glance, so
she could not read his thoughts. He kissed her lightly once
more, then rose and held out his hand.

"Come, 'Sabelle," he said. "It grows late. We must return
to the keep."

"Aye," she breathed, then, for one moment, ceased to
breathe at all as her hand touched his.

Lionel had kissed many women, but Isabella did not
know that. Nor did she know what had caused the brief
shadowing of his handsome visage or the agony it fore-
boded. She knew only that her first kiss was as beautiful
as she had dreamt it would be and that she would love
Lionel Valeureux until the day she died.

The great hall was still. Isabella sat quietly, embroidering
on the tapestry she had begun, which would chronicle Giles's
adventures. The girl was clumsy and impatient with her
needle when it came to such work, and her task was made
even more difficult by the tears that stung her eyes, blurring
the design.

The trees had shed their leaves. Autumn was upon them,
and Giles and Lionel must journey north to join the Duke
of Gloucester. Isabella's brother stared glumly into his wine
cup, for he knew how their coming departure had saddened
his sister. Lionel, morose as well because he had not thought
of some means of extricating himself from his betrothal to
Gilliane Beaumaris, plucked idly at the strings of his lute.
He knew that Isabella and Giles both fully expected him

to ask for the girl's hand before leaving, and he knew too that he could not. His position was made even more uncomfortable by the fact that he could not even explain his dilemma to them. The Ashleys were a proud and honorable family. They had taken Lionel into their home and hearts and let it be known that he would be welcome as Isabella's husband. They would scorn and despise him if they discovered how he had deceived them by wooing the girl when he could not wed her; and Lionel found he could not bear the thought of their contempt.

"Give us a song, my lord." Giles spoke with forced cheerfulness, at last, to break the silence, slurring his words just a little, for he was half-drunk.

"Oh, aye!" Isabella cried.

Anything to break the awful stillness of the chamber! Anything so the two she loved most deeply would not see the tears that threatened to spill from her sorrow-filled eyes.

Happy to comply, Lionel strummed a few chords on the lovely lute, which was fashioned of mellow wood inlaid with mother-of-pearl.

"I shall play ye a song I wrote myself just yesterday eve," he informed them, his eyes upon Isabella's face before he began to sing.

> "Scarlet lips hath my lady fair.
> Soft as silk her flaxen hair.
> Her beauty lies beyond compare.
> A white rose is my lady.

> "Dusk-pink the cheeks upon her face.
> Black-lashed eyes of grey-green lace.
> Fair is she; I rest my case.
> A white rose is my lady.

> "Cupid hath let his arrow fly.
> I love this maid, I'll not deny.
> To kiss her lips, I'd gladly die.
> A white rose is my lady.

> "To thee, fair maid, a troth I'll plight.
> If thou knowest of the trysting site,

Meet me there in pale moonlight.
A white rose is my lady."

The plaintive notes of the lover's lament died away slowly.
Isabella lowered her eyes to her embroidery, her heart
pounding with anticipation. The meadow! The meadow in
the woods where the swing hung. Lionel wanted her to meet
him there, tonight! She was sure of it. And there, he would
ask her to marry him. Tears filled her eyes again, but this
time, they were tears of joy.

It seemed as though Isabella had waited forever, but at
last, Rushden Castle was quiet. In the small antechamber
of the girl's room, old Alice was snoring gently; and farther
down the corridor, in his own chamber, Giles was deep in
wine-steeped slumber. Lord Oadby and Lady Shrewton
had retired hours ago to the Countess's room and had
not reappeared. Silently, Isabella rose, pulled on her robe,
then, on stealthy, hushed feet, tiptoed downstairs to the
great hall, where Sirs Eadric, Thegn, and Beowulf lay
sprawled upon pallets on the rush-strewn floor. Half-
consumed tankards of ale sat beside the knights, and a
pair of dice was thrown carelessly to one side amid a scattering of coins. The girl breathed a sigh of relief at this
evidence of the men's earlier activity, for she knew they
too had passed from drunken stupor to a sleep from which
they would not easily awaken. Normally, the three knights,
who had taken to guarding her, would have been roused by
the slightest disturbance and leaped to their feet, swords in
hand. But tonight, they didn't stir as Isabella crept over
them.

Still, the girl's fingers trembled as she lifted the heavy
wooden shaft that barred the front doors, and for an instant,
she froze, her heart thudding horribly in her breast, as Eadric
snorted suddenly in his sleep and rolled to a more comfortable position. Then she was out into the darkness, her
bare feet flying over the cobblestones to the postern gate.

The night was as still as Rushden had been, the silence
broken only by the faint sigh of the wind that rustled the

dying leaves of the trees and sent the tall wet grass rippling, scattering the dewdrops so they glistened like prisms beneath the stars. Above, the frosted moon shone down like a halo, lighting the path that led to the meadow.

When Isabella had reached the place, she paused, glancing around expectantly for Lionel.

"Lionel?" she whispered, but there was no response.

Her heart plummeted in despair, thinking she had misunderstood the words of his song after all.

"Lionel?"

"Enchanté, demoiselle," he answered softly, grinning as he stepped from the shadows.

"Oh, my lord! Ye—ye frightened me," Isabella said, exhaling with relief at the sight of him, then giving a small, nervous laugh and putting one hand to her breast, where her heart was beating rapidly.

"Forgive me, my dearest heart, but I wanted to be certain 'twas ye and not some other who didst seek our trysting place."

The moonlight shone down upon his golden hair, making him seem like some young god in the darkness as he took her hands in his, and she thrilled to his words of endearment and caressing touch. She could hardly believe he was hers, that this handsome man who stood so boldly, so gloriously, before her would someday be her husband, that they would pledge their troth to each other here and now, for always.

Isabella gazed around the meadow, wanting to engrave its every detail upon her memory: how the moon streamed down like glowing mist through the branches of the gnarled trees; how the grass sparkled as though a thousand diamonds lay upon the earth; how the swing, hanging from the old oak, moved gently in the wind, which was crisp and clean with the smell of autumn. The girl could almost imagine fairies dancing in the darkness, for the clearing seemed suddenly mystical and filled with the magic of love.

"'Sabelle," Lionel breathed. "'Sabelle."

His voice was low and thick with passion, and he kissed her with an urgency she could not deny, did not want to deny. Feverishly, she clung to him, her breasts pressed against his chest so she could feel their hearts pounding as

one, even as their mouths met; their tongues entwined; their
bodies embraced. Isabella could taste the wine he'd drunk
earlier, sweet upon his lips, and smell the fragrant trace of
sandalwood soap upon his skin; and she knew, from this
moment on, that she would always associate those things
with Lionel and this night, just as the meadow would forever
be their special place.

Lionel's mouth left hers to travel across her cheek to her
temple, to the silky strands of her hair. He buried his face
in the cascading mane, inhaling the deep rose scent of her
as he crushed her to him; then suddenly, he swept her up
and whirled her about as though he heard some wild and
poignant melody played for them alone. Isabella found she
was laughing and crying at the same time, the tears streaming down her face as she smiled down at him, caught up
in the bittersweet ecstasy of the moment.

"Oh, Lionel, my love," she said ardently when, at last,
he had released her, and she could breathe once more.
"'Twill be like dying when ye leave me."

"I shall come back, 'Sabelle," he told her earnestly.
"Never doubt that, my dearest heart."

Then, perhaps moved by the wine and the headiness of
the night, he yanked his sword from its scabbard and plunged
the blade into the ground dramatically. It fluttered there
gently for an instant, bright and gleaming like a molten
silver cross where the moonbeams struck it, sending lambent
rays in all directions. Lionel dropped to one knee, laying
his hands upon the hilt.

"Aye, I shall come back, 'Sabelle, and I shall make ye
mine or die trying. By all that is holy, this I swear."

She gasped at the seriousness of the vow, touched to the
very core of her soul, as he had known she would be. The
laughter left her countenance, leaving only the tears glittering like raindrops in her wide grey-green eyes. How he
must love her to make such a pledge! A strange chill of
foreboding possessed her. 'Twas tempting fate to love like
that!

Isabella sank to the earth before him, placing her hands
over his and looking up raptly into his deep blue eyes.

"Oh, Lionel. Lionel! Take it back! I wouldst not hold ye to such a vow. 'Tis wrong! Take it back!"

"Nay," he refused, his golden visage suddenly hungry and defiant. "'Tis done. Oh, God, 'Sabelle!" he cried, flinging the sword aside. "Thou hast bewitched me!"

Then somehow, they were lying upon the grass, and he was loosing the lacings of her robe, pulling at the straps of her shift. She shivered as he bared her breasts, and the cold night air touched them. For a moment, she was startled, for no man had gazed upon her so; and she was young and afraid.

Lionel seemed to sense her uneasiness, for he muttered, "Christ, ye are so beautiful." Then he groaned, "Oh, 'Sabelle, I cannot wait to have ye. I have tried. . . . God knows, I have! But each day with ye has but made me more determined to have ye. Say ye will be mine . . . now . . . tonight!"

Isabella quivered in his warm embrace, uncertain, frightened, yet wanting him so.

"I—I am a maid," she whispered.

"'Sabelle"—his voice was urgent in her ear—"I do not know when Gloucester will give me leave to come again. God's wounds! Ye have stirred my blood all summer. Ye cannot deny me now! Have I not pledged, on my oath, my troth to make ye mine?"

"Aye, oh, aye. But I am afraid, so afraid. Oh, Lionel!"

"Do not fear, my dearest heart," he murmured reassuringly. "There is naught to fear. I shall be gentle with ye."

His hands wrapped themselves in her tangle of silvery tresses as he kissed her deeply once more, his tongue parting her resisting lips savagely until they yielded to him. His fingers swept down to cup one firm, budding breast, and then it seemed his hands were everywhere, touching her, setting her body ablaze with a hot flame of desire as she writhed beneath him. His mouth left hers to cover the rosy tips of her breasts with sweet caresses of moisture. His tongue flicked the rigid little peaks lightly. Isabella stirred in his grasp and moaned, trembling with slowly awakening passion. Her body arched against Lionel's. In minutes, she would be his. . . .

A cloud passed across the face of the moon, and somewhere in the distance, a lone hawk screamed in the darkness, startling them.

Frightened again, Isabella wrenched herself free and sat up, clutching her garments to her naked chest. To her fanciful nature, the momentary shadowing of the moon, followed by the bird's piercing cry, seemed an ill omen. She shuddered, and the magic spell of the night was broken. Lionel inhaled sharply and shook his head, trying to clear it of the madness that had possessed him: for surely, that is what it had been. Dear God. He had nearly seduced the King's ward! To take Isabella now, under false pretenses, would be to dishonor her for all time and bring Edward's wrath crashing down upon his head. The girl was a marriage prize, and until she was wed, His Grace would not look pleasantly on the absence of her maidenhead—or the man who had taken it. Not until Lionel was free of his betrothal to Lady Gilliane Beaumaris could he dare to dream of making Isabella his.

Slowly, Lionel helped the girl reassemble her nightclothes, then brushed the twigs from her hair, each knowing the moment of her surrender had been lost.

Chapter Six

LORD OADBY'S BEADY, RED-RIMMED EYES WERE GLAZED with lust as he watched the two lovers from the shadows. How fortunate that he had seen Isabella slipping from her chamber and had stealthily followed her—the little slut. Now that he had learned of her willingness to lie with the first handsome courtier who had come along, the Earl felt less apprehensive about his own plans for the girl. After all, she could hardly protest against his taking of her maidenhead when, like a common serving wench, she had been ready to give it away to Lord Lionel Valeureux, a mere, inexperienced youth who had flattered her with a few pretty phrases. Lord Oadby smiled sourly. The boy had bungled things badly, carrying on with his sword in that ridiculous fashion instead of simply taking Isabella before she'd a chance to consider the full import of the act. Virgins always hesitated unless one dealt firmly with them, paying no heed to their outcries of fear.

Thank God, the Earl was not a romantic fool, bothered by stupid notions of honor and property. *He* would know how to handle the girl, and she wouldn't be running to the Duke of Gloucester with any tales now either. Christ's son, but she was beautiful. Just the thought of how her pale, naked breasts had gleamed in the moonlight was enough to make Lord Oadby's manhood harden rapaciously once more. He had been stirred earlier by the sight of Isabella's rosy nipples and had eased the ache in his loins with his hand, but there had been little satisfaction in it. Now, the Earl was so excited, he was trembling. He could scarcely wait to make the girl his. Greedily smacking his lips together with anticipation, he hurried after the two lovers as quietly as possible.

Oh, what luck! Providence had indeed smiled upon Lord Oadby tonight. Some animal in Isabella's menagerie had mewed pitifully, and instead of returning to the keep, she was heading for the stables, parting from Lord Lionel with a few whispered words and a brief kiss. The Earl could hardly believe his good fortune. Surely, his possession of the girl was meant to be. He pushed the last of his qualms about the Duke of Gloucester from his mind and, suppressing the desire he felt to chortle aloud with glee, slowly swung open the stable door.

He glanced about eagerly, then frowned with puzzlement. Isabella was nowhere to be seen, and yet, Lord Oadby knew, with certainty, that he had indeed observed her entering the stables. Then the low sound of her voice crooning softly reached his ears, and he realized she was in the loft. He cursed silently to himself, for he would have to climb the ladder that led to the upper story of the stables, and his painful gout would make that difficult. Nevertheless, the throbbing bulge in his hose drove him on. As best he could, he clambered up the rungs, huffing and puffing until, red-faced from exertion, he attained the top. Once there, he paused momentarily to regain his breath, then staggered toward the girl.

Isabella gazed up with fright as, without warning, the Earl's fat figure loomed toward her menacingly from the shadows, and for a moment, she was so stunned, she couldn't move. She had thought Lord Oadby in bed with his mistress. To suddenly see him lurching toward her so purposefully, his intent plain, was a shock that took her some minutes to absorb. Then, with a small cry of terror, she pushed the whimpering kitten she'd been soothing from her lap and leaped to her feet, frantically searching for someplace to run to. But there was nowhere to hide, and the Earl was standing between her and the ladder. She was trapped. Wild-eyed with panic, the girl cast about desperately for some sort of weapon, then seized upon a nearby pitchfork. She turned, wielding the tool threateningly.

"Get away," she warned her warden, whose evil pig eyes were blinking rapidly with surprise. "Don't come near me, or I'll use this, I promise ye."

"Now, my dear," Lord Oadby wheedled, "there's no need for such hysterics. I did but see the light"—he indicated the torch that Isabella had lit upon entering the stables—"and come to investigate to discover whether or not there was aught amiss here. 'Tis my duty, ye know, as your warden to be certain all is well at Rushden."

"Well, there's nothing wrong," the girl hissed, refusing to relinquish her hold on the pitchfork and backing away warily as the Earl sidled toward her. "'Twas but one of the new kittens, crying out with loneliness and fear, so ye may return to your chamber at once."

"Why, I cannot possibly leave ye alone here, my dear. What if one of the men-at-arms were to find ye and take advantage of your solitude here in the stables? 'Tis a ways from the keep, and no one would hear if ye screamed for help," Lord Oadby noted blandly. "'Tis my obligation to conduct ye safely to your room."

"I have no need of your escort, I assure ye. There is no

man at Rushden who would do me harm—except yourself, my lord."

"I?" The Earl looked hurt. "Why, my dear, I am indeed sorely grieved that ye would believe such a thing of me when I have done my best to see ye were properly cared for all these years."

Isabella snorted with contempt.

"Don't make me laugh, my lord," she sneered. "Ye and your whore have done naught but desecrate the memory of my parents and stuff your purses with Rushden's gold. My brother and I are not as stupid as ye would wish, my lord. We are well aware that were it not for the Duke of Gloucester, by now, we would be little better than paupers. Indeed, 'tis only your fear of Richard that has prevented ye from impoverishing us. We do but wait until Giles reaches his majority to call for an accounting of our estate and seek redress from the King for your treatment of us. We are Ashleys, my lord, one of the oldest and most powerful families in all of England and staunch Yorkists besides. We are not pigeons for your plucking, and we shall not be left penniless when ye depart here. No matter how cleverly ye have concealed your thievery, we shall discover what has been stolen from us, and ye shall be made to repay it down to the last tuppence, I promise ye!"

The Earl shrugged.

"I do not think so, my dear," he said. "Your brother will not be the first young man to suffer a tragic accident, and ye will not be so high and mighty, I'll wager, once ye find yourself in a Moorish whorehouse. But first, I shall have a taste of what ye almost wasted on Lord Lionel, ye stupid little tart."

Lord Oadby grabbed the pitchfork so suddenly from Isabella's hands that she was taken by surprise and lost her hold on the weapon. She had not thought his gluttonous, gout-ridden figure capable of moving so fast. Then, before she realized what was happening, the Earl dealt her a cruel blow with his fist. The girl reeled, falling to her knees, her head spinning dizzily from the impact of the punch as she cowered upon the floor, petrified. Blindly, she attempted to crawl away, but before she could escape, Lord Oadby was upon her, straddling her, pinning her down beneath the weight of his considerable bulk. His fat, groping fingers caught her wildly clawing hands easily and pinioned them above her head. Then, with a jeering smile of satisfaction and triumph, he ripped open the lacings on her robe and tore her shift in half, exposing her heaving breasts to his leering stare.

"I'm going to enjoy taking your maidenhead, my dear," he told the terrified Isabella crudely, his slack mouth fairly drooling as he gazed down at her stricken countenance.

She screamed hysterically, and he slapped her hard across the face to silence her outcries. Then, with his free hand, he began to fondle her breasts, squeezing them and pinching her nipples. Tears of shame and horror and rage at her helplessness streamed down the girl's cheeks as she moaned and tried to stifle the ragged sobs that rose in her throat, choking her. This couldn't be happening. This just couldn't be real!

Lord Oadby, thinking the fight had gone out of her at last, groaned and rose slightly, fumbling with his hose. Isabella seized the opportunity to bring one knee up sharply between his legs. The Earl gasped with pain at the unexpected assault and rolled off her, doubled over in agony. Unsteadily, the girl managed to get to her feet. She began to run, but Lord Oadby, forcing himself to recover, heaved his gross body up and grabbed her hair, yanking her back. Isabella struggled furiously against him, and as they spun about crazily, locked in mortal combat, the Earl lost his footing and, nearly taking the girl with him, toppled over the edge of the loft. His lips parted with incredulity, his arms flailing wildly, he fell, striking his head against the solid wooden door of one of the stalls below. He crumpled into a large heap and was still.

Still dazed with shock and terror, Isabella leaned cautiously over the precipice, not quite believing her tormentor had been bested. The odious Lord Oadby lay slumped beneath her like a pile of blubber. His neck was twisted at an odd angle, and blood was seeping from a huge gash at the back of his head. He was, the girl recognized with mingled horror and relief, quite dead.

She sank to the floor of the loft, sobbing uncontrollably as she clutched the torn remnants of her nightclothes to her and rocked back and forth like a dull-witted child. After a time, she giggled nervously, then laughed and laughed hysterically until the tears ran down her face. With difficulty, she forced herself to stop. She gasped raggedly for breath, then, upon realizing, at last, that something would have to be done, attempted to rise. Her knees buckled, but she caught herself and made her way slowly down the ladder, not daring to glance again at the Earl's inert, sprawled form.

Minutes later, she was shaking her sleeping brother awake.

"Giles!" she whispered urgently. "Giles, wake up!"

"Hmmm," he moaned, then licked his lips to moisten them and swallowed, making a soft, sucking noise. "Hmmm." He stirred and shifted his position while Isabella looked quickly at her brother's tutor to be certain that Master Jaksone still slept soundly in the antechamber of Giles's room.

"Giles!"

"What? What? What is it?" He suddenly sat straight up in bed, wide-eyed as he stared about in confusion. He blinked, rubbing the sleep from his eyes, and then cried, "'Sabelle! What are ye doing here? What's wrong?"

"Shhhhh. Keep your voice down!" she warned lowly. "There's been an accident in the stables. Lord Oadby is dead, and I need your help."

Wide awake now, he took in the state of her apparel and inhaled sharply.

"Godamercy, 'Sabelle! Did he rape ye?"

"Nay, but 'twas only by the grace of God that I escaped. Come quickly. We must think what is to be done."

Her brother was already hauling on his clothes as silently and rapidly as possible. In moments, the two were out in the corridor.

"Wait, 'Sabelle. I'll get Lionel. We may need him."

Briefly, she paused, considering, then nodded in agreement. Her beloved would not betray them. Giles slipped down the hall, only to reappear a short time later with his foster brother. Lionel was still tucking his shirt into his hose, and his golden visage was shadowed with anger and concern. He strode forward worriedly upon spying Isabella and took her hands in his.

"'Sabelle! Art hurt?" he asked.

"Nay." She drew comfort from the warmth of his touch, glad he was there, holding her close.

"By God, the whoreson bastard!" Lionel's voice shook with rage. "I should never have let ye go to the stables alone!"

Giles stared at them sharply at that but said nothing. Lionel was his foster brother. If he had been trysting in the moonlight with Isabella, it was with honorable intentions, Giles was sure. Besides, the girl had had little enough happiness in her life as it was. He did not begrudge her a few moments of stolen joy.

"Come," Isabella urged. "We must hurry, else someone may find the body."

"Jesus Christ!" Giles cursed when they had reached the stables. He kicked the Earl's corpse viciously. "The pig!" he spat.

"Oh, Giles, what are we to do?" Isabella inquired anxiously, biting her lip. "We dare not let anyone discover what has happened, for many know of Lord Oadby's perfidy to us; and perhaps none would believe my story, thinking we wished our warden ill. And, oh, Giles! We *didst* swear to have our revenge upon him! *Fiat!* Let it be done. Remember? We cannot risk having anyone investigate the Earl's death and find some reason to bring the King's wrath down upon us."

"No one who knew Lord Oadby would doubt your word, 'Sabelle," Giles assured her. "Still, perhaps 'tis best not to take any chances. In truth, we do not know what sort of friends the Earl may have had at Court, and if they are at all like him, we would not be safe from their vengeance."

"I have thought of a plan," Lionel announced. "We must dress the swine in his hunting clothes and take his body out to that ravine—ye know, Giles—the one in the woods, where the waterfall runs down into that little stream. We must throw the corpse down into the gully, as though the whoreson bastard suffered a fall from his horse while out hunting and broke his neck. How fortunate for us that the pig didn't ride well and was as fat as a toad besides. No one will doubt that the clumsy glutton pressed his over-burdened steed and took a fatal tumble. The churl used his spurs often enough most cruelly on the poor beast, did he not?"

"Aye." Giles nodded. "It might work. It might indeed. The whoreson bastard often hunted alone—although me-thinks his prey was but poor wenches, with whom he made savage sport." Her brother's face looked deadly in the flick-ering torchlight, and Isabella shivered uncontrollably for a moment. "We shall have to hurry," Giles continued, "for already, dawn draws near; and we must leave here in the morning as we'd planned."

"Oh, Giles, nay!" the girl cried.

"Aye, dear sister, we must. 'Twould seem odd to change our plans at the last minute, and 'twould give cause for suspicion if we stayed, and then Lord Oadby's body was discovered. Ye must be brave enough to face, without us, whatever tomorrow may bring."

"Giles is right, 'Sabelle," Lionel declared, giving her hand a gentle, reassuring squeeze. "Come. We have much to do and scant time in which to do it."

"'Sabelle, go back to the keep," Giles ordered, "and fetch Eadric, Thegn, and Beowulf. I know, from your let-ters, that they love us well and can be trusted. Inform them of what has happened. Then tell them they are to relieve the sentries on guard duty at the main gate and that, in the morning, they are to say they saw the Earl ride out early, alone, to go hunting. When Lord Oadby does not return, they are to lead a search party to find him. Be certain they understand that they—and they alone—are to search the area around the ravine. 'Twill be simpler if they are the ones to discover the body, as they will know how to answer any questions put to them.

"Lionel will go with ye and get Lord Oadby's hunting

clothes whilst I strip the corpse and saddle the Earl's horse. Hurry now!" Giles reiterated urgently. "Each moment we delay does but bring the dawn closer."

At last, after what seemed like hours, the conspirators had carried out their scheme and, exhausted, sought their beds. Though as weary as the rest, still, Isabella lay awake, numbly going over and over again in her mind the events of the night. It was with difficulty that she pushed the horrible memory of Lord Oadby from her thoughts and tried to concentrate instead on Lionel, her beloved.

Thus, it was only later—much later—that she recalled that though the heir of St. Saviour had sworn to make her his, he had mentioned no word of marriage. And though Isabella tried desperately to ignore it, to reassure herself of Lionel's love for her, a small, fearful doubt about his feelings toward her crept into her heart and mind—and would not be banished.

Chapter Seven

The Hills, Wales, 1453

THE NIGHT WAS AN EBONY VELVET BACKDROP, AGAINST which the pale sheen of the ghostly grey fog, which hung low and thick over the land, swirled with an unworldly shimmer. Above, the mist-ringed moon shone through the branches of the trees with a silvery haze that drifted across the well-worn paths twisting like a maze through the savage Welsh hills. From the distance came the cry of some lone animal, but other than this, the darkness was still save for the quick, ragged gasps of the woman who now leaned against an aged, bent tree for support and tried to catch her breath. The pause in her flight was brief. After casting a furtive glance over her shoulder, she began once more to run, her bare feet as fleet as the hooves of a deer bounding through the forest.

This morn, she had been the daughter of a powerful

Welsh chieftain, Owein, and the wife of a handsome Welsh lord, Bryn-Dyfed. Tonight, she was naught but a captive of her enemies, the English. After the bloody battle, her father had managed to get away to some hiding place, where those of his men who remained would join him. But her husband had been slain—she had seen him fall, his head split open by the blade of an enemy ax—and she had been taken prisoner to be held for ransom. Only her wits had allowed her to escape. She smiled grimly to herself as she thought of how easy it had been to fool the two stupid sentries who had guarded her. Still, the lord who was her captor was not so easily deceived.

Even now, from behind, the sound of pursuit was audible to her keen ears, and spurred her on. The path grew steeper. The woman's pace slowed as she clambered over the sharp rocks that jutted from the earth. She screamed as the echo of laughter rang out through the night, and a man's hand grabbed her ankle from below, hauling her down to the flatter ground. She struggled desperately in his arms, but at last, he pinioned her wrists behind her back, then dealt her several sharp slaps across the face.

"Bastard!" she hissed, knowing now that escape was impossible. "English dog!"

The man only laughed again, his teeth flashing whitely in the moonlight.

"Ah, Hwyelis"—he caught her tangle of rich brown hair, forcing her face up to his—"what a merry chase ye have led me! But now . . . ye are mine!"

He ground his mouth down on hers hard, then abruptly flung her to the earth. For a moment, he stood towering over her like some tall golden god, noting the way her long lithe legs gleamed where her skirts had ridden up to her thighs; the way her full soft breasts heaved beneath the thin material of her gown; the way her generous, lush mouth parted and trembled; the way her mysterious, pale blue eyes glittered as she pulled the knife at her waist to defend herself. The man glanced at the dagger carelessly, as though it were little more than a pin to prick him.

"Dost mean to use that on yourself or me, my lady?" He lifted one eyebrow devilishly, as though amused.

"On ye, Tremayne!" she spat. "Think ye that I wouldst let ye touch me—ye, an enemy of my people?"

"But not *your* enemy, Hwyelis," he purred softly, "not after tonight. After tonight, I shall be your lover, and when I am through with ye, ye will beg me to take ye and make ye so."

"Nay!"

"Shall we see, my lady? I will even make ye a wager to add spice to the sport."

"What sort of wager?" Hwyelis gazed up at her captor suspiciously, wondering if he had thought of some means to trick her as she had his sentries.

"I will wager ye this: If, even once, during my taking of ye, I cause ye to cry out with wanting for me, then when the child of our mating is eight years old, ye will bring him to me, to be raised as I see fit."

"Child? How can ye be so sure there will come a babe of our mating, Tremayne?"

"I feel it, Hwyelis—in my bones and in my blood. I knew, from the first moment I saw ye, that I must have ye, my lady. That is why I have not yet ransomed ye back to your father. Aye, ye will give me my son, Hwyelis; have no doubt about that."

She tossed her head scornfully.

"And if I do not cry out?"

"Then ye may keep the child—a bad bargain for me, since the puny brats my wife has bred are sickly lads, like their mother, not likely to survive till manhood; and since my previous mistresses—God, curse my luck—proved barren. I need an heir, my lady. I am the last of my name."

"Dost think me a fool?" she asked, sneering. "A half-Welsh bastard is not likely to inherit the earldom of a powerful English lord, Tremayne. 'Tis a trick! Ye do but lie to deceive me!"

"There is a little-known clause in the Hawkhurst charter that permits such a descendance if there are no legitimate males of the line remaining. On my honor, I swear 'tis so," he continued when she remained silent. "Ah, that sweetens your temper toward me, Hwyelis, does it not?" The Lord grinned wryly as he saw her eyes suddenly narrow with calculation.

"Ye must have me first—and win the wager!" She pointed her knife at his heart threateningly, defensive again. "And I shall slay ye before ye do either!"

"The wager stands then?"

"Aye."

"Your word on it, my lady."

"Ye have it."

Lord Hawkhurst laughed loudly once more, then kicked the dagger from her hands and fell upon her.

"Ah, ye will be a fit mother for my son, Hwyelis. Thou art as wild as a savage hawk, my lady, but I shall tame ye nevertheless; never ye fear, my sweet Welsh witch," he breathed, his lips silencing any response she might have made.

Then there was nothing for her but his lovemaking and, sometime later, her single cry of surrender as he drove strongly between her thighs and smiled down at her with triumph in his strange amber eyes.

As though he could not believe his ears, the sentry stared down at the lone woman and four young lads who stood outside the portcullis of the old castle.

"Did ye hear me?" the woman called angrily. "I am the Lady Hwyelis uerch Owein, and this boy"—she pushed one of the children forward—"is Waerwic, son of Lord Hawkhurst. I demand ye admit us at once. I warn ye: Tremayne will have your head on a platter if ye turn us away."

The young guard was new at this post and did not know what to do. At last, he summoned the master-at-arms, who boxed the sentry's ears smartly for keeping the Lord's former mistress and his child standing outside in the hot sun. Nine years had passed since the master-at-arms had laid eyes on the Lady Hwyelis, but he would not soon forget that rich cascade of tangled brown curls or those mysterious, pale blue eyes that had so enchanted his lord.

"'Tis indeed the Lady Hwyelis, one of the Lord's favorites!" the master-at-arms informed the guard. "Ye will

be lucky if the Lord does not put ye in the stocks! Why,
the poor Lady is nigh to fainting from her long journey and
the heat. Raise the portcullis at once, fool!"

"But—but, sir, how was I to know? She is without an
escort—or even a horse!"

"No matter. It be the Lady Hwyelis right enough."

Once inside, Hwyelis and her children were taken to a
chamber where they could refresh themselves before Lord
Hawkhurst, who was out hunting, returned. There, Hwyelis
stared at her reflection in the looking glass and sighed. She
had donned her finest garments for the trip to Devon, but
now, they were bedraggled, stained with salt water from
her crossing of the Bristol Channel and dirt from the roads
she had walked upon after leaving her small boat. With the
help of a serving maid, she did her best to repair the damage,
for there were no ladies-in-waiting to attend her. The Lord's
wife had died, along with the two small sons she had given
him.

Hwyelis gazed at Waerwic. 'Twas good she had kept her
bargain and brought the boy here, to Hawkhurst Castle. One
day, he would be its lord; and despite the fact that the keep
was old and, from what she had seen, in sad disrepair, it
would offer him a far better future than the savage hills of
Wales. Here, Waerwic would become an earl, a man of
property and importance. In Wales, the most he could hope
to attain would be service to some lord. She smiled at the
eight-year-old, solemn-faced lad, who did not yet fully
understand why they had journeyed so far from home.
All he knew was that his grandfather, Owein, had been
very angry at their going.

"Hwyelis, thou art a fool!" Grandfather had thundered
upon learning of their plans to travel to England. "Dost truly
think the English dog will recognize the brat? Ha! 'Tis more
than likely the pig will not even recall your name! God's
blood! Have ye not shamed us enough already? Three bastards ye have borne, and both Powys and Newyddllyn willing to marry ye!"

Hwyelis had tossed her head proudly, unmoved by her
father's wrath and his tirade.

"I am not a woman to be bound to any man. I told ye I'd no wish to wed when ye gave me to Bryn-Dyfed, though I didst love him well. My life is my own. Tremayne will remember; he is not a man to forget. He will claim the boy as his and make Waerwic his heir. I shall not throw away such an opportunity for my son simply because his grandfather chooses to be a fool!"

And so they had come to Hawkhurst.

Aye, Tremayne will remember, Hwyelis thought as she continued to study her son.

The boy had her rich brown hair, streaked with the gold of his father's, and his father's odd yellow eyes, filled with mystery like Hwyelis's own. There could be no mistaking the child's heritage.

"Hwyelis!" Lord Hawkhurst burst into the chamber at last, and one glance at him told her she need not worry that he would cast the lad aside. "Ye came! After all this time, ye came!"

Then he swept her into his arms and kissed her; and a thousand memories of the long sweet nights they had lain together in the Welsh hills, before she had been ransomed, flooded her very being. In her fashion, she had loved Tremayne, as she had loved all those with whom she had shared her body. It was good to feel his arms about her again. Lord Hawkhurst's eyes glittered as they raked her eagerly, and he remembered too. In the end, he had been forced to let her go, but he had never forgotten her, for she was a woman a man did not forget.

"Hwyelis," he said once more, scarcely daring to believe she was here, was real.

She gave a little tinkle of laughter, as though guessing his thoughts, and flung her head back in that arrogant manner he recalled so well.

"Tremayne. I have come, as promised."

He sighed.

"After all these years, I am still Tremayne to ye. Why dost not call me by my Christian name? 'Tis James, as well ye know, my lady."

She smiled.

"Tremayne suits ye better, methinks."

He chuckled with amusement at this, then embraced her again before, at last, he turned to the children.

"Why, what's this, Hwyelis? Am I supposed to choose which son is mine? Ah, my lady, didst think I wouldst not know my own spawn? Ye, lad"—he pointed to Waerwic— "step forward. What is your name, lad?"

The boy bowed.

"'Tis Waerwic, my lord," he answered boldly, without a trace of fear of this big, muscular man who had so heartily caressed and kissed his mother.

"Ye have taught him well, Hwyelis," Lord Hawkhurst observed. "Dost know who I am, Waerwic? *Waerwic!* Ah, ye cannot go through life here with such a name. After all, ye are half-English and my heir. From now on, ye shall be known as Warrick. Well, Warrick, dost know who I am?"

The boy glanced at his mother and then back.

"My father, my lord."

Lord Hawkhurst's booming laughter rang out once more.

"Aye, and so I am."

The days that passed were happy ones, for Lord Hawkhurst was much taken with his son and had no objection to the boy's half brothers either. It was good for the lad to have such close ties to Wales. They would serve him well in the future, Tremayne thought, though even he did not know just how well his son was to profit from his heritage and childhood bonds. That was to come later, much later, long after the Earl lay buried in his grave, and a war-torn England proclaimed a Welsh upstart King.

Lord Hawkhurst showered all the boys with a careless, haphazard warmth that stemmed from his deep fondness of and affection for Hwyelis, who again shared his bed. He would have taken her to wife and said as much, but she only laughed gaily and shook her head.

"Nay, Tremayne, I am a wild thing, not meant to be caught and caged. I must be free to love where I will and part without care. Ye know that."

Aye, how well he did. He had tamed her once, for a

time, but only because it had pleased her to be his. He had never bound her to him. He could not. It would have killed her spirit and left her but an empty shell. The Earl held her as long as he could, but eventually, the time came when Hwyelis grew restless and longed for the hills of Wales and gave thought to the future of her other three sons. 'Twas not right that they remain in England, the land of their enemies. They were pure Welsh, and Madog was Bryn-Dyfed's heir.

She told Tremayne she must go, and though he was sorrowed by her leaving, he realized he could not keep her. It was as she had said. She belonged to no man, for she was a woman meant to be free.

Warrick, however, was too young to understand this. He was bereft with emptiness and fright as his mother hugged him to her breast in farewell, enveloping him in the fragrant forest scent of the wild roses and moss that belonged to her alone. He clutched her frantically, clinging to her tightly, as though he would never let her go. 'Twasn't true! She just couldn't be leaving him! She was his whole world, everything he knew; and yet, she was actually smiling and ruffling his hair as though he were but a stray pup for whom she had found a home.

"Mama, please," he begged, "say 'tisn't true . . . that ye aren't going away."

"But 'tis true, Waerwic," she told him gently. "I must return to Wales, and ye must stay here. 'Tis our fate to be parted from each other."

"Nay. Nay! Don't leave me, Mama. Oh, please don't leave me!"

But she only set him from her, straightened her back, and mounted the mare that Lord Hawkhurst had given her. She spared Warrick not even a single glance as she rode through the iron portcullis of the keep, so he never saw the tears streaming silently down her cheeks. Bitterly wounded, he ran to the stables and hid, flinging himself down upon the hay in the loft and weeping great, wrenching sobs. The only woman he'd loved and worshiped all his life had deserted him.

After a time, in a small corner of his mind, something hard and cold was born at the cruel thought and lay in icy dormancy, waiting to flourish.

At ten years of age, Warrick was sent to a neighboring estate for fosterage. Lord Drayton, one of Lord Hawkhurst's closest friends, was pleased to have the Earl's heir given into his care and did his best to see the boy was well trained. Warrick worked hard at the tasks put to his doing—harder than most, for though he was recognized as his father's heir, the boy was taunted unmercifully by his foster brothers for being a half-Welsh bastard. "Savage," they called him—and worse—when there was no one to interfere, often making him the butt of vicious jests and beating him when they wished to teach him a lesson.

Such harsh treatment might have broken a gentler, weaker lad, but it only served to make Warrick strong, firing him with a grim determination to succeed in besting them all. This he did by mastering his weapons—the broadsword and shield, the battle-ax, the lance, the morningstar, the crossbow and longbow, and the dirk—so proficiently that soon all were afraid to challenge him. He walked among them without fear then, his head held high, his pride his only comfort in his lonely existence.

Whenever he could, Warrick slipped across the Bristol Channel to Wales too, to learn a different form of fighting—the guerilla warfare with which the Welsh had managed to keep the English from conquering Wales. There also, he grew close to his half brothers, his only friends, and dutifully visited his mother, Hwyelis, though he could never quite forgive her for deserting him. It was there as well, in the wild hills of his early childhood, that he met Brangwen, the woman to whom he later gave his whole heart.

Warrick asked her to marry him, not realizing that beneath her outward facade of breathtaking beauty lay a black core of evil. Unlike Hwyelis, who gave herself freely for the joys of loving and sharing, Brangwen gave only to lure and ensnare and finally destroy. She took pleasure in wielding her wicked power over men and seeing them brought to their knees. She used Warrick, promising to wed him, then when she was certain he was hers, she laughed in his face.

"Didst truly believe I wouldst marry the bastard spawn of an English dog?" she sneered. "Thou art a fool, Waerwic. Why should I settle for that crumbling old heap of stones, to which ye are heir, in the land of my enemies, when I can be mistress one of the finest keeps in all of Wales? Get ye hence, ye son of a churl. Ye have ceased to be of amusement to me."

Warrick was stunned; his heart was broken. The cold worm of hatred for all women that had crawled into his soul at his mother's desertion grew to monstrous proportions at his beloved Brangwen's cruel betrayal of him. He was only nineteen, but already, he was a man grown hard from the wounds his life had inflicted on him. His pride and arrogance were all that sustained him—those, and his vow never to love again.

When, two years later, his father was killed in battle, Warrick knew only that he wanted to get away from Devon and Wales. He had won his spurs, and blind with grief, he left Lord Drayton's service and made his way to London, where he sought a place for himself at Court. There, he distinguished himself in service to the Crown and became one of His Grace's favorites.

Now, at twenty-five, as he stood before Edward, the only liege to whom he had sworn fealty, Warrick cursed the day that had ever brought him to the palace: for the man the King had chosen to act as the new warden to the Ashleys was none other than Lord Warrick James ap Tremayne, now Earl of Hawkhurst; and he felt nothing but rage upon learning of his appointment to the office, despite the honor of the position. 'Twas Dorset or Hastings who had suggested the idea—he had no doubt—for those two favorites of His Grace were always trying to rid themselves of their rivals at Court.

"With all due respect, Sire—I am well content here at the palace," Warrick protested stiffly, trying to think of some way in which to extricate himself from the unwanted chore.

Edward only laughed and bent to fondle the voluptuous

breasts of his latest mistress, who lay at his feet and who was gazing too raptly for the King's liking at the handsome countenance of the courtier who stood before him.

"Come, Hawkhurst," His Grace chided softly, his crystal blue eyes filled with the cruel deviltry that, of late, his subjects had come to know only too well. Edward liked his gifts to be accepted with gratitude, and Warrick's attitude irritated him. "I award ye an office most men would have paid handsomely for, and still, ye are not pleased. Rushden is a rich estate. Its revenues are quite sizable, I am told, and your share will be most generous. Though ye are hardly a pauper, I would not have thought ye would scorn so fair a prize. What ails ye, my lord? I fear I do not understand your reluctance in accepting the position."

"Begging your pardon, Sire, but with all due respect— I am *not* a nursemaid. I do not believe I am a man fit for such a task."

"Christ's son, Hawkhurst! Is that all?" Edward laughed again. "Godamercy! The Ashleys are hardly in swaddling clothes, and even if they were, they would have a nanna to attend them. What are ye thinking of, my lord? Ye will scarcely see the lad, Giles, who is fostered to my brother Gloucester. And the girl, Isabella, is a pretty maid of thirteen and quite a taking little wench—or so Dickon informs me," the King added as an afterthought. "In fact, I have decided she would make ye an excellent bride."

"Bride, Sire!" Warrick gasped, stunned and angered by this announcement. And then, forgetting whose presence he stood in, he burst out, "But I have no wish for a wife!"

His Grace's eyes hardened slightly, though still, he smiled.

"But *I* wish for ye to have one, Hawkhurst. 'Tis time ye gave thought to the matter of producing an heir. The idea of your lands descending to one of your Welsh half brothers strikes me ill, very ill indeed. 'Twould ease my mind greatly if ye were not so tied to that lot."

"Except for my older brother, Madog, my brothers are bastards like myself, Your Grace, and not likely to inherit. After all, I am hardly in my grave, Sire! Does Your Grace have cause to doubt my loyalty?" Warrick inquired coldly, lifting one eyebrow demoniacally.

There were not many who insulted the Earl—and lived.

"Nay, of course not," Edward answered. "I would scarcely have awarded ye such an honor otherwise. Oh, come, my lord. The boy is the last male heir of his line. If aught should happen to him—if he should die—the maid would inherit all and become a very rich woman in her own right. Even now, she is no mean prize, for her dowry alone is a fortune.

"Rushden has always been a Yorkist stronghold, Hawkhurst—and one of importance. I must have a man I can trust there to be certain that does not change. The late Lord Oadby, though greedy, knew his duty to his king. 'Tis unfortunate he lost his life in a hunting accident. Ye have served the Crown well, my lord. 'Twould be a pity if that were not to continue. Of course"—the King shrugged when the Earl remained silent—"if ye still have no desire for the appointment or the Lady Isabella, I am sure I can find other tasks—and women—to take your fancy. The Lady Nan was recently widowed"—His Grace mentioned one of his previous whores—"and though her estate is small, the keep is still of some military value. . . ."

"I understand perfectly, Sire." Warrick spoke through clenched teeth, his face white with ire, a muscle working furiously in his jaw as he fought himself for control.

"I thought ye would," Edward intoned dryly. "Guard my wards well, my lord, and let me know how ye find the Lady Isabella. Dickon *does* have excellent taste in women, even though he seems to prefer them on the quiet side. Ye have my permission to go now and begin the preparations for your journey."

Warrick bowed low, then turned abruptly on his heel and wrathfully quit the chamber.

Once outside, he leaned against a wall for support, shaking all over with impotent ire. The unwelcome thought of leaving Court paled before the even more disastrous news he had just received. *Marry!* He was to be married—and to a wench he had never laid eyes on! It was either Lady Isabella Ashley or one of the King's cast-off whores. His Grace had made that quite clear.

Women! A plague take them all! Warrick cursed silently, recalling Brangwen, beautiful Brangwen, his

once-betrothed, who had played him false and left him
for another.

The Earl ground his teeth with rage and frustration, thinking hard, but he could see no avenue of escape. Edward
was his liege, and Warrick's duty to the Crown had been
made plain. He had no choice; he would have to accept the
position at Rushden as the new warden to the Ashleys, and,
worse yet, he would be forced to take the Lady Isabella to
wife. The first would at least enrich his purse. But the last
. . . The Earl's lip curled with distaste. He had no wish for
a bride, but since he must wed her, Warrick determined he
would bend the Lady Isabella to his will, or he would break
her. He would not be made a fool of again!

Chapter Eight

ISABELLA CHEWED THE TIP OF HER QUILL ABSENTLY AS SHE
gazed up from the large account books spread before her.
She had been poring over the records for a number of hours,
trying to set them straight. Lord Oadby had juggled them
cleverly, and it had taken her many months to determine
just how he had managed to make the ledgers seem square.
She sighed, then laid aside her pen and closed her eyes,
rubbing them tiredly for a moment.

After the Earl's death (the manner of which, mercifully,
none had questioned), the girl had, with no small measure
of delight, sent the highly distraught and suddenly frantic
Lady Shrewton packing, despite the Countess's shrill whines
that she had no place to go (her husband having cast her
off when she'd taken up with Lord Oadby).

"Poor Percy," Lady Shrewton had wailed tearfully and
wrung her hands as though bereft with grief for the late
Earl, though Isabella had known the Countess was concerned only about her own fate. "He was all I had. Oh,
what is to become of me?"

The girl had eyed Lady Shrewton coldly and replied, "I
neither know nor care, my lady. Ye have one hour to be

gone from Rushden—taking only those possessions that are rightfully yours—after which time, if ye have not departed, ye will be forcibly removed by my brother's men-at-arms."

"Oh, ye are cruel. Cruel!" the Countess had cried. "And after all I have done for ye too, ye ungrateful wench!"

"Ye have done nothing for me but usurp my proper place as mistress of Rushden and make my life miserable," Isabella had rejoined, trembling with quiet rage. "So do not think to shame me with any reminders of your many kindnesses to me, for there were none. Ye never cared for me or made one attempt to ease my unhappy lot. Had it not been for your fear of the Duke of Gloucester, I would not even have had what little I received. 'Tis your own greedy folly that has brought ye to this pass. Had ye but taken pity on me, I would do the same for ye now. As 'tis, I do but despise ye. The sooner ye are gone from Rushden, the better."

Following Lady Shrewton's hasty, ignominious departure, Isabella had written the King to inform him of the Earl's untimely demise and to request guidance in the matter. As she had feared, His Grace had responded that he would send a new warden to take Lord Oadby's place. But as it had, by then, been the dead of winter, and the snow-covered roads had made travel difficult, the girl had surmised the Earl's replacement probably would not arrive until after the spring thaw—or later. In the meanwhile, she still had several weeks left in which to establish herself as mistress of Rushden; and Isabella had vowed that, this time, she would not be so easily dislodged. She was no longer a child but a woman.

She had begun by scrupulously going over Rushden's numerous account books to familiarize herself with the state of her brother's lands. It had been the first time the girl had seen the records, which Lady Rushden had kept before her death and Lord Oadby's arrival, and it had taken Isabella over a fortnight just to figure out the system her mother had originally devised and employed; the ledgers had been so altered by the Earl. Nevertheless, the girl had persisted in her task, angered but not surprised when she had finally discovered the extent of Lord Oadby's misappropriations. Afterward, she had written her brother to advise him of the

condition of his estate and to inquire what steps he wished
her to take with regard to their new warden, whose identity
was as yet unknown.

*We cannot allow this new warden to think we are so
young and ignorant that he may fill his purse with our gold
without risk too, 'Sabelle,* Giles had written back, and she
had realized that, for all his words of encouragement contained therein as well, he was worried also. *From what ye
have told me, Rushden is still a very rich estate, despite the
sums that Lord Oadby embezzled over the years. I shall not
see the profits of my inheritance further pilfered by another
thief or squandered by a fool. Ye must keep a close watch
on this new warden, dear sister. Remember—ye are mistress at Rushden now. If he does aught ye find the least bit
suspicious, ye must write to me of it at once. In the meantime, Eadric, Thegn, and Beowulf will know what to do.*

Isabella had glanced at the three faithful knights and
shivered. They had not been at all shocked by the manner
of Lord Oadby's death. On the contrary, they had admitted
having discussed slaying the odious Earl themselves and
had actually seemed disappointed that Isabella had inadvertently prevented them from carrying out this scheme. If
the new warden proved as dreadful as the old, the girl was
certain that this time, the three knights would not hesitate
to murder him and dispose of his body without a trace!

Aye, she had no cause to fear the new warden. She had
only to whisper the command, and he would somehow "accidentally" meet his end at Rushden Castle, with none the
wiser as to the true manner of his death. Isabella shuddered
and grew faint at the thought of giving such a terrible order
but knew, if forced to, she would. For all her sweet nature,
she could be strong and unyielding if the occasion demanded. Giles was everything to her. He had entrusted his
inheritance to her. She would do whatever was necessary
to hold it safe. She had assured her brother of that.

And in response, he had written: *Aye, dear sister, I know
if need be, ye wouldst even wield a sword for me, though
'twas too heavy for your grasp.*

The girl sighed, closing the account books as the tears,

which came quick of late, stung her eyes. Oh, if only her
parents had not died, and Lord Oadby and Lady Shrewton
had not come to Rushden! For a moment, Isabella wept
bitterly with grief for her childhood, then, at the sound of
footsteps, hastily dried her tears.

"Beggin' yer pardon, m'lady"—one of the serving maids
entered and bobbed a curtsy—"but there be a bit of a ruckus
in the cookhouse."

The girl sighed again as she followed the wench downstairs and out into the inner ward of the keep to the kitchen.
There was so much to do at Rushden; Isabella had not
realized how much until after Lady Shrewton's departure.
Perhaps the Countess had not been to blame for her ill nature
after all.

After the difficulty in the cookhouse had been settled,
Isabella ordered her horse saddled, intending to ride out to
the cemetery, where she now often knelt at her mother's
grave, seeking counsel. The upkeep of Rushden was no
easy matter, especially for one who had not been properly
trained since childhood for such a task; and the girl found
her new responsibilities a heavy burden. She wished for an
older and wiser head than her own to guide her, but there
was none. She alone was now mistress of the castle, as
Giles had said.

"And where be Eadric, Thegn, and Beowulf?" the grizzled master-at-arms, Sir Lindael, questioned when she
reached the portcullis.

Isabella glanced up inquiringly.

"Why, I do not know, sir. Why do ye ask? I have ridden
by myself in the past. Is there some reason now why I
should not?"

"Aye, that there be my lady," old Lindael answered, to
her surprise. "Ye no longer be a child, my lady, but a young
maid—one old enough to be wedded and bedded," the
master-at-arms said bluntly. "And ye be a marriage prize
besides. And though ye be the King's ward as well, your
warden be dead, my lady; and the times be hard and uncertain. When life is difficult, it does strange things to men,
even the best of them. There be many rough lords and

knights abroad who might take advantage of your innocence, my lady, noble born though ye be, and force ye into wedding them to seize your dowry."

Isabella thought of Lord Oadby and shuddered. He had wanted her—though not as his wife.

"But—but surely, the King would not countenance a match made in such a fashion, Lindael."

"He might not, my lady, but then again, he might simply fine your unwanted husband for marrying ye without His Grace's permission. Either way, 'twould not be a pleasant experience for ye, my lady."

"I—I've changed my mind, Lindael. I'll not be riding out today after all."

He nodded.

"'Tis best, my lady."

Thereafter, whenever the girl was forced to go beyond the castle walls to oversee the estate or to nurse ailing crofters, she was accompanied by no less than twenty-five heavily armed outriders. In addition, the villeins in the fields kept a sharp eye on the land. If there were a man who sought to capture the Lady Isabella and force her to yield to him, he would find it extraordinarily difficult to do so.

Nevertheless, the girl missed the freedom of galloping over the moors and through the forests. She wondered how the creatures of nature fared without her and was touched when the crofters, suspecting her worry, began to bring injured animals they had found to the keep for her to tend. First, it was an old hound dog belonging to one of the knights, then a bushy-tailed red fox a poacher had attempted to ensnare, then a young deer wounded by a poorly aimed arrow. Had they not been trying to brighten Isabella's spirits, the villeins would have quietly killed these last two beasts and tossed them into the stew pot. The girl knew this and saw that none who delivered the injured creatures to her went away without reward, thereby gaining the love and trust of even the most wary of Rushden's tenants.

"Have ye decided, my lady?" Alice inquired, rousing the girl from her reverie.

Isabella looked at the gowns that had been laid out for her inspection and at which she had scarcely glanced earlier.

"Aye, Alice, I shall wear that one"—she pointed to the most unattractive of the three.

"But—but, my lady," the nanna protested vigorously, "that dress has always made ye look too pale...washed out, if I may say so, my lady. Ye know the new warden will be arriving any day, perhaps even today. Surely, ye want to make an effort to find favor in his eyes...."

Regretfully, for she loved pretty things and had possessed few of them under Lord Oadby and Lady Shrewton, Isabella shook her head.

"Nay, I wish no man to gaze upon me with favor save for two, Alice, and they are not here or likely to be soon, lest Gloucester gives them leave once more to come. The new warden may deal honestly by me and my brother, but then again, he may not. I shall do naught to gain his interest until I determine what sort of man he is. If he harbors no ill plans toward us, we may be comfortable again. If not, why, then, he will soon feel the bite of steel between his ribs!"

"Oh, my lady!"

Alice was aghast. Surely, this was not her gentle mistress, who wished harm to none, speaking.

Abruptly, Isabella remembered with whom she was conversing. She gave a soft strange laugh that was most unlike herself.

"Nay, do not fear, Alice. I shall do naught to bring the King's wrath down upon us, but I must take whatever steps are necessary to guard Giles's inheritance."

And his life, she added earnestly to herself.

Chapter Nine

LORD WARRICK AP TREMAYNE, EARL OF HAWKHURST, was tired, his temper, foul. He had ridden long and hard beneath the unseasonably warm spring sun, and he had been forced to suffer his younger half brother Caerllywel's teasing jibes the entire journey as well. Warrick wished he had never informed his brother of his new office and betrothal, much less asked Caerllywel to join him at Rushden: for his brother, knowing the Earl had no desire to leave Court and even less wish to be wed, had seized upon these announcements as a means of jabbing at Warrick's pride, which Caerllywel always thought in sore need of a few pricks. Much to the Earl's irritation, his brother had proceeded to set about this task by likening Warrick to a hog farmer and Lady Isabella Ashley, whom neither had ever laid eyes on, to a sow. As, despite the King's comments to the contrary, this was the same mental picture that Warrick himself had sourly drawn, he was not at all pleased by his brother's observations. Thus, though the Earl was relieved to see the towers of Rushden rising ahead in the distance, his ill mood did not abate.

"Well, Waerwic"—Caerllywel gave the Earl's name its Welsh pronunciation and grinned broadly, not in the least dismayed by his brother's forbidding countenance—"at last, we may discover whether or not Edward has set ye to tending a pig in a poke!"

Warrick's jaw hardened, for of his three half brothers, Caerllywel was the only one who would have dared to taunt him in such a manner—especially in his present frame of mind.

"If ye value your life, Caerllywel, ye will cease jesting about my bride," the Earl warned. "I do not even know that I will wed the maid."

"Oh, ye will," Caerllywel rejoined easily. "Ye have too much pride to stomach one of His Grace's whores, Waerwic. 'Twill be your downfall someday, that pride of yours."

"Well, when that day arrives, ye may gloat to your heart's content," Warrick intoned sarcastically. "Till then, I pray ye hold your tongue, for I am sore tempted to cut it out!"

"Be my guest, brother, if ye think ye can," Caerllywel said softly.

The Earl gave him a sharp glance at that but made no reply. Warrick would not have cared to cross swords with any of his brothers, with the possible exception of his youngest brother, Emrys, who was the least adept with a blade. Of the other two, however, his older brother, Madog, would probably kill him, and Caerllywel would certainly stand a fair chance. They had not lived most of their lives in the wild Welsh hills for naught.

Savagely, the Earl dug his heels into his stallion's sides and galloped on ahead, his brother's laughter ringing mockingly in his ears.

"I—I came as soon as I found it, m'lady. Be it—be it hurt bad?"

"Nay, Wat, I think not." Isabella reassured the lad with a smile as she examined the wounded lamb carefully. "Its leg is broken, but 'twill soon mend if I can but set it properly and keep the poor babe still for a while."

"Oh, m'lady"—Wat's young face was puckered up dreadfully—"indeed, I—I do not know how I came to lose it. I could have sworn the count was right. . . ."

"'Tis naught, Wat. Such things happen, even to the best of us. I am just glad the injury is not worse. 'Tis a wonder the lamb was not killed, falling into such a pit. 'Tis the second one that has been found. Some poacher's trap, no doubt. I shall have Eadric and the others fill it in immediately. Ye will show them the place, Wat. Now fret yourself no longer. If ye had not been so quick to discover the poor babe's absence, searched for it, and heard its bleating, the lamb would have been dead by now."

"Aye, m'lady."

"Fetch me that bucket of water over there, and look through that woodpile for a stick that will serve as a suitable splint. Then bring me my unguents and linen strips."

"Aye, m'lady."

The lad scampered off to do her bidding while Isabella crooned soothingly to the wounded beast. She was so absorbed in calming the frightened animal, she paid no attention to the commotion outside the castle walls; indeed, 'twas doubtful she even heard it.

Warrick's dark visage was ominous in appearance. He had called his name to the sentries, stated his authority and business plainly, and had been politely but stoutly refused admittance to Rushden Castle.

"Mind ye, I'm not saying ye aren't who and what ye

claim to be, my lord," Sir Lindael called down from one of the two towers that flanked the entrance to the keep. "But I have my lady's safety to think of, and for all I know, ye might be brigands wishing to carry her off. These be hard and uncertain times, my lord, and there be many ruffians abroad."

"Poor Waerwic," Caerllywel taunted, his voice choked with muffled laughter, "it seems your swine of a bride is as reluctant as ye. Quick, brother, find out which chamber is hers, and give a hog farmer's call in that direction. Perhaps then she can be induced to let us inside. My throat is well nigh parched from eating your horse's dust."

The Earl favored his brother with a withering glance.

"My bride knows nothing of the proposed match between us. Now cease your prattling, fool. God's blood! I do not know why I brought ye with me!"

"Because ye would have died of boredom otherwise. Really, Waerwic, ye would do well to develop a sense of humor. I'll warrant that frown of yours will send your bride scurrying for her sty—"

That was as far as Caerllywel got. The next moment, he was flying through the air, then landing with a thud in the dirt, a large dent in his armor from the flat side of his brother's sword. The Earl's men were laughing uproariously, having long endured too many of Caerllywel's sly jokes themselves not to be delighted in seeing him get his comeuppance. Slowly, Caerllywel got to his feet and brushed himself off, still grinning nevertheless, for he knew how to laugh at himself as well as others.

"I shall repay ye for that low blow, Waerwic," he promised, ruefully gazing down at his battered mail. "This was a new breastplate too, damn ye! If your bride turns out to be a beauty instead of a pig, I shall steal her away. Unless she wants for sense, she'll see straight off I'm a much better bargain than ye."

Warrick, some of his anger having been vented, only snorted.

"Despite your tall tales of your prowess with wenches, I have yet to lose one to ye," he pointed out.

"True. Sad but true," Caerllywel agreed, remounting his

steed. "I don't know what 'tis the maids find in that ugly mug of yours to attract them. Well, have ye thought of some means to get us inside yet? I'm like to die of thirst."

The Earl's face hardened once more.

"Sir Lindael, I shall have your head if ye do not lower the drawbridge, and raise the portcullis at once!" he shouted wrathfully.

"I'm sorry, my lord, but I cannot. However, I have thought of a plan," the master-at-arms yelled, beginning to let down a bucket by rope from the tower. "If ye will put the King's writ in this pail, I shall have a clerk examine the scroll, and we will determine whether or not ye may be admitted."

Warrick fumed and cursed mightily under his breath, but it seemed there was naught else to be done.

"Rhys," he barked sharply to one of his squires, "can ye swim?"

"Aye, my lord."

"Then take this writ, and put it in the bucket that damned fool has lowered for our benefit," the Earl snarled sarcastically. "By God, he shall find himself removed from his post and placed in the stocks before this day's end; I swear it!"

"Do not be too harsh with the man, Waerwic." Caerllywel's voice was suddenly serious. "They may, in truth, have had trouble here, and there is no point in getting started off on the wrong foot in your new position."

"When I want your advice, I shall ask for it!" Warrick snapped, but Caerllywel saw the tense muscle working in his brother's jaw relax slightly and was relieved.

The Earl had a fearsome temper that could frighten even his brother Madog at times. If the young Lady of Rushden Castle were to witness it ... Caerllywel shook his head and sighed. Even the wicked Brangwen, who had married Lord Gryffydd and made his life hell, was afraid of Warrick nowadays.

The Earl waited in silence while the clerk read the contents of the scroll. At last, as Rhys was being hauled, dripping wet, from the moat, the drawbridge was lowered and the portcullis raised. Warrick clattered inside and dismounted with an arrogant sweep of his dark brown, gold-lined cloak.

"Take me to your mistress at once!" he demanded imperiously, his eyes narrowed, his voice cold.

"But—but, my lord," the master-at-arms protested vigorously, "surely, ye will want to go first to the keep and bathe and—"

"At once, I said. Do not keep me waiting," the Earl warned grimly. "Ye have already caused my temper to grow most foul by your delays."

Sir Lindael stiffened. There were not many men who had spoken so to him in his life, and he feared now, despite his earlier hopes to the contrary, that the new warden was going to be as bad as Lord Oadby had been.

"As ye wish, my lord," the master-at-arms stated, his manner distant and disdainful as he began to lead the way toward the stables.

"Christ!" Caerllywel groaned, his eyes wide with amazement. "She really *does* live in a sty!"

"I said to take me to your mistress," Warrick growled, giving his brother a covert look and glancing around with some uneasiness.

The faces of the Rushden men were closed, unreadable, and watchful. Was this a trap? The Earl had been informed that his predecessor, Lord Oadby, had lost his life in an unfortunate hunting accident, but perhaps that had been only a tale. Warrick laid one hand warily on the hilt of his sword, beginning to grow faintly alarmed. What on earth would a wench of good breeding be doing in the stables?

"The Lady Isabella be inside, my lord"—Sir Lindael indicated a half-open door at one end of the stables.

The Earl stared at the master-of-arms icily.

"If this is a jest, sir, I find it a poor one," he drawled.

Sir Lindael drew himself up to his full height.

"I assure ye I would play no trick on the King's warden, my lord. Ye insult me by the suggestion."

"Very well then," Warrick declared and strode inside.

He was so unprepared for the sight that met his eyes that he gasped and stopped short, causing Caerllywel to run right into him. Both men gazed around themselves with astonishment. It was as though they had stumbled into a menagerie, as indeed they had. Birds of every kind twittered and squawked upon perches here and there. Three rabbits in cages sat up, noses twitching, at the entrance of the two men. A deer, tied in one corner, bounded and thrashed, startled by the intruders. An old hound dog barked and proceeded to chase a bristly porcupine across the hay-strewn floor. Two cubs romped at the heels of a snapping, bushy-tailed fox in a pen. From the loft, a furry, one-eyed badger glared down, its long claws showing wickedly. Countless kittens mewed, scattering this way and that when a goat bleated and shook its head, causing the bell about its neck to ding loudly.

"Dear Lord, Waerwic," Caerllywel whispered, his voice choked with muffled laughter, "can *that* be your sow?"

The Earl's eyes fell upon the young maid who sat in the midst of all this cacophony and confusion, a whimpering lamb across her lap. What he could see of her hair was pinned up haphazardly beneath a filthy kerchief, from which tangled strands straggled and that the girl now brushed from her eyes with a grimy hand. Smudges of dirt covered her cheeks and the tip of her nose. The gown she was wearing was of fine muslin, but at first glance, it looked like a rag, for it was spattered with dried blood, some sort of greasy ointment, and what appeared to be—Warrick was almost afraid to sniff and find out for certain—animal dung.

He swallowed hard, opened his mouth to speak, then closed it, dumbfounded. Only Caerllywel's snigger behind him brought him to his senses.

"My—my lady Isabella?" The Earl managed to find his tongue at last.

The girl, intent on binding up the splint she had fashioned for the lamb's broken leg, glanced up irritably.

"Wat, I thought I told ye . . . Oh, marry-go-up—" she broke off abruptly, staring at the man before her.

At twenty-five years of age, he was tall and strongly muscled, his body as lithe as a whipcord. From his broad shoulders hung a cloak fastened with rosettes bearing the badges of brown-and-gold hawks, their wings spread, their talons poised to strike. His powerful chest, beneath his white

linen shirt and dark brown satin doublet slashed with gold
was protected by the only armor he wore, a savage sort of
breastplate. From there, his body tapered down to a firm
flat belly and a narrow waist, from which hung a gleaming
silver sword. His well-formed legs were encased in gold
hose. The tops of his high, black leather boots shone glossily
in the sunlight that streamed in through the stable door.

He was handsome enough—in a cold hard way that
reminded Isabella of the hawks upon his badges, for his
hair was a rich tobacco-brown streaked with gold. He wore
it parted in the middle and shagged back on the sides in
wings. His skin had been bronzed by the sun, weathered
by the wind. Above his full, sensual lips, his hooked nose
jutted with proud nostrils, flared now at the stables' stench.
The set of his lean jaw was sure and haughty, as though he
were accustomed to being obeyed—and without question.

But it was his eyes that caught and held Isabella's attention, for she had never before seen their like. They were a
tawny shade of amber, more yellow than brown, lined with
thick dark lashes and framed with swooping brows; and they
were gazing at her with disgust—and, to her surprise, intense dislike.

There was an odd, animal magnetism about the man that
attracted yet frightened her. Isabella shivered with apprehension, for suddenly, she knew, some way, somehow, that
the lord's coming would affect her for all time. She took a
deep breath, marshaling her courage. So this was the man
who was to guard Giles's inheritance; the stranger could be
none other. Well, if he had meant to intimidate Isabella
from the start, he had failed.

"My lady Isabella," he repeated, "I am—"

"I can guess who ye are," the girl said frostily, matching
his own tone of voice. "The new warden sent by the King.
Ye are blocking the light, my lord, and, as ye can see, this
is a delicate operation"—she indicated the lamb's broken
leg. "Please be good enough to go to the keep, as I'm sure
that Sir Lindael requested ye politely to do. I don't allow
others besides myself in here. They scare the animals, as
ye must be aware ye and your men have done. Sir Lindael

will attend to your needs quite adequately until such time as I myself can wait upon ye."

Dismissing him, she turned back to the lamb. For the second time that day, Warrick opened his mouth to speak, then abruptly closed it. He was consumed by ire. By God, how dare the wench talk to him in such a manner—and before Caerllywel too, who would doubtless taunt him unmercifully about it later? The Earl pivoted on his heel and walked rapidly from the stables, shouting orders to his men, his mind on Isabella all the while.

So *that* was the maid the King would see him wed and bed. God's wounds! A taking little wench indeed! Damn Edward to hell and back! Well, there was nothing to be done. Warrick would just have to give her a thorough scrubbing and blow out the candles when making love to her; that was all. As for the girl's attitude toward him—well, that would change soon enough after he had administered her a few richly deserved slaps for her impudence!

It was then that the goat, which, unbeknown to Isabella, had chewed through the frayed rope that kept it tied to a post, gave another cry and, bell ringing, head lowered, charged straight through the half-open door and into Warrick's posterior. The Earl, unprepared for such an attack, staggered, lost his balance, went flying through the air, then tumbled facedown upon the cobblestones in the bailey. Instantly, the ward was filled with an ominous silence as everyone stared, horrified. Then, quite pleased with itself, the goat bleated again, tossed its head, and pranced a few nimble steps before scampering off, its bell chiming like laughter in the stillness. Caerllywel turned away, stuffing the folds of his cloak into his mouth to smother the peals of mirth that bubbled to his throat. Isabella, horrified and yet seeing the humor of the situation also, was torn between the lamb and the goat and wailed, "Tinker! Tinker, come back!" in a voice that wavered unsteadily before she too succumbed to a badly muffled fit of giggles.

Several of Warrick's men, regaining their senses at last, ran forward to assist the Earl up, but irately, he knocked away their outstretched hands, rose, and brushed himself off, his face a distorted mask of rage. By God! The ignominy of it all! He had not been at Rushden half-a-day, and already, the wench had succeeded in making a fool of him! Warrick whirled toward Isabella, his fists clenched tightly at his sides. Wisely, she lowered her gaze, turning her attention back to the lamb.

"Madam," the Earl began accusingly, his tone clipped and harsh, "madam, ye did that a'purpose!"

"Did—did what, my lord?" Isabella asked, trying desperately to retain command of her voice and looking up at him now, eyes wide with pretended innocence.

"Provoked that goat into assaulting my—my person!"

"Oh, nay, my lord! I—I assure ye I did not! Indeed, I— I do not know how the wretched beast managed to free itself—Oh, nay!" She suddenly held one hand to her mouth in mortification. "Oh, nay, not again! Oh, my lord—"

"Waerwic! Waerwic! Look out!" Caerllywel shouted in warning as Warrick snapped around just in time to see the goat charging once more.

The Earl caught the full force of the animal's blow in his stomach. With a loud "Oof!", he sprawled backward into a pile of hay, limbs flailing as he banged his head against one of the bird perches.

The raven sitting thereon, violently startled, squawked, flapped its wings wildly, then croaked chatteringly again, the noise sounding amazingly like a chortle, as it settled back onto its perch.

"Awk!" it chirruped, then whistled, cocking its head at Warrick quizzically. "Another one down the hatch! Another one down the hatch!"

At this, Isabella could no longer restrain herself.

"Oh, Ma—Matey!" she stammered with despair to the sly, mischievous bird, which belonged to a knight who, before coming to Rushden, had spent a great deal of time at sea. "Not—not ye too!"

Then, much to Warrick's fury, she burst into uncontrollable laughter.

Isabella lay back in the huge, hammered-brass bathtub and closed her eyes. She had not yet seen the new warden again, although she had learned his identity from a much-rattled Alice. He was Lord Warrick ap Tremayne, Earl of Hawkhurst, said to be one of the King's favorites. Godamercy! There could have been no worse welcome for such a man than the shocking contretemps at the stables.

Isabella wondered if the Earl would ever forgive her. It seemed doubtful—he had indeed been very angry—but nevertheless, she must try to make amends at once. Otherwise, Lord Hawkhurst might take his unmistakable desire for revenge, which the girl had seen plainly upon his face, out on Rushden. She shivered slightly as she recalled the way those strange amber eyes of his had raked her with distaste. Briefly, Isabella wondered why the Earl had disliked her on sight, even before the disastrous occurrence at the stables. Naturally, he must have been disgusted by her appearance—after all, she *had* looked a fright—but that did not account for Lord Hawkhurst's initial coldness to her. At last, unable to think of any reason why the Earl should hold her in contempt (apart from the awful incident with the recalcitrant goat and the impertinent raven), Isabella gave up trying and called for Alice.

"Aye, my lady?"

"Lay out my sea-green gown with the little cap, please."

"Aye, my lady."

Alice beamed, relieved. After the highly awkward and unfortunate meeting this morning, she had feared that Isabella had decided to continue her scheme for appearing as unattractive as possible. Now, it seemed perhaps Lord Hawkhurst's dark, handsome visage had caused the girl to change her tactics. She always looked especially beautiful in that particular dress.

Indeed, Isabella could not have been more lovely as she descended the main stairs to the great hall below. The sea-green silk was shot through with silver thread, bringing out the silvery highlights of her pale blond hair, which shimmered, unbound, to her hips. Cut low at the bodice, the gown showed a generous display of Isabella's ripe breasts, offset by the many slender, fragile-linked silver chains she had draped around her neck. A silver filigree girdle encircled her waist; its jeweled dinner knife gleamed in the soft candlelight. The dress itself fell in gentle folds to the floor; the tight sleeves, which ended in points upon her wrists, were complemented by her silver surcoat. The little sea-green cap, fringed with silver bangles, sat close upon her head. The coloring of the costume served to make the grey-green of Isabella's eyes stand out like twin oceans in her face, and she seemed more wraithlike than ever, appearing to glitter as she walked.

Warrick and Caerllywel stared at her with amazement as she moved toward them slowly, gracefully, from across the hall. Surely, this could not be the same filthy, ragged maid they had seen in the stables earlier, who had so insultingly laughed at the antics of the goat and raven and unwisely kept both men idly waiting all day—no doubt afraid to face Warrick after the injury to his pride and posterior! Isabella fluttered an enchanting curtsy, holding out one slim hand to first the Earl, and then his brother.

"My Lord Hawkhurst"—she smiled, showing even white teeth that shone like pearls—"and Sir Caerllywel—have I pronounced that correctly? The Welsh tongue is difficult to command, I understand, and, alas, I have not been trained in the language."

"Ye said my name more beautifully than I have ever before heard it spoken, my lady," Caerllywel told her, his eyes appraising her with open admiration, despite his brother's frown.

"My lord"—Isabella turned back to the Earl—"I'm afraid I owe ye an apology for the manner in which my brother's men and I greeted your arrival. We had not expected ye so soon, and since the King, in his letter, did not apprise us of the new warden's identity, Sir Lindael, fearing for my safety, was perhaps overzealous in his duties. I wish ye will not judge him too harshly. I myself was concerned for the lamb and hope I can make amends for my earlier rudeness and the—the terrible mishap in the stables."

This was all said sweetly, without guile or suppressed amusement, but Warrick, to whom nothing in life had ever come easily and who was therefore suspicious of everyone and everything, was not deceived. The wench wanted something from him. What was it?

"Of course, my lady," he droned, his eyelids lowered so she could not guess his thoughts.

His reply was not encouraging, but despite his ill humor, Isabella forced herself to continue to smile as they made their way to the high table for supper.

All through the evening meal, she chattered to both men with a brightness that hid her despair, for although she rapidly won Caerllywel's affections, the Earl remained silent and distant. Still, Isabella persisted, for it was important to her to know Lord Hawkhurst's thoughts toward herself, Giles, and Rushden.

"Have ye ever been a warden before, my lord?" she inquired curiously, reaching for the thick yellow butter and spreading some upon a slice of rich, crusty bread.

"Nay, but I have been well informed of my duties," the Earl answered tersely, his mouth turned down sardonically at the corners as he remembered, with distaste, the King's orders.

"Ye—ye do not relish the position," Isabella stated, her eyes suddenly wide with apprehension, her spirits faltering: for if such were the case, Lord Hawkhurst would doubtless be apt to deal harshly with her and her brother. "My lord, I—I know ye are angry about what happened this morning, and rightly so, but I pray ye do not judge me and mine too sternly for it. I—I assure ye that Giles and I will not be a charge on ye, my lord. Indeed, ye will scarcely see my brother, as he is fostered to my lord Duke of Gloucester; and—and the estate is well run. Ye will have only to determine that the revenues paid to the King are fair. . . ."

Her voice trailed off at the glint in his golden eyes. She shuddered. The way the Earl was looking at her reminded her of the way a hawk gazes fiercely at its prey before ripping its hapless victim to shreds. Even so, there was something more in those amber eyes as well—a mocking appraisal that made Isabella feel as though she were little better than a slave upon a block, to be bought—and bedded—by Lord Hawkhurst if and when it pleased him.

She turned away, sipping her wine in the tense silence and trying to still the quivering of her fingers upon the chalice. When she spoke again, it was to Caerllywel, who squeezed her hand briefly under the table. Isabella gave him a grateful smile, thereby missing the dark, threatening glance the Earl threw at his brother.

Caerllywel only grinned and leaned closer to whisper in Isabella's ear.

"Do not mind Waerwic," he said. "He is wroth because the King sent him here instead of keeping him at Court, where my brother wished to remain. That is all," Caerllywel lied without qualm. "It has naught to do with ye, my lady, despite the unfortunate occurrence at the stables. Waerwic's ire will cool soon enough—for 'twas only his damnable pride that was injured—and ye will see he is not truly such an ogre as he pretends."

Though still uncertain of this, Isabella breathed a small sigh of relief.

"I—I did not know. I thought perhaps he—he might bear a grudge against me and wreak ill upon Rushden for it. Marry-go-up. I shall never forget the look on his face when he strode from the stables. He was so angry, I feared he would strike me! I should not have laughed so; 'twas indeed too bad of me. I am not usually so unkind, but—but, oh, *'twas* funny."

"Aye, indeed, 'twas, my lady. Do not fear. Though he may be mad for a time, I assure ye that Waerwic will not deal injuriously with ye and yours nevertheless. That is not his way. He is hard and arrogant and ofttimes cruel, but he is seldom unjust—stubborn perhaps but rarely unfair. He will not bleed your brother's estate for any real or imagined slights—if that is what ye fear."

"I—I *was* afraid. . . . Giles has entrusted Rushden to my care, ye see, and I do not take my responsibilities lightly, sir. I know that Lord Hawkhurst and I got off to a most miserable start, but I had hoped to make amends. . . ." Her voice trailed off, and Isabella bit her lip.

"And so ye have, my lady. Twice, this day, I have discovered myself dumbfounded at the sight of ye." Caerllywel spoke more loudly, his eyes warming with amusement and desire.

Despite herself, Isabella smiled, her fears temporarily abating.

"I can only hope 'twas because ye found my appearance so improved the second time, sir. 'Twas indeed too bad of ye to invade my menagerie and frighten all my animals. Indeed, now that I think of it, *ye* are to blame for what occurred this morn!"

"Oh, come, my lady. Surely, ye jest. We did no more than walk inside—"

"Aye, but nevertheless, 'twas the sight of ye that provoked the goat so. Usually, he is the gentlest of creatures—"

"Oh, come, my lady!" Caerllywel repeated.

"Well, I must admit that Tinker has a great dislike for cloaks, sir. Ye see, when he was young, some of the lads thought 'twould be a good jest to bundle him up in a blanket so he couldn't see. Naturally, the poor beast ran about wildly, quite blind with terror, and the nasty imps yelled and beat him with stout sticks on top of it all to prod him along. 'Twas very mean of the boys, of course, and they were severely punished for the prank, but the damage had been done. Tinker was dreadfully frightened and never recovered from the shock of the incident. Now he is ready to attack anything even remotely resembling a blanket. That is why I keep him in the stables."

"Along with that tart-tongued bird and various other assorted animals who are, no doubt, as ill-mannered as—"

"Their mistress?"

"Oh, nay, my lady!"

"Oh, come now, sir. Has my master-at-arms been telling fables, or did ye not refer to me as your brother's sow this morn?" Isabella inquired and pretended to pout.

"Christ's son! How dare Sir Lindael repeat such a thing? I'll have his head for it—"

"Ah, then 'tis true!" the girl crowed, much to Caerllywel's discomfiture.

"Nay, my lady—"

"Mayhap ye confused me with my brother then, who serves the Boar of Gloucester," she suggested cleverly.

"Aye, that was it!" Caerllywel clutched this straw gratefully, thereby missing the pun that had been intended.

"Oh, come now, sir!" Isabella persisted, her sides now

shaking with silent laughter. "Even so, ye would hardly have referred to Giles as a sow, a piglet perhaps. . . ."

Finally, Caerllywel saw the joke and realized she was shamelessly making fun of him as punishment for the impertinent remark that had been huffily (much to her amusement) imparted to her by the highly offended Sir Lindael.

"Isabella—may I call ye Isabella?—ye are a most tempting and terrible tease," Caerllywel stated firmly, his eyes dancing ruefully. "Doubtless, had your master-at-arms informed ye earlier of my observation, which was made, may I remind ye, before I had seen your true and most lovely self, 'twould have been *my* posterior that capricious goat assaulted instead of the undeserving Waerwic's."

"Aye," she admitted, her eyes twinkling as her natural gaiety gurgled forth at last.

"Poor—poor Waerwic," Caerllywel gasped, joining in her mirth. "I'm afraid he was made the butt of the jest in more ways than one this day!"

At the thought of Tinker ramming into Lord Hawkhurst—not once, but *twice*! and what Matey had had to say on the subject—Isabella very uncharitably but helplessly went off into another fit of giggles and dared not glance, even surreptitiously, at the Earl, whose face, she was sure, was that of a man who is contemplating murder.

This was indeed the case, for Warrick could not help but overhear these ill-timed remarks of both Isabella and his brother, and he was wondering, quite seriously, whether or not he would be hanged for throttling the two of them with his bare hands. How dare Caerllywel sit there, flirting outrageously with the brazen hussy and so obviously enjoying her company, when he knew the maid was betrothed to Warrick?

The Earl steamed inwardly at the thought as he studied Isabella covertly, wondering what kind of wife she would make him. His first impression of her had been wrong. She *was* beautiful after all, once all that dirt had been washed off, beautiful in a strange, haunting manner he found oddly disquieting.

She's like Brangwen, he thought, or Mélusine. His mouth

tightened as he remembered the wicked silvery mermaid from whom the Woodvilles claimed descendance. She would bewitch a man, laugh at him, and lead him to his death. Well, she will not find me so easily caught in her net, to be speared by her trident. I suffered once for such a wench; I shall not do so again, he vowed.

"Ye will like my brother Emrys," Caerllywel was saying to Isabella as Warrick brought himself back, with a start, to the present. "He is a healer like yourself, although he practices the art upon people, not beasts."

"Is he to come here, then . . . Emrys, I mean?" Isabella queried innocently.

"Well, n—nay," Caerllywel stuttered, suddenly realizing his mistake, for the Earl had strictly forbidden him to speak of the betrothal, which the King had ordered, until such time as Warrick himself decided to tell the girl. "Ye will meet him when—when—"

"Ye babble, brother," Warrick noted warningly. "Methinks ye have drunk too much ale. Come, my lady." He took Isabella's hand, pulling her to her feet. "I fear my brother is no longer fit company for a maid such as yourself."

She barely had time to bid Caerllywel good night and dip him a slight curtsy before the Earl was leading her from the great hall, his fingers closed about her own so tightly, her hand ached, despite the electric shock that seemed to jolt through her at his touch. Isabella stumbled after his tall, forbidding figure, nearly falling.

"Please, my lord. Ye—ye hurt me, and ye go too fast," she breathed.

Although he stared down at her without reply, he did loosen his grip somewhat and shorten the length of his strides so she could keep pace more easily as they climbed the main stairs and wound through the long corridors of the castle.

The flickering torches along the walls cast eerie shadows upon Warrick's cold, chiseled profile, making him seem like some demon and momentarily scaring Isabella. Where was he taking her? What did he mean to do to her? Oh, why hadn't she held her tongue at supper? Perhaps she had

truly enraged him! Did he mean to beat her? Her father had
never struck her mother, but Isabella knew other men were
not so kind. Mayhap the Earl too was drunk and wanted
to—to—

The girl shivered with horror at the last unfinished thought.
She remembered Lord Oadby, and without warning, panic
engulfed her. Perhaps Lord Hawkhurst was no better than
her previous warden. Suddenly, Isabella shrank back, trying
desperately to yank away from him.

Warrick turned, cūrsing under his breath as he hauled
her struggling body toward him once more.

"What ails ye, madam?" he asked irritably, once he had
stayed her flight. Then, seeing the expression on her face,
he laughed softly, jeeringly. "Dost think I mean to ravish
ye here in one of these halls? Aye, ye do," he said when
she didn't respond. He grinned wickedly, the first smile she
had seen from him, his teeth flashing whitely in the dim,
wavering light. "'Tis not my intent, I assure ye," he told
her, his glittering eyes suddenly raking her boldly, as though
he knew what she looked like unclothed, lingering on the
rapid rise and fall of the swell of her breasts beneath her
bodice. He lifted a strand of her hair that had tumbled over
the ripe mounds. "But even if 'twere," he continued, caressing the tress deliberately, as though to make her aware
of his power over her, "there would be naught ye could do.
I am master here now, and 'twould be little enough payment
for the insult delivered to me this morn!"

The girl was shocked by his crude words and behavior.
How dare he treat her in such a low fashion, as though she
were no better than a tavern wench—or worse? She glanced
down the corridor uneasily, suddenly very much aware that
they were totally alone here. There was no one to defend
her but herself.

"How dare ye touch me? Take your hands off me at
once!" Isabella hissed, terrified. "My brother's men wouldst
slay ye for less than ye have done! I have but to give the
command, and ye will die most unpleasantly here at Rushden, with none the wiser as to the truth of the matter.
Accidents happen, my lord, even to the most careful of
men."

"Do they now?" he questioned softly, dangerously. "And did ye give Lord Oadby fair warning too?"

It was a shot in the dark, but the girl didn't know that. She blanched, sick with fear, as she realized the foolishness of her remarks, then instinctively reached for her dagger, having some desperate notion of slaying the Earl if he had guessed her secret and attempted to expose her.

"Lord Oadby was cruel and often used his spurs most harshly on his horse," she said by way of explanation, praying that Lord Hawkhurst would believe her. Then she shrugged lightly, as though the matter were of no concern. "'Tis no wonder the poor beast threw him. Now leave me be, my lord, else I shall kill ye myself!" Isabella suddenly wrenched free from him and pulled her blade.

The Earl's yellow eyes narrowed at the quick, defensive gesture and her threat.

"So the rose *does* have thorns," he purred, his voice silky and low, "and wouldst see me murdered before surrendering her virtue."

"As I wouldst see any man who tried to take me by force," the girl declared fervently, recalling Lord Oadby again.

Warrick stalked toward her until she stood against one wall of the corridor. Then he placed his hands on either side of her so she could not escape, mocking her still and seeming unconcerned for his life, though Isabella now held her dagger at his throat, albeit somewhat waveringly.

"Are ye so sure I would have to take ye by force, my lady?" he queried, one eyebrow lifting.

He laughed again as she blushed hotly, confused, his very nearness causing her heart to pound violently in the strangest manner. Her fingers, which held the blade, trembled. With a swift movement, he knocked the knife from her grasp and pinioned her arms behind her back roughly so she was pressed against his chest. He caught her hair painfully with one hand, twisting her countenance up to his.

"Are ye so sure, madam?" he demanded again, his lips inches from her own.

"My—my lord, please," Isabella gasped, mortified, "ye

are my warden. Surely, the King did not give ye leave to trifle with an innocent maid...."

The Earl's eyes glinted oddly at that, filling with cold amusement, anger, and yet a sudden, hot desire as well: for he found the girl's nearness aroused him, and the sense of power he felt at knowing she was helpless against him filled him with a strange thrill of triumph besides. She would not deceive him as Brangwen had done. Warrick would see to that.

"Where ye are concerned, Edward has given me every liberty," he told her, tightening his steely hold upon her possessively, as though to accentuate this. "Aye, every liberty," he repeated.

"What—what do ye mean?" Isabella asked nervously, a slow, ominous foreboding suddenly filling her being.

"Why, only that His Grace has decided ye would make me an excellent wife," he responded sarcastically, his words like a slap in the girl's face.

"Nay!" The cry burst involuntarily from her lips as she stared up at him, numb with shock. "Nay! Ye lie! 'Tisn't true! It can't be true!"

"I assure ye 'tis, madam, much as we both may dislike the matter. Though I did attempt to dissuade him from the match, the King has already signed the contracts betrothing ye to me. I had not meant to tell ye yet—or in such a manner—but perhaps 'tis best. Now that ye know where ye stand with me, mayhap ye will be less inclined to play me for a fool."

"I would not do such a thing in any event." Isabella's voice was tinged with a quiet dignity that made him feel slightly ashamed.

Then he remembered Brangwen, and his purpose once more hardened.

"See ye do not, else ye will suffer for it, I promise ye. Which chamber is yours?" he inquired abruptly, releasing her, giving her no time to absorb the awful impact of his words.

"That one," the girl answered dully, blindly pointing out her room, still unable to comprehend the brutally delivered announcement of her betrothal to this man.

No wonder he had dared to treat her as he pleased. She felt as though she had received a stunning blow and been sent sprawling. Her stomach lurched sickeningly, as though the earth had suddenly dropped from beneath her feet. She stood there stupidly, her mind a blank daze until Warrick spoke again, recalling her to the present.

"Then get ye to it, my lady, and tease my brother no more. I find I mislike the idea greatly. Ye are not meant for him."

"Nor for ye, my lord," Isabella choked out pleadingly, her eyes begging him to say he did but jest. "Please tell me 'tisn't true. I do not wish to be your wife—"

"Nor do I want ye as such!" Warrick spat, his nostrils flaring at the insult she had unwittingly delivered to him. "But there is naught to be done. 'Tis Edward's command."

"Godamercy," Isabella whispered, clasping her hands and pressing her forehead against them, as though in prayer. "Then I am lost. Lost," she reiterated, her voice a small, ragged sob.

Helplessly, she looked up at the Earl. This man was to be her husband, would share her bed, would have the right to put his hands upon her and—and—Oh, Lionel. *Lionel!* She gave another strangled cry of despair.

"Nay! Nay! Ye will never have me," she vowed irrationally.

"It seems ye are certain of a great many things, madam," Warrick sneered, his eyes roaming lewdly over her body again as he returned her dagger. "I have always found 'tis most unwise to be so sure of oneself. As unwelcome as the prospect is, ye *shall* be my wife, my lady—and in every way," he added crudely, mockingly, his meaning plain. "'Tis the King's wish that I get an heir. That is the whole purpose of our marriage."

"Then—then surely, some other maid would serve as well." Isabella bit her lip. "Ye do not want me, my lord—"

"Not as my wife, nay. But ye are infinitely preferrable to one of Edward's cast-off whores, which is what he offered me otherwise—as though I, Hawkhurst, would be content with some sullied slut! At least *ye* are a maid"—he paused deliberately, as though waiting to see if she would deny it, then went on more intently—"and I find the thought of bedding ye does not . . . displease me."

He laid one hand upon the girl's throat, then let his fingers slide slowly down the hollow between her breasts, smiling jeeringly at her obvious distress.

"Don't. Please don't," Isabella whispered, the words echoing like a whimper through the hall.

To her surprise, Warrick ceased the sensuous movement, shrugging carelessly, for the point had been made.

"How much time? How much time do I have before we are wed?" Isabella inquired, thinking feverishly.

"I am in no hurry, madam, nor am I in the habit of bedding children. Ye are young yet. A year or two perhaps."

"Once, I thought that was a long time," the girl said.

"And so 'tis, my lady. Who knows what may happen in such a time? His Grace might change his mind; I might be slain in battle. . . . Though I confess I find these two possibilities unlikely."

"My lord, please. There must be *some* means of extricating ourselves from this unwanted betrothal. I simply cannot marry ye. I—I love another."

There. She had said it, her true reason for not wanting to wed the Earl: for though he was handsome and rich and a favorite of the King, Isabella did not love him. She loved another, and despite the fact that the impassioned letters the girl had received from Lionel since his leaving had contained no mention of marriage, she still hoped her beloved's intentions toward her were honorable. Aye, surely, they were! She just couldn't believe otherwise. It would break her heart.

Warrick inhaled sharply. His eyes narrowed.

"Then that is your misfortune"—his voice was low and threatening as he responded to her confession. "Don't even think of deceiving me with another, madam, for I shall kill ye if ye do. Remember that—and well—and take no other to your bed, thinking some brave lover will save ye from your plight. I am deadly with my broadsword and will not be betrayed again. Forget this man. Ye are mine," he breathed. "Whether ye wish to be or not—ye are mine. Good night, my lady. Pleasant dreams."

Then he bowed, turned on his heel, and left her.

After he had gone, Isabella scurried to her chamber, slammed the door, and did something she had rarely done in her life: She shot the bolt home—fiercely, as though her very well-being depended on the Earl hearing the echo of the lock sliding shut. Then she leaned against the door, shaking all over, feeling as though she were going to be violently ill.

Married! She was to be married to Lord Hawkhurst! The thought chilled her to the bone. God's blood! She would not do it! She would have Giles's knights slay the Earl at once! Then Isabella remembered she had warned Lord Hawkhurst that he might easily meet his end at Rushden and had aroused his suspicions about Lord Oadby's death besides. She bit her lip, cursing her foolishness. After tonight, the Earl was certain to be on his guard, and too, there was his brother Caerllywel to be thought of—Caerllywel, who had been kind. If Isabella gave Giles's men orders to kill Lord Hawkhurst, they would surely slay his brother as well. There could be no chance of Caerllywel investigating the Earl's death and possibly bringing the King's wrath down upon Isabella and Giles.

Dear God. What was she to do? What was she to do?

Oh, Lionel. Lionel, my love! How can I live without ye? 'Tis too cruel! It cannot be!

Isabella pressed her face against the hard wooden door— and wept.

Chapter Ten

THE NEXT MORNING, ISABELLA WAS GLAD SHE HAD NOT acted rashly, for the Earl was polite but withdrawn at breakfast and made no mention of their betrothal. It was inconceivable to the girl that Warrick could sit there so calmly, ignoring her, when their lives had been so disastrously changed. Had he no feelings, this man who had said he would wed her, though he did not wish to have her as his wife? She thought of Lionel and the look on his face when he had sworn to make her his. The Earl had not looked at her like that last night . . . would never look at her like that.

Oh, God, oh, God, she prayed fiercely. Don't let it be true. Please don't let it be true that this man is to be my husband. 'Tis Lionel I love. Oh, Lionel. *Lionel!*

Caerllywel too was silent, and Isabella wondered whether it was because of his aching head born of the liquor he had consumed the previous evening or the fact that he and his brother had quarreled fiercely long after she had retired last night. The girl had heard them arguing, but their voices had been low, and she had not learned anything, despite pressing her ear to her chamber door for what had seemed like hours. The soft tones had not been loud enough to carry intelligibly. Isabella would have crept down the corridor from her room or sent Alice to spy on the two men, but the girl had been so frightened by Warrick that she had sought comfort instead in the gentle snoring of the old nanna, who slept in the small antechamber of Isabella's room.

The girl would have been only faintly surprised to learn she herself had been their topic of conversation.

"For all her sweet temper, she is no fool," the Earl had growled. "She has eyes that can see into a man's soul, and her ears are attuned to the slightest nuance of his voice. If ye persist in your attentions to her, she will cause trouble between us. I am warning ye, Caerllywel: Keep away from her."

"Oh, come, Waerwic. Ye speak ill of my Lady Isabella only because Brangwen has soured ye for all women. My Lady Isabella was but pleasant—"

"Nay, she is a witch—like all the rest! Ye do not believe me?" Warrick had asked, then laughed shortly when his brother had remained silent. "God's wounds! She threatened to slay me this eve."

"What?" Caerllywel's eyes had widened with disbelief, then narrowed. "Nay!"

"Aye, 'tis true. The Lady Isabella pulled her knife and swore she would kill me or set her brother's men to the task. Doubtless, that is what really happened to Lord Oadby. Oh, aye, she is a pleasant maid indeed, brother," the Earl had sneered, "one who, at the slightest provocation, is likely to stab me whilst I sleep or command her brother's men to arrange a fatal 'accident' for me."

"Nay, I cannot believe that of her, Waerwic. One who sets her hand to healing does not murder in the dark of night." Caerllywel had suddenly stared at his brother accusingly. "Ye must have frightened her—deliberately!"

"Oh, aye." Warrick had smiled wolfishly. "I told her we were to be wed, then intimated what I expected from our marriage. I very much fear my sweet bride is not at all looking forward to sharing my bed."

"But—but why on earth did ye set about to terrify the girl, Waerwic? Surely, there was no need for such."

"I do not aim to be saddled with a wench who knows no fear of me, Caerllywel. Had I dealt with Brangwen as I should have, she would have been too afraid to cast her eyes upon another man and would yet be mine."

"Nay, even that would not have held her, and my Lady Isabella is not Brangwen, Waerwic," his brother had reminded him grimly.

"Perhaps not, but they are alike nevertheless—all of them! Deceitful, lying bitches, one and all—good for one thing only! And fools are men who cannot see the rotten black hearts that lie beneath their facades of outward beauty!"

"Waerwic, Waerwic. Ye are wrong, *wrong*! One wench played ye false; 'tis true. But 'twas her nature, brother. She was sick and evil. Our mother warned ye of it from the start, but ye would not listen. Even had ye threatened Brangwen with death, she would have laughed in your face and lain with her executioner before your very eyes! My Lady Isabella is not like that, Waerwic. She is a woman to be won with love and treasured, methinks; and once her heart is yours, 'twill have no room in it for another man— I know it! Waerwic, Waerwic! I pray ye: Do not allow your hatred of one wicked maid to blind ye to the attributes of a wench who is naught but gentle and good. Ye will regret it, and bitterly, I promise ye."

"Thou art a fool, Caerllywel."

Warrick's mouth curled with contempt as he remembered the words of last night this morning. His brother *was* a fool.

The Earl had been right to frighten Isabella. Already, she behaved more modestly, her eyes downcast at her plate instead of flirting with Caerllywel.

That Isabella had *not* been teasing his brother the previous evening had not occurred to Warrick. He had no sisters and was not close to any woman. Thus, he had not recognized that Isabella's manner was that of a girl who had been raised primarily by and among men and so conversed easily with them, without the coyness or restraint that would have marked another woman. Indeed, because of her deep love of animals and Lady Shrewton's mean behavior toward her, Isabella had spent far more time in the stables than the sollar. She could stitch a wound like no other, but when it came to embroidering a sampler, her skillful fingers grew awkward and clumsy. She could boil herbs for an unguent, but when it came to steeping petals for perfume, she invariably spoilt the mixture. She could cradle a beast in her lap for hours without moving, but when it came to sitting at her studies, she fidgeted after a few minutes. She could carry on a lively discussion with the knights of the castle, but when it came to talking with the maids of the keep, Isabella was at a loss, for their interests were not her own.

But the Earl knew none of this and would not have believed it if he had. He had become too accustomed to thinking of women as mere bodies to warm his bed—to be dismissed with a handful of coins or a pretty bauble if they had pleased him, a few sharp words and sometimes a slap or two if they had not.

Warrick pushed away his plate and rose to his feet.

"I intend to ride out over the estate today. Do ye wish to accompany me?"

He had directed the question to Caerllywel, but Isabella did not know that.

"But of course, my lord," she answered politely, looking up at him with some surprise. "I have already given instructions for my mare to be saddled. Sirs Eadric, Thegn, and Beowulf will escort us, along with whomever of your own men ye may choose."

If Caerllywel's head had not been throbbing so badly from the ale he had drunk last night, he would have chortled aloud at the expression on his brother's face. In Warrick's mind, women did not meddle in the business affairs of men, and so Isabella had inadvertently insulted him again.

"Madam"—the Earl spoke coldly, disdainfully, wishing to put the impudent witch in her place—"I am sure there is no need for ye to trouble yourself in such a manner. The services of your chief bailiff will be quite adequate, I assure ye, as I am certain he knows far more about the management of your brother's lands than ye."

"I—I do not think so, my lord. Indeed, he will find it quite odd that I do not accompany ye. However"—Isabella quickly desisted, not wishing to provoke him—"if that is your desire . . ."

"Aye, 'tis," he informed her loftily, and nothing further was said as the girl left the hall to send a messenger for the bailiff.

But Master Potter, when summoned and told why he had been called from his duties, protested vigorously, shaking his head.

"My lord, I have a bad leg," he whined, "and 'tis difficult for me to ride any great distance. When 'tis necessary I oversee the farthest reaches of the estate, I travel by cart. Sometimes, it takes many days just to get from one point to another. Ye will do better to take the Lady Isabella. 'Tis she who keeps the account books anyway, and she is the only person, besides Lord Rushden, who knows the true worth of his lands. That, I assume, my lord, is what ye wish to know, is it not?"

"What do ye mean—the Lady Isabella keeps the account books? Do ye not see to the matter yourself with the aid of a clerk?"

"Oh, nay, my lord. The Ladies of Rushden have always kept the records and known as much of the castle's affairs as the Lords themselves. The Rushden charter, my lord, permits descendance to females if there be no legitimate male issue to inherit. For this reason, the daughters of Rushden are as learned in many areas as its sons are. In my time, my lord—with the exception of when Lord Oadby oversaw the estate and prevented the Lady Isabella from taking her rightful place as its mistress—there has never been a daughter of Rushden who could not hold and manage the keep as well as any of its sons."

Warrick inhaled deeply and thought if he heard Caerllywel laugh—even once—the Earl would slit his brother's throat. Fortunately, Caerllywel must have suspected this, for he made no sound, although if Warrick had spared him a glance, he would have seen his brother's eyes were filled with merriment.

"Master Potter, I desire ye to fetch the Lady Isabella here to me at once," the Earl ordered grimly.

"Aye, my lord."

Presently, Isabella appeared, her hands clasped demurely before her, her eyebrows raised in gentle inquiry. Warrick was not deceived. He suspected that beneath her outward demeanor, Isabella was secretly laughing at him. With difficulty, he quelled the strong desire he had to box her ears and silently cursed her for a witch.

"My lord?" she queried.

"I—I have changed my mind, my lady," Warrick stated stiffly. "I desire ye to ride out with us after all."

"Very good, my lord," Isabella responded smoothly.

"And cease 'my lording' me. There is no need for it when your rank is as great as my own, and ye are to be my wife besides! I have a name; 'tis Warrick. Use it hence, madam!" he snapped wrathfully.

Christ's son! The wench sought to make a fool of him at every turn!

The soft light that shone always in Isabella's eyes died, and her heart sank with despair at his words.

Oh, Lionel, my love, my dearest heart and soul!

"As—as ye wish, my—Warrick," the girl replied at last, her voice so low, they almost didn't hear her.

Neither the Earl nor Caerllywel missed the sudden shadowing of her face before dumbly she turned away from them and once more left the hall. Caerllywel threw his brother an angry glance, but Warrick only stared back at him coolly until the younger man swore under his breath, then abruptly followed Isabella from the chamber. The Earl frowned, watching with narrowed eyes as his brother caught the girl's arm and bent to speak to her. Reluctantly, she ceased her blind, hurried stride, earnestly gazing up at Caerllywel as he talked. Then she shook her head slightly and tried bravely to smile, but it was a pitiful attempt at best. Fuming inside, Warrick joined them and, with a single dark look, curtly put an end to their conversation.

There was another tense moment of anxiety as Isabella's little grey mare, Cendrillon, was led forth, and the Earl's strong hands closed around the girl's waist to assist her into the saddle. His fingers were like a steel band, deliberately possessive, as though to remind her she belonged to him and not to Caerllywel—or any other. And as with the previous evening, Isabella found Warrick's touch strangely disturbing to her. Briefly, the girl saw his eyes gleam with that odd light of desire that had frightened her so last night, and she trembled slightly as she gathered up her reins.

"I—I am ready, my—Warrick," she said.

Only then did the Earl release her to swing up onto his own mount, a huge brown destrier with a golden-cream mane and tail. Slowly, they cantered beneath the iron portcullis and over the drawbridge to the terrain beyond, Caerllywel and the rest following behind.

The day had dawned brightly and was now clear, for the early morning mist had long since lifted, though here and there, dewdrops sparkled still, like prisms, upon the spring grass. Before the small party, the road stretched out in a ribbon that wound its way through the forests and fields, just beginning to bloom. The branches of majestic oaks and sturdy pines intertwined with those of the tall ashes and slender poplars, forming canopies of multicolored green above the gnarled limbs of the spreading yews and thick, tangled gorse, at whose bases a riotous cascade of wild roses, gillyflower, ferns, and moss grew. Acres of newly planted wheat, oats, and barley gleamed in the sunlight and rippled in the slight breeze that stirred now and then, whispering softly to the crofters who dotted the countryside, hoes and scythes in hand. In the distance, cattle mooed lowly, and sheep and goats bleated on the hillsides.

All about him, Warrick saw nothing but signs of prosperity, cleanliness, and health: for Isabella had put her months as mistress of Rushden to good use, righting many of the wrongs that Lord Oadby had perpetrated, despite the Duke of Gloucester's pointed warning to him. After her previous warden's death, the girl had found that although, on the surface, Rushden seemed well cared for, its tenants had been even more badly treated than she and Giles. Isabella had been horrified upon learning of the hardships the villeins had endured, and she had set about to ease their lots as best she could, winning the crofters' love and gratitude. Now, they hailed her warmly when they spied her, laying aside their hoes and doffing their caps with respect.

Several women worked alongside their men in the fields, but others tended the neat vegetable patches the Earl saw behind every single cottage. Older children aided their mothers at this task, but the little ones, Warrick noted, played under the watchful eyes of a few young maids.

He turned to Isabella questioningly.

"Why are they not all in the fields, where even the youngest of them ought to be?" he asked, his voice disapproving. "And who gives them leave to plant gardens for themselves and care for them when there is other work to be done?"

"I do," Isabella answered calmly, "as my father did and his father before him and his father before him. Our ways here at Rushden are different, my lord."

"So I see," the Earl remarked dryly.

"My lord—Warrick—the manner of life ye observe here has long been the custom at Rushden—despite Lord Oadby's many wicked and miserly attempts to change it," the girl added coolly, and Warrick, wisely, did not miss the hint. "Our tenants are well cared for and take pride in their work. I ask ye, my lord: Of what use is a villein who has been beaten and starved into submission, who is likely to run away, rebel, or fall prey to any number of illnesses and die? Of what use is a child who, put to work in the fields at two, is likely to be emaciated and malformed at eight and dead at fifteen? Of what use is a crofter who, having managed to survive the hardships of such a childhood, grows to manhood angry and resentful or broken in spirit and bereft of pride? I tell ye such tenants are of value to no one, Warrick;

and I was hard pressed to right the many wrongs that Lord Oadby did to break the spirits of my brother's people." Again, there was a warning in her words.

"Your ways encourage them to have ideas above their stations!"

"Perhaps, but what is a man without hope and dreams? Do ye not see what a rich estate is Rushden? Do ye think 'twould be even half as wealthy if our ways here were otherwise? Nay, 'twould not be, methinks. There would be cruelty beyond measure and crime without end. Those who could not bear it would flee; those who stayed would suffer; and thus, Rushden would suffer too, as it did during Lord Oadby's time. Now—I'll warrant that one of Rushden's villeins does the work of three on another estate—and does it better and does it willingly, with a gladness born of love and security. There is not a man here who must wonder whether or not he will have enough food to feed the hungry mouths of his children. There is not a man here who must cheat the castle of its rightful due or steal from his neighbors in order to survive the winter. I have seen to that. 'Twas my ancestors' belief that a man was bound more surely with honey than vinegar, my lord, and so it has been here at Rushden. There is not a man here who would not freely and happily lay down his very life for me if I asked it. Can ye say the same of your own crofters?"

The Earl thought of his own tenants, a poor and bedraggled lot who worked sullenly and watched him slyly out of the corners of their eyes. He thought of his own estate, Hawkhurst, a crumbling-down ruin, which produced little and was grossly encumbered by debt, despite his own personal wealth. The contrast with Rushden was not pleasing, and he was consumed with envy and wrath that this small slight girl at his side ruled a domain where the villeins met one's eyes without fear, where the fields were greening richly beneath the spring sun, and where the herds were vast and well tended. She was only a woman. How did she know of such matters? 'Twas most unseemly. A wench's place was at her spinning wheel or embroidery frame in the sollar—or beneath a man in bed. Warrick felt like a fool in the face of her knowledge and wealth, the fact that she was succeeding where he had failed.

That his failure was due primarily to his not spending any time at his estate only rankled him further. He had no one to blame but himself for the current condition of his lands and castle. Like his father, he preferred life at Court and in battle, retiring to his domain only upon receipt of his steward's messages that matters could be neglected no longer. Even then, like his father, Warrick spent more time hunting than overseeing his estate. No wonder the number of his tenants lessened each year, as more and more of them dared to forsake their small plots and brave the world in hopes of finding a better lot.

The Earl set his heels to his stallion's sides and galloped on ahead, not trusting himself to speak, but now determined to make more than just the cursory examination of Rushden that he had originally planned.

At the village, he was met with further evidence of how well Rushden was run. Even the dirt roads were clean, the garbage and offal being periodically removed and used to fertilize the fields. The priest and the bailiff were summoned to show him their ledgers, and one old man among the crowd that had gathered to view the new warden tugged on the priest's robe and asked in a querulous voice if the village folk should fetch their papers.

"Papers? What papers?" Warrick inquired suspiciously.

"Why, the papers the Lady has the priest write for us to show we have paid what is due the Lord," the man answered simply.

"He means his receipts, Warrick," Isabella explained as she reached the throng. "At harvest time, each villager and tenant is given a receipt for the revenues he has paid to the Lord. That way, a new priest or bailiff cannot force the people to pay again what they have already fairly paid once. 'Twas my father's idea. The times are hard, what with the civil war and not knowing who may wear the Crown to-morrow; and 'tis not right for the commonfolk to suffer for the quarrels of the nobility."

"Aye." Warrick's golden eyes narrowed. "That, at least, I can understand, for the Welsh too have long been afflicted by such. The Ashleys have always been Yorkists, have they not?"

"Aye, since the beginning of the civil war. And ye, my lord?"

"I, madam?" The Earl raised one eyebrow mockingly and smiled strangely.

His brother laughed.

"Waerwic is always for the winning side, my lady," Caerllywel said.

Isabella was shocked.

"Why, that's terrible! Have ye no honor?"

"I am half-Welsh and a bastard besides, madam," Warrick drawled, his tone a trifle bitter. "What kind of honor would ye expect me to have? I am a savage—or worse—or so I have been told."

Isabella turned those fathomless grey-green eyes upon him.

"Even a savage must have some code of honor," she noted softly. "Without such, a man is nothing."

The Earl's nostrils flared whitely, and for a moment, Isabella thought he would hit her with his whip; then, his jaw set, he hauled on his reins and spurred his horse forward, galloping out of town.

Isabella bit her lip in despair.

"I have angered him, and 'twas not my intent," she said.

"Do not fret yourself, my lady," Caerllywel told her. "Ye didst but speak the truth, as well Waerwic knows. He will get over it soon enough."

"I wish—I wish I understood why he dislikes me so. 'Tis something more than just our betrothal, methinks. I know he doesn't want to wed me, that 'tis the King who commands our marriage; but surely, Warrick must know I desire this match no more than he does. Last night—last night, after he told me of it, I even prayed 'twas but a drunken jest." She paused, then sighed. "I'm sorry. 'Twas unkind of me to tell ye such a thing, but, oh, Caerllywel! 'Tis true! To be forced to marry a man I scarcely know . . . Ye cannot understand how the thought appalls me! I hoped I would have a choice in the matter. Now everything is so changed, and there is nothing I can do. Nothing!" she reiterated bitterly. "Oh, surely, the Earl cannot hold me to blame for our betrothal; surely, he cannot! Why, then, does he treat me so? Do ye know, Caerllywel? Will ye tell me?"

"'Tis—'tis simply Waerwic's way, my lady," Caerllywel responded, turning his face away so she could not see his expression. "He does not mean to be cruel. 'Tis just that he has little liking for any woman. He was not always thus. Once, he laughed as easily and gaily as any other man—and loved too—but the object of his worship was ill chosen. Brangwen, his betrothed, was like the belladonna plant, beautiful but poisonous at her core. In time, all of us came to see it—all except Waerwic, who was blind to her evil, despite our mother's attempts to warn him of it. Even my brothers and I could not reason with him. Brangwen used Waerwic, and when she had done with him, she scorned him and played him false. The wound of her betrayal went deep. I pray ye be patient, my lady, and not judge him too harshly for his ways."

"I—I shall try."

"Thank ye, Isabella." Caerllywel smiled soberly. "Ye are a gentle maid. Perhaps, in time, ye may heal Waerwic as ye do the creatures of the woods and moors."

"Mayhap. After all"—her voice caught in a ragged little sob—"I shall have a lifetime to try. The King has seen to that."

They rode on in silence, Isabella lost in sorrow and Caerllywel having no further words of comfort to offer.

Chapter Eleven

IT WAS NIGHT WHEN THEY REACHED THE OUTLYING KEEP of Oakengates, which belonged to one of Giles's vassals, Sir John Debolt. But the dark was not sufficient to disguise the fact that all was not well at the castle. By the light of the moon, the small party could see that several of the fields had been burned, leaving great patches of blackened ruin upon the land, and the herds that would normally have ranged upon the sweeping heaths were nowhere to be found.

Isabella was distraught.

"What can have happened?" she asked as she stared, horrified, at the ravage that had been wrought. "'Twas not thus the last time I visited here with my brother's men."

"I do not know," Warrick told her, his earlier enmity toward her vanishing now in the face of the destruction that threatened them both. "But we shall soon discover whatever may be wrong, I promise ye."

To her surprise, he gave her a small, reassuring smile before calling back orders to the men behind who accompanied them. Instantly, all snapped to attention, eyes and ears alert, hands laid warily upon hilts of swords. The entourage would not be taken unaware if there were any who sought to wreak ill upon it.

At last, the fortress came into view. It was not large, but it was capable of being efficiently defended, and it had served Rushden well in the past. After Caerllywel had shouted their names to the sentries, the party was admitted without difficulty. Once they were inside, Sir John himself came forward to greet them, his warm welcome doing little to hide his dismay at knowing the state in which they had found Oakengates. He assessed Isabella's new warden sharply.

"I have heard of ye, my lord," their host announced as he ushered them into the great hall and gave orders for food and drink to be brought. "'Tis said ye are a hard man— but just—and your sword arm is strong. I trust ye will do well by Rushden and the Lord and Lady."

"As well as I am able insofar as my office permits," the Earl replied. "I am, after all, the King's agent and must do as he wills."

"As must we all," Sir John observed smoothly. He turned to Isabella. "And how fares England's prettiest rose? Well, I trust." His keen eyes surveyed her critically, as though searching for some sign of ill-being.

"Aye," Isabella answered, avoiding his piercing gaze. "I am well, sir."

Sir John was silent for a moment, then nodded, apparently satisfied. Something was troubling the girl, but she

had no wish to speak of it; he could tell and so did not pry.
Instead, he continued, changing the subject.

"And your brother, Lord Rushden—he does well under
the tutelage of Gloucester?"

"Aye, sir. He has won his pennon and is one of the
Duke's personal attendants. He loves Richard well."

"'Tis good. Come," he said brusquely, the amenities out
of the way. "No doubt your day has been long and tiring.
Ye must refresh yourselves, for doubtless, ye will wish to
view the estate tomorrow; and as I'm sure ye must have
noticed, all is not well at Oakengates."

Sir John sounded tired, as though he had battled a foe
who had yet to be beaten, and he was now at his wit's end
to discover some means of prevailing over his enemy.

"Aye, we saw. There has been trouble here, Sir John,"
Isabella stated, coming straight to the point. "Though 'twas
dark when we arrived, the moon didst show us the
destruction that has been wrought. What has happened,
sir?"

"Reivers, my lady." Sir John's voice was grim. "The
attacks began shortly after Lord Oadby's death. I had hoped
to settle the matter before ye could learn of it, but so far,
I have not been successful."

"Your reticence was unwise, Sir John," Isabella chided
gently. "'Tis my business to know what is amiss here. If
ye needed help, why did ye not send to Rushden for it?"

"I did, my lady, but Sir Lindael informed me ye had
enough problems as 'twas, and as 'twas likely ye would
insist on riding to Oakengates, he did not wish ye to learn
of the difficulty here. He sent what men he could spare,
but none knows the identity of the outlaws, my lady, and
Sir Lindael feared for your safety. Though 'tis probably
unlikely, the men may be disguised knights of some lord,
who plans to carry ye off and gain your riches through a
forced marriage and who has set upon this scheme to lure
ye from Rushden."

"Nay, surely not. 'Twould be a poor plan at best, its
means haphazard and its outcome uncertain. Besides, if such
were the case, we would doubtless have been set upon on
the road. Methinks that Sir Lindael has taken a great deal

upon himself lately in order to shield me," Isabella noted. "I can see I shall have to speak to him."

"Do not be too harsh with him, my lady, I pray ye"—Sir John spoke with the liberty of an old and valued retainer. "Indeed, I am as much to blame as Sir Lindael, for once he told me of his fears, I agreed wholeheartedly to keep the matter from ye: for ye know, my lady, that ye would have come, regardless of the consequences to yourself."

"And despite your attempts to keep me at home, I am here anyway. Oh, Sir John, not ye too! However am I to guard Giles's inheritance if his men are determined to keep me in ignorance of Rushden's affairs at every turn in order to protect me from any evil that might befall me?"

"Lord Hawkhurst will see to the estate, my lady. 'Tis his duty, and I hope ye will not be playing any of your tricks upon him." Sir John eyed her sternly.

"Ye are quite correct, sir," Warrick remarked, giving Isabella an unfathomable glance. "Do go on with your tale. Ye say ye have yet to capture the robbers?"

"Aye, they are many and clever, and I am starting to suspect there is a traitor in my household. I have laid many traps for those who plunder the lands, yet still, they manage to outwit me at every turn, escaping into the forests, where the hiding places are many."

"Ye have questioned everyone here, of course," the Earl said.

"Aye, but without result. Naturally, all claim to be innocent of aiding the accursed thieves, and none here, to my knowledge, has behaved in a sly and unnatural manner. In addition, I find it difficult to believe any of my men are involved in the matter. Those who serve me have been with me many years and have long since proven themselves trustworthy and faithful retainers. 'Tis indeed a most exasperating puzzle to me."

"If your men are as ye say, I think we can discount them"—Warrick spoke thoughtfully—"and must look elsewhere for the answer."

"A rebellious tenant perhaps," Caerllywel suggested. "Has aught occurred that one might hold some grudge against ye?"

"Nay, I do not believe so. Did not ye yourselves see evidence today of how well all at Rushden and its outlying lands are treated? Our ways may seem strange to ye, but they are good ways nevertheless—despite what Lord Oadby used to say." Sir John sniffed, as though offended.

"Aye, the crofters did indeed seem well and content," Warrick admitted, marking the vassal's dislike of Rushden's previous warden. Isabella was not the only one who had loathed the man, it appeared. "Nevertheless, if all is as ye said, the reivers cannot be working alone. Someone, not a villein of the fields, but a servant inside the castle walls, must be abetting them. In the morning, we shall set about to discover who 'tis."

Oddly enough, Isabella had no doubt at all that her new warden would accomplish this task. Though she did not like him, he seemed a man of purpose; and Sir John, whose opinion the girl trusted and who had not cared for Lord Oadby, did not appear to find any fault with Warrick. Indeed, the vassal's attitude toward the Earl was one of deference and respect.

Isabella sighed and handed her wine chalice to a servant so he might refill it. She was so deep in thought, she scarcely noticed the bitterness upon the boy's face, and later, when she tried to recall it, the impression was fleeting, and she decided she must have imagined it after all.

Chapter Twelve

THE NEXT MORNING, IT WAS DECIDED THE PARTY WOULD split into three groups, with Caerllywel staying behind at the keep to interrogate the servants, Warrick setting forth with Sir John to question the crofters, and Isabella going with the bailiff of Oakengates to survey the damage that had been done. The girl was oddly pleased that Warrick apparently now trusted her knowledge of the lands enough to allow her to continue her responsibilities as mistress of Rushden (though she had meant to do so in any case).

Because of this, her spirits were brighter than they might otherwise have been, for it could only mean that Warrick did not intend to wrest her power from her grasp by upsetting the manner in which Rushden was run. She might be forced to become the Earl's wife, but at least Giles's inheritance would be safe.

Isabella had to curb the strong impulse she felt to sing softly as they rode along, as it would have hardly have been seemly in the face of the destruction that Sir John and his castle had suffered.

Now that the day had dawned, she was able to view the full extent of the ruin clearly, and the girl was appalled. Oakengates had been extremely hard hit by the reivers. Major portions of its just-beginning-to-ripen crops had been burned; its herds of cattle, sheep, and goats had been reduced to a mere few beasts. At once, Isabella saw the fortress would not glean enough from its harvest to pay the revenues due Rushden, much less to survive the winter. Swiftly, she determined that she would levy no fees on the keep this year. Then mentally, she began adding up the contents that, with the coming autumn, would fill her own storehouses, trying to figure out how much might safely be spared for Oakengates. The girl sighed, her heart going out to Sir John and his villeins, for they would have to work doubly hard next year to repair the damage that had been done and to bring the castle up to date on the revenues that would then be owing. She hoped fervently that Warrick and Caerllywel succeeded in discovering the identity of the culprit responsible for aiding the outlaws.

The traitor will have to be hanged, Isabella thought, then shuddered, not knowing if she would be able to uphold such an order, though she knew the penalty would be justified and necessary to prevent such from happening again.

At last, the inspection was completed, and the windswept moors stretched out before her in a wild sweep of rolling green, broken here and there by winding jumbles of pale rock and crevices through which babbling rivulets sometimes coursed. In the woods, quiet pools lay clear and blue beneath the spring sky, their cool waters disturbed only by the trailing branches of the trees. Far to the east would be the jagged cliffs and sandy beaches that lined the coast and then the sea that Isabella knew of only from tales sung by the castle bard and told by Giles and Lionel and others who had journeyed to places far beyond the shores of England.

"Do ye wish to return to Oakengates now, my lady?" Sir Beowulf inquired, interrupting the girl's reverie.

"Nay, let us ride on a little longer," Isabella said.

She had missed galloping freely over the heaths, and surely, there was no threat of her being kidnapped as long as she was well escorted. Besides, the thought of returning to Oakengates—to Warrick—was unwelcome to her. She needed time to think about the betrothal that had so changed her life. Despite the Earl's comments on the matter, Isabella was certain there must be some means of securing her release from the match, and she intended to find a way to free herself. She had already written to Giles and Lionel to inform them of the new warden's identity, although she had said nothing of the betrothal, wanting to tell them herself of the match; and she dared not involve Sir Lindael or any of the other knights in the matter until Giles could advise her what to do. Sirs Eadric, Thegn, and Beowulf especially might take it into their heads to murder Warrick, thinking they were doing the girl a favor. Isabella must remain silent until her brother arrived. Perhaps Giles and Lionel would speak to Gloucester. . . . Aye, the Duke had been kind. He might be persuaded to plead her case before his brother the King, particularly in favor of Lionel, whom Richard loved dearly.

Lost in thought, her spirits lifting a little, the girl rode on, forgetting the thieves that lurked at hand, until Sir Thegn asked if she considered it wise to stray so far from the fortress with robbers skulking about. Even then, Isabella discounted them, her voice slightly scornful.

"Why, 'tis broad daylight, Thegn, and we are well armed. Surely, those who plunder the lands have not grown so bold as to attack a party such as ours by the full light of day. Nay, they strike at night, like the cowards they are."

"Very well, my lady, but at least let me ride back and warn Lord Hawkhurst of your intent," Sir Eadric put in.

"As ye wish." Isabella shrugged. "However, I do not think he will be much alarmed."

But she was wrong. Warrick, when Sir Eadric gave him the news, swore mightily under his breath, then began shouting orders to his men.

"Damn her!" he cursed in between commands. "Has she run mad—to even think of such a thing in light of what has happened here? Sir Eadric, I shall hold ye and Sirs Thegn and Beowulf responsible if aught ill has occurred to the Lady Isabella. How *could* ye have agreed to let her go beyond sight of the castle walls?"

"We—we did try to dissuade her, my lord, but she has been so confined of late, and she is such a—a fey creature, my lord. She pines for the fields and the forests as others hunger for food and thirst for drink. We did our best, my lord, but we could not reason with her, and—and 'twas not as though she were alone."

"If she would not listen, ye ought to have forcibly returned her to the keep! She is scarcely more than a child—and an ill-behaved one at that!"

"My lord!" Sir Eadric gasped, horrified at the thought of laying rough hands on his mistress. "Surely—surely, ye cannot mean what ye just said."

"I most certainly do. Your mistress is a brat. . . . Oh, ye mean about using force to restrain her. Nay, I spoke in haste. Ye are in no position to lay hands upon her. . . . But *I* am."

The Earl's eyes narrowed at the thought. Not only was he Isabella's warden, but, thanks to the King, her betrothed as well. Warrick had every right to touch her and in whatever manner he pleased.

"I am sore tempted to give her a sound thrashing!"

"Oh, my lord, I pray ye: Do not be too cruel with the Lady. She is, as ye said, little more than a child, and—and, except for Lord Oadby, she has been used with kindness by the men in her life. 'Twas not her father's way to handle his women with his fists. The Lady is not accustomed to being struck—"

"Then 'tis high time someone *did* deal her a few sharp

slaps—several of them, in fact! Mayhap then she will learn her place! I am master here now."

"Oh, nay, my lord! She will not understand if ye beat her. Please, my lord, I beg ye—"

"*I am* no fool to be bewitched by the charms of a pretty maid, however fey she may be!" the Earl snapped, then set his heels to his destrier's sides and was gone.

Isabella, her ears attuned to every sigh upon the wind, every rustle of the brush, was the first to hear the shrill cry of pain in the distance. Abruptly, she reined in her mare to listen for the sound again. Aye, there 'twas!

Some animal is hurt, she thought and, without warning, urged her horse to a gallop, leaving Warrick's and Sir John's men, who did not understand her sudden, wild flight, staring after her in confusion.

Only Sirs Thegn and Beowulf, who, out of long familiarity, guessed the cause of her unexpected start, were able to gather their wits quickly enough to follow, and even they lagged behind, for Isabella's steed was small and fleet, better able to traverse the rocky, gorse-strewn moors than were the ponderous destriers the men were mounted on.

"My lady! My lady!" Sir Thegn called futilely as he saw they could not possibly keep pace with Isabella. "My lady, come back!"

"'Tis no use. We'll never catch her," Sir Beowulf observed with a sinking feeling in the pit of his stomach as the image of Lord Hawkhurst's cold hard face suddenly filled his mind. "God's wounds! The Earl will have our heads! Did ye see where she went?"

"Nay, did ye?"

"Aye. Ride back to the others. Tell them to spread out and to listen sharp for the cry of a wounded beast. That is where the Lady will be. I shall go on, since I saw the place where she entered the forest."

"Agreed," Sir Thegn said as he too thought fearfully of Lord Hawkhurst's wrath if aught ill befell the King's ward.

Isabella, meanwhile, was galloping recklessly through the woods, heedless of the low branches that slapped at her face and tore at her clothing, scratching her chest and arms.

She could hear the injured animal's squeals of agony even more clearly now, and her only thought was to reach the wounded creature as quickly as possible.

At last, she burst into a clearing and abruptly reined her mare to a halt at the sight that met her startled eyes. She was horrified, for never in her life had she seen such filthy men as the three who stood before her. They seemed old, for their grimy faces were unshaven; and the girl saw, as their shouts and laughter rang out, that their gums were foul and rotten, and many teeth were missing from their mouths. Their shoulders were stooped beneath their ragged garments, but they could not have been as aged as Isabella had, at first, thought, for they were possessed of a wiry strength that seldom belonged to the elderly commonfolk. The men were crouched around a pit into which a boar had fallen and over which they hovered with an unnatural glee. The hole was not deep, but it was enough to contain the furious beast. The poachers (for Isabella was certain now that this was what they were and not the reivers, as she'd feared) were jabbing the creature unmercifully with spears that, although stout, had not yet proven sturdy enough to penetrate the animal's thick hide deeply enough to kill it.

"Stop that! Stop that at once, I say!" Isabella shouted, her face white with anger at their cruelty, for although the wounded boar was mean and ugly, it was still a beast of nature and thus, to her, something to be protected.

The men glanced up fearfully and half-rose, frightened by Isabella's sudden appearance and intending to take to their heels, but upon perceiving it was only a young girl who threatened them, they cackled loudly again instead, momentarily diverted from their harassment of the creature.

"Hey, Bo," one cried, "look there! 'Tis a better prize than this old pig, methinks," the man gloated, his eyes glittering oddly. "What say we ferget about the boar and grab us that maid instead?" He pointed toward Isabella. "I ain't had me a wench since that old hag we took off'n that blind beggar, and she weren't much good anyways. But I'll warrant this one knows how to please a man. Aye." His eyes raked Isabella appreciatively. "I wouldn't mind getting betwixt them there pretty legs of hers at all."

"How do ye know they's pretty, Wyatt?" the poacher called Bo croaked.

"Got to be—with a mug like that."

"I am Lady Isabella Ashley of Rushden," Isabella announced coldly but calmly, for surely, the men would not dare to harm her! Nevertheless, she backed Cendrillon away slightly before continuing. "And ye are trespassing on my vassal's land. I order ye to be gone from here at once or be hanged for your thievery."

The men only guffawed raucously at her statement.

"Ye going to take us prisoner all by yerself, little lady?" the third poacher asked, his lips twisted in an ugly sneer.

"My men-at-arms are on their way here now." Isabella forced herself to continue to speak composedly, though a little shiver of fright now ran up her spine. "They will see ye are properly punished for your crimes."

"Ha!" the man snorted, tilting a flask up to his lips. "That's a likely story, I'll wager! 'Pears to me like ye's all by yerself."

The girl watched, mesmerized, as the dark liquid ran down his dirty chin, and he wiped it off with the sleeve of his torn shirt. Why, they were drunk, all of them! Isabella knew then that she ought to get away at once, to ride back to her men for help; but still, the boar thrashed sickeningly in the pit, and she could not leave it.

"I'll warrant yer right about her being by herself, Fess," Bo said after glancing around uneasily for a moment. "I don't see nobody else, and I don't hear nobody else. Still, does seem peculiar though, a wench like that riding all alone in these here woods. Looks like she's gentlefolk to me. Mayhap we'd best get on out of here after all. I don't like it."

"And I'll wager she jest said that to scare us off," Wyatt jeered, "what with even a rabbit being able to tell ye's a'feared of yer own shadow! Ye can get on if'n ye want, but I'm fer seeing what's under them fine skirts of hers myself. What about ye, Fess?"

"Well"—he scratched his head, as though considering— "I wouldn't mind taking a peek. Hell, once we're done with her, we can throw her in the pit, and that old pig'll take care of the rest."

Isabella gasped, shocked that the men would even consider such a thing.

"I warn ye: You'll pay for it with your lives if ye dare to touch me!" she threatened, edging Cendrillon even farther away as the poachers started to sidle slyly closer. "If ye wish to save yourselves, you'd best be off before my men-at-arms arrive," she went on, looking around and listening desperately for some sight or sound that would tell her that Sirs Thegn and Beowulf and the rest were somewhere near at hand.

The men only chortled. Then suddenly, without warning, they rushed toward her, grabbing at her legs and Cendrillon's bridle. Instinctively, Isabella raised the whip she always carried but never used, slashing at the poachers fiercely. Bo and Wyatt howled with pain, but Fess only grunted.

"Ye think yer going to beat us to death with that little stick?" he queried with a leer, snatching at Isabella's skirts and ripping the material.

The girl kicked out at him viciously, catching him a blow on the jaw that sent him staggering; then she urged Cendrillon forward, intending to gallop from the clearing. But Fess thwarted her plans, rolling to one side and springing to his feet with a rapidity that surprised her. He yanked her from the mare's back as she passed. Isabella screamed and struck him again with the crop, but finally, he managed to wrest the whip from her grasp. He broke the slender crop over his knee and flung the bits into the forest, then caught hold of her bodice, ripping it down to expose her shift beneath which her breasts heaved. Then he dealt her several sharp slaps.

Isabella gasped once more, then screamed hysterically, putting up her hands to try to ward off the painful blows as they rained upon her face. She thought of Lord Oadby, and tears streamed down her cheeks: for by now, all three poachers were pawing at her lustfully, and she could smell the fumes of their breath hot and fetid upon her cheeks. Scarcely conscious of what she did, the girl jerked her dagger from her girdle and stabbed blindly, wildly, at the hands that assaulted her. She heard a shriek of pain and saw that Bo had fallen back before she plunged the blade into Wyatt's shoulder. She was only dimly aware that Fess had now succeeded in tearing her gown and girdle from her body, leaving her clad in just her thin white undergarment as she turned to face him like a cornered animal, knife poised with determination. Seeing the damage done to his friends, he stepped away warily and grinned, a horrible, lewd, hateful smile.

"Wicked little bitch, ain't ye?" Fess growled before moving toward her again—slowly, evilly.

Warrick paused to give his panting destrier a chance to catch its breath, then bade the snorting war horse be silent as the strangled cries of a terrified woman reached his ears. *Isabella!* The Earl's heart leaped to his throat with fear and anger. Though Warrick did not want her as his wife, Isabella was still his, by God, and no man would touch what belonged to the Earl. Besides, he was the girl's warden as well and responsible for her safety. With a savage snarl, he dug his spurs viciously into the stallion's sides.

Like an avenging demon, Warrick galloped into the clearing from the cover of the woods. He took in the situation at a glance. Blinding rage consumed him, and he did not hesitate. His broadsword caught Fess right across the throat, severing the poacher's head from his shoulders. Once more, Isabella screamed as blood spewed from the man's neck in a crimson gush that splashed her in dreadful, mind-numbing spurts. She gazed down at herself, stricken, her hands spread wide and dripping with the warm, sticky red liquid. To her utter horror, the poacher's trunk remained standing briefly before crumpling in a heap on the ground, where the blood now bubbled forth in a rivulet that ran over the earth to where Fess's head lay, brain still functioning, his eyes flickering momentarily with shock before mercifully, at last, they glazed over, sightless. Dear God! For just that one terrible, fleeting instant, the man's head had still been alive, and he had known what had happened to him! Isabella's knees buckled beneath her as she retched violently onto the grass, bracing herself against a tree for support. She dropped her knife, holding her shaking hands to her face to hide her eyes, then was sick again as she realized her fingers had smeared the poacher's blood across her cheeks and lips.

Bo and Wyatt turned to flee, but the Earl showed them no quarter, cutting them down in the same manner as he had their friend. Bo's head toppled from his shoulders, bouncing along the ground before it rolled to a stop some distance away from where Isabella huddled. Wyatt's head seemed to spring from his torso, flying high into the air before it landed with a thud upon the earth and tumbled to a halt.

His dark visage grim with fury, Warrick wheeled his destrier, yanked the war horse up fiercely, then dismounted to hurry to Isabella's side. The Earl too was covered with blood, and the liquid ran slowly down the blade he still held in one hand, dripping upon the grass in droplets of red, to make a tiny puddle upon the ground.

The girl stared at him, her eyes still wide with horror, before she turned away and buried her face against the trunk of the tree that still supported her. The muffled sobs choked in her throat as she gasped raggedly for breath, trying to force the awful, unreal scene from her mind.

Warrick laid one hand upon her shoulder, his touch curiously gentle.

"Art hurt?" he inquired, his voice raw with concern, for he saw that her gown had been ripped from her body, and he feared she had been raped.

Isabella shook her head negatively in reply, continuing to weep as the Earl stood there silently until the boar squealed once more and thrashed sickeningly in the pit that contained it. At the sound, the girl moved slowly, dazedly, toward the hole, peering over its edge at the wounded creature. There, Warrick joined her.

The animal lay on its side, heaving with pain, legs flailing wildly, spears protuding from its body. Blood thickened and congealed around the many punctures, where already flies had begun to settle, adding to the beast's terrible agony.

The Earl's immediate instinct was to kill the creature at once in order to put it out of its misery, but oddly enough, he **found** himself instead saying to Isabella. "Can ye save it?"

"**Nay,**" he answered, her voice quivering. "Be merciful, and **slay it** quickly."

Warrick was not insensitive to the ache in her tone.

"**Turn** aside," he commanded softly.

She did as he told her and heard the boar shriek once. **Then, moments** later, all was still, and the Earl was leading her **away from** the pit, shielding her eyes from the dreadful carnage of the bloody, decapitated poachers lying scattered on the earth. He called to his stallion, Gwalchmai. After the steed had approached, Warrick took a flask from his **saddle, wet** his handkerchief with the ale, and began to sponge the blood from Isabella's body. She bore his ministrations without protest, standing mute before him, and he realized she was still in a state of shock. When he turned her lovely countenance up to his, he saw the purplish-blue marks that had begun to show upon her cheeks.

"What happened to your face?" he asked.

"One of the poachers struck—struck me," Isabella explained, her voice hurt and confused.

"Then I am glad I killed him," the Earl said, forgetting he himself had sought Isabella out with the express purpose of dealing her a few sharp slaps.

Now, to his surprise, the idea of someone hitting her filled him with wrath and indignation. She was too small and fragile to be used so. Warrick found he could not even scold her for riding beyond sight of the castle walls, for her punishment had been more than even he would have wished. When he had finished cleansing the blood from her trembling body, he held her close, sensing she needed physical contact to be comforted, stroking her hair and whispering to her soothingly as her tears began anew, and she wept against his chest.

The Earl did not know how long they remained thus before, at last, he became aware of Isabella's near-nakedness in a different manner, of the soft curves of her flesh pressed against him enticingly, of the heady scent of her perfume bewitchingly pervading his flaring nostrils. Roses, it was—white roses; he was sure. The fragrance reminded him faintly of his mother. He stirred and swore, attempting gently to disentangle himself from the girl's arms: for the bloodlust of his having killed the three men was upon him still, and he knew of but one other way to ease it. The thought that it was his right to have Isabella occurred to him, but instantly, Warrick shoved it from his mind. It would be tantamount to rape in the girl's present condition, and God knew, she had suffered enough horror this day. Besides, he sensed instinctively that to take her by force would be to turn her against him for all time, and oddly enough, the Earl found the thought of that disturbed him. Once more, he tried to push the girl from him, but Isabella gave a tiny, constricted cry, clutched him, clung to him, and again buried her face against his chest, finding solace in his nearness.

Warrick saw that one strap of her shift had fallen from her shoulder, exposing a generous amount of her full ripe breasts, which he could see plainly anyway beneath the thin cloth. Somehow, the undergarment had ridden up too, displaying a flash of long leg and thigh. The Earl groaned and swore once more as he felt his loins quicken and his manhood harden. Again, he tried to thrust Isabella away, but once more, she resisted, snuggling against him, her face turned up to his as she looked at him, hurt, puzzled, and inquiring.

His amber eyes darkened, for he wanted her; and suddenly, as his thighs pressed against hers, the girl realized what was happening to him. Her eyes widened; it was she who now attempted to pull away, but she was too late.

"Witch!" Warrick breathed. "Dost tempt me?" And then, "Oh, sweet Christ, Isabella," before his mouth swooped down over hers, and his arms tightened, imprisoning her like an iron band.

The girl struggled in his grasp, but still, the Earl held her fast, his lips searing hers, his tongue probing, parting her mouth to slip inside, swirl about her own tongue deliciously and then more demandingly as his passions intensified. Isabella was engulfed by a whirlwind of emotions. She was startled and somehow excited and afraid all at the same time. She tried to resist, but the sudden desire that flamed through her blood was too strong; and soon, she felt herself, against her will, melting in Warrick's embrace. Her head pounded dizzily, and her heart beat too rapidly in her breast. She did not understand the strange feelings that possessed her. It was Lionel she loved. Why, then, was she responding to the Earl with this fire that seemed so wanton and alive, this blaze that filled her very soul?

'Tis only a kiss! she told herself wildly. Only a kiss. But Lionel's lips had not felt like this. Lionel's mouth upon hers had been warm and inviting. Warrick's kiss was hot and savage—filled with the years of age and experience that Lionel had yet to live through; but Isabella did not recognize that. She knew only that there was nothing of the dashing romantic in the Earl, that he would never kneel at her feet to pledge his love as Lionel had done. Nay, Warrick was pure power and passion; he would take what he wanted— as he was taking her lips now—and dare her to defy him, to deny him....

"Nay," she murmured, mortified. "Nay, my lord, do not do this. Please."

But Warrick only went on kissing her, his mouth burning across her cheek to her temple, trailing down her silken hair to her silvery throat and breasts. His fingers pushed blindly at the strap of her shift that yet remained upon one shoulder. The riband fell. The undergarment slid down, despite Isabella's attempts to clutch it to her, for the Earl caught her hands and pinioned them behind her back with one of his own, baring her breasts for his eyes and fingers and lips.... The girl moaned and renewed her struggles as Warrick's free hand cupped one ripe mound; his mouth found one rosy crest, and his tongue teased the bud to a taut little peak.

"Please, my lord," Isabella begged, horrified by and ashamed of her uncontrollable response to him. "I—I am a maid, and—and—" She intended to tell him again of her love for Lionel and beg once more for release from her betrothal. But instead, her ears discerned the approach of her men-at-arms, who had finally discovered her whereabouts, and she finished lamely, "And my escort comes."

Again, the Earl swore, then lifted his head, his dark golden eyes raking her in a manner that made her blush and tremble and turn away from his gaze. Hastily, he rearranged her shift, then unfastened his cloak and draped it about her to hide her near-nakedness from the men who were now emerging into the clearing from the woods.

"My lady!" Sir Beowulf reined in shortly his heavily panting destrier, aghast as his shocked and disbelieving eyes surveyed his mistress, her new warden, and the horrible carnage in the clearing. "Art harmed?"

Isabella shook her head, still shaking in Warrick's arms, and prayed the faithful knight would think she quivered out of fear—instead of the bewildering, frightening passion the Earl had unleashed in her.

"The Lady Isabella is safe—no thanks to ye," Warrick stated, his voice hard with anger at having had his love-making interrupted, but Sir Beowulf did not know that.

"My lord," the knight began defensively, "we followed as quickly and best we could, but my lady's horse is fleet and far outstripped our own; she galloped away so suddenly—"

"That is no excuse," the Earl told him grimly. "Ye are to guard your mistress closely at all times, even at the cost of your life! 'Twas only that Sir Eadric had sense enough to warn me of the Lady Isabella's intention to ride beyond sight of the castle walls that I found her before she was ravished. She might have been killed by those three ruffians ye see lying there!"

"Aye, my lord."

"Warrick, please," Isabella pleaded, her voice low, one hand upon his arm. "'Twas indeed my fault. The men didst try to warn me, but I would not listen; and when I heard the boar's cry of pain, I didst ride heedlessly from my escort, though they called for me to wait. Sir Beowulf and the others are not to blame. I alone am the one ye should punish."

The Earl glanced down at her, noting her wide grey-green eyes filled with penitence—and something more—and her soft, vulnerable lips, now bruised and swollen from his stolen kisses. He remembered the feel of her curves pressed against him and the taste of her pink nipple in his mouth. Despite himself, he found the very nearness of her still intoxicating.

What has she done to me? he wondered. 'Twas naught but a few kisses I took from her, and even now, I grow weak with lust at just the sight of her, would grant her every desire—the forest nymph, the water sprite! She has bewitched me as she has the others! How can I hold the knights to blame when even I cannot resist her charms?

He shook his head, as though to clear it.

"Very well, then, madam. Ye will be confined at Oakengates until we discover the traitor within its walls and the hiding place of the reivers; is that clear?"

"Aye, my lord."

"Sir Beowulf, ye and the rest of Lord Rushden's men will bury the bodies, and take the heads back to the keep to be displayed upon pikes along the road as a warning to others who may seek to poach upon the lands."

"What about the boar, my lord? Sir Debolt will surely wish it for his table."

The Earl saw Isabella's face blanch at the thought of eating the animal that had been the cause of her horror and Warrick's slaughter of the poachers.

"The beast is to be divided among the crofters, for they have suffered the most from the thieves' attacks. If Sir John questions ye about it, ye may say it is upon my order that the creature finds its way into the cooking pots of the villeins rather than Sir John's."

"Aye, my lord."

"Ye will also fill in that pit. Sir John's men will set out to search for the Lady Isabella's steed. It must have run away during the melee. My men will accompany me and the Lady Isabella back to the fortress. Report to me there once ye have finished."

"Aye, my lord."

Warrick turned, placing his hands around Isabella's waist to lift her onto his saddle. The contact was like an electric shock jolting through them both. Isabella gasped, and the Earl too inhaled sharply as her eyes fell before his own piercing ones. He noted the pulse beating rapidly at the hollow of her throat, and it was all he could do to keep from ravishing her right then and there.

The ride back to Oakengates was sheer torture for them both, for it was necessary that Warrick keep one arm about Isabella to prevent her from falling off the destrier; and once, his fingers accidentally brushed her breast, causing her to blush with mortification as her nipple hardened at the brief touch.

When they reached the castle, Isabella hurried away to her chamber as quickly as possible, not daring to glance at the Earl again and ignoring the cries of distress that rose from Sir John's womenfolk at her appearance. Once there, she bolted her door and sat down upon the bed, quivering all over and wanting to be alone with her confusion. Something had happened to her, and she did not understand it. Was her nature base? Was she a wanton that she trembled with wanting for her new warden when 'twas Lionel she loved? Oh, sweet *Jesù*! What was wrong with her? And how would she ever be able to face Warrick—or Lionel— again?

Chapter Thirteen

WARRICK TOO STRODE DIRECTLY TO HIS ROOM BUT FOR another purpose. His slaying of the three poachers had driven him to a blind frenzy of rage and passion, and his male instinct to protect a female he considered his had been highly aroused. In addition, the way in which Isabella had stood almost naked in his arms, pressed against him so enticingly, had reminded the Earl that he had gone without a woman for many weeks. His loins ached. He wanted Isabella, and he had every right to take her, but instinct warned him against her.

She was as fey as her brother's knights had said, and though Warrick had thought himself on guard against her charms, somehow, he too had fallen under her spell. He must put her from his mind. The girl was a witch—like

Brangwen. She would steal her way into his heart, with her grey-green eyes and yielding lips, and then she would destroy him. He glanced at the serving maid who had entered to attend him.

"Come here, lass," Warrick said, and then, when she stood before him, waiting expectantly, he asked, "Are ye a virgin?"

The girl smiled boldly, invitingly.

"Nay, my lord."

"Then take off your clothes, and get into that bed."

"Aye, my lord."

The girl was dark and comely enough in a blowsy fashion, and she was, very definitely, *not* a virgin. The things she did to him with her hands and mouth eased his physical torment, but even so, Warrick found himself comparing the wench to Isabella. The maid's breasts were small and firm, her nipples, brown, so unlike Isabella's full ripe mounds and rosy crests. The girl was rawboned too and her body, generous, not at all like Isabella's delicate frame and slender build. The wench's hips were broad and met the Earl's own vigorously as he drove into her and pretended it was Isabella's slight, curved hips that arched so wantonly against him. He groaned, shuddered, and was still. After a moment, he rolled off the wench, gave her a few pieces of silver, and sent her on her way, his mind still on Isabella.

Minutes later, Caerllywel knocked upon the chamber door and entered. His eyes took in Warrick's nakedness and the state of the bed at a glance. Caerllywel grinned.

"Methinks slaking your lust upon another will not help what ails ye," he remarked, his voice a trifle too casual for his brother's liking.

The Earl looked at him sourly.

"And just what would ye know about what ails me?" Warrick snapped.

"Like everyone else in the great hall, I saw the Lady Isabella when ye returned. The others may believe she still trembled with fear of the poachers, but they do not know ye as I do, brother; and 'twas your cloak that shielded her near-nakedness. What did pass between ye, I wonder, before the others arrived?" When the Earl made no response,

Caerllywel raised one eyebrow and shrugged, his eyes glimmering faintly with speculation. "She is yours, ye know," he observed, "and ye want her. So why do ye tarry in carrying out the King's command? Why do ye not wed the girl, and have done?"

"Because, though 'tis Edward's order, I've no wish for a bride, especially one who seeks to bewitch me as Brangwen did."

"Brangwen, always Brangwen. Christ's son! I wish to hell you'd never met that bitch! Waerwic, when will ye learn that all women are not the same?"

"Never, for they *are* the same, despite what ye say. The Lady Isabella is no different from the rest. I would as lief have had the serving wench; she pleased me just as well."

"Did she? I wonder. Well, now that ye have eased the lust in your loins—if not your heart—do ye have time to attend to business?"

"Aye, what is it?"

"I have discovered the identity of the traitor at Oakengates. He is being held below, in the dungeons. Do ye wish to join me in the questioning of the boy?"

"Aye."

"Then I shall await ye in the great hall."

Though the flickering torches of the men-at-arms lighted their way, the passage to the dungeons was still dark and eerie. The long, winding steps that led to the cells far below the castle were steep and covered with oozing green slime. Now and then could be heard the faint trickle of water where the moat seeped in through the stout stones of the keep, making the air damp and rank with foul-smelling moisture. Warrick's nostrils flared momentarily before accustoming themselves to the stench. Ruthlessly, he kicked at the mean, chattering rats that scurried away, tails slithering over the wet stones, at the men's intrusion.

Sir John's face was stern in the wavering light as he selected a key from the huge ring he carried and turned it in the old, rusted lock of one of the cubicles. Slowly, the door groaned open.

"The prisoner, my lord," he said, indicating the boy

inside, who stood up defiantly as they entered. "His name is Ham. So far, he has refused speak."

"Then how did ye discover he was the traitor?"

"Sir Caerllywel, when he questioned the servants, thought the lad's manner strange. He accused Ham outright of being the reivers' accomplice, and the boy tried to flee. Naturally, he didn't get far."

"Do what ye will to me! I'll tell ye nothing!" Ham suddenly cried boldly. "I be innocent, no matter what that stupid Welsh bastard says!"

Warrick smiled at this reference to his brother, but it was a wicked smile, and Sir John shuddered as a shiver of fright chased up his spine.

"Mind your tongue!" the vassal ordered. "This is Lord Hawkhurst, brother to Sir Caerllywel and the new warden of Lord Rushden and the Lady Isabella."

"So? I suppose ye mean to kill me. Well, I ain't afraid to die, so ye may as well hang me, and have done!" the lad spat.

"Aye." The Earl nodded. "If ye are the traitor, as my brother claims, ye will most certainly hang—but not until ye have given us the information we desire."

"I won't tell ye anything, I told ye! I be innocent!" Ham asserted.

"Then why did ye attempt to run away when my brother accused ye of being the reivers' accomplice?"

"I—I was afraid."

"Oh?" Warrick raised one eyebrow as though amused, for he was sure the boy was lying. "But if ye are innocent, as ye say, ye had no cause for fear. Do ye still wish to remain silent?" The Earl paused, but Ham said nothing, and presently, Warrick went on. "Then I am sorry for ye, for your life will be most miserable until ye talk." The lad's eyes grew wary and slightly scared at this, but with false bravado, he thrust his jaw out stubbornly and continued to refuse to speak. "Caerllywel, bring the boot," the Earl ordered.

At that, Ham began to struggle, fighting the men-at-arms desperately until finally they managed to manacle him to one wall and jam his foot into the iron boot. Almost casually,

Warrick took the flask his brother held out to him and poured the oil from it into the boot. Then he recorked the vessel.

"Tell me the names of your accomplices and where they are hiding, and ye need not suffer before your hanging," he told the boy, but still, Ham remained mute and rebellious. "Very well then." The Earl sighed, for he disliked torture, although he knew it was necessary. "Caerllywel, your torch."

Warrick pressed the flaming torch against the boot. Soon, the iron grew hot, and the oil within began to bubble. The lad cried out with pain at the searing agony of his burning foot, and the Earl was glad that Isabella was far above in her room, where she would not hear Ham's outburst. Even Sir John and the men-at-arms blanched. Warrick removed the torch to allow the boot to cool.

"Give me the names and the hiding place," he said grimly.

"M'lord, please!" the boy begged. "I don't know! I be innocent!"

Once more, the Earl held the torch to the boot, and Ham fainted. Caerllywel dashed the lad with a bucket of cold water to revive him, and the torture continued.

For the past few days, the sounds of the ax and hammer at their work had thrummed in Isabella's ears. Now, all was silent, and, to her, the stillness was even more horrifying. She shivered as the reivers who had not been slain in the battle between them and the men-at-arms were marched forward, and what pitifully remained of the boy Ham was dragged forth. She was shocked as she recognized, at last, the strange serving lad who had filled her chalice that first evening at Oakengates. For a moment, the girl feared she would swoon as the stench of the burned and rotten stumps that had once been his feet reached her nostrils. Isabella pressed her scented handkerchief to her face, her body swaying slightly with dizziness and nausea. Warrick put one arm firmly around her waist in order to steady her.

"Ye must not faint!" he hissed.

"God's blood! What have ye done? What have ye done, ye monster? He—he's only a boy!"

"He is a traitor to all of Oakengates and Rushden!"

"But—but why?"

"His family died of the sweating sickness, and he has blamed Sir John all these years for not being able to save them. 'Twas only recently the lad was given an opportunity for revenge."

"But—but no one could have helped his people. Even my own parents' lives were taken."

"Aye, but sometimes, things play strange tricks on a man's mind."

Isabella knew her warden spoke the truth, but still, it did not lessen the horror she felt at the sight of the boy.

"Ye are cruel, my lord," she said.

The Earl gazed down at her coolly, his face closed and unreadable.

"Dost truly think I am without feeling, madam?" he asked. "Dost truly believe I enjoyed torturing a confused and half-mad lad? Before God, I gave the boy every opportunity to speak, to spare himself the agony that followed when he remained silent. Ye called me a monster, my lady, but was it not better for one to suffer than the hundreds who would have, had the reivers' attacks continued?"

"Aye, ye are right, of course," Isabella answered quietly at last, ashamed. "But still, it seems so harsh. . . ."

"That is life, madam," he told her. "And one must be strong to survive."

"Aye, I suppose so, and yet, I would it were otherwise. I do not think I was meant for such a life. Warrick, must I—must I stay and watch? I have never witnessed a hanging before. I have no desire to do so now."

"The traitor and the reivers must be duly punished for their crimes. Sir John has given the order, and as mistress of Rushden, ye must uphold it or undermine your vassal's authority here. Do ye understand?"

Slowly, Isabella nodded in assent.

As the castle looked on, the outlaws were led to the gibbets that had been built, and nooses were placed firmly around the thieves' necks. One or two of the robbers struggled, but the men-at-arms soon subdued them. Each reiver was given a chance to confess and repent his crimes, then was blessed by the priest. After that, Sir John nodded to the executioners. With a few strangled cries and several loud cracks, the condemned men were hanged. Isabella gasped sharply and turned away, knees buckling at the awful sight; but the Earl's arm about her waist tightened, forcing her to remain standing. Her heart thudded at her new warden's nearness. Briefly, that strange electric shock sparked between them, and Warrick swore softly under his breath. Then silently, without touching, they walked back to the keep, Isabella taking care not to glance again at the lifeless forms on the gibbets, where the bodies would hang until they rotted.

Chapter Fourteen

ISABELLA COULD BEAR NO MORE. SHE TOLD HERSELF IT was the incidents with the poachers and the reivers that had overwhelmed her, but in her heart, she knew this was not the truth. It was the strange attraction to her new warden that had been a part of her ever since he'd kissed her that drove her away, away to Grasmere, a manor house that had been willed to her by her maternal grandmother.

As the spring turned to summer, the girl, like a fawn seeking refuge, left Rushden Castle to journey to Grasmere. There, she awaited her brother, Giles, and her beloved, Lionel—especially Lionel. She was convinced that if she could but see him again, this confusing desire that burned in her for Warrick would fade.

For the first time in her life, Isabella did not understand herself, could not explain the feelings that drew her to the Earl, in spite of her love for Lionel. It was wicked and wrong of her. She knew that. She could not have felt worse if she had betrayed her own dear brother, and in a way, she supposed she had; and that too weighed heavily upon her conscience.

Eagerly, the girl fled to Grasmere, but it was not so much because she longed for the manor house, although, in the past, she had spent many a happy hour there, but because she wished to escape from Rushden Castle, her home, and the man who now ruled there. Isabella was afraid to stay, afraid that Warrick would somehow succeed in his mocking assault upon her defenses. She had no wish to become his wife, but she was bound to him by the King's command; and though the Earl might not desire her for his bride, he wanted her still—wanted her in a carnal fashion that had aroused her on some ancient, primitive level she did not understand and could not control. He had but to look at her, his amber eyes gleaming speculatively, hungrily, and she caught fire inside, her bones melting like molten ore, her body trembling hotly, frightening her with the heat of its passion.

And so she ran away and hoped her new warden would not pursue her.

The ride to Grasmere passed without incident, for which the girl was very grateful. She had had enough of killing and death. It was too much for her gentle nature, which so joyed in life and the living. Though she knew the slaying of the poachers and the hanging of the reivers had been necessary and justified, she could not help but feel pity for them all the same. She was sharply aware of the fact that once, each had come to a fork in the road of his life—and had chosen the wrong path to follow. Why? Isabella wondered. What had gone amiss to lead their footsteps toward the sorry ends they had reached? She knew the answer was nothing more than a simple decision to choose one road over another; and the girl shivered, knowing even the best of men might select unwisely and be brought to folly for their foolish mistakes.

How hard life was; its decisions were never easy. Isabella prayed that when the fork in the road of her life came, she would choose the right path. She did not know then that she had overlooked one important fact: Sometimes, one has no choice in the matter.

At last, Isabella spied Grasmere looming ahead in the distance, and she urged Cendrillon to a quicker pace. The manor house was her special place, and she had not seen it since before her parents had died.

To see Grasmere at its best was to see it standing tall and proud against a summer sky, as it did now. No walls enclosed it, marring its beauty, for it was only a simple manor house and had not been built for defense. It stood on a gentle crest upon the land, the vividly green grass sloping down and away from the house like the flowing skirts of a woman seated upon a stool. At the edge of the vast lawn, a riotous cascade of flowers nestled at the bases of the saplings, which rose up to give way in turn to the denseness of the old woods that clustered upon the wild, windswept moors that stretched for miles in all directions.

The house itself was built of dark grey stone and was three massive stories square, flanked on either side by smaller wings. With its four machicolated towers, the widow's walk, and the lofty turrets that sat upon the corners of the wings, it resembled a castle. The front was lined with long, narrow casement windows, with diamond-shaped, lead-glass panes that shone like prisms when touched by the summer sun, reflecting a thousand dancing rainbows upon the lawn, which shimmered like some fairyland when the morning dew lay yet upon the grass. Between the windows, trellises climbed the walls, and roses—white roses—grew intertwined upon the lattices, lifting their fragile, fragrant petals to the sky.

She breathed a sigh of relief as the stout oak doors of the manor house were flung open wide, and she stepped into the hall. She was safe. Naught could harm her here—or so the girl thought. She did not know that it would be here, at Grasmere, that not once, but twice, the course of her life would be changed for all time; and she would have no choice in the matter.

Giles came, at last, in response to the letters that Isabella had written to him—the first to inform him of their new warden's identity, and the second to beg her brother to come to her at Grasmere with all haste. With him came Lionel, her love.

Still, as always, it was to Giles's arms that Isabella moved first, for her beloved brother would always hold a special place in her heart, set apart from other men. She saw he looked older—and tired, so very tired. There were lines of strain around his eyes that had not been there before, as though the years had finally wearied him, dimmed the eager light of youth that had once blazed in his hazel orbs, leaving naught save embers of smoldering sorrow and pain. Where once he had looked outward at the world, he now looked inward instead, as though he had found life wanting and had retreated from it.

Isabella knew instantly that something had happened to change him, and she was disturbed by the alteration in him, for she had always thought of Giles as a tower of strength. Now, for the first time, she saw her brother as he really was: just a man, like any other; a man who had done his duty, and well, but whose heart was no longer in it. For Giles was somewhere far away, in some corner of his mind where all was sweetness and light, and men did not suffer. Suddenly, the girl knew she could not burden him with her troubles. She would only be adding to the pain he was already enduring. He would be saddened by her unhappiness, torn apart by the idea that she was to marry Lord Hawkhurst. She loved Giles. She could not bring such hurt to him—not now.

So Isabella smiled brightly in welcome, and though the lilt of her lips did not quite reach her eyes, her brother did not see that. He saw only that she was as beautiful as always, a haven of peace and serenity, of harmony and grace, in a world that was often ugly and cruel. His hazel orbs filled with warmth as he walked toward her, limping slightly.

Startled and concerned, the girl ran to his side at once.

"Giles! You're hurt! Let me help ye!"

"'Tis naught. A broken bone that did not set properly; that's all. I manage very well now."

"Oh, Giles, ye should have told me."

Isabella bit her lip with sorrow that he should have been wounded so; and yet, somehow, the lameness suited him, adding a certain poignancy to his romantic nature and appearance. Her heart welled up with love for him. It didn't matter that he was not the pillar of invincibility she had once imagined; in her quiet way, she had always been strong enough for them both. Fervently, Isabella enveloped her brother in her arms and kissed him sweetly, brushing back a strand of hair that had fallen into his eyes.

"Oh, Giles, 'tis good to see ye," she said.

"And ye, dear sister," he replied.

She longed desperately to ask him what was wrong, but now was not the time or the place. So instead, she turned to Lionel, her love, her glorious golden god of the moonlit meadow.

But curiously, Lionel's blinding brilliance had been dimmed too for the girl in the year since she'd seen him, been tarnished in some manner she could not explain. He was as handsome as ever, surely, but somehow, he seemed lacking when, unbidden, Warrick's dark, masculine image; his cold, chiseled countenance; and his hard lean body filled her mind. Isabella lowered her gaze quickly, lest Lionel should guess her guilty thoughts as he bowed and kissed her hand.

"Art not glad to see me, 'Sabelle?" he asked softly, startling her back to the present.

"Of course," she assured him. "Welcome to Grasmere." But even to her ears, the stilted words sounded like an obedient child reciting by rote.

She turned away, thereby missing the sudden, troubled frown that marred Lionel's features and his speculative gaze as he and Giles followed her into the house.

Isabella studied her brother quietly, worriedly. He had said little throughout supper, scarcely even commenting on their new warden or the state of Rushden's affairs. It was as though Giles could not bring himself to concentrate on the matter, and once more, the girl had the feeling that his mind was far away. She waited silently for some explanation for her brother's subdued manner, but at last, when none was forthcoming, she broached the subject herself.

"Giles, what is wrong?" she asked gently. "Thou art not yourself. What has happened, dear brother, to change ye so?"

To her horror, a ragged sob burst from Giles's throat.

"Oh, 'Sabelle," he whispered, turning away so she would not see the agony upon his face. "How can I tell ye when, even now, it pains me so to speak of it?"

"What is it, Giles? What is it?" she questioned fearfully. "Art ill?"

"Aye." He rubbed his eyes tiredly, then ran his hand through his hair carelessly, almost tearing at the silvery strands. "But not in the way ye imagine. I am sick; 'tis true. But the ache is here, in my heart, 'Sabelle." He struck his chest with one clenched fist, then sighed wrenchingly again, trying to master his emotions. After a time, he spoke dully. "How do I begin . . . and where?" He paused. "'Twas winter, and the first snow of the season had fallen. Oh, 'Sabelle, ye should have seen it! The naked branches of the trees glistened with icicles, as though they were encrusted with diamonds; and that strange white mist of Scotland hung low and thick over the Borderlands, so the hills seemed almost alive with some enchanting, mythical magic. Even my lord Duke was caught up in the spell.

"One morn, he woke and, smiling, bade me fetch those closest to him. We would go hunting, he said, for we were low on supplies, and the barbarous Scots had retreated farther to the north. We needed to replenish our stores before following them.

"Ah, 'twas a grand day, 'Sabelle, the finest of my life: for somehow, I became separated from the rest of the hunting party, and in the forest, I met a maid. A snow queen, she was, or so I thought. How can I explain to ye, dear sister, the feeling that came upon me when first I saw her? 'Twas as though an arrow pierced my heart, for I loved her from the first moment of our meeting."

"Aye," Isabelle murmured, understanding. "'Twas thus for me with Lionel."

"Her name was Catriona," Giles went on as though the girl had not spoken, "and she was a Scotswoman. Oh, aye, we knew, from the beginning, that there was no hope for us," he answered the unspoken question in his sister's eyes, "but still, we dared to dream, for she too had somehow been touched by love. For over a fortnight, while my lord Duke tarried in the area, gathering supplies and preparing to do battle yet again, Catriona and I met in the woods and walked and talked and made love beneath the snow-laden branches of the pines. She must come away with me, I told her, though the life of a camp follower would be hard. 'Twas no longer safe for her in the Borderlands: for if her family discovered her love for me, they would kill her, thinking her dishonored by an enemy—"

His voice broke, and suddenly, the girl knew what was coming.

"Oh, Giles, nay!" she breathed.

"Oh, aye, 'Sabelle. Ye do not know the Scots. They are indeed a most heathen race, and the clans are laws unto themselves. Why, the chiefs of families are regarded almost as kings! Can ye imagine? 'Tis as though civilization has left them untouched, for they are always feuding with each other, as well as with us, and they make battle with the crudest of weapons, 'Sabelle. Why, I've scarcely seen even the meanest of bombards among them! And what little black powder they have managed to acquire, they use improperly, so more often than not, they blow their own men to bits. God's blood! How someone as precious as Catriona came from those savages, I'll never know."

He was silent for such a long time after that that Isabella, though by now having guessed the end of the story, prompted quietly, "Go on, Giles. Finish it. 'Twill do ye good to speak of it. What happened?"

He inhaled sharply, as though it had suddenly become difficult for him to breathe, but at last, he nodded and continued.

"I went back for her, as we'd planned, the day we were to leave; and I found her there, in the forest, a dagger through her heart." And though Isabella had prepared herself for this, still, she gasped. "Aye"—Giles's mouth twisted bitterly. "Her whoreson Scots clan had slain her. Oh, 'Sabelle!" he suddenly cried out. "She was so beautiful, even in death, like some sleeping fairy princess lying there in the blood-reddened snow! I dismounted and knelt to touch her, still daring to hope she didst yet breathe and not knowing her menfolk waited there for me. They charged at me from the trees, the murderous cowards. I drew my sword, blind with grief and rage . . . oh, such rage, dear sister, as I hope never to feel again. The urge to kill overwhelmed me. I slew them one and all. I even struck down one man's destrier. The beast staggered and fell upon me, breaking my leg. The pain brought me to my senses at last, and I was sickened unto death by the carnage I had wrought, for Catriona would not have wished it . . . would have been appalled by it. . . ."

Giles fell silent once more. Anguish for her brother tore through Isabella like a sharp blade. She bit her lip and blinked the tears from her eyes, trying to think of some words of comfort to offer. Finally, she took his hand in her own and held it tightly, recalling what Giles had told her one day at their parents' graves.

"I am sorry, dear brother, so very sorry. But methinks that Catriona would not have wished for ye to grieve so for her, Giles," the girl said.

"I know. 'Tis just that—that her death was so senseless, and I thought of what ye once told me years ago, in the stables, when ye said something about war being so senseless, with men dying and women being left alone to mourn. I—I paid it no mind at the time; I was too young and thoughtless to see the wisdom of your words. . . . But, oh, 'Sabelle, how right ye were! I can glory no more in war, and the thought frightens me. Of what use am I to a man like my lord Duke if I cannot serve him with my whole heart and soul?"

"Oh, Giles. Hast talked with Gloucester of this? Dost truly think he joys in battle? Dear brother, how wrong ye are if that is what ye believe. He does his duty, aye, and does it well; but he suffers for it all the same, Giles. One has but to look into his eyes to know 'tis so."

"Ye seem so certain of that, 'Sabelle."

"'Tis because I am, dear brother. I say again: Speak to Gloucester of your fears. He will understand."

"'Twould comfort me greatly if I knew that to be so. Thank ye, 'Sabelle, dear sister. I knew ye wouldst help me, for ye are truly the most gifted of healers. Surely, God will smile upon ye all your life."

"Have no fear for me, Giles," Isabella reassured him quickly, more determined now than ever to keep him in ignorance of her own unhappiness. "I am content. Sleep now, dear brother. Sleep, and let peace fill your heart and soul."

Quietly, she left the hall, signaling to Sirs Eadric, Thegn, and Beowulf that they should take Giles upstairs now, and put him to bed. Exhausted by the wine he'd drunk and the telling of his story, his eyes had already closed, and his breathing had become deep and even.

"'Tis the first time I have seen him rest well since it happened," Lionel remarked, joining Isabella. "I knew he did but need to speak of it; but the Scotswoman's death grieved him beyond measure, and then the shock of the killings ... Godamercy, 'Sabelle! I do not know how he managed to slay them all, for there were five of them, and Giles was but a squire alone against them. Gloucester was for knighting him at once for the deed, but Giles would not hear of it. He said 'twas no brave act at all but the work of a madman, and my lord Duke did not press the matter, saying that Giles needed time to heal. 'Twas why Richard sent him here, I think, in response to your summons, and bade me accompany Giles. Gloucester believed 'twould do your brother good to get away from the fighting for a while."

"Aye," Isabella agreed. "The Duke is truly a most kind and sensitive man. Methinks when ye return, if Giles will but speak to Gloucester of the fears with which he is beset, Richard will understand and set my brother's mind at ease."

"Would that I could do the same for ye, dearest heart," Lionel professed and took her hand. "Come, 'Sabelle. Walk with me upon the moors, and tell me what is troubling ye. 'Tis something more than just the change in Giles that ails ye, I'll warrant."

"Aye. Oh, Lionel, something dreadful has happened, and though I prayed for Giles's arrival and assistance, I see now that he must not be burdened with my troubles on top of all else he has suffered."

"Nay, ye are right, of course, but can ye not tell me what is wrong, dearest heart? Whatever 'tis, I shall try to make it right. I love ye, ye know."

"I know," Isabella stated ardently, for she wanted so much to believe it was true. "That is what makes it so hard. ... Oh, Lionel!" the girl suddenly burst out. "I am to marry Lord Hawkhurst!"

"Nay! It cannot be true!" Lionel was stunned by her announcement.

"I assure ye 'tis," Isabella told him bitterly. "The King has ordered it and has already signed the betrothal contracts binding me to Warrick."

"Oh, 'Sabelle, nay. Nay!"

But even as he spoke the words, Lionel's body was pervaded by a small sense of relief: for though he had attempted to disentangle himself from his commitment to Lady Gilliane Beaumaris, he had failed. He sighed as he thought of his father's wrath upon receipt of the letter informing Lord St. Saviour that he wished to have the contracts with the Lady Gilliane annulled so he might wed Isabella instead. Lord St. Saviour had replied curtly that Lord Devizes, Gilliane's father, was his oldest and dearest friend, that the marriage had been arranged since birth, and that 'twas impossible for the contracts to be broken. How dare Lionel even suggest his father do such a thing? 'Twould be the deepest possible insult to both Lord Devizes and the Lady Gilliane! In fact, Lord St. Saviour had continued, he believed 'twould be best if Lionel would ask Gloucester for a leave of absence and return home immediately in order that the wedding might take place as soon as possible.

Even now, Lionel's sojourn at Grasmere was but a postponement of his marriage vows. As soon as he left the manor house, he must continue his journey to St. Saviour-on-the-Lake, where, at the neighboring estate of Devizes, he would be wed.

He had dreaded breaking the news to Isabella and seeing her love for him turn to contempt. Now, he need not tell her after all. Her announcement, as unwelcome as it was, had spared him the humiliation of making his own. Still, Lionel was not content. Isabella was his, by God. The thought of her marrying Lord Hawkhurst angered him, even though Lionel could not wed her himself.

"Oh, 'Sabelle"—he hugged her close so she might not see the expression on his face—"to lose ye before ye are even mine..."

"I know, I know. I thought perhaps ye wouldst speak to Gloucester. He loves ye well. Mayhap he would attempt to persuade the King against the match if ye asked him to."

"I shall try, dearest heart, of course, if that is what ye desire. But I do not have much faith that such a plan will succeed. Lord Hawkhurst is one of Edward's favorites, and ye are indeed a prize worth having, 'Sabelle."

"The Earl does not want me; he has said as much. 'Tis only by the King's command that he weds me."

"He is a fool then." Lionel spoke bluntly, the wheels in his mind churning furiously. He might yet prevent Isabella's marriage—but then, what of his own? "Oh, 'Sabelle, if only—"

"What, my love? If only what?"

"Nothing. 'Twas nothing. Do not despair, dearest heart. I shall find some way out of this sorry tangle for us; I promise ye that. If it takes a lifetime, I shall make ye mine, somehow, one way or another."

He turned her lovely countenance up to his then and kissed her, claiming her lips demandingly, possessively, as though to be certain he would leave his mark upon her. Feverishly, Isabella clung to him, molding herself to him, willing him to set her afire as Warrick had done. But although Lionel ravaged her mouth savagely with his tongue in a manner designed to delight and excite her, Isabella felt not even the inviting warmth of awakening she had known with him before. She was too scared.

At Lionel's touch, Warrick's dark, hawklike image had flitted through her mind, filling her with a cold, frightening dread at what the Earl would do if he discovered her perfidy, and she found she could not respond to Lionel because of it.

Oh, my love, my love! Warrick has spoilt even moments such as these for us, she thought bitterly.

She drew away, the back of one hand pressed to her lips, as though to eradicate the feel of Lionel's mouth upon her own.

"What is it, 'Sabelle?" he queried, his deep blue eyes puzzled and glittering slightly with rage, for he had sensed her lack of response to him. "What is wrong that ye seek to deny what we both desire?"

She shook her head a little, as though to clear it, and turned away.

"'Tis Warrick," she explained dully. "Already, he has come between us."

"Why? How? What do ye mean, 'Sabelle?" Lionel questioned wrathfully, then inhaled sharply, his eyes narrowing in sudden understanding. "He has made love to ye, the bastard! He has already taken ye and—"

"Nay!" Isabella whirled as Lionel caught her roughly and shook her. "Nay! I am still a maid; I swear it!"

"But he has held ye like this and tasted your lips, as I have, has he not? Nay, do not deny it, 'Sabelle, for I can see in your eyes 'tis true. God's wounds! How could ye let him touch ye, the whoreson?"

"Dost think I wanted him to? He is my betrothed!" Isabella cried, distraught. "'Tis his right. What wouldst ye have me do? Oh, Lionel. Lionel! I told him I loved another and pleaded for release from the betrothal, but he only laughed and mocked me cruelly and told me he would kill me if I betrayed him with my lover! Do ye wonder now why I am frightened so? If he knew I were with ye, he would—"

"Christ's son! I shall slay him, the bastard! Is he daft to think he can lay hands upon what is mine?"

"But I am *not* yours! And now, if ye do not speak to Gloucester and ask him to persuade the King against this match, I never shall be. Oh, Lionel. Lionel! Ye swear ye love me and wouldst make me yours, and yet, ye do not speak to me of marriage—"

Isabella broke off, her heart constricting with fear at his silence. Had she been right, after all, in doubting him?

"I cannot," he admitted at last; then, at her stricken glance, he rushed on to forestall the questions that tumbled to her lips. "Oh, 'Sabelle! I have made such a mess of things; I do not even know where to begin to explain. . . . Forgive me, dearest heart, and trust me. In time, I shall straighten everything out, I promise ye."

"But I do not understand—"

"Shhhhh. Trust me," he reiterated. "I love ye. Is that not enough?"

And though the girl knew, somehow, in her heart, that it was not, still, she tried desperately to banish her doubts and replied, "Aye, of course. I am sorry. I know ye will do your best to right whatever is wrong. Ye are not to blame for what has happened."

And though Lionel's conscience smote him guiltily at that, he made no attempt to deny her statements. He had entangled himself in such a web of hypocrisy and lies that even had he wished to unravel it, he could not have done so now. He had thrown away his opportunity to speak, to explain, and to beg Isabella's understanding, instead demanding she trust him and using her faith in him to deceive her. That was unforgivable.

"I shall speak to Gloucester," he said abruptly. "'Tis the least I can do."

"Oh, Lionel, my love, thank ye," the girl breathed, her aching fear receding. "Thank ye so much. I knew ye wouldst not fail me."

What he would do if the Duke persuaded the King to release Isabella from her betrothal to Lord Hawkhurst, Lionel did not know. As with everything he did, he determined to cross that bridge when he came to it. For now, it was enough that he had managed to retain Isabella's love and trust. He wanted her and meant to have her, as he'd said, one way or another.

Chapter Fifteen

THE DAYS AT GRASMERE PASSED SLOWLY THAT SUMMER, as though autumn were in no hurry to make her appearance, and for that, Isabella was grateful. Giles needed the serenity of those peaceful, languid days to recover, to forget the horror of his beloved Catriona's tragic death and his mad slaying of her clansmen. Each morning, he and Isabella walked and talked as they had of old. Like children, they explored the woods and the moors, finding joy in the simple discovery of a foxhole or squirrel's hideaway; and the girl's heart lightened as some of the sorrow in her brother's eyes began to dim. Now and then, Giles even spoke of Catriona, and Isabella was relieved to find the telling was not as painful for him as, at first, it had been.

"I shall never love again, 'Sabelle," Giles told her one morning, "for my heart will always lie with Catriona. How strange it should be thus, but perhaps 'tis the way of us Ashleys. I sometimes think that Father died more from a broken heart over Mother's death than from the sweating sickness that took them both."

"Aye, I too have often wondered if 'twas not so. Still, ye are young yet, Giles. Despite what ye say, methinks ye will love once more."

"Would ye, if Lionel were taken from ye?"

"I—I do not know."

"I pray to God ye need never find out, 'Sabelle. Which reminds me: I have been so engrossed in my grief that I have forgotten my duties. 'Tis time ye were wed, dear sister. Methinks I had best ask my foster brother his intentions toward ye," he said teasingly, his face lighting up a little at the jest.

"Nay," Isabella said quickly, too quickly; then, at her brother's puzzled, inquiring glance, she smiled brightly. "There is no hurry, Giles. Let us wait until ye are well before we talk of my leaving ye. I could not bear to be parted from ye at this moment; I see ye so little as 'tis."

"Ah, 'Sabelle, methinks your world still revolves too much around me. However, I am selfish enough to let it remain so a while longer. So. Tell me of Rushden and our new warden. I fear I paid little attention to ye earlier when ye sought to speak of them."

"Rushden does well, as always, and our new warden, though hard, is fair."

"Yet, ye shiver when ye talk of him, 'Sabelle."

"Nay, dear brother, 'twas but a sudden cooling of wind. It seems autumn draws nigh after all."

"Riders approach, my lady." Sir Eadric made the announcement as he entered the hall and bowed respectfully. "'Tis Lord Hawkhurst and his men. Beowulf, who has the eyes of an eagle—or so he claims—managed to discern the banners of the party."

"Art—art sure, Beowulf?" Isabella queried, one hand fluttering to her throat.

"Aye, my lady. It be the Earl right enough."

"But why does he come here, I wonder? Oh, I hope nothing is wrong at Rushden. Thank God, Lionel has taken Giles hunting. Thegn, please have my mare saddled and brought around at once. I shall ride out to meet his lordship and discover what is the matter. Beowulf, if Lords Rushden and Lionel return, detain them here until I can find out if anything is amiss. Eadric, ye will accompany me."

"Aye, my lady," the three knights chorused as one.

Once outside and mounted up, Isabelle urged Cendrillon to a rapid pace, her heart pounding nervously in her breast. Why was Warrick coming here? The girl did not truly believe there was trouble at Rushden. The Earl was too arrogant to consult her over such a matter; he would have handled the difficulty himself. Nay, there was some other reason he sought her out at Grasmere, invading her haven, her refuge. Had he somehow learned about Lionel? The thought sent a shudder down Isabella's spine. Though Warrick did not want her as his wife, he still considered her his and had made it quite clear what he would do if he discovered she had betrayed him.

Cendrillon's thudding hooves rushed over the moors, trampling the tall grass rippling in the wind and the last of the wildflowers that still bloomed before the onset of autumn. Recklessly, Isabella flung her head back, letting the breeze stream through her tangled mass of silvery hair as she galloped over the hard earth. There was always a strange sense of freedom that pervaded her being when she rode this way. It made her feel wild and alive, able to face anything—even her new warden. She was glad that Sir Eadric had warned her of Warrick's coming, for it had given her time to prepare herself, to gain control of the small fear at the back of her mind. At least she would not be taken unaware, for no doubt, the Earl had meant to surprise her!

She spied Warrick, at last, and cantered toward him, slowly reining her mare to a halt. The Earl seemed even more darkly handsome and forbidding than she remembered, and oddly enough, Isabella's heart caught in her throat at the sight of him. She turned away so he would not see the confused expression on her face, then, after gathering her composure, she smiled warmly at Caerllywel, who had spurred his horse forward to meet her.

With a sly, triumphant grin at Warrick and a courtly flourish designed to melt even the hardest of hearts, Caerllywel swept off his cap and bowed low in the saddle.

"My dear Lady Isabella," he greeted her, his eyes twinkling, despite his brother's frown, "ye are even more beautiful than I remembered."

"And ye, Sir Caerllywel, are still as silver-tongued as ever," Isabella noted archly with pretended disapproval, though the corners of her mouth quirked ever so slightly. And then, more coolly, she greeted the Earl. "My Lord Warrick," she said as he drew his destrier up and motioned for his men to stop. "We are honored. What brings ye here, to my humble manor house, Grasmere, when ye have all of Rushden at your disposal?"

The Earl smiled mockingly, that jeering grin she recalled so well, as his yellow eyes raked her body hungrily, then returned to rest upon her countenance.

"My lady, 'tis I who am honored," he professed, his tone tinged with just a hint of sarcasm. "Do ye normally ride out to greet your guests in this manner, or"—he lowered his voice slightly—"can it be that ye missed me far more greatly than I imagined?"

"If that is why ye have come, ye have wasted your time, Warrick," Isabella rejoined with mock sweetness, continuing to smile for the benefit of his men and a laughing-eyed Caerllywel, who had urged his steed closer in order to overhear the soft exchange, which soon grew more heated.

"Have I?" the Earl drawled, then shrugged. "Ah, well, 'tis my time to waste, after all."

"What brings ye here, my lord?" Isabella questioned again impatiently. "Is aught amiss at Rushden?"

"Nay. 'Tis as ye told me, my lady: The castle is well run. 'Tis merely that I feared perhaps Grasmere was not equally as efficient, that mayhap there was trouble here; ye have lingered so long at this place."

"My brother is here and ill. I wrote ye as much in response to the messages ye sent."

"Aye." Warrick nodded, his gaze still ravishing her speculatively. "And I am touched by your sisterly devotion. Still"—his piercing eyes narrowed—"I find it hard to believe 'tis your brother alone who commands your attention at this place, as unwell as he may be."

"I knew it! Ye came here to spy upon me!" Isabella hissed.

The Earl raised one eyebrow demoniacally.

"Is there aught for me to spy upon, madam?" he queried softly, intently.

The girl inhaled sharply, realizing suddenly how foolish she had been. Had she greeted Warrick normally, she might have allayed his suspicions. Now, she had only succeeded in arousing them. Doubtless, the moment he saw Lionel, the Earl would recognize him as the man whom Isabella loved. She bit her lip, then attempted to shrug casually.

"Grasmere is my home, my lord," she responded at last, "not a place of intrigue. However, ye must suit yourself in the matter."

"I intend to, my lady."

The ride back to the manor house was a nightmare for Isabella, for she could think of no way in which to warn Lionel of their predicament and beseech him to do nothing rash. She recalled his reckless announcement that he would slay the Earl, and she prayed the two men would not come to a duel. As disloyal as the thought was, Isabella knew that Lionel could not possibly hope to prevail over Warrick's age and experience, and she feared the man she loved would be killed.

What the Earl was thinking, she had no idea, for his dark visage was closed and unreadable except for the glint in his amber eyes when he looked at her. It was almost as though he could read the thoughts chasing frantically through her mind, and the idea unnerved her. For a moment, Isabella believed she would swoon. To her dismay, Warrick drew his steed near and reached out one hand to steady her, his arm deftly encircling her waist. She trembled in his grasp and knew he could not help but notice, the wretch!

"There is no need for ye to faint, madam," he told her, his eyes filled with cool amusement. "I am certain ye have been faithful to me—with your body, if not your mind."

Suddenly, the Earl's possessiveness and arrogant assumption angered Isabella. Even if Warrick did not want her as his wife, he might at least show her a little respect. After all, it was not her fault she was betrothed to him. She gazed up at him from beneath half-closed lids.

"And what makes ye so certain of that, my lord? Someone once told me 'twas unwise to be so sure of things," she taunted quietly.

For just an instant, his grip about her tightened, and his nostrils flared whitely, thinking she had betrayed him. Then he relaxed and laughed, knowing she had not.

"*Touché*, my lady," he acknowledged the point. "I see ye are clever as well as beautiful. However, 'twas not my intent to insult ye, as it seems ye were, but rather to compliment ye instead. Mayhap I should have spoken more plainly. I meant only this: There are ways in which a man can tell if a woman is still a maid, and do not think ye are so foolish as to attempt to deceive me on our wedding night with any of the tricks less virtuous wenches often employ."

Isabella blushed furiously.

"Oh! How dare ye speak to me in such a fashion?" she snapped.

"Wouldst rather I whispered words of love like the moon-struck swain I shall doubtless discover here?"

"I don't know what you're talking about," the girl retorted stiffly.

"Don't ye?"

"Nay. There is no one at Grasmere save for myself, my brother, Giles, and his foster brother, Lord Lionel Valeureux, whom Gloucester didst bade accompany Giles on his journey."

"Ah." The Earl pounced upon this last. "Ye must tell me more about this Lord Lionel. Is he not the heir of St. Saviour-on-the-Lake?"

Isabella quivered once more with apprehension.

"Aye, and Giles's foster brother, as I have said. There is nothing more to tell. I have seen him but a few times in my life. My lord—I beg of ye—my brother has only just begun to fully recover from a terrible shock. He does not yet know of our betrothal, and 'twould only upset him. Please, say nothing to him, and do naught to bring him further unhappiness. I wouldst not see him hurt again, especially now, when he is yet so vulnerable. There will be time enough later, when he is well, to speak of the matter. After all, ye said yourself 'twould be some time before we would be wed...." The girl's voice trailed off as she glanced up at Warrick pleadingly.

"Very well, madam," he agreed at last, "but my silence has a price—Nay, do not look so alarmed, my lady." His eyes lingered on her mouth. "'Tis but a kiss, one kiss, given willingly from your lips—a small price to pay, surely, for your brother's well-being."

Isabella flushed, her gray-green orbs suddenly downcast, her heart beating too fast in her breast. For a moment, she did not trust herself to speak. Why should the Earl wish such a thing from her? 'Twas but meant to humiliate her; she was certain of that.

"Well, madam?" He lifted one eyebrow inquiringly. "Is it a bargain or nay?"

"Aye—aye, my lord." Her voice was so low, he almost didn't hear her.

"Your word on it, my lady."

Her eyes flashed dangerously at that.

"Do ye not trust me, Warrick?" she asked defensively.

"Nay. I trust no woman, madam, least of all one as... bewitching as ye."

"I am no sorceress, my lord, but even if I were, ye wouldst need have no fear of me. There is no spell that would win your heart, for ye have none; and even if ye did, I would not want it."

The Earl's golden eyes narrowed ominously at that, for there was only one other woman who had dared to scorn him so.

"Ye speak boldly for a wench who is one day to be at my utter mercy," he observed. "'Twill be interesting to see if you are so brazen then, my lady."

Isabella shivered slightly at his words, but still, determined not to let him get the best of her, she answered bravely—if a trifle bitterly.

"Methinks ye do but delay that day in order to make sport of me, my lord. 'Tis but a cat and mouse game that ye play."

"'Tis the Valeureux who wears the cat's badge, madam," he reminded her silkily. "I bear the hawk's rosette. I do not stalk my prey. When I strike, 'tis swift—and sure. Remember that."

Isabella swallowed hard, then suddenly spurred her mare ahead, Warrick's soft, jeering laughter ringing in her ears.

Isabella had, after all, worried in vain, for the Earl, if reserved, was at least courteous to both Giles and Lionel; and Caerllywel put forth his best effort at charming all. Indeed, he won the girl's heart for all time by succeeding, with his preposterous jests and antics, in making Giles laugh aloud brightly and naturally for the first time in months.

"Oh, Caerllywel," Isabella sighed. "I cannot tell ye how grateful I am for your kindness to my brother. Every day, he grows more like the Giles I remember of old."

Caerllywel smiled.

"Now if I could but lighten the shadows that darken *your* eyes, 'Sabelle, I wouldst be the happiest of men."

"How good to hear ye address me as 'Sabelle," she said, gently turning away from the inquiry in his eyes. "Methinks I shall enjoy having ye for a brother after all, Caerllywell, though ye are the worst of rogues."

"And Waerwic, 'Sabelle?" He continued to probe searchingly. "Will ye enjoy having him as your husband?"

"My feelings toward the Earl do not matter. He is my betrothed. Please, Caerllywel"—Isabella laid one hand upon his arm—"let us speak no more of my marriage. I am content," she lied, then laughed lightly, as though to dispell any lingering doubts he might have. "Come. Ye promised us the arrangements for your treasure hunt would be finished this morn, and I expect ye to keep your word, sir!"

The idea for the infamous treasure hunt, as Warrick called it, had somehow jokingly arisen one evening at supper; and Caerllywel, being immediately stricken with the possibilities of the suggestion, had proposed to carry out the scheme. He would, he had told them, undertake to work out the basic details of the plan, such as the rules and so forth, then would request that Sirs Eadric, Thegn, and Beowulf think up the necessary clues, draw up maps, and hide the treasure. That way, all would be certain that Caerllywel was not pulling another one of his awful jests on them. Seeing Giles's face light up with excitement at the thought of a treasure hunt, Isabella had readily agreed to it.

Warrick, Giles, and Lionel were already mounted and waiting impatiently when she and Caerllywel stepped outside. Both Giles and Lionel were shouting for them to hurry and laughing with anticipation, and even Warrick was smiling with wry amusement.

"Come, brother," he called dryly. "Ye have kept us in suspense long enough. Ye must explain this mad plan of yours at once."

"Patience, Waerwic, patience." Caerllywel grinned and paused deliberately, causing everyone to groan. "All right, all right!" He raised his hands for silence, then queried mischievously, "Are we all assembled?"

"Ye can see we are!" the Earl snapped tartly. "Get on with it, brother!"

"There is no need to get huffy about it, Waerwic," Caerllywel drawled with mock wrath. "Beware, lest I give ye a false map! Now. The game is this: Somewhere, out there"—he indicated the sweep of terrain—"the very good Sirs Eadric, Thegn, and Beowulf have buried a treasure, and we must find it. The rules are simple." He reached into his doublet. "These, my dear players, are our maps. We do but have to decipher the clues contained herein and follow them to the treasure. Are there any questions?"

"Only one," Warrick said. "Just what is this treasure we are seeking? We must be certain 'tis worth all the effort we are about to put forth."

"Oh, come, come, Waerwic," Caerllywel chided. "Even *I* do not know the answer to that! Where is your sense of adventure? 'Tis the very fact that ye do not know what the treasure is that lends the game its spice. However, Giles's faithful knights have assured me 'tis something we shall be most grateful for, once we have found it. Are we ready? Then let us proceed at once!"

The pale grey mist that had cloaked the moors earlier had faded with the slow onslaught of the mellowing sun, and the air was cool and crisp with the clean scent of the late-coming autumn as the small party rode forth from Grasmere. Here and there, the leaves of the trees had begun to turn colors, the red and gold mingling with the green like flickering flames in the forest.

All were in high spirits as they studied the cryptically detailed maps, which Caerllywel had given them, and attempted to decipher the clues leading to the treasure. Isabella, who was most familiar with the vicinity surrounding Grasmere, was the first to figure out the starting point and set off with a little cry of triumph, the others galloping close behind.

"Not fair! Not fair!" she wailed laughingly over her shoulder and urged Cendrillon to a faster pace.

Presently, she was deep into the woods and had lost the rest, who, one by one, gradually split up in order to follow their own hunches, each certain he alone was on the right track.

It was late afternoon when Isabella finally reached a small clearing wherein stood an old, abandoned well that was said to have existed from the time of the Druids and that the girl had decided was the hiding place of the treasure. Few sought the well out nowadays, however, for it was believed to be haunted; so despite her enthusiasm, Isabella approached it cautiously. She shivered as a soft cry floated to her on the wind and almost turned back before she recognized it was only the whicker of a steed. Someone else had beaten her to the treasure! For a moment, the girl knew only disappointment at having lost the game; then her heart began to pound excitedly in her breast. The winner was probably Giles, as, next to her, he knew the area best; but there was also a chance that it was Lionel, and she would have a few precious minutes alone with him before the others arrived. Eagerly, Isabella touched her heels to Cendrillon's sides, guiding the mare into the clearing.

"Ye!" she cried as, much to her dismay, she discovered

it was Warrick who awaited her. "What are *ye* doing here? This place is little known, even to my brother and myself. How did ye find it so quickly?"

"I determined 'twould be easier merely to decipher the last clue while the rest of ye wasted your time getting through the entire map. And as your three knights kindly employed a Welsh word in the final puzzle—no doubt in order to assist my brother and me a little since we do not know this region—'twas not that difficult for me to discover this place. I had but to search for a well."

"Aye, but how did ye know that?"

The Earl pointed to his map and quoted, "'Ride ahead of the sun to a place where its worshipers once drew cain from a ring of stone.' In order to ride ahead of the sun, one must travel west, naturally," he explained. "Sun worshipers were, of course, the ancient pagans, so I assumed the location of the treasure was old and probably abandoned. But the real key to the riddle was *cain*, which, in this instance, refers not to the biblical Cain, but a Welsh word meaning 'clear bright water.' 'A ring of stone' thus translated as a well."

"Very clever, my lord. I have to admit 'twas the *cain* that puzzled me. I wasted a great deal of time searching the land east of a place called Eden's Folly before I realized the sun worshipers were doubtless Druids, and I thought of this place. 'Tis said they haunt this well, ye know."

"Really? Well, shall we see if they disturbed the treasure?"

"All right." Isabella nodded.

Warrick helped her dismount, and together, they hauled up the bucket from the well. The rotten timbers on which the pail's frayed rope was wound creaked ominously, but at last, the two had the treasure in hand. It soon proved to be nothing more than a huge picnic lunch and a couple of bottles of wine, but Isabella, who was by this time famished, only laughed and set about preparing the meal.

"Christ's son," the Earl cursed, gazing down at the now-open basket as though he would like to have kicked it. "Do ye mean to tell me we searched all morn for this?"

"I'm sorry," Isabella apologized ruefully from where she

knelt. "I imagine this was Eadric, Thegn, and Beowulf's idea of a jest—in which they were doubtless aided and abetted by your brother. Nevertheless, 'twas thoughtful of them to provide this repast. I'll warrant they realized how hungry we would be after our exertions, and I am starved, so all is not lost."

"Aye." Warrick's eyes suddenly darkened speculatively. "Ye are right, of course. All is indeed not entirely lost," he said softly. "We are, after all, quite alone here; and ye do owe me a kiss. I think now, madam, is the time to collect it."

Isabella's chest constricted without warning; for an instant, she found herself unable to breathe. In the next moment, she was inhaling sharply, practically gasping for air. The Earl had been so long in demanding payment that she had thought he had forgotten all about the price of his silence. She should have known better!

"Warrick, please," she whispered.

"Come, sweetheart," he coaxed strangely, holding out one hand and smiling down at her oddly. "I am waiting, and ye did promise."

Slowly, fearing what he might do to her otherwise, Isabella laid her palm in his and rose to her feet, wondering at the peculiar glint in his eyes and the endearing manner in which he had spoken to her. Why, he had made it sound as though they were lovers! But why? Why this sudden change in attitude toward her? Somehow, it frightened her. Though Isabella feared and disliked him, she was honest enough with herself to admit that Warrick had a strong animal magnetism that attracted her to him, no matter how hard she fought against it. What would happen if he turned the full depths of his charm upon her? She did not think she could stand such an assault upon her senses. She half-turned, as though to flee, and felt the Earl's hand tighten on her own.

"I am waiting, my love," he murmured, still gazing down at her with the strange light in his eyes. "It has been far too long since I last tasted the sweetness of your lips."

Still hesitant, a pulse now beating rapidly at the hollow of her throat, the girl pleaded once more for release from the price of his silence, but he only laughed and shook his head.

"Come, come, 'Sabelle." He spoke the intimate version of her name as though caressing it. "Do not play coy with me. Ye know full well that I desire ye. This will not be the first time I have held ye in my arms—nor will it be the last. We shall share many such moments together, and I know ye await them as eagerly as I. 'Tis only your maidenly virtue that causes ye to blush and deny it. Now, come. Where is the kiss ye promised me?"

Tentatively, trembling slightly, Isabella wrapped her arms about Warrick's neck and placed her mouth on his. She had meant only to kiss him lightly, then withdraw; but suddenly, he crushed her to him, tangling the fingers of one hand roughly in her hair so she could not free herself. Alarmed, the girl began to struggle, not realizing it appeared as though she were pressing her body even closer to the Earl's and writhing against him suggestively. But Warrick knew and took full advantage of the situation, bending her backward so her knees buckled, and she was forced to stop fighting him, to cling to him tightly, almost wantonly, for support. Her head began to spin dizzily as the blood rushed to it hotly, and from somewhere deep in her throat came a low, animalistic moan—a soft cry of passion and surrender that she was unable to prevent.

Only then did the Earl let her go. And only then did Isabella hear the smothered gasp of outrage that came from the edge of the clearing. Horrified, the girl whirled in time to see Lionel, his face a distorted mask of anger and disbelief, yank his horse about cruelly and gallop heedlessly through the woods.

"Lionel!" she sobbed brokenly, understanding, at last, the reason for the scenario just past. "Lionel!" But he was gone. Desperately, she tried to run after him, but Warrick caught her possessively and yanked her back. Her eyes flashing with pain and rage, Isabella stared up at him dazedly, hating him, wanting to kill him. "Ye knew!" she accused him feverishly. "Ye swine! Ye knew that Lionel was there all the time! Ye made it seem as though ye and I were lovers—that I—that I *wanted* ye—"

"Aye," he said, grinning, but the smile did not quite reach the narrowed shards of his amber eyes. "I warned ye, madam: Ye are mine, and I will not have ye trysting with another."

"Oh, God, I despise ye! I despise ye, do ye hear?" Isabella cried.

"Dost think I care?" the Earl queried sharply. "'Tis enough that ye obey me. I do not ask for your love."

"Even if ye did, I wouldst never give it to ye. *Never!*" the girl vowed.

Blindly, uncontrollably, she struck out at him like a wild thing, her fingers curled into tightly clenched fists. But Warrick only laughed, easily pinioning her arms behind her back and claiming her mouth once more, kissing her searingly until her lips were bruised and swollen from his violent lovemaking, and her body was melting against his, her wrath turning, against her will, to desire.

Chapter Sixteen

SOMEWHERE, IN THE DISTANCE, THE VAST, WINDSWEPT moors seemed to meet the even more endless sky, the vivid autumn reds, golds, and greens of the earth and the pale, washed blue of the firmament running into each other, like watercolors in the rain, until they became as one; and the far horizon had no beginning, no end.

That is what the end of the world will be like, Isabella thought as she gazed out across the land. The heavens will meet the earth, and somewhere, the stars will fall into the sea. Perhaps if I ride far enough, I will find it has already begun, that somewhere, beyond the distant blurring of the horizon, the world is dying even now... dying, as I am dying inside, nevermore to be....

She sighed slowly, deeply, as though to inhale sharply would be to cause the dull, throbbing ache in her heart to stab more painfully, hurting her beyond what she could bear.

Lionel had gone, and she had been given no chance to explain to him what had really happened that day at the well. Warrick had seen to that, watching her constantly from beneath half-closed lids and waiting, waiting, unnerving her with the savagery and desire she knew lay coiled within his being. The girl trembled as she thought again of how he kissed her that day at the well and how she had melted in his imprisoning arms, surrendered to his demanding lips. Oh, God. He could have taken her there, and she would have given herself to him willingly, shamelessly, not caring that she despised him, that he had turned Lionel against her, had wounded both her and her beloved to the very depths of their souls. Only Giles's arrival had prevented the Earl from making her his. Oh, God. What was wrong with her?

Surreptitiously, Isabella looked over at Warrick, who rode beside her. He had done something to her to make her want him, despite her hatred of him. What was it? She studied him covertly, as though she could somehow discover the answer, but she could not. He was handsome, aye, but she had known many handsome men, Lionel among them. What was it then? The way those suddenly hot yellow eyes seized upon her hungrily, possessively, mentally stripping away her clothes and ravishing her fiercely, passionately, so she quivered all over just thinking about how it would be if Warrick actually made love to her? Aye, that must be it, for even now, she shivered uncontrollably with wanting at the thought. He had seduced her with those knowing eyes that seemed to say, "Come hither, and I will make ye feel as ye have never felt before. Ye are mine . . . mine!"

Christ's son! The very arrogance of the man. Who did he think he was anyway? His rank and riches were no greater than Lionel's, so what was it that drew Isabella to Warrick then, despite her love for the heir of St. Saviour? Surely, 'twas more than just a pair of eyes, no matter how compelling they might be. But . . . had it—had it not been Lionel's eyes that had won her heart? Aye, in truth, it was so. Isabella was stricken with despair at the thought. Was she but a fool then, to fall for a desire-filled glance? Nay, 'twas more than that. Lionel was her golden god, the sun and the sky. And Warrick . . . Warrick was a dark devil, the shadows and the earth. Aye, that was it.

We all have a darker side, the girl realized, and she knew that somehow, some way, Warrick had seen hers and claimed it as his own. Nay, I shall not be his Persephone, she thought, rebelling against the idea. I shall get Lionel back and find some way to free myself from Warrick's spell. Oh, if only I had been able to talk to Giles!

But her brother had gone back to the Borderlands to rejoin Gloucester and to battle the barbarous Scots who dared to raid upon England's soil. There was no one left to talk to except Caerllywel, and Isabella could not bring herself to speak to him of her troubles. No matter how kind he was, he was still Warrick's brother.

So she rode on silently toward Rushden and said nothing of the ache in her heart.

Beside her, the Earl watched the girl intently, guessing the depth of her pain and feeling a momentary flash of guilt at the hurt he had done her. Then he remembered Brangwen, and he forced himself to remain hard and unyielding. He would have no bride who would betray him. He would not be made a fool of again. He was sorry for Isabella, for by now, he had learned how cruelly Lord Oadby had treated the girl and her brother and how they had suffered as children, even as Warrick had suffered during his own youth. But the knowledge did not lessen the Earl's unrelenting purposefulness toward Isabella. Indeed, it made it more stern. She had been allowed to run wild, had virtually been raised in the stables of Rushden, under the care of Sirs Eadric, Thegn, and Beowulf, who, out of love and pity, had indulged her every whim. As a result, her behavior toward men was too free and easy for Warrick's liking. At Rushden, it mattered little, as her brother's knights knew their place and would never have dreamt of taking advantage of Isabella's charms. But at Court...

The Earl's mouth tightened. The girl would encourage every courtier at the palace; and rakes like Lord Thomas Grey, Marquis of Dorset and the Queen's son, would not hesitate to make Isabella theirs and then boast of their conquest of her for all to snigger about behind Warrick's back! Doubtless, her fear of what he would do if he discovered she was not a virgin on their wedding night was the only thing that had prevented her from lying with Lord Lionel. But after the Earl had married her, and her maidenhead no longer remained to serve as proof of her faithfulness... Aye, that was when she would betray him, would seek to revenge herself on him for all real and imagined slights. Then she would give herself to any man just to spite him, as Brangwen had done.

Even now, Isabella was probably already contemplating her vengeance, Warrick thought as he stared over at her still figure on Cendrillon. Well, she would not have it, he vowed. He would keep a close watch on her while they were betrothed and after they were wed, he would kill her if she even so much as looked at another man. As for the girl believing herself in love with Lord Lionel—well, the Earl hoped he had ended the affair before it had become too serious. But just in case he had not, Warrick had sent his squire Rhys to St. Saviour-on-the-Lake to discover all there was to know about its heir. If, despite all that had occurred, Lord Lionel still persisted in his attentions to Isabella, the Earl would know how to deal with that moonstruck swain most efficiently. Arrogantly, Warrick dismissed Lord Lionel Valeureux from his mind.

Moments later, the Earl's musings were abruptly interrupted by a startled cry from Isabella. The sound brought him back sharply to reality, but before he could discover what was amiss, the girl had urged her mare to a gallop and was heading away from the road to the moors beyond.

"'Sabelle!" he shouted angrily, but she paid him no heed.

Warrick swore under his breath, then yanked his horse about to follow Sirs Eadric, Thegn, and Beowulf, who had already hastily pulled away from the procession.

"'Tis some animal in distress, my lord," Sir Eadric called back over his shoulder. "'Tis the only thing that sets my lady Isabella off like this."

This was soon proven to be the case, for by the time the Earl had reached her, the girl had dismounted and was bent over a stray dog that lay upon the ground some distance from the road. How she had spied the hound, he did not know, for it was little more than a crumpled heap of bones; it was so starved. She talked to the animal quietly for a moment, then, as it seemed docile and friendly enough, she held her hand to its nose to let it accustom itself to her scent. Tentatively, the beast licked her fingers. It was only then that she began to examine it. Once finished, she raised her head.

"Thegn, have some of the men bring a cart," Isabella ordered, gazing up at Warrick as though daring him to defy her command.

But he said nothing. There was no pressing need to return to Rushden, and besides, the Earl knew that Isabella had a special penchant for injured creatures and would not have obeyed him in any event, had he ordered her to leave the hound. At least it would give her something to think about beside Lord Lionel Valeureux.

The cart was brought, and the girl carefully lifted the unprotesting dog into the vehicle, covering the animal up with an old horse blanket and crooning soothingly to the beast all the while.

"Poor old hound dog," she said, patting its head and scratching its ears. "Poor old hound dog. Ye just got too old to be of use to your master, I guess, so he turned ye out to fend for yourself, I'll wager. Eadric, tie Cendrillon to the back of the cart, please, and, Beowulf, fetch me a little bit of meat from your pouch. I know ye had saved it for later, but this poor creature is in greater need of it than ye."

"Aye, my lady."

"Surely, madam, ye do not mean to ride the rest of the way to Rushden in that cart," Warrick stated. "'Twill be most uncomfortable, and 'tis filthy besides."

"What is a little dirt and discomfort compared to how this poor dog has suffered? Can ye not see how starved 'tis? 'Tis frightened as well and needs to be reassured, although I am certain ye cannot understand that, my lord, being so bold in your manner," Isabella told him, her voice tinged with sarcasm and double meaning.

The Earl raised one eyebrow and grinned.

"I didst not hear ye complain of my bold manner that day at the well, my lady," he reminded her softly, causing

her to blush with shame and fury as she recalled once more
how she had so willingly acquiesced to his desires.

"Oh! How dare ye mention that day to me?" she snapped.
"Ye are no gentleman, my lord."

"Oh, I can be gentle, 'Sabelle, most gentle, if only ye
wouldst stop fighting me."

"I shall never yield to ye, Warrick, and ye are a fool if
ye believe I will. And cease calling me 'Sabelle! I have not
made ye free to name me thus."

"Ah, well. 'Tis no matter. I will not need your permission
much longer. I have decided we shall be wed as soon as
possible after returning to Rushden."

Warrick had not meant to say that. Indeed, he did not
know why he had. He had no wish for a bride. It was just
that Isabella always seemed to get the best of him, and the
thought had pricked his pride and vanity.

"Nay!" the girl cried sharply with sudden fright, her heart
pounding anxiously in her breast. "Nay," she reiterated,
forcing herself to remain calm. "'Tis a lie. Ye do but lie
to fret me. Ye said 'twould be a year or more at least."

For a moment, the Earl was tempted to agree that he had
only been taunting her; but upon reflection, he realized,
because of the King's command, that he was going to have
to wed Isabella sooner or later. It was unlikely that Edward
would annul the betrothal, having already signed the contracts; and the chance that either Warrick or Isabella would
die before the marriage could take place seemed equally
remote. Besides, as Caerllywel had said, the Earl wanted
the girl. He decided he might as well wed her and have
done. She was fourteen now—old enough to be bedded—
and perhaps once she was his wife and at his utter mercy,
she would be too frightened to betray him after all.

"I have changed my mind, madam. I grow weary, as
your warden, of trying to silence your insulting tongue
and wouldst still it, as your husband, in another manner,
one that will prove far more pleasing to the both of us,
methinks."

"God's blood! Do ye dream I will let ye touch me, ye
whoreson bastard?"

"Aye," Warrick's eyes ravished her crudely, mockingly, as though to punish her for the aspersion she had cast upon his birth. "And more. Do *ye* doubt 'twill be so?" He laughed lowly when the girl made no response to him. "Comfort your hound, madam," he directed before turning away. "It trembles—as do ye."

The first thing that Isabella did upon returning to Rushden was to see that the stray dog she had found was settled comfortably in one of the empty stalls in the part of the stables that served as her menagerie. She fixed a pallet of straw inside the stall and arranged the old horse blanket over it, then laid the hound tenderly upon the bed. After that, she brought food and water and placed them within easy reach of the animal. As she had done in the cart, the girl patted the beast kindly and spoke to it encouragingly as it raised its head to sniff its new surroundings, then rose slowly to wolf down the meal that Isabella had provided. While the creature was eating, the girl examined its painfully thin body carefully, tending a number of cuts and scratches and one particularly deep wound that looked as though the dog had been viciously bitten. Then, after a few more reassuring words to the hound, who wagged its tail feebly and lay down again upon the pallet, she gathered up her rags and many unguents, replacing them in her basket, and left the stall. Isabella took care to lock the door securely behind her so the animal could not escape: for over the years, it had become her practice to isolate each new beast from the other creatures in the menagerie until the newcomer had grown accustomed to the others, and the girl was certain it would not attack any of its fellow companions.

The dog having been cared for, Isabella walked slowly to the keep, allowing her thoughts, for the first time, to dwell on Warrick's words during their journey. Did he really mean to wed her now instead of waiting? Or had it indeed been only a lie to fret her? She must discover the answer as soon as possible, for if the Earl meant them to be married at once, there would be no time for Lionel to speak with the Duke of Gloucester and ask him to persuade his brother the King against the match.

The girl sighed with despair. It seemed that nothing in her life had gone right since the deaths of her parents.

"Why so glum, 'Sabelle?" Caerllywel joined her, his eyes kind and filled with concern. "Is aught amiss with the hound?"

"Nay, nothing more than what some decent food won't cure, methinks. The poor animal has numerous cuts and scratches and one particularly nasty wound, but those will heal with time."

"Then what is it, my lady, that brings such sorrow to your face?"

"'Tis naught, Caerllywel, truly."

"Oh, come, 'Sabelle. Am I not your friend?"

"Aye, but ye are also Warrick's brother."

"The fool," Caerllywel muttered under his breath, then asked more loudly, "what has he done?"

"Nothing really, except to say we are to be married at once." Isabella's voice was bitter at the thought. "In the beginning, he told me 'twould be a year or two at least before we would wed, and now it seems he has changed his mind."

"Mayhap 'tis best, my lady. Sometimes, when a thing is unpleasant, 'tis better to get it over with, for waiting only prolongs the agony."

"Aye, but I had hoped—I had hoped something would happen, in time, to prevent the marriage from taking place. Now that will be impossible."

"'Tis unlikely that such would have occurred in any event, 'Sabelle," Caerllywel observed slowly, then paused. "I know ye dislike Waerwic, but it could be worse. At least he is handsome and rich and a favorite of the King. And in his own fashion, my brother will treat you well. He will not beat ye or otherwise abuse ye, as some men would."

"But he will not love me either!" the girl cried.

"How do ye know, my lady? As Waerwic often says, 'tis unwise to be so certain of things. Oh, 'Sabelle, my brother's heart is cold; 'tis true. But 'tis because he was so deeply wounded by Brangwen's betrayal of him. Your heart is warm, and ye are a healer of those who have been hurt. There is magic in these tender hands"—Caerllywel took them in his own and studied them intently for a moment.

Then he looked into her eyes. "Can ye not set them to curing the ache in Waerwic's soul? If ye can, ye may find he will love ye more truly than ever a man has loved a woman."

Isabella bit her lip and turned away so that Caerllywel could no longer see the expression on her face.

"But how—how can I, when I—when I love another?"

"Lionel Valeureux?" he inquired softly.

"Aye. Oh, aye," the girl sobbed quietly, trying to pull her hands free, but Caerllywel hung onto them gently but firmly.

"'Sabelle, look at me," he ordered. "Look at me. Despite his many charms, Lord Lionel is not the man for ye; and methinks, in your heart, ye know it. Oh, 'Sabelle, ye are woman capable of deep and lasting passion. When ye love— truly love—ye will give your whole heart and soul. Tell me, is there not some small part of your being that ye have held back from Lionel Valeureux?"

"Nay! Nay, 'tisn't true!" Isabella protested, but her eyes were haunted by shadows of doubt all the same.

"Isn't it?" Caerllywel queried, then shrugged lightly when she refused to reply. "Perhaps not, then. But if 'tis, ye must ask yourself why, my lady. Look to your heart, 'Sabelle, for therein lies the answer."

Lost in thought, Isabella made her way to the stables, opening the door and automatically gathering up her basket of linen strips and unguents as she began her morning rounds.

Warrick had not lied to her. Preparations for the wedding were, even now, being carried out by the excited servants at Rushden, all of whom thought Isabella extremely lucky to be marrying such a rich and handsome man. One of the King's favorites too! Imagine being blessed with such good fortune.

Lucky, the girl thought bitterly, her mouth curling with scorn. Lucky to be wedding a man who does not love me. Lucky to be torn from the man *I* love.

But even as the reflection came to her, she remembered Caerllywel's words of the other day and was troubled by them. Was he right? Could Warrick come, in time, to love her if she set about to heal his wounded heart? He wanted her, aye; that much she was sure of. But could his desire for her grow and deepen to something more lasting, and did Isabella want that to happen? She thought of Lionel and wondered why, despite his fervent reassurances of his love for her, she could not banish that small fear of doubt about him that still clouded her mind. Was Caerllywel right? Was her heart indeed trying to tell her something?

The girl sighed and shook her head. There were no easy answers.

Most of the inhabitants of her menagerie appeared to be doing well, and she turned, at last, to the stall wherein she had kept the stray dog, which she'd named Faegen, the past few days.

"Well, Faegen, my boy," she greeted the hound, who raised his head at the sight of her. "And how are ye doing today?"

To Isabella's surprise, the animal laid its ears back and growled at her.

"Here now. What's wrong, Faegen? Are ye hiding something ye don't want me to discover? That old soup bone mayhap? Did ye bury it under your pile of hay?" she teased. "Well, I promise not to disturb it. Come on now. Let's take a look at ye."

Basket in hand, she moved toward the beast, gave it a few tender pats, then bent to examine the nasty injury on its body, which had stubbornly, despite her treatment, refused to heal. She touched the wound gingerly, probing gently to see if the infection was growing worse. Faegen growled once more, then barked and snapped at her. Isabella gave him a light, reproving thump on the nose to quiet him. He certainly was restless today.

"I know it hurts," she said, "but I'm only trying to help ye."

Faegen was not soothed by the sound of her words. Suddenly, without warning, he turned and bit the girl on the leg.

Although she winced as the sharp teeth dug into her calf, Isabella was not at all frightened by this assault, for she had been bitten before when dealing with the creatures of her menagerie. She merely assumed the dog's injury pained him more than she had realized, and he was only defending himself against further ache.

"All right." She gave Faegen's ears a friendly scratch. "We'll leave the wound today then, and see how it does tomorrow."

Once outside the stall, the girl glanced at the bite on her leg. It did not appear to be serious, so she washed it with some soap and water and thought no more about it.

The next day, Faegen refused to allow her inside the stall. He growled and barked and ran at the door threateningly when she attempted to open it. Slightly alarmed now by his behavior, Isabella slammed the barrier shut and bolted it, a puzzled frown on her face. Inside, the hound continued to run about wildly, snarling, yelping, and lunging at the stall door as she stood there, studying him thoughtfully. Why, it was almost as though he had gone berserk.

"Madam."

She turned at once at the sound of that faintly mocking voice and the rap of knuckles upon the open stable door. Warrick's tall dark figure filled the entrance, blocking the shaft of autumn sunlight that grew paler each day with winter's approach. He had been hunting, she saw, for he still wore his hunting jacket and falconer's glove. He tapped the side of one high, black leather boot absently with his whip.

"Is something wrong?" he asked. "I thought I heard some sort of scuffle—Oh, 'tis the dog. May I come in?"

"Aye." The girl nodded. "I do not know what is the matter with him. He—he seems to have suddenly gone quite mad."

"Mad?" The Earl's eyes widened. "Stand away from the stall, 'Sabelle!" he commanded, striding quickly to her side and yanking her back when she didn't move. Filled with foreboding, he stared down at the hound grimly. "How long has he been like this?"

"Just—just this morning. Why? Oh, yesterday, he was a little snappish; in fact, he bit me, but—"

"What?"

"He—he . . . Faegen bit me. On the leg. But I'm sure 'twas just because his wound pained him so when I touched it," Isabella added hurriedly by way of explanation, thinking that Warrick would make her get rid of the animal otherwise. "'Twasn't his fault. I don't believe he really meant to hurt me. . . ." Her voice trailed off at the ominous look upon the Earl's face.

"Let me see the bite," he ordered curtly. Then, "Oh, for Christ's sake, Isabella! I have no intention of ravishing ye. Now pull up your skirts so I can see your leg!"

Warrick bent and examined the small wound closely, but he didn't touch it. After a moment, he stood, his visage shadowed with anxiety as he glanced once more at Faegen.

"Don't let that dog out of the stall," the Earl told the girl. "Has it come in contact with any of the other creatures in this place?"

"Nay. I don't think so, except perhaps the cats. They and the birds are the only ones free to roam about the menagerie. They catch rats . . . the cats, I mean, not the birds. But I do believe 'tis rather unlikely any of them have entered the stall. They aren't yet accustomed to Faegen; and as he was most likely a hunting dog at one time, he would surely have killed any cat or bird that got into the stall. That's one of the reasons I locked him up. I keep all my newcomers isolated from the rest until I am certain they understand they are not to attack their fellow inhabitants. Why, Warrick? What's wrong?"

"I'm not sure," he said. "I've only seen one other beast in my life that behaved in such a strange fashion, as though it had suddenly lost its mind. Have ye never before viewed such, my lady? Oh, surely, ye must have, as many animals as ye have tended. Think hard, 'Sabelle!" His voice was urgent.

"Aye, there—there was one that behaved oddly, growing vicious, without warning, as Faegen has done. I found it upon the moors. A ferret, 'twas. It had been in a fight and was badly injured. It seemed friendly enough when I approached it, but as I drew near, it suddenly snarled and began to run about quite wildly. Then it charged at me. Eadric was there, and he slew it before it reached me. 'Twould have attacked me otherwise, he said. I—I cried over its death all the same."

"The animal I saw was a badger," Warrick spoke. "I thought it peculiar at the time because it was not at all frightened of me and my brothers. To our surprise, it came right up to us; and Caerllywel and I decided it must have been caught and tamed by someone. I remember Emrys bending down to pet it—for he was fascinated by its fur and claws—and then Madog, some instinct for danger, perhaps, warning him, snatched my brother's hand away before he could touch the beast. The creature went berserk moments later. We climbed into the trees to escape from it. A few minutes after that, 'twas dead. I am worried, 'Sabelle. We must keep a close watch on that dog."

She looked at Faegen, who was still acting crazily, and then, as though she were afraid to, glanced down covertly at her leg. The Earl did not miss the gesture.

"If the hound dies . . ." he began, then stopped.

"You're—you're saying I could die too," Isabella whispered, "because Faegen bit me. Oh, Warrick, nay. Nay!" she cried, her eyes wide with horror.

"I shall summon a physician—"

"Why? Why should ye care?" the girl spat bitterly. "If I die, ye will be free of me!"

Then she turned and ran so he would not see the sudden tears streaming down her fear-filled face.

"'Sabelle!" Warrick called, starting after her. "'Sabelle, wait!"

But she had gone.

The following day, Faegen's condition had worsened, and he was foaming at the mouth. Convulsively, he attempted to swallow but could not. The day after that, he was subdued, almost suspiciously quiet; and though Isabella's hopes had been raised, at first, upon seeing his calmed state, they plummeted to the depths of fright and despair when she realized the animal was paralyzed.

Several hours later, Faegen died.

Chapter Seventeen

THE CASTLE WAS PREMONITORILY SILENT AND FILLED WITH grief. The happy preparations for the forthcoming wedding had ceased. The physician had come and gone; and now, where none dared to disturb him, Warrick sat alone in the great hall, his eyes closed, his head resting in his hands.

There is nothing to be done, my lord. I have seen this before. The lady Isabella will soon grow quite mad, as the dog did, and then she will die. I am sorry. There is nothing to be done.

The doctor's words hammered in the Earl's mind, and a terrible sense of guilt chiseled at his soul. He had not wished to marry Isabella, and now, he would not have to. Oh, God. To live with that on his conscience for the rest of his life! Never had he thought he would live to see the day when he was sorry he would not be wed.

There is nothing to be done....

"Nay! There must be something that can be done!" he muttered fiercely to himself, slamming one fist down upon the high table, causing Isabella's empty plate beside him to jump and clatter, a sharp and painful reminder that she had not joined them for supper.

Since Faegen's death, the girl had kept to her chamber, distressed by the eyes of the servants, who watched her apprehensively, waiting for some sign that the madness was upon her. Warrick inhaled deeply, his chest constricting painfully as he recalled Isabella's words to him.

"I don't want to become as Faegen did, my lord. Please, Warrick, if I—if I *do* go mad, slay me quickly, oh, quickly," she had begged. "'Twill take but one blow from your sword, and ye are the only man here I can trust to do it. The others will go on hoping that I—that I won't die, and they will spare me a merciful end...." Her voice had trailed off pitifully.

"God's blood!" Warrick swore as he remembered the

brave facade that Isabella had managed, despite her fear.
"There must be *something* that can be done!"

"Why do ye care, brother?" Caerllywel was suddenly
standing there before him. The mysterious blue eyes that
Caerllywell had inherited from Hwyelis, their mother, bore
no trace of their usual merriment. Instead, they were quietly
accusing. When Warrick made no answer, Caerllywel deliberately repeated the question. "I ask again: Why do ye
care, brother?" The word "brother" was almost a sneer. "If
she dies, ye will be rid of her. 'Tis what ye wanted, is it
not? After all, she's good for but one thing only, and there
are plenty of other women for that."

The Earl's dark visage, when he looked at his brother,
was deadly.

"I ought to slay ye for those words," Warrick said.

"Why don't ye try? Is it because I do but fling your own
back into your face?"

"Christ's son! I *shall* kill ye!" the Earl snarled, suddenly
springing to his feet and drawing his sword.

Caerllywel laughed, but the sound was not pleasant. He
pulled his own blade from its scabbard.

"As I told ye once before, ye can try, brother," he goaded
softly.

The two men faced each other warily, forgetting, for the
moment, the blood bond between them. Briefly, they saluted, and then there was nothing but the clash of steel upon
steel that echoed ominously through the great hall. The
brothers were evenly matched, and the duel was made even
more murderous by the fact that neither man was armored.
Again and again, the swords engaged, thrust, and parried
until both men were panting from their exertions, wiping
the sweat from their brows. This was no childhood game
of pretense; it was a furious battle to the death; and either
way, both brothers would be losers. Somewhere, deep in
their hearts, they realized this; but they were beyond caring.
Each meant, with grim determination, to slay the other.

"Stop!"

The single cry rang out authoritatively through the great
hall. The two men paused and turned to where Isabella
stood, stricken, having been summoned by the frightened

servants (mad or nay, the girl was still their mistress) to put an end to the fight.

"Stop, I say. I am still mistress here at Rushden, and I command ye to lay down your weapons at once. There will be no blood shed here, in my brother's keep."

The two men stared hard at one another for a time, then slowly, their rage having drained from them at the sight of Isabella's pale but lovely countenance, they sheathed their blades. The great hall was silent.

"Lord Hawkhurst! Lord Hawkhurst!" Sir Beowulf burst into the room. "Oh, my lady, I did not expect to see ye...." The knight's voice trailed off lamely as he became aware of the stillness. He looked rapidly at the Earl, then Caerllywel, then finally, Isabella. He took a deep breath. "Is—is aught amiss, my lady?"

"Nay, Beowulf," she said quietly. "What is it ye wish?"

"My lady, I have found an old woman in the village. Her name is Maude. Oh, my lady! She claims she can cure ye!"

For just an instant, the girl's heart stopped, then suddenly, it began to soar in her breast as though it had wings. She gazed at Beowulf incredulously.

"'Tis—'tis true, Beowulf? Ye—ye do not jest!"

"Nay, my lady."

"Fetch this beldam here at once," Warrick ordered, causing Isabella and Caerllywel to stare at him with astonishment.

"Aye, my lord. I will, my lord. 'Tis just that—that—"

"Well, what is the problem?" the Earl demanded impatiently of the knight.

"Begging your pardon, my lord, but the villagers—the villagers," Beowulf stammered, "well, they swear she's a—a witch, my lord."

"Witch or nay, if there's a chance the Lady Isabella can be saved, we must take it. Fetch the woman immediately. 'Sabelle, go upstairs, and wait for us in your chamber."

The words were curt, but for the first time since his coming, Isabella thought she saw a spark of caring for her deep in Warrick's golden eyes.

* * *

The night was black. The brisk autumn wind, touched by winter's icy fingers, soughed eerily through the long corridors of Rushden Castle. Here and there, along the hall, the torches flickered, when caught just so by the draft, and cast strange, dancing shadows upon the walls.

Warrick gazed at the bent old harridan who trudged beside him, and despite the fact that he had always considered himself a brave man, he shivered slightly. The wavering flames of the torches and the corners of darkness suited the hag, he thought: for if ever there really existed a witch, he would not have been surprised to learn it was Maude.

Small in frame and wizened in body, her pointed bones sticking out at sharp angles where they joined, she looked as though she were a hundred years old, and every day of her hard life had been etched into her skin. Never had the Earl seen such a wrinkled face. The loose folds sagged down from her sunken eyes and cheeks; the eyes themselves were as black as obsidian and glittered just as brightly. Her large, humpbacked nose jutted out prominently above a thin, cracked, and drooling mouth that gaped to show several missing teeth. Those that still remained were black with rot, and the beldam's breath was foul. Coarse dark hairs grew upon her upper lip and chin. Wispy grey strands straggled from her head. The ragged gown she wore was none too clean.

How can I let this horrible creature examine Isabella? Warrick asked himself for the umpteenth time. How can I not?

"'Sabelle." He knocked softly upon her chamber door. "'Sabelle, the woman called Maude has come."

Old Alice opened the door and bade them enter, frightened though she was by Maude's appearance. Like the Earl, the faithful nanna would not throw away any opportunity to save her mistress's life. Alice alone at Rushden understood just how deeply the girl had suffered during her childhood. In Alice had Isabella confided her joys and fears about Lord Lionel Valeureux and how much she dreaded her forthcoming marriage to Warrick. Alice alone knew now just how terribly afraid Isabella was that she would die, for it had been the nanna who had been wakened by the girl's screams that night after Faegen had died.

Isabella had clutched her pillow to her breast and wept and gasped, "I don't want to die! I don't want to die!" over and over again while Alice had stroked the silvery cascade that had tumbled about the girl's shaking shoulders.

"There, there, my lady," Alice had crooned soothingly to Isabella in the darkness. "You're not going to die. Whether ye like it or not, you've got a wedding to attend."

Now, the girl surveyed with dismay the ancient, hunched harridan who had entered the room. Was *this* the woman who was to heal her? Why, the hag wasn't even clean! But she was all that Isabella had, her one chance to survive. The girl squared her shoulders determinedly.

I'm not going to die, she told herself. I'm not going to die. Please God, just let me live through this, and I'll marry Warrick and never look at another man as long as I live.

"Thank ye for coming, Maude," she said and, repressing a shudder, held out her hand.

"Now show me the place where the mad dog bit ye, m'lady," the beldam commanded, once the amenities had been gotten out of the way.

Slowly, Isabella raised her skirts and extended her leg slightly.

"Ah." Maude nodded. "It be well below yer heart. That be good. 'Twill take the madness a while to travel through yer veins. When did it happen?"

"Three days ago."

"Then I may yet be in time to save ye."

"Can ye—can ye really cure me? The physician said there was nothing to be done."

"The old fool," Maude snorted contemptuously. "What does he know of the ancient ways and powers, the secrets that have been handed down from one generation to the next? Because of educated fools like him, who scorn the old and grasp eagerly the new, the knowledge of the past will soon be fergotten, lost fer all time. Put yer trust in God, m'lady: fer though the Lord gave us many illnesses to test our faith, He also gave us the means to cure such.

There be many plants that grow upon this earth, m'lady, and each one has a special purpose. It be only fools like yer doctor who do not understand this wisdom. Lie down, m'lady, and I will begin my preparations. Ye"—she turned to Alice—"set a kettle of water to boiling on the hearth."

In silence, Maude opened the burlap bag she carried in one hand and drew forth some recently picked foliage, just now beginning to wither; a handful of gnarled roots and tiny seeds; and a mortar and pestle. With a sharp dagger, she sliced the roots and threw them into the pot of water the nanna had put to heating on the fire. Then, muttering under her breath to herself, the hag placed a few of the plants and some seeds into the mortar and, with the pestle, started to grind them up thoroughly. To the crushed flora, she added a bit of the dark brew that now bubbled in the cauldron. Once the paste was finished, the woman donned a pair of thick work gloves, such as those used by the crofters in the fields, and approached the massive canopy bed, where Isabella lay.

"Why—why do ye need the gloves?" the girl asked.

"To confound the madness, m'lady," the stooped harridan cackled. "The gloves do not breathe like the body. The madness will not enter them."

Then, beginning to chant in a strange, singsong voice, the beldam smeared the mixture, which she had concocted, on Isabella's leg. After that, Maude covered the bite with some of the whole leafage that remained and then bound the girl's calf up securely.

"Now ye must drink some of the brew, m'lady," the hag directed.

Slowly, Isabella took the offered chalice. The dark liquid was bitter, but somehow, she managed to choke it down. Almost instantly, she felt nauseated and longed to vomit into her chamber pot, but she did not. Maude nodded with satisfaction, then carefully packed away her things and slung her burlap bag over her shoulder.

"I shall come again tomorrow and each day after that until the madness be gone," she told Isabella.

"How—how long will it take for me to get well?" the

girl inquired timidly, for to some extent, she was frightened by Maude. The woman was indeed a witch!

"Many days, m'lady. It depends upon when the first symptoms of the madness appear. Mayhap by the time the moon be full, ye will be healed."

Isabella gasped raggedly for air and tried to scream, but her throat constricted horribly, and no sound came out. She was choking, choking. She could not swallow; but still, the evil hawk, with its macabre black talons, hovered over her, forcing bilous liquid down her throat. She struggled furiously against the bird, but her attempts to fight it were futile, for her hands and feet had been securely tied to the hawk's perch.

She couldn't breathe. She was so hot; she was burning up. The bird was smothering her, roasting her alive, trying to drown her, anything, so long as it slew her, its helpless prey. She screamed and screamed and screamed, and still, there was no sound. The bitter brew trickled down her throat. She could not swallow. She gagged convulsively. The feathers of the hawk's wings scraped her throat, compelling her to down the vile liquid.

And, oh, the pain! The incredible, terrible pain. It tore wrenchingly through her body, shards of unbearable agony shooting up and down her spine, pounding in her head, her limbs. She flailed about sickeningly, spasmodically, her muscles twitching violently, uncontrollably. Oh, God, someone, please stop the pain!

"Oh, my lady. My poor, poor lady," Alice wept and wrung her hands as she stared with horror at Isabella, who writhed wildly upon the bed, tearing at the strips of linen that bound her to the posts, contorting her body grotesquely, unnaturally, in a frenzied effort to free herself.

Slowly, Warrick drew off his black leather hunting gloves and washed his hands, scrubbing them thoroughly, as though they were tainted. Sweet *Jesù!* He could not bear the girl's madness. It was killing him inside, and yet, he still could not bring himself to slay her as she had pleaded with him to do. In the final reckoning, even he, whom Isabella had trusted to end her life mercifully, had failed her. He turned accusingly to the old beldam, Maude, who stood watchfully nearby.

"She is worse." He spoke grimly.

The harridan nodded.

"The madness be strong, m'lord, but we will yet prevail."

"How can ye be so sure?" the Earl asked angrily, his face haggard and drawn with worry.

"It be the fifth day the Lady Isabella has been like this since the first symptoms of the madness appeared."

"So?"

"There be no foam about her mouth, no paralyzing of her limbs, and she be yet alive. She be one of the lucky ones. Aye, we caught the madness in time, m'lord. The Lady Isabella will get well."

"If you're lying to me . . . If she dies, ye old witch, I shall kill ye," Warrick snarled.

But Maude was not afraid. Her black eyes snapped, and she chortled maliciously as she gathered up her bag.

"I shall come back tomorrow," she said.

"Waerwic, ye must get some rest now," Caerllywel stated gently, "else ye will fall ill yourself. Ye have done all ye could do—and more. I shall sit with 'Sabelle for a while."

"Nay." The Earl shook his head, rubbing his eyes tiredly.

"As ye wish, then." Caerllywel pressed his brother no further, knowing it would be useless. "Come, Alice," he addressed the nanna kindly. "'Twill do ye no good to remain here. Waerwic will call us if there is any change."

Once he was alone, the Earl moved again to Isabella's side. There, he stood gazing down at her and despising himself for the first time in his life. *He* was to blame for her condition. Somehow, *he* had brought this on the girl because he'd had no wish to marry her. If only he had cared about her, had forbidden her to touch that Goddamned hound that day—Oh, Christ, Christ! Caerllywel was right. Isabella was but kind and good; taking pity on all in need, no matter the consequences to herself. And Warrick had treated her with contempt—taking the kisses she had refused to give him, mocking her, frightening her—when he might have won her love instead. Well, God had punished him for it. The Earl was eaten alive with guilt. If the girl died, he would never forgive himself.

Damn ye, Brangwen! he cursed silently to himself. Because ye turned out to be naught but paste, I have scorned a jewel. Godamercy! What a fool I have been, hard and cruel, wanting to hurt Isabella so she would not hurt me; she, who gives of herself so freely to all those in pain. Caerllywel tried to tell me of her sweet nature, just as he tried to warn me about the evil in ye, Brangwen. Why didn't I listen? I was too proud, too stubborn. Oh, sweet *Jesù*, let her live. Just let 'Sabelle live, and I'll make her happy; I swear it!

With this vow, Warrick turned away. It was time again to give the girl some more of the bitter brew and change the compress on her leg. After the first onslaught, the symptoms of Isabella's madness had worsened rapidly, and Maude had not proven strong enough to force the girl to drink or to restrain her wild thrashing while the bite was cleansed and dressed. Only the Earl had the power now to accomplish these tasks. Even Caerllywel could not control Isabella, so Warrick had ordered Maude to instruct him in what must be done. None knew why he succeeded in managing the girl when his brother could not—for Caerllywel was built as powerfully as the Earl—and Warrick did not tell them that his terrible sense of guilt would have given him the strength of ten men, had it been necessary. Donning the black leather gloves, he moved once more to Isabella's side.

The girl opened her mouth and screamed soundlessly again as the macabre hawk with the ebony claws swooped toward her. Once more, she fought him with all the power of her madness, but still, he forced the hateful liquid down her throat, compelling her to swallow, swallow, swallow, not caring that she was choking.

Far off, in some sane corner of her mind, she thought she heard a voice sobbing, "'Sabelle, Oh, God. 'Sabelle." But she pushed the image away. 'Twas the malevolent bird, trying to trick her. It did not love her. It would never have whispered her name so hoarsely, so brokenly, so tenderly.

Once, there had been a golden god who had spoken her name like that, but he had gone. Oh, come back! Come back, my golden god. . . .

But even now, far across England at Devizes Castle, unbeknown to Isabella's tortured mind, Lord Lionel Valeureux was repeating the vows that would bind him till death to his betrothed, Lady Gilliane Beaumaris.

Chapter Eighteen

Grasmere, England, 1480

ISABELLA ASHLEY PERCHED SILENTLY UPON THE STONE coping of Grasmere's widow's walk, gazing out over the vast sweep of the moors below. The terrain seemed to stretch out endlessly before her, like a distant sea, its tall grass rippling like waves when touched by the cool fingers of the spring breeze. Lightly, the wind caressed her still-wan face and tangled the silken strands of her silver-blond hair. Gently, she brushed the billowing tresses from her wide, fathomless grey-green eyes, then stared down with wonder at her trembling hands. Her heart swelled in her breast with joy and awe. She was alive! She could not believe it; miraculously, she was alive. How strange that it should be so and that it was Warrick who had saved her, for Caerllywel had told her how the Earl alone had restrained her wild thrashing to force the bitter brew down her throat, had changed the dressing on her leg two or three times a day to draw out the madness that had possessed her. Now, only the slight, occasional quivering of her limbs remained to remind her she had nearly died. The girl drew her shawl more closely about her, shuddering a little as she pushed the unpleasant thought from her mind.

"'Tis indeed peaceful here, my lady," Jocelyn said, recalling Isabella to the present. "No wonder Lord Hawkhurst sent ye here to rest and recover. Grasmere is like a balm that soothes the battered senses."

Isabella turned and smiled at the maid by her side. Jocelyn was Maude's granddaughter, as difficult as it was to believe, for except for the sly mystery that tinged her dark sloe eyes, Jocelyn was nothing at all like her grandmother. She was tall and graceful, with slender curves and rich russet hair that hung freely to her waist. Her mother, dead now, had been Maude's daughter; her father's name, Jocelyn did not know, though it was said he had been a fine lord.

"Aye, just one night, my ma lay with him," Jocelyn had told Isabella ruefully, "and nine months later, I was the result. Ah, what a handsome man she used to say he was, bold as brass, and the price of the tumble well worth it. She said I took after him. I suspect it must be true, for I've little enough resemblance to her—God rest her soul—and Gram. Gram said she reckoned the Thatcher blood was just getting too thin to hold its own, and I guess she was right, because Ma died young. She caught a chill and just faded like a winter rose, went so fast, Gram couldn't save her. I wish I'd known Ma longer; she was as gay as a lark in springtime. Even when she was lying there dying, she still had that same sunshine smile on her face. I'll wager that's why Pa took such a fancy to her that night. Anyway, 'twas she who taught me how to speak proper and read and write some. She kept house for the village priest a long time ago, and he gave her lessons now and then. At any rate, I'll work hard, my lady, and ye won't be sorry ye took me on, I promise ye!"

Upon recovering, Isabella had summoned Maude to Rushden Castle and had offered the old harridan whatever reward she desired.

"Ah, m'lady," the beldam had wheezed. "There be but one thing I ask of ye. I be getting on, ye know; even now, sometimes, late at night, I can hear that old Grim Reaper outside my cottage, a'knocking at my door. Well, I can't say as how I won't be glad to go, fer my bones be getting dry and brittle and my soul powerful weary; but I worry about my granddaughter. Except for me, Jocelyn ain't got any other folk, and she be a prideful wench besides; too good to marry the stonecutter's son, she were, though I boxed her ears for her disobedience, and the poor lad's heart were well nigh broke. If'n ye'd take her on, m'lady, I'd rest easier in my grave; I would."

And so the girl had acquired Jocelyn, who now served as her maid and companion.

"I don't know of any place on earth more beautiful than Grasmere," Isabella responded, at last, to Jocelyn's earlier words. "I feel at home here, even more so than I do at Rushden. I guess that's because Rushden truly belongs to Giles, and Grasmere is mine, all mine."

"La, it must be heaven to own a place like this, my lady," Jocelyn sighed. "Mayhap someday . . . nay—" she broke off with a little laugh and shook her head. "Nay, that's just wishful dreaming; I know. I'll never in my life own a house like this." Her voice was wistful.

"But riches aren't what make a person happy, Jocelyn," Isabella said gently. "'Tis the love and joy in your heart that do that."

She bit her lip and thought of Caerllywel's words that day. *Look to your heart, 'Sabelle,* he had told her, *for therein lies the answer.*

Well, she had looked, but even so, Isabella wasn't sure she knew the answer. That was why she had come to Grasmere—to find it.

Lionel Valeureux studied speculatively the tall towers of Grasmere rising up in the distance before him. With the diamond-shaped, lead-glass panes of its windows reflecting the gleaming rays of the spring sun, the manor house appeared almost like some magical fairy castle shimmering there upon the crest of the windswept moors—the perfect setting for the silvery nymph it contained.

Damn ye, 'Sabelle! Lionel swore silently to himself.

For months, he had tried to put the girl from his mind, but he had been unable to forget her nevertheless. Despite all that had happened, he wanted her still; and his marriage to Lady Gilliane Beaumaris had only intensified his desire for Isabella.

Lionel's mouth tightened angrily when he thought of his wife, the timid brown mouse he had been forced to wed.

Christ's son! Had there ever lived a more pathetic creature? Painfully shy and inadequate, she had been mortified by the boisterous, customary ritual of bedding on their wedding night and had actually burst into tears when her maids had disrobed her to show all present that her small thin body was without deformity or flaw. Her racking sobs had ruined everything for everyone. The drunken jests and ribald laughter that were normally such a good-natured part of the bedding had ceased as the guests had gradually, one by one, uncomfortably fallen still. Lionel had felt like a fool as the men had glanced at him covertly, amusement and pity mingled plainly on their faces. By God, the ignominy of it all! How dare Gilliane disgrace him, Lionel Valeureux, in such a fashion? Embarrassed and furious, he had taken her viciously to punish her for her idiotic behavior, then left her the following day.

"You'd best accustom yourself to my lovemaking, ye stupid little slut!" he had snarled cruelly to his terrified bride, obtaining a mean delight from the way she had cringed in fear. "For when I return, ye shall have more of the same! Aye, every night I spend with ye shall be as last eve—or worse! You'd best pray I get a brat on ye—and quickly— if ye have no desire to suffer my future visits to your bed!"

Lionel smiled wolfishly to himself as he remembered how poor Gilliane had wept and cowered before him, shuddering uncontrollably at the thought of his touching her as brutally as he had done on their wedding night. And he would, despite the fact that there would be little satisfaction in it. Oh, God. If only it had been 'Sabelle who'd lain beneath him!

His loins stirred achingly at the thought. How Lionel wanted her. He must have her; he must!

He paused for a moment, glancing back over his shoulder and cursing himself for not having come directly to Grasmere, going first to Rushden instead. But he'd had no way of knowing that Isabella was at the manor house, rather than her brother's keep.

She had been ill, Lord Hawkhurst had told Lionel coldly when he'd asked for Rushden's mistress, and the Earl had sent her to Grasmere so she might recuperate in peace. Icily,

Lionel had thanked Lord Hawkhurst for the information, not missing the spark of antagonism that had flared in the Earl's eyes toward him at the mention of Isabella's name, then continued on to the manor house.

Briefly, a muscle quirked in Lionel's hard, determined jaw. No doubt Lord Hawkhurst was hot on his heels to Grasmere, for even if he did not want the girl, the Earl would not relinquish easily that which he considered his. Well, there was no help for it.

Lionel dug his spurs into his stallion's sides and galloped on toward the manor house in the distance.

"Why have ye come, Lionel?" Isabella asked again as they made their way across the moors, Lionel having insisted on the stroll in order to escape from the curious eyes and ears of the servants. And if Lord Hawkhurst had indeed pursued him, it would take the Earl a while after his arrival to discover Lionel's and Isabella's whereabouts and put an end to their tryst.

"I wanted to see ye, of course," the heir of St. Saviour said.

"But—but why? After that day at the well—"

"I know, I know." He spoke impatiently, not giving the girl a chance to explain what had happened that afternoon. "I despised ye for that, but even so, I've not been able to get ye out of my mind. God knows, I have tried. But ye fill my thoughts every waking hour of the day, and at night, I dream of nothing save ye." Lionel suddenly stopped walking and forced Isabella to face him. " 'Tis as though ye have bewitched me, for I grow more obsessed with ye with every passing day. I tell ye, 'tis driving me mad! I want ye, 'Sabelle. Christ! How I want ye! I forgive ye for what happened that day at the well. Only say that Lord Hawkhurst means naught to ye, that ye are mine, now and for always!"

Hurt that he trusted her so little and could believe she had encouraged Warrick, as well as him, yet still want her, she turned her head away so he could not read the expression on her countenance. What kind of love was that?

"Did ye—did ye speak to Gloucester?"

"Nay," Lionel admitted at last. "But I shall, 'Sabelle, I

promise ye! 'Tis only that Richard has been much preoccupied of late with this battling of the Scots. There has been no time to approach him. . . ."

"Then I am sorry, Lionel, sorry for both of us: for I made a vow to God, when I was ill, that if He would but spare my life, I wouldst marry Warrick and think no more of ye."

"Nay, 'Sabelle! Ye cannot do this to me! Ye are mine. Mine! God's blood—" Lionel swore and, without warning, suddenly took her in his arms, raining searing kisses passionately upon her face, claiming her mouth possessively, demandingly, compelling her lips to yield to him, though she struggled against him.

"Take your hands off my betrothed!"

Lionel and Isabella jerked apart as though they had been shot at the sound of the frostily delivered command. Warrick stood before them, grimly slapping the side of one black leather boot with his riding crop. His dark visage was a distorted mask of anger, though he held himself in check.

Godamercy! Isabella thought. What was he doing here, at Grasmere, and what must he be thinking?

Jesù! What a fool he had been! Warrick was infuriated by the idea. Because of the dreadful guilt he had felt when Isabella had fallen sick, he had almost convinced himself of her sweet nature. Well, thank God, he had discovered his mistake in time! She was as wicked as Brangwen had ever thought about being—worse—for he had saved Isabella's life, and for that alone, she had owed him her loyalty. Well, that was gratitude for you, using her illness as an excuse to slip away and meet her lover! Only, somehow, the two had gotten their messages mixed up, and Lionel had gone to Rushden by mistake. No wonder the young fool had been in such a hurry to leave!

"Well, well," the Earl drawled, his voice harsh and seething with rage. "Isn't this a pretty sight?"

"Warrick, please, let me explain—" Isabella began, mortified that he should have discovered her with Lionel and in such a fashion.

Oh, dear God. What must he be thinking? she wondered again. That she was a wicked, deceitful, ungrateful bitch who, though he had saved her life, had played him false at the first opportunity. Nay, oh, nay! 'Twasn't true. 'Twasn't like that at all. If only he would give her a chance to explain. . . .

"Warrick—"

"Be silent, witch!" he hissed, moving toward her threateningly, as though he meant to strike her, causing her to cringe from the wrath upon his face. "What a fool ye are, madam," he jeered hatefully, and her worst fears were realized. "Did your lover promise to wed ye and save ye from my bed? Is that why ye ran so eagerly to his arms?" Warrick snorted with contempt when the girl made no reply, understanding now that it was useless to try to explain, to attempt to reason with him. "Nay, I thought not," he sneered. "Do ye know why, madam?" he went on ruthlessly, wanting to hurt her, as she had hurt him. "Nay? Shall I tell ye then?" The Earl smiled mockingly, nastily, as he thought of the report his squire Rhys had delivered to him on Lord Lionel Valeureux. "Your lover cannot wed ye, because he is already married!"

"Married!" Isabella cried involuntarily, stricken to the very core of her being.

She turned and stared at Lionel with shock, as though she'd never really looked at him before. Her grey-green eyes begged him silently to deny the Earl's accusation. But Lionel did not.

"Oh, aye, 'Sabelle," Warrick continued, hammering the words like nails into her heart. "He is wed to Lady Gilliane Beaumaris of Devizes, a plain brown wench, I'm told, nothing to compare to your silver beauty. But she is still your lover's wife all the same."

Isabella's head spun dizzily until she thought she would swoon. She reeled slightly on her feet, her limbs trembling violently with agitation and the aftermath of her sickness.

"Oh, Lionel," she breathed. "Lionel! Say 'tisn't true! Please," she pleaded desperately. "Say 'tisn't true!"

But he could not.

"I'm sorry, 'Sabelle." He confessed his duplicity at last.

"Oh, God, oh, God!" she wailed miserably, her world crumbling down about her. She had loved him—loved him—and all the time, he had been deceiving her. "Ye bastard!"

she spat bitterly; then, with all her small might, Isabella slapped the heir of St. Saviour hard across the face.

He never flinched from the blow, just stood there staring at her with an anguish to match her own in his eyes. The girl's hand flew to her mouth in horror as she saw the red mark that her palm had made on his cheek.

"Oh, God," she moaned again.

In that moment, despite himself, Warrick's heart ached for her, for he knew the desperate hope, the torment, and the agony she was feeling. Had he not felt as much when Brangwen had laughed in his face?

"'Sabelle," he said and held out one hand to her; but she ignored him and, picking up her skirts, ran blindly across the wild moors toward Grasmere.

Woodenly, the two men watched her go, neither making any effort to detain her flight. Then slowly, Lionel turned back to the Earl.

"Ye whoreson Welsh bastard." The heir of St. Saviour spoke lowly, his blue eyes glittering with hate. One hand went instinctively for his sword. "I shall slay ye for what ye have done."

Warrick only laughed, and the sound was not pleasant.

"Fool! Think ye I would sully my steel by engaging ye?" he asked. "A whip is good enough for the likes of ye"— the Earl indicated the riding crop he held in one hand— "and I shall be sore tempted to use it if ye do not leave Grasmere at once. Ye may be Gloucester's man," Warrick continued silkily when Lionel made no move to depart, "but I am the King's. Ye would be wise not to press me further," he warned.

Briefly, Lionel's fingers tightened on the hilt of his blade, but he did not draw the weapon after all. Reason had begun to set in, cooling his rage slightly. To draw steel on one of Edward's favorites would indeed be the act of a fool. There would be another time, another place; and perhaps then, Lord Hawkhurst would not rank so high at Court. The King was notoriously fickle.

"We shall meet again, my lord," Lionel promised the Earl vehemently, both men understanding the duel had only been postponed.

"And on that day, I shall kill ye," Warrick vowed softly. "Till then, remember that the Lady Isabella is mine."

Chapter Nineteen

THE LAST OF THE SMALL, DRUNKEN WEDDING PARTY HAD gone, closing the chamber door firmly behind them. Isabella was alone at last—alone, with her husband. She lay quite still beside him in the massive canopy bed they occupied, clutching the fine, white linen sheet to her naked body desperately, as though it might offer some protection against him. Earlier, she had consumed a great deal of wine to give herself courage for this night; but though the liquor had been warm, she still felt cold inside. She tried to tell herself there was naught to fear, that surely, the man who had married her would not abuse her now that he had her at his utter mercy; but still, she was afraid. As much as she had attempted to overcome the feeling, she could not bear for him to touch her, even though she owed him her very existence. Her reluctance to give what was legally his seemed poor payment indeed for the saving of her life, but Isabella could not help it. If he touched her, took her, she would belong to him for all time, be bound to him forever by more than just the vows they had spoken. And yet, how could she refuse him? Surely, her body was little enough to offer in exchange for her life. Nevertheless, she trembled a little, tears glistening on her cheeks, as she awaited the assault that was her husband's right.

Slowly, Warrick rolled over on his side, propping himself up on one elbow to study his bride. She was so hauntingly beautiful in the candlelight that it almost took his breath away. Her wide grey-green eyes were like seas before a storm, with their mysterious depths. Her long black lashes made dark, crescent smudges upon her cheeks when she closed the orbs to avoid his gaze. The Earl longed to trace the line of her straight, finely chiseled nose, to follow it down to her full pink lips, which quivered slightly, soft and inviting, yielding, exciting. He could almost taste them now, feel the tiny pulse beating at the hollow of her throat, kiss the pale breasts that swelled above the sheet she held so tightly to her chest. God, how he wanted her. But Isabella did not want him, Warrick knew.

She married me in a daze, he thought, because she was bitter and hurt and didn't care what happened to her. It is only now, in my bed, that the shock of Lord Lionel's perfidy has receded in her mind, and the full import of what it means to be wed to me has dawned on her. Now, she cares what becomes of her. She doesn't want me to touch her. Though I saved her life, she hates me: for I am also the man who exposed her lover for what he really was, breaking her heart with the knowledge. I am the man who is now her husband, not he.

The Earl stretched out one hand and caught the girl's jaw, gently turning her face toward him. Blindly, through the blur of her tears, she stared up at him, her eyes dark and shadowed with pain. For a moment, her fear stirred him to pity. She had borne so much. He could wait a few days before making her his. Then he recalled the sight of her nakedness when her maids had disrobed her, and his loins quickened once more. Isabella was his wife, by God. She had no right to say him nay, and Warrick would not let her deny him in any event. He would take her by force if necessary, for sooner or later, he intended to have her. Aye, 'twould be better if he took her now, despite her fright. To wait would only prolong her agonized suspense.

"'Sabelle."

She stiffened at the word and attempted to turn away, but he compelled her to go on looking at him.

"'Sabelle . . ." He bent to kiss her.

She inhaled raggedly.

"Warrick, don't. Please. Please don't touch me."

"I saved your life," he reminded her sharply, drawing back a little, his eyes narrowing slightly. "And ye are my wife besides."

"Well, I wish ye had not. I wish I were not."

"Do ye? Dost truly think ye wouldst be better off dead? Dost truly believe *he* would have loved ye any better?" The

Earl's amber eyes flashed with anger as he thought of Lord
Lionel Valeureux.

Isabella bit her lip.

"Perhaps not, but at least he would not have despised
me."

"I do not despise ye, 'Sabelle," Warrick told her.

"Don't ye?"

"Nay."

"Oh, God," the girl breathed with anguish. "Let us at
least have honesty between us—if nothing else. Ye never
wished to marry me."

"'Twas nothing against ye, 'Sabelle. I had no desire to
wed any wench. But as the King commanded me to marry,
I would as lief have wed ye as any other. At least I wanted
ye . . . still want ye. . . ." His voice trailed off meaningfully
as he moved to take her in his arms once more.

"Wouldst rape an unwilling maid?" Isabella suddenly
cried out in protest against him.

He must not touch her; he must not! She would be lost,
she thought again, lost to him forever. Somehow, deep in
her heart, she knew it was true. He would waken that dark
side of her, set it aflame with desire, and she would never
be free of him, not as long as she lived.

He laid his hand upon her throat, his eyes glittering
strangely.

"Willing or nay, have ye I shall," he vowed with fierce
intent.

Afterward, Isabella never remembered just exactly how
it had happened; but somehow, suddenly, Warrick was kissing her, kissing her as she had never been kissed before in
her life, draining her very soul from her being, then pouring
it back in again, filling her to overflowing, blinding her to
everything but him. Her heart pounded jerkily in her breast
with a hope she feared to feel and something akin to pain
that came with it: for the promise of a love that would last
for always was on his lips, and she knew it was but a lie.
No man loved like that. Lionel had not loved her like that.
Warrick did not love her like that, would never love her
like that; so why was his mouth kissing her like this, as
though he were giving every part of himself to her and

asking for every part of her in return? Oh, why did he want her heart when he did not love her? Wasn't it enough that Lionel had hurt her deeply? Must Warrick tear her apart inside too?

"Nay, oh, nay," she whimpered, trying to free herself from his all-enveloping embrace, but his arms only closed about her more tightly, holding her near, pressing her to him.

Oh, Christ, sweet Christ, what had she done to him? He had meant only to take her, as he had taken countless other wenches; but from the moment he had kissed her, Warrick had been swept away by something stronger than lust, deeper than desire. It was as though Isabella had been made for him, for she fit against him perfectly, her gentle curves just right for the length of his hard, muscular body. The rose scent of her perfume invaded his flaring nostrils, engulfing him with its sultry, enticing fragrance. He felt as though he were drowning in it—and he did not care. The taste of her lips was sweeter than the wine he had drunk earlier. How was such possible? Surely, the girl had bewitched him in some manner, drugged his liquor with some potion. Why else would his head be spinning in this fashion? Why else would his flesh feel as though it were on fire where it pressed against her yielding softness? Why else would he be filled with this strange, all-consuming presentiment that his destiny for all time lay in Isabella's arms? The idea was ridiculous! She was only a wench, like any other. But still, he could not halt the tide of overwhelming passion that rushed through him, making him long to take her savagely and make her his, daring her to deny that she belonged to him— and him alone. He wanted her—all of her—not just her body, but her heart and soul as well; and yet, if someone had asked him why, he could not have replied. He knew only that the night was suddenly filled with magic, and he yearned for Isabella as he had never desired another woman in his life.

"'Sabelle, 'Sabelle," he moaned hoarsely against her mouth.

He kissed the trembling corners of her lips, thrilled by the manner in which they quivered beneath his mouth. Then he teased them gently with his tongue, tracing the outline of her lips as though he were memorizing every curve, every detail, of their so sweetly vulnerable shape. Though she tried to resist him, still, he parted her mouth, forced it open with his tongue, ravaged it tenderly, at first, caressingly, tasting every drop of the nectar within, savoring it lingeringly until the fever in his blood drove him to be more demanding. He ground his lips down on hers hard, almost savagely, so she was compelled to kiss him back, did not even realize she was doing so. Her mind was a blank, a heady swirl of dizzying sensations that flooded her being like a maelstrom, sweeping all thought away. Her mouth grew warm, tingling inside, where his tongue pillaged it, devoured it, as though he could not get enough of her. And like a piece of driftwood, she was carried away by the tide of emotions he was unleashing inside of her. Oh, God. What was he doing to her?

'Tis the wine, she thought. Aye, 'tis the wine. Surely, 'tis only the wine.

But she knew, in her heart, it was not.

"Warrick . . . Warrick," she murmured his name aloud, a sigh of wanting that fell plaintively in the silence, and she did not even hear it. She was melting inside, her bones turning to liquid ore as unconsciously she molded herself against him, her hands reaching up to entwine themselves in the rich tobacco-brown waves of his hair.

Impatiently, roughly, he yanked away the sheet to bare her nakedness to his raking gaze, but she did not care. She did not even see how his eyes darkened with hot hunger at the sight of her creamy flesh. She knew only that his hands were moving on her body, stroking her lightly: her throat, her breasts, her belly, her thighs. His fingers were like feathers everywhere upon her skin; she was shivering all over from his touch, shuddering with the delight and desire he was arousing in her.

He was so gentle with her; why had she ever feared him? Truly, no maid had ever had a more tender initiation into the rites of lovemaking. How strange that it should be so. He did not love her. He had married her only to fulfill the King's command. Why, then, was Warrick taking her as though she were a beloved bride? And why was she responding so wantonly to his kisses, his caresses? It was Lionel she loved—wasn't it?

Warrick's heart raced as he explored her body. He marveled at the softness of her skin, like velvet beneath his hands, and the smallness of her frame, so very fragile, she seemed almost like a will'o-the-wisp in his arms. He was so strong and powerful; he could have conquered her easily, without effort. But her willing surrender had become important to him. Warrick wanted her to want him as much as he desired her.

His palms cupped her breasts, tightened gently upon the full ripe mounds that filled his hands. Lightly, he brushed her nipples, over and over, until they were hard little peaks of excitement, aching for his caresses, his kisses. His fingers slid slowly over the rosy crests; his thumbs flicked at the tiny buds. He took one small firm button in his mouth. Languidly, he sucked it until Isabella felt a strange yearning begin to grow inside of her. His teeth closed gingerly about the pink tip, nuzzled it, nibbled it. His tongue teased it moistly, licking it, swirling about it in the most delicious manner, sending ripples of ecstasy radiating from it in all directions. He could feel Isabella trembling and saw her fling her head back in exultation as the quicksilver waves washed through her body. She felt as though she were floating, floating like spindrift upon a sea of rapture. Oh, sweet *Jesù*. How she wanted him!

His lips closed over her other nipple, stimulating it as he had done its mate, then traveled deliberately down the length of her to her belly. His hands slipped down her legs, fingers trailing along the insides of her thighs, then back up, then down again, taunting her.

A tormenting ache started deep in the secret place of Isabella's womanhood and spread through her blood like wildfire. She burned for Warrick to quench the heat of urgency within her, the blaze that scorched her so tempestuously, craving release. Instinctively, she arched against him, whimpering a little.

In response, his hand sought her *there* at last, found the downy curls and pliant folds of the valley wherein no man before had ever trod. His fingers caressed her rhythmically, tantalizingly, until she was warm and wet, pulsating with the mounting beat of frantic desire that thrummed in her veins. Slowly, sensing her need, he eased the ache, filling her inside, stroking the depths of her with tiny, fluttering movements of his fingers that wakened her passion to its fullest, roused it to a feverish pitch that was almost unbearable.

He pressed his mouth to the unfolding petals of her woman's flower, tasting the honeyed nectar of her being. He tongued her deliberately until she writhed beneath him, moaning down low in her throat, her hands drawing him even nearer. She inhaled sharply with shock and pleasure at the intimate contact as the slow, throbbing tremors within her started to build with an intensity that made her think she would surely explode if they continued. And then suddenly, without warning, it was as though a thousand stars had burst within her, sending bolts of white-hot coruscation through her body. She gasped breathlessly once more, exhaled, panted raggedly for air.

No longer able to contain himself, Warrick rose, covering her body with his own. His hard maleness sought and found her, entered her forcefully, so she barely felt the sudden stab of pain that accompanied his assault, though she cried out until he silenced her lips with his own, kissing her fervently, as though again, he could not get enough of her. His mouth slashed like a brand across her cheek to her temple and then the silvery tresses of her long damp hair. His breath was warm in her ear, where he muttered thickly, brokenly, words that Isabella only dimly heard, only half-understood; she was so filled with rapture. Deliberately, he withdrew, then drove into her once more; and this time, he did not leave her but lay atop her instead, accustoming her to the feel of him inside of her.

She could feel the sinews in his powerful arms standing out like cords, supporting his weight as finally he began to move again, plunging into her over and over, gyrating down into the moist, molten core of her.

Never interrupting the motion, he rolled slightly to one side, taking her with him so she rested upon one hip. He draped her free leg in the crook of his arm and grasped her buttocks, helping her meet his now-rapid thrusts. Isabella could feel the muscles in his sweating back ripple beneath her calf as she tightened her leg more firmly about him and put her arms around his neck.

Warrick threw his head back, breathing heavily, his hawklike face naked with desire as he stared down at her.

"Do ye want me?" he asked, his amber shards dark with passion and filled with a strange expectancy. "Tell me ye want me, 'Sabelle!"

The girl shivered with an odd thrill of vulnerability at the words, for it was as though Warrick were demanding her surrender, as though she no longer belonged to herself but to him. . . .

"Aye, I want ye," she whispered, unable to deny him.

His eyes closed. He groaned and crushed her to him possessively, burying his face in her shoulder, kissing that sensitive place at the curve of her neck, spiraling into her faster and faster until she cried out once more at the scintillating suns that flared within her, turning her to brilliant flame. The earth seemed to rock beneath her. Her head reeled. For one blind, exhilarating eternity, Isabella thought she would faint. As though from a distance, she heard Warrick's low moan of joy, felt the racking shudders that shook his body until, at last, he was still.

It was over.

He kissed her gently, lightly, several times on the mouth, then laid his head again upon her shoulder. Quietly, they rested together, waiting for the frantic pace of their breathing and hearts to slow. Finally, Warrick moved from Isabella's body, though still, he held her close, cradling her tenderly in his warm embrace.

They did not speak, for neither knew what to say. They had been swept away by the unexpected magic of the night, and now, they were confused and a little frightened by what had happened between them. It was not love. Nay, it could not be love. Love was but a lie that only fools believed.

For a moment, Warrick stared at Isabella intently, searchingly, as though seeking something he had not previously thought to find. But she closed her eyes and turned away from his gaze so he could not see the expression on her countenance. Physically and emotionally drained, she was too vulnerable to face him now, this instant. He was so clever at guessing her thoughts; he would know immediately how his lovemaking had affected her, the strange hope and yearning for him that had risen in her heart; and he would use the knowledge to hurt her. To the girl's surprise, Warrick did not force her to look at him once more, as he had done earlier. He merely lay there beside her, playing idly with a strand of her silky, tangled hair and thinking.

It was only later, much later, that, despite her whispered protests, he took her in his arms again, this time teaching her about himself and the things he desired as well.

Chapter Twenty

ISABELLA STIRRED GENTLY AS THE FIRST PALE STREAKS OF the rose dawn lit the sky. There was something different about the day; she knew. But it was not until she felt the tightening of Warrick's arms about her that she realized what it was. In a rush, the events of last night came flooding back to her, causing her to blush painfully with shame and mortification. God's blood! How could she have behaved so wantonly, allowed herself to be so completely conquered by this man who lay beside her, surrendered so willingly to his strong, enveloping embrace?

'Twas the wine, she thought dully. 'Twas only the wine.

But the girl knew, in her heart, it was not true. Oh, sweet *Jesù*. What had Warrick done to her?

Cautiously, so as not to waken him, she turned her head slightly to study him curiously, as though somehow expecting to find him changed; but he was not. Though the hard lines of his face were not as pronounced in sleep, there was still an arrogance about his dark, handsome visage that could not be denied. But strangely enough, Isabella felt no fear of him now. Caerllywel had been right. Warrick had not beaten or abused her, as the girl had been half-afraid he might; and though she suspected the Earl would not be above dealing her a few sharp slaps in a rage, she knew now that he would not physically ill-use her, as many men did their wives. Had Warrick been as cruel as she had first thought, he would not have taken her with such tenderness last night, taking the time to be certain she knew pleasure too. He would simply have raped her instead, brutally, without care for her feelings. But he had not. There was some kindness and compassion in him. At least Isabella could be grateful for that. At least she would not have to spend the rest of her life with a man who would savagely torment her.

The rest of her life. How strange that sounded. How strange to think that every morning now, for as long as she lived, she would awaken with Warrick lying beside her, one arm about her possessively, one hand tangled in her cascading mane of hair. In the past, the girl had always slept alone. Now, unless her husband were gone, she would never sleep alone again, for Warrick was not a man who would not claim what was rightfully his. He had made that quite clear last night. Isabella shivered a little as she recalled the words he had spoken.

Willing or nay, have ye I shall.

Aye, Warrick would take her whenever he wished, and she would be helpless against him. Worse yet was the terrible knowledge that, despite what she felt in her heart and mind, her body wanted him; and he knew it. Yet, there had been more than just lust between them last night; surely, there had been. Did a man truly take a woman as Warrick had taken her if there was not some spark of caring in him for her? Isabella bit her lip. Her knowledge of courtship and lovemaking was so limited that she did not know. Perhaps all men were liars and cheats, masters of deception and duplicity who stole your heart, then shattered it into a million pieces. The girl sighed wistfully, her heart aching at the depressing thought. She wondered how it would have been, had it been Lionel who had taken her last night, Lionel, whom she had loved.

Warrick, who had awakened and was watching her silently, saw her face soften briefly, dreamily, and guessed the cause. His nostrils flared whitely. Isabella was his wife, by God; and though he had taken her fiercely last night, with a torrid passion that had inflamed them both, he had been gentle with her, and she had responded to him in a manner he had not believed possible. He had almost dared to hope she did not truly hate him after all, that they might yet make something of this marriage they had not wanted. Now, this morn, though he held his bride in his arms, Warrick knew her heart and mind were with Lionel Valeureux. The thought filled him with rage.

"Do not even think of him, madam," the Earl ordered coldly, startling the girl. Marry-go-up! How long had he been awake, and how had he read her mind so easily? It was uncanny, and for a moment, all her fear of him returned. Was she to have no secrets from this man? "Like it or not, ye are mine," he continued warningly, "and I will have no other in your thoughts. Do ye understand, 'Sabelle?" His golden eyes pierced her own grey-green ones, as though he could see into her very soul.

Isabella shuddered slightly and turned away.

"I—I do not know what ye mean, my lord," she said. "My thoughts were of no one special."

"Do not lie to me, madam!" Warrick snapped, catching her jaw and compelling her to look at him. "I saw your face, and 'twas easy enough to read. Well, ye will never know the answer to your question, for ye will never share the bed of Lionel Valeureux or any other man save me. Is that clear? Ye are my wife—"

"Well, I wish I were not!"

Warrick's mouth tightened with anger. His eyes narrowed.

"No more than do I, my lady; I assure ye. Nevertheless, 'tis done, and we must live with it. And if ye wish to find some semblance of happiness in our relationship, ye had best learn to obey me."

"Happiness! What do ye know of happiness, my lord? Ye, who are bitter and cruel! Ye know naught of joy. Naught!" Isabella cried out in defense.

Warrick smiled hatefully, mockingly.

"Do I not?" he asked. "Once more, ye lie, madam. Tell

me, if ye can, that I didst not give ye joy last night and receive it in return."

The girl gasped and flushed with embarrassment. God-amercy! How could he speak so openly of the intimate act they had shared last night? 'Twas indecent!

"Ye dare to remind me—" she began.

"That ye surrendered to me willingly?" He raised one eyebrow devilishly, then laughed. "Oh, I shall do more than remind ye, 'Sabelle." His eyes raked her meaningfully. "Aye, I shall do much more than that."

"Nay," she breathed, trying to yank away from him. "Don't touch me!"

Easily, he retained his hold of her.

"Why so eager to flit away, my fairy queen?" he inquired jeeringly. "The morn is early yet, and I lust for thee."

"Lust, aye," Isabella hissed. "That is all 'tis!"

"Did ye expect something more, my lady? Love mayhap? Alas, how wicked of me to crush your hope—"

"I hoped for nothing, do ye hear? I want nothing from ye!"

"Well, that's too bad, 'Sabelle, because I want something from ye," Warrick told her intently. "Come, madam," he coaxed. "Ye know 'twill do ye no good to fight me; and though ye will doubtless find it difficult to believe, I really have no desire to hurt ye."

"Don't ye?"

"Nay, my lady. I wouldst but give ye pleasure, as I didst last night."

"Pleasure! I knew no pleasure, my lord—"

"Didn't ye?" Slowly, Warrick pulled the sheet from her body, exposing Isabella's nakedness to his hungry eyes. He laid one hand upon her breast. Almost immediately, to the girl's shame, the rosy crest hardened at his touch. He laughed once more. "Didn't ye, 'Sabelle?" he queried again.

And then he was kissing her, ravishing her, despite her struggles, setting her afire as he had done last night. When it was finished, he moved from her slowly, then rose and began to dress.

"'Twould be wise, in the future, madam, if ye did not lie to me," he said. "Now summon your women, and start packing the best of your clothes and jewels. We leave Rush-den Castle within the week."

Surprised, Isabella sat up, drawing the sheet up to cover her nakedness.

"Leave Rushden! But—but where do we go, my lord?"

"To Court, of course. Things are well in hand here—Master Potter and Sir Lindael can oversee the keep quite adequately until our return—and I have tarried far too long from the palace as 'tis. There is no telling what Dorset and Hastings may have done in my absence to discredit me. Besides, His Grace would be deeply offended if I did not present ye at Court. Ye are, after all, his ward; and as 'twas he who insisted on this marriage, I am certain he will wish to be assured our wedding has indeed taken place."

Isabella bit her lip as she remembered the ceremony that had been nothing at all as she had sometimes imagined during her childhood. She and Warrick had been married quietly in the chapel at Rushden, with only a handful of the castle's knights and maids present to witness the rite. Giles had not even been there, for Isabella had feared he would do something rash to prevent the wedding from taking place, had he known about it. She would write him today, informing him of her marriage, saying only that it was by the King's command she had wed their warden, Lord Warrick ap Tremayne, Earl of Hawkhurst, and that she was well content with her husband. It would be enough. It had to be, for the girl could not bring herself to explain about Lionel and how he had deceived her. The heir of St. Saviour was Giles's foster brother and dearest friend. No matter how deeply Lionel had hurt her, Isabella could not destroy the bond between him and her brother.

"'Sabelle." Warrick spoke, bringing her back, with a start, to the present. "Why dost thou linger in bed? Do ye wish me to rejoin ye?" He grinned wickedly, as though he were already contemplating this.

"Nay. Nay," she answered hastily. "I was—I was but waiting for ye to leave."

"Why?" he inquired and then, at her blush, drawled with amusement, "Oh, for Christ's sake, Isabella! How can ye be so shy of me after what we shared last night and this morn?"

The girl flushed even more painfully with embarrassment.

"Oh! How can ye speak of such things to me?" she asked, mortified.

"And just why should I not? There was naught wrong in what we did. In fact, I enjoyed it very much. Besides, ye are my wife—"

"So ye keep reminding me, my lord," the girl put in dryly.

"And I may discuss what I choose with ye," he went on as though she had not interrupted him. "I'm afraid you'll just have to get used to it, sweetheart."

The endearment came naturally to his lips, surprising them both; and for an instant, the magic of last night sparked between them once more. This time, it was Warrick who turned away.

"Arise, my lady," he growled, his voice sounding oddly constricted. "Ye have lain abed long enough to set the whole fortress gossiping about my virility and your nature. No doubt I shall have gained the admiration of every man in the keep for my prowess and your willingness to receive me."

To Isabella's horror, she recognized this was probably the truth. She glanced at the little clock that sat upon the table by the bed. Why, 'twas nearly noon! All would realize the marriage had long been consummated—and not just once, but several times! She could already picture the sly, knowing looks of merriment that would be directed toward Warrick and herself, the bawdily insinuating jests that would be told. She could have wept with vexation and despair as she fairly flew from the bed and scrambled hurriedly into her robe so she might summon her maids.

She was just reaching for the chamber door when Warrick's arm suddenly shot out, preventing her from sliding the bolt back.

"Wait!" he commanded curtly, striding to the bed.

Briefly, he stared down at the fine white linen sheet upon

which they'd lain. He raised one eyebrow coolly as, at last, he spied the blood stain he was seeking.

"What is it, Warrick? What's wrong?" Isabella queried, puzzled.

"I wanted to be certain the proof of your virginity was plain upon the sheet," he informed her.

Isabella blanched, as though he had struck her. Her hands clenched tightly by her sides.

"Did ye doubt ye wouldst find it, my lord?" she questioned icily, hurt and indignant.

"Nay, 'Sabelle. I knew last night I was the first. 'Twas only that I wished to be sure others would not doubt it. If there had been no proof of your virginity for them to see, ye wouldst have been publicly disgraced. Ye know that."

Aye, she did. She was ashamed she had been so quick to judge her husband unfairly when he had only been thinking of her.

"I—I'm sorry, Warrick."

The apology was stilted, but at least she had spoken it. He gazed at the woman who was now his wife, and for a moment, Warrick wanted desperately something he could not name.

"'Sabelle—" he began, but the almost pleading word had come too late.

Isabella had gone.

BOOK TWO

*Rose
of
Rapture*

Chapter Twenty-one

The Road to London, England, 1480

ALTHOUGH HER HUSBAND RODE AT HER SIDE, STILL, ISA-
bella was more excited than she'd ever been in her life as
they traveled toward London. Never had she journeyed so
far from Rushden and viewed as many wondrous sights as,
to her delight, she saw now. Eagerly, her eyes, wide with
marvel, took everything in, awed and overwhelmed by the
towns through which they passed, much larger than any she
had ever seen. She was skeptical and dumbfounded when
Warrick told her that London was even bigger, for the girl
could not conceive of such, even in her imagination. New
too was the deference all showed to her as the Earl's bride.
Though Lady Isabella Ashley of Rushden had commanded
respect, the Countess of Hawkhurst, wife to one of the
King's favorites, wielded a power that was almost intoxicating. Isabella found herself petted and pampered and waited
on hand and foot as she had never been before; and she
thought wryly to herself that there was something to be said,
after all, for having a man like her husband at her side.
Warrick had but to lift an eyebrow in that devilish fashion
of his, and all quailed before him, scurried to do his bidding,
and grew faint if everything was not to his liking. As his
bride, Isabella lacked for nothing; and to her surprise, in
all things, she came first and foremost with the Earl.

Each morning, Sir Bevan, Warrick's master-at-arms,
made certain the girl was accorded a place at the head of
the cavalcade, so she would not be smote with grit from
the horses' flying hooves as they rode along, and saw that
her flask was filled with cool fresh water to quench her
thirst as the day wore on. Every so often, the knight would

appear at her side to inquire if there was aught she needed, and she had but to ask a thing, and it would be done. Several times, Isabella was forced to turn away to hide her smile when Sirs Eadric, Thegn, and Beowulf grumbled under their breath about Sir Bevan's attentiveness to her.

At midday, the party would stop at some roadside inn for lunch, and there, Warrick never failed to hand Isabella down from her saddle, escort her inside, and demand a private room, where she might dine and rest. Usually, he took his meals with her as well, as did Caerllywel, and made certain she received the choicest of the food and drink that was served them. At night, he engaged the finest of chambers for her; and Alice, Jocelyn, and the two other maids who attended the girl were kept busy unpacking Isabella's coffers and laundering and airing her own personal linens before they were put on the bed, Warrick being of the firm opinion that all inns' sheets were infested with lice and bedbugs and unfit for him and Isabella to sleep on.

She wondered at his consideration for her, for she had not expected it; and once, when she questioned him about it, the Earl glanced at her impatiently, frowning.

"Ye are my wife," he said for the hundredth time, as though this explained everything. "Didst think I would ill-treat ye?"

"N—nay, at least I hoped ye would not. But then, neither did I believe ye wouldst go out of your way to be kind me. I—I know ye didst not wish to wed me."

"We have been over this before, madam. Whether we like it or not, the deed is done. We are married, and I would scarcely abuse ye for that when 'tis no fault of your own. God's wounds! I am not a monster, my lady, though ye have accused me of being such in the past. As long as ye are mine—and please me—ye will want for naught. Much as ye may believe otherwise, I do not desire your unhappiness."

Thoughtfully, Isabella considered this last remark as the days passed, and the entourage rode toward London. It seemed a strange thing for Warrick to have told her when he had hurt her so deeply by exposing Lionel's deceit. But gradually, as she pondered the matter, the girl realized the only times the Earl had truly wounded her had been when he'd believed her unfaithful to him, either in body or mind. She recognized then that Caerllywel had been right about his brother. Warrick had been so terribly injured by Brangwen's betrayal of him that he found it difficult to trust any woman, and he was too proud to be made a fool of again. That was why he watched Isabella so fiercely, so intently, like the hawk whose badge he wore, growing angry and jealous if even her thoughts strayed to another man.

At last, I think I'm beginning to understand him, the girl decided. He is afraid to love. How strange that it should be thus when he does not even fear death. Yet, 'tis true. He is afraid to love, for to love, one must risk being hurt. Warrick cannot bear that, so he asks only for loyalty instead. 'Tis as Caerllywel told me. Warrick is hard—and sometimes cruel—not because he is unkind or unjust, but because he is so vulnerable. As long as I am true to him, in both body and mind, he will be a good husband to me, just as he is a good lord to the men who serve him so faithfully. And perhaps, in time, as Caerllywel said, Warrick may even come to care for me a little, and my life with him will not be so bad after all. Even now, I really have no cause for complaint, for he sees to my every need, even in bed.

Isabella blushed with mortification at this last unbidden thought, glancing quickly, surreptitiously, at her husband to discover if he had discerned the direction her silent musings had taken. To her relief, he was conversing with Caerllywel and appeared to be paying her no heed. She exhaled thankfully, for Warrick seemed to have an uncanny knack for knowing what went on in her head, and it was difficult for her to hide her innermost feelings from him. How horrible it would be if her husband were to learn how— now—just the sight of his muscles rippling beneath his doublet stirred her, making the girl long for the evening, when they would close their chamber door and shut out the rest of the world, and Warrick would take her in his strong arms and make love to her. Now, after so many nights of lying in his warm embrace, she made no protest against him when he took possession of her. It was useless to deny him;

he would have her anyway, despite her struggles; and it was pointless to fight him when her body so obviously desired him.

Aye, she wanted him, just as he wanted her. It was not love, but it was more than many had.

Warrick saved my life, Isabella reminded herself, *and despite all that has occurred between us, he is trying to make our marriage work. Can I do any less? Nay. I must put Lionel from my heart and mind and devote myself to being a good wife to Warrick, as I promised when I knelt before the priest and plighted my troth.*

Still, it was so difficult to do. Though she now longed to despise him, Isabella had loved Lionel deeply, and she found even the pain of his duplicity could not completely obliterate her gentler feelings toward him. Again and again, she told herself she hated him. But then, just when she thought she was over him, something would happen to make her recall the love they'd shared, and a thousand treasured memories would flood her very being before the anguish of Lionel's perfidy pierced her anew. The gleam of sunlight upon a young man's golden hair, a pair of laughing blue eyes looking into her own grey-green ones, a white rose handed to her by a child, a fragrant bar of sandalwood soap given to her by an innkeeper's wife—such small, unimportant things, they were, that made her remember and yet yearn to forget.

Oh, Lionel. Lionel!

Only at night, in Warrick's arms, did the ghost of Isabella's first love cease to haunt her, driven away by her husband's kisses, his caresses. Once more, the girl gazed at Warrick searchingly.

Aye, at last, she could understand the hard shell he had built around himself in order to survive. The betrayal of one's love was not a wound that was easily healed.

There is magic in these tender hands. Can ye not set them to curing the ache in Waerwic's soul? If ye can, ye may find he will love ye more truly than ever a man has loved a woman.

"I will try," Isabella vowed softly to herself. "Before God, I will try."

* * *

Vast and cluttered, the city of London sprawled along the
River Thames in a haphazard jumble of cacophony and
confusion. The air reverberated with the lusty cries of merchants hawking their wares, each trying to out-shout his
competitors as he advertised the bargains available at his
stand. Candlewick Street was a close huddle of cloth shops,
before which the peddlers had set up their carts to display
bright bolts of material of every color and weave. On West
Cheap were the more elegant establishments and stalls of
the goldsmiths and jewelers, which contrasted sharply with
the marketplaces of the fishmongers, ironmongers, and vin-
ters that could be found on Thames Street, where the tangy
smell of freshly caught fish pervaded the nostrils, and the
violent pounding of hammer upon anvil assaulted the ears.
Often, the bolder of the vendors could be seen accosting
passersby; and the unfortunate, captive customers would be
forced to listen to a barrage of demands, pleas, and whee-
dling before they either purchased the wares arrayed for
their inspection or escaped from the persistent merchants
by threatening to call the guard.

Occasionally, fights broke out here and there upon the
streets and especially around the docks, where exotic goods
from far-off places were being busily unloaded from the
boats and barges that clogged the wharves. Isabella discerned the fragrant scents of cinnamon and clove among
the many other spicy odors that wafted deliciously through
the air, mingling with the enticing aroma of newly baked
bread and pastries that emanated from the bakeries. From
the Thames itself came that peculiar, dank smell always
associated with rivers, accompanied by a slightly damp breeze
that stirred faintly, sending tiny waves rippling across the
waters that lapped gently at hulls and piers alike.

With the wind rose the gay trill of the flute and twang
of the lute as wandering minstrels moved from corner to
corner, pausing, now and then, to pass their caps for small
donations. There were mimes and mummers, acrobats and
jugglers too, and once, Isabella saw a man with a monkey
that danced to the tune of a carillon and held out a battered
tin cup for coins. The jingle-jangle of the sovereigns was

lost in a smattering of applause that gave way, in turn, to the sounds of raised voices warning, "Make way, make way," before the clatter of horses' hooves and carriage wheels, which rumbled over the cobblestones and paving blocks, sent the gathered crowd scattering rapidly. There had been more than one poor, unwary townsperson trampled to death by the steed of a careless, impatient lord or crushed beyond all recognition beneath the churning, rimmed wheels of a fast-moving vehicle. Isabella's breath caught in her throat as she saw a ragged child barely escape from such a fate, and she pressed her mare close to Warrick's stallion for protection, somewhat frightened by the hustle and bustle of London.

There was naught to fear with her husband at her side, however, for the throng seemed to melt away before Warrick's hawk-adorned banner and the cries of his men.

"Make way! Make way for the Earl and Countess of Hawkhurst."

Then, at last, they were entering the royal residence, the palace known as the Tower.

Designed by a monk named Gundulf, and built by William the Conqueror, the original structure of the palace, which formed the core of the residence, was named White Tower. It was not beautiful, for it had been intended to stand as evidence of the power of the Normans. Its tall, thick, whitewashed walls were constructed of giant slabs of pale blond limestone, which had been imported from the quarries of Caen, in Normandy, and hard, rough Portland ragstone, which had been brought from Kent. The walls were topped by four turrets, three of which were rectangular, one of which was round and used as an observatory.

Over the years, around this primary fortress had been built a series of gateways, walls, bastions, and towers that made the palace one of the most formidable strongholds in all of Europe.

They entered the residence by means of the Lion's Gate, riding across a stone causeway and the wooden drawbridge that spanned the outer moat. Then came a barbican known as Lion Tower (for it was there the King's royal menagerie was housed), followed by another drawbridge and portcullis that barred the way to the Middle Tower. Beyond the Middle Tower was yet another causeway and drawbridge that stretched across the inner moat to the Tower at the Gate, the gatehouse of the outer ward. After passing through that portcullis, they reached the Bell Tower, which guarded the inner bailey and housed the warning bell that called the fortress to arms. Then came the towers that were built into the inner wall. There were so many of these that Isabella, as Warrick pointed them out to her and told her their names, thought she would never get them all straight.

On the western wall was Beauchamp Tower, where Thomas Beauchamp, third Earl of Warwick, had been imprisoned in 1397. On the northern wall were Robyn the Devylls Tower; Flint Tower, which contained the most horrible dungeons in the fortress and was sometimes called Little Hell; Bowyer Tower, where the King's bowmaker had his workrooms and lodgings; Brick Tower, and Martin Tower. On the eastern wall were Constable Tower; Broad Arrow Tower; and Salt Tower, which had formerly been known as Julius Caesar's Tower, because it was said the Romans had built their first wooden fortress on the site. On the southern wall were Lanthorn Tower; Hall Tower (which was sometimes called Record Tower, as it was there the official records were kept); and Garden Tower. On the outer wall, opposite Hall Tower, were St. Thomas's Tower, named for Thomas à Becket, which stood guard over Traitor's Gate and whose stairs led directly to the Thames; Cradle Tower, which also had a gate that opened onto the river; Well Tower, which contained the vault; the Tower Leading to the Iron Gate; and the Tower Above the Iron Gate.

In the center of all this stood White Tower, flanked on either side by Cole Harbour, which was actually two towers joined by a walkway, and Wardrobe Tower.

Isabella was certain she would become lost several times before learning her way about the vast palace, so once they were comfortably installed in their lodgings and had bathed and eaten a light repast, she asked Warrick to show her about the residence. The tour started off pleasantly enough, but the girl was soon sorry they had not kept to their chamber after all when several of the courtiers, spying Warrick's return, foisted their unwelcome presence on the newlyweds and began flirting outrageously with Isabella. Though she did nothing to encourage their attentions, still, they persisted, not in the least daunted by her attempts to rebuff them or Warrick's darkening frown. The final straw came when one brash young cavalier, made heady by several cups of wine, worshipfully fell to his knees and dubbed Isabella the Rose of Rapture, then proceeded to strew in her path a bunch of white roses, which he had picked earlier from the King's gardens, reminding her, painfully, of Lionel for a moment.

At this point, Warrick lost his temper and, grabbing the squire up by the scruff of his neck, shook him roughly before sending the young man on his way with a well-aimed kick to his posterior. Red-eared, the courtier snatched up his cap, which had fallen off, and, bowing and muttering his apologies to Isabella amid the laughter of the rest, hastily made his departure. Shortly thereafter, the remainder of her cavaliers also found it prudent to make their adieus, and the girl was left alone with a highly enraged husband.

"Madam," Warrick growled as he faced her wrathfully, his hands clenched tightly by his sides, as though he were trying to prevent himself from striking her. "Ye purposely encouraged those men to dangle after ye as though ye were no better than an East End trull!"

"My lord, I did not!" Isabella gasped, hurt and angered by the unfairness of the accusation. "I was but pleasant, as well ye know. 'Twas your jealousy of the courtiers' attentions to me—and not my behavior—that caused your temper to grow so foul. Now ye do but seek to vent your ire on me because ye made a fool of yourself over a young lad's drunken flattering of me. Doubtless, the tale will be all over Court by this eve! How I will hold my head up, I do not know," the girl sniffed disdainfully.

Her eyes flashed as she tossed her head, seemingly impervious to her husband's blackening visage, though inwardly she quaked and thought it most unfortunate they were standing at the top of the steps that led down to Traitor's Gate. Below, the River Thames rushed through the iron bars of the barricade, lapping at the stone stairs that were green with slime; and for a moment, Isabella thought of all those who had been rowed through that gate to ascend the steps and then had rarely left the Tower alive. Briefly, she shuddered, and Warrick, guessing her silent musings, frowned sardonically.

"Not being a king, I can hardly send ye to the block on Tower Green, my lady. Be glad of that and the fact that we are not in Lion Tower, for I wouldst be sore tempted to feed ye to the wild beasts there!"

"Would ye?" Isabella asked, picking up one of the roses that lay at her feet and pressing its blossom to her nostrils. She inhaled deeply of the sweet fragrance, then looked again at her husband. "Would ye, my lord? Art so eager to be rid of me then?"

For a moment, Warrick stood silently, staring at her. Then he swore under his breath and muttered, "May God burn ye for a witch, 'Sabelle!"

The girl turned away from the intensity of his gaze, not at all displeased by his answer. Her husband might not love her, but he did want her. It was a beginning, she thought. The beginning of a seed that might grow with time and flourish into the most lasting of flowers.

She tossed the rose into the Thames and smiled softly to herself as Warrick suddenly took her in his arms and brought his mouth down over hers hard.

Chapter Twenty-two

THE GREAT HALL WAS CROWDED TO OVERFLOWING WHEN Isabella and Warrick reached it that evening for supper, but the Earl quickly found places for them at one of the trestles near the high table. There, they shared a trencher together, as was the custom at Court, and were waited on by Warrick's squire Rhys, who stood just behind them and served them well.

Warrick introduced her to many of those seated at the trestle. Among them were two of his rivals, Lord Thomas

Grey, Marquis of Dorset and the Queen's older son by her
first marriage, and Lord William Hastings; Sir Richard Grey,
the Marquis's younger brother; Lord Thomas Stanley, who
was called the Fox, for his ability somehow to be always
on the winning side, and his wife, Lady Margaret Stanley
(née Beaufort), whose son by her first marriage, Henry
Tudor, lived in exile, in Brittany, because he had a distant
claim to the throne, and the Plantagenets were notorious for
eliminating their adversaries; and Lord Dante da Forenza,
Conte di Montecatini, who was one of the Italian ambassadors to England and who was directly on Isabella's right.

The Count was an extremely vain and breathtakingly
handsome man, with dark skin, jet-black hair, and ebony
eyes that glittered appreciatively every time they fell upon
the girl. He was built slenderly, but Isabella guessed that
his body was like finely tempered steel beneath his expensive, exquisite clothes, for though his artistically formed
hand closed lightly around his chalice when he lifted the
cup to his lips, she had the uncanny impression that he
might as easily have crushed the goblet between those slim
fingers. There was a strange magnetism about him that
attracted yet repelled her, for it was as though he were some
sort of sleek, exotic snake, silkily coiling and uncoiling
himself next to her on the bench upon which they sat. Every
movement he made was languid and graceful, almost too
sensuous for a man; and Isabella discovered herself faintly
disturbed by him, although she could not have said why,
for there was no fault to be found with his manners. The
Italian seemed to sense her unease and turned the full depths
of his striking charm on her to win her favor, but still, the
girl continued to feel vaguely discomforted by his presence.
Once, she had to repress a slight shudder when he smiled
at her disarmingly, his eyes glinting with a cold admiration
that held no desire. It was almost as though he admired her
as a beautiful object, detachedly, without wanting. He flattered her prettily, expertly, but somehow, Isabella felt there
was a note of insincerity in the words; they came too easily
to his lips for her liking. Nevertheless, she forced herself
to converse pleasantly with the Count, thinking that perhaps
she was being unfair, that mayhap his strangeness was due

only to the fact that he was foreign and therefore different.

"So, *signora*, I have heard ye are called the Rose of Rapture, and now I see, with my own eyes, why the courtiers have named ye thus," the Italian told her. Isabella flushed, mortified that the tale of what had occurred that afternoon had already spread so quickly through the palace, though she had expected as much. Upon viewing her red-stained cheeks, the Italian smiled apologetically. "I am sorry, *signora*," he said. "Please forgive me. I did not mean to embarrass ye, though ye are even more becoming when ye blush so shyly. Perhaps I should not have brought up the matter."

"Nay." The girl shook her head. "'Tis quite all right, my lord, I assure ye. Doubtless, all here know the story by now and will make mention of it, for 'twill seem a good jest to many. Being newly wed, my husband and I have borne our fair share of teasing. 'Tis only that I hoped this particular tale would not become grist for the gossips' mill; 'twas such a foolish incident."

"Oh, nay, *signora*," the Count protested. "'Twas most romantic—or at least so I have been informed. They say your husband loves ye so much, he cannot bear for another man's eyes to gaze upon your beauty and so guards ye most jealously. And indeed, 'tis easy enough to see why it should be so."

Again, Isabella's cheeks grew pink, their soft warm glow almost matching the color of the gown she had chosen to wear that night. Of pale damask silk, the dress was cut low across the bodice to reveal the gentle swell of her creamy breasts and fell in narrow folds that clung to her slender waist and rounded hips. The gown was complemented by a silver surcoat and steepled *hennin*, from which swirled yards of billowing pink-and-silver material. Isabella's long mane of hair was piled atop her head beneath the hat, exposing the clear, lovely lines of her face and throat.

Her fathomless grey-green eyes darkened slightly at the Italian's words. Oh, if only it were true that her husband loved her beyond all reason; but she knew it was not so. Still, 'twas far better the Court believe such than learn the veracity of the matter.

"Warrick is a good husband to me, my lord," she murmured, then turned away, only to find her husband's amber eyes watching her speculatively from beneath half-closed lids.

Isabella quivered a little as a small shiver of desire chased down her spine. In a few hours, perhaps less, if Warrick were impatient for her, they would be alone in their chamber, and he would make love to her. But tonight would be different. Tonight, they would recapture the magic they had known that first time of their mating. Somehow, the girl felt certain of this. She glanced down at her hands, remembering Caerllywel's words. Aye, tonight would be different. She would lay to rest, at last, the shadows of Brangwen's and Lionel's ghosts, which stood between them, and set about slowly to win her husband's heart. She had vowed as much, and if she was to be happy with Warrick, Isabella knew she could do no less. It was not the path she would have chosen to follow, had a choice been given her, but it was the fork in the road she had taken nonetheless; and there was no turning back for her. She did not know if she could ever gain her husband's love and trust; she did not even know if she desired it. She knew only that she had to try.

"Lord Montecatini appears to find ye most enchanting, 'Sabelle," Warrick spoke, startling her back to the present.

"Does he? I hadn't noticed, my lord."

"Hadn't ye?"

"Nay. As your wife, I have eyes only for ye, Warrick."

He was surprised and faintly puzzled by her words; she could tell. But she saw he was intrigued as well, if a trifle suspicious.

"What manner of game do ye seek to play, madam?" he asked.

"No game at all, my lord." For life and love are not games, she thought. "No game at all."

For an instant, her eyes met his over the rim of the chalice she had raised to her lips. She held his gaze momentarily, as though they were truly lovers; then her lashes swept down to hide her thoughts, and she turned away, feeling somehow awkward. She was not a sorceress, no matter what her husband thought, and trying to bewitch him into falling in love with her was not going to be easy. Warrick was so clever. What if he discerned her intentions toward him? How horribly amused and hateful he would be. Well, Isabella would just have to take that chance.

She was glad that Lady Margaret Stanley had spoken, claiming Warrick's attention.

As the Baroness talked softly to Warrick, Isabella studied the woman covertly, for Margaret interested her. The Baroness was small and plain: for though her features were handsome and elegantly chiseled, she wore no paint and was somberly dressed, being an extremely pious woman. But Margaret's dark eyes, though often modestly downcast, were shrewd, missing nothing; and Isabella suspected that a highly intelligent brain lay beneath the Baroness's outwardly saintly facade.

Though now titled Lady Stanley, Margaret still referred to herself as the Countess of Richmond. It was as though she found it difficult to remember the title had been stripped from her by the Yorkists, and she had had two husbands since the death of Edmund Tewdwr, Earl of Richmond, a Lancastrian who had died a prisoner of the Yorkists in Carmarthen Castle, leaving Margaret, at thirteen years of age, a widow. Shortly after Edmund's death, the Baroness had given birth to her only child, a son whom she had named Henry and whom she adored above all else. Though his claim to the throne descended through his mother, through the illegitimate line of John of Gaunt by his mistress Katherine Swynford, Henry Tudor was now the sole surviving Lancastrian heir.

Isabella glanced uneasily at her husband at the thought, for she had suddenly recalled too that Henry was a Welshman. His paternal grandfather had been Owein Tewdwr, a Welsh bard who had secretly married Katherine of Valois, the old King Henry VI's mother. His father, Edmund, had been the old King's half brother. Henry himself was the old King's nephew. Aye, Henry Tudor was a Welshman. Isabella was sure of it, for even now, Warrick was calling Margaret's son not Henry, but Harry. Lord Harry Tewdwr, Earl of Richmond, though the title was no longer rightfully his, any more than his claim to the Crown was legitimate. Still, King Edward IV thought Henry enough of a threat to have attempted to capture him in the past. But so far, Henry had managed to elude the King.

As I would have, Isabella thought, if my ambitious, loving mother were my eyes and ears at Court.

She gazed again at Margaret and wondered what clever schemes the Baroness plotted and planned behind those large dark eyes so often turned upward toward heaven. There were those at Court who foolishly dismissed Margaret as a good but simple woman, but Isabella, as she watched the Baroness surreptitiously, was not one of those so easily misled.

Following her first husband's demise, Margaret had married Sir Henry Stafford, whose nephew, another Henry Stafford, was now the Duke of Buckingham and wed to the Queen's sister Katherine. Isabella looked at the young Duke seated at the high table. He too held a claim to the throne, she remembered, legitimately, through Thomas of Woodstock.

His Grace the Duke of Buckingham, Henry Stafford; Henry Tudor, the last of the Lancastrians; Lady Margaret Stanley, his ingenious, doting mother; and Lord Thomas Stanley, the Fox, the Baroness's third husband. Without warning, Isabella shivered at the thought of such a dangerous combination.

And what of Warrick, her husband, who was half-Welsh?

Waerwic is always for the winning side, my lady.

"Art cold, 'Sabelle?" Warrick inquired curiously, noting her faint shudder and observing how still and silent she had suddenly fallen.

"Nay." She managed a small laugh as she stared up at him, stricken, her heart constricting in her breast.

Richard. Oh, Richard, my lord Duke who is so kind. They would wrest the Crown from your beloved brother the King if they could. I know, somehow, 'tis true.

"'Twas nothing, my lord, a slight draught; that's all. 'Tis gone now," the girl lied, for the strange feeling that had possessed her still persisted, chilling her to the bone.

Only a fortnight past, she had vowed to love, honor, and

obey the man who had knelt beside her before the priest. Only tonight, she had determined to win the heart of that same man who had become her husband. But Isabella had not realized then that someday, Warrick might also become her enemy.

She could no longer look into his eyes, those amber orbs that would search out relentlessly her innermost thoughts: and she was glad when a knight, bearing a covered silver dish ornately encrusted with jewels, approached the table, though she wondered at the sudden tittering of the courtiers that just as quickly faded to a strange, expectant silence.

"My Lord Hawkhurst"—the knight spoke and bowed with an exaggerated flourish—"His Grace begs ye accept this small token of congratulations on your recent marriage." He lifted the lid to reveal a brown-and-gold hawk, which, though still alive, had been securely bound up and lay helplessly amid a bed of white rose petals.

Isabella gasped, then gave a small cry of horror at the bird's plight and what she knew was a nasty jest on the King's part: for none present, having heard the story of what had occurred that afternoon, could have mistaken the meaning of Edward's wedding present to the couple.

"Oh, cruel. Cruel!" the girl whimpered and attempted to spring to her feet, intending to release the poor hawk at once.

Warrick's arm, however, shot out rapidly to encircle her waist—lovingly, it seemed, to those who watched—but to Isabella, it was as though she had been imprisoned by an iron band: for her husband's grip had tightened warningly, almost painfully, around her, restraining her impulsive action.

The Earl smiled wryly at the knight who had delivered the trussed bird, then glanced casually about the great hall.

"I see that His Grace has not lost his sense of humor during my absence," Warrick said loudly enough for all to hear. A smattering of appreciative laughter rang out but then died as still the courtiers watched and waited, like animals stalking their prey. "Come, 'Sabelle." Warrick rose and offered his arm to her, his eyes cautioning her to do nothing rash. "Methinks the King would like to meet ye."

Trembling with rage, she stood, her grey-green orbs flashing defiantly; and though she was desperately frightened by the idea of bringing Edward's wrath down upon herself and her husband, she made no move to lay her hand on Warrick's arm.

Instead, in the breathless silence that had once more fallen over the great hall, she took the heavy plate dish from the knight and set it on the table. Then she drew the dagger at her waist and, crooning soothingly to the hawk all the while, deftly cut the thongs that tied it. The bird stirred and struggled to rise but could not. The girl saw, with fury, that one of its wings was broken. Having, by now, learned how hateful those at Court could be, Isabella knew they would not hesitate to mock both her and Warrick unmercifully if the hawk continued to fail in its pathetic attempts to fly. It was not to be borne. She would not have Warrick made a fool of again. Swiftly, she caught the jesses that trailed from the bird's sharp talons and, with a graceful motion, swung the hawk upward to settle upon her wrist. The bird wavered unsteadily for a moment, then gained its balance, its yellow eyes meeting hers fiercely for just an instant, as though in recognition of the bond that had been borne between them. It lifted its head proudly to gaze about the room and gave a shrill sweet cry of victory. A few white rose petals that had clung to its claws drifted down to scatter heedlessly upon the floor, then all was once more still.

For perhaps a minute more, the great hall was hushed, then suddenly, a wild cheer accompanied by a burst of admiring applause for a deed well done swelled from the courtiers, echoing to the rafters as Isabella raised the hawk high for all to see.

Flushed with triumph, she turned to her husband and, to her surprise, for she had feared he would be angry, saw his eyes were glimmering with pride and approval instead.

"*Brava*, 'Sabelle," he whispered, lifting her free hand to his lips to kiss it. "*Brava*, my lady."

And in that moment, Isabella could have sworn he loved her.

On her husband's arm, the girl walked nervously toward the high table. Whether or not Edward was wroth, she could not tell. She had glimpsed the King and Queen earlier upon entering the great hall, of course, but she had not realized she would be presented to them this evening. She had thought such would take place upon the morrow, at Westminster Palace, where formal Court was held. Anxiously, Isabella bit her lip and glanced down at her gown, wondering idly if it was grand enough for the occasion, though it seemed the least of her worries right now.

"Smile, 'Sabelle!" Warrick suddenly hissed in her ear, startling her. "Ye look as though ye are on your way to be executed at Tower Green. There is naught for ye to fear. Ye were magnificent, and Edward has shown us both great favor."

"Marry-go-up, my lord! How? By mocking us before the whole Court by giving us this pitiful hawk on a bed of white roses?"

"Nay." Again, Warrick grinned sardonically. "That was merely a jest on Edward's part. The real gift was the plate, of course, and it must be worth a small fortune."

"Oh. *Oh!*" Isabella's eyes widened as, at last, she understood. "Then—then the King is well pleased with our marriage?"

"Aye."

"Well, he certainly chose a cruel way of showing it! My lord Duke of Gloucester would never have been so unkind. Methinks your Edward is not the man his brother believes him to be."

"Be that as it may, he is still my liege—and yours. Do not be so foolish as to spoil the victory ye have won, 'Sabelle."

"Nay, my lord. I shall not. But do not ask me to love the King, for I cannot."

Warrick's eyes gleamed speculatively at that, but he said nothing further.

Edward Plantagenet, the King, was thirty-eight years old but looked older. He had been but nineteen when he'd won his glorious victory at Towton and claimed the throne for his own. England's tall golden god, he'd been then, a brilliant military commander who had wrested the Crown from

King Henry VI and whom the commonfolk had welcomed with open arms and adoration. But Ned's subsequent years of dissolute living had taken their toll on him, tarnishing his splendor. The body that had once been so lithe and powerfully built had thickened and coarsened from over-indulgence in rich food and drink. The handsome face had grown slack and soft from the easy, careless years of late. The eyes that had been as clear and blue as a summer sky were now bloodshot from too many late nights of carousing with a string of never-ending women. Only the glossy mane of blond hair remained to tell Isabella why England had once looked upon their King as a golden god and taken him so dearly to their hearts. Had Isabella known him then, she might have loved him. But she had not, and so she felt nothing but an odd sense of tragic waste as she knelt before her liege.

This was Richard's brother, and yet, how unalike the two men were. There was nothing of Richard's somberness, his kindness, his haunting sadness, about Edward. Nay, just as Dickon was the darkness, so Ned was the light, a dying sun, perhaps, but a sun just the same, a passionate fire that was consuming itself, burning itself out with its own intensity. There was a cruel deviltry in the King's eyes that made the girl shiver slightly as he bade her rise; and she did not miss the way he appraised her body and desired what he saw.

Her heart gave a little lurch of apprehensiveness, for even at Rushden, rumors of Edward's insatiable lust for women had reached her ears. There were many at Court who, at one time or another, had been the King's mistress; and Isabella had no wish to share his bed.

"So ye are my ward the Lady Isabella," Edward was saying as, with a guilty start at having allowed her thoughts to wander in the King's presence, the girl came back to the present. "I did not realize what a favor I had done Warrick by choosing ye for his wife. Not only are ye beautiful, but clever too." He indicated the hawk that still perched upon her wrist. "'Twas indeed a deed well done, my lady."

"Thank ye, Your Grace." Isabella spoke at last, glad the

King was not angry with her. "My lord and I are most appreciative of your wedding present and hope ye are well pleased with our marriage."

"I am, my lady, though I confess a small regret at your loss. Dickon told me ye were quite a taking little wench, but I'm afraid I failed to recognize my brother's taste was more exquisite than I thought. I can see indeed why my courtiers have dubbed ye the Rose of Rapture."

"Ye flatter me, Sire." Isabella blushed faintly, not wanting to encourage the King, particularly as the Queen was staring at her most venomously.

Elizabeth Woodville was older than her royal husband but looked younger, for she had taken great care to preserve her cold, haughty beauty. Even now, it was easy to see why Ned had been bewitched by her. Her smooth skin was as fair as cream, and her regal face appeared as though it had been sculpted from the finest of marbles. She shaved her brow, as did most of the Court women, so little could be seen, beneath her *hennin*, of the famous silver-gold hair that was said to cascade, like a shimmering waterfall, to her knees. But her high forehead set off to advantage her delicately arched brows and wide, pale blue eyes, which glittered like ice. Her straight, classical nose flared proudly above a slightly pouting, rosebud mouth whose lips, at the moment, were thinly compressed with ill-concealed jealousy.

Isabella knew instinctively that the Queen hated her, for the girl's own silvery beauty rivaled Elizabeth's—and Isabella was much younger than the Queen. Elizabeth was barely civil to the girl, and Isabella was glad when, after talking with Warrick for a time, the royal couple allowed the newlyweds to depart.

Much to the disappointment of the courtiers, who had hoped to become better acquainted with the girl, Isabella and Warrick did not remain for the dancing that followed supper but instead sought their chamber. There, Isabella set about at once to mend the hawk's broken wing while Warrick ordered his squire Rhys to go down to the mews and see if a bird perch might be obtained from the King's falconer. Finally, Ragnor, as the girl had decided to call the hawk, was settled in for the night; and Isabella turned shyly to her husband.

She wanted to make love with him, to begin her campaign to win his heart, but she did not know how to make her wishes known. Silently, she took the cup of wine he offered her and sipped it nervously, trying to think of something to say. The words, however, did not come easily to her.

"Warrick, I—I" She broke off abruptly, biting her lip.

"Aye?" he asked, raising one eyebrow as though amused.

Suddenly, she knew he knew what she wanted. She stiffened a little, squaring her small shoulders proudly, believing he intended to mock her. The soft, pleading light in her eyes died, and she turned away, a sharp stab of anguish piercing her heart. It was no use. Even if she succeeded in putting Lionel from her heart and mind, she could never win Warrick's love. The shell he had built around himself was too impenetrable, and he was too afraid of being hurt ever to let down his guard and invite her inside the walls that protected him from the world.

"Nothing," she whispered. "'Twas naught."

She set down her chalice and moved toward the antechamber of their room, intending to summon Jocelyn or one of the other maids to help her undress. But Warrick stopped her, coming up behind her and placing his hands on her shoulders.

"I do not believe 'twas naught, 'Sabelle," he murmured in her ear, running his hands down her arms caressingly. "If ye want me, ye do but have to speak the words," he told her. "There is no shame in desiring your husband. And ye do desire me, 'Sabelle, do ye not?" he queried softly, turning her around to face him.

"Aye," she breathed at last. "I do not understand how or why, but ye have wakened something in me that has made me want ye."

"'Tis called passion, 'Sabelle." His voice was low and husky; his golden eyes were dark with hunger and gleaming with an odd light. "It pleases me that ye want me," he said. "Go, and tell your maids ye will have no need of them this evening."

When she returned, she found her husband had blown

out most of the candles and stripped down to his shirt, which hung open to reveal his sun-bronzed chest matted with dark hair, and to his hose, beneath which she could see plainly the evidence of his desire for her. Slowly, he walked toward her, taking the steepled cap from her head, allowing her hair to fall in a shining silvery stream to her hips. Then languidly, he began to strip the garments from her body. When finally she stood naked before him, he lifted her in his strong arms and carried her to the bed. Briefly, he towered over her, watching her as he cast away the remainder of his clothes, then joined her.

Already, Isabella could feel her body trembling with anticipation, and she knew her husband could feel it too. For a moment, he studied her intently, one hand drawing tiny circles on her belly.

"Why didst thou come to me this eve, 'Sabelle?" he inquired curiously, for though before, after the first few nights of their mating, she had received him willingly enough, this was the first time she had sought to initiate their lovemaking.

"I—I wished to please ye, my lord."

"Why?"

"Because—because although I had not thought it possible, ye are a good husband to me, Warrick. And much as ye dislike our marriage, ye are trying to make it work. It seemed I could do no less."

"I see." He was silent for a moment, then, "And what of Lionel Valeureux, madam?"

"He betrayed my love for him, my lord. I—I try to think of him no more."

"If what ye say is true, then ye have pleased me, my lady, for I wouldst have your loyalty—nay, I *demand* it."

And my love, Warrick? she wanted to cry out. Wouldst ye have that too if I can ever find it in myself to give? But she did not ask the question. It was enough, for now, that Warrick believed she had put Lionel from her heart and mind. She must go slowly and give their relationship a chance to grow if there was to be something more than desire born of it.

Gently, she touched her husband's face.

"How could I refuse to give ye my loyalty, my lord? Ye saved my life, Warrick. For that alone, I wouldst give whatever ye asked of me."

"Would ye?"

"I—I wouldst try, my lord. I am trying."

"Then put your arms around my neck, and make love with me, 'Sabelle."

Slowly, she moved into the circle of his warm embrace and met his lips eagerly, if a trifle shyly. Her mouth quivered vulnerably just a little at the intimacy of the kiss, for Warrick's tongue parted her lips demandingly, possessively, as a man who knows it is his right. Savagely, he sought the sweetness that awaited within, pillaged her mouth until her lips clung desperately to his, craving still more. Almost cruelly, he wrapped his hands in her silver-blond tresses, which billowed out over the pillows, as though to draw her even nearer while he went on kissing her deeply, fiercely, setting her aflame with passion. His tongue darted hotly in and out of her mouth, ravaging her, tracing the outline of her lips searingly until she knew they were bruised and swollen with desire. But she did not care. More boldly now, Isabella followed where his tongue led, licking, caressing, entwining, as she tasted the inside of his mouth, exploring it just as he had done her own. Warrick moaned with pleasure, the low sound mingling with her own whimpers of delight as their mouths pressed feverishly to each other; their breathing became as one.

They gasped for air as Warrick's lips left Isabella's to slash like a whip across her cheek to her temple and the damp, silky strands of her hair. He buried his face in the cascading mane, inhaling sharply the fragrant rose scent of her. Hoarsely, he muttered in her ear, his warm breath sending shivers down her spine.

"Witch!" he snarled, then, more gently, "'Sabelle, sweetheart."

She thrilled to the words and flung her head back in exultation; her eyes closed; her mouth parted slightly as his lips slid down her throat, his teeth grazing lightly the pale slender column offered up, so bare and trustingly, to him. He laid one hand there, fingers tightening momentarily, possessively, before both palms swept down to cup her breasts.

His mouth found that small, soft, sensitive place on her shoulder and teased the spot tormentingly with teeth and tongue while she writhed beneath him, her blood like quicksilver as it pounded through her veins. He could feel the pulse beating crazily, jerkily, at the hollow of her throat and her nipples growing hard and rigid as his fingers played with them, his thumbs brushing the flushed little peaks.

He lowered his head, pressed his lips to the swollen crests, first one, and then the other. He sucked the ripe buds deliberately, took them between his teeth, his tongue flicking the rosy tips rapidly, swirling about them tauntingly so they stiffened even more with excitement. Tiny electric tingles rippled like shock waves through Isabella's body as she cradled Warrick's head in her hands, stroking his hair gently as his tongue continued to titillate her nipples, his fingers to fondle her breasts.

Something soft and warm stirred in her as she opened her eyes to watch him, and for a moment, she longed for a child of his making to fill her belly, suckle at her breast. Then his mouth began to travel even lower still, and the feeling passed to be replaced by one even more primitive.

Somehow, he had his wine cup in his hand and was pouring the liquid over her; she could feel it trickling down between her thighs, intertwining with the soft curls and folds of her womanhood, where, even now, his lips were kissing her, his tongue was tasting her, lapping at the wine and honey of her. She trembled uncontrollably at the sweet sensations he was arousing in her, opening the gentle swells of her valley, caressing her rhythmically until she was wet and warm where he touched her, and she yearned for him to fill her deep inside.

His fingers slipped in to stroke the length of her with small, fluttering movements that made her loins quicken unbearably. The little flower of her secret place budded beneath the heat of his tongue, its tiny petals furling and unfurling until suddenly it blossomed wildly, the bursting of its bloom making her arch her hips frantically against his hand that cupped her. Over and over, she cried out with wanting as the throbbing tremors shook her; then, momentarily content, she sighed and breathed deeply with pleasure. She was sated but not yet satisfied. It was she who had wanted to do the taking this eve! How could she have let him sweep her away so utterly when 'twas she who had wished to conquer him?

Her hands sought her husband, drew him up so she could kiss him, taste the moist, musky scent of her that clung to his lips. He moved to enter her, but she denied him, her small palms pushing against his chest until he lay upon his back beneath her, gazing up at her curiously. He started to speak, but she put her hand over his mouth, silencing him.

"Be quiet," she told him softly. "And let me do my will. Ye will not regret it, I promise ye."

Gently, she wrapped her fingers in his hair and kissed him tenderly, at first, as though she were yet a shy maid, who had not lain with him before. She kissed his eyelids and his nose and his mouth. Lightly, very lightly, her eyelashes swept, like butterfly wings, over his cheeks, exciting him in a strange way with their feathery touch, for Warrick had never experienced such before. Then her lips were upon his ear, parting as she breathed a low sigh into the curved shell. Her breath was warm and made him tingle with desire that quickly sharpened as she nuzzled his lobe and bit it gently with her teeth.

His loins stirred, raced. This was an Isabella he had never seen before, an Isabella who had learned well the lessons he had taught her and was boldly applying her talents to please him. For a moment, he again wondered why. But the thought was fleeting, for soon, she had driven all but his lust for her from his mind.

Lingeringly, sensuously, she pressed the length of her body over his. Then slowly, very slowly, she undulated against him, her flanks rubbing his briefly, enticingly, as her mouth seared its way down his chest, tickling the soft mat of dark fur there. Her lips found his nipples, stimulating them as he had her own, nibbling at them with her teeth, teasing them with her tongue until they hardened as rigidly as her own had done; and she wondered if he felt the same radiating ripples of delight she had known earlier. It seemed he did, for he gave a small groan, and his fingers dug into her back, kneading the sinuous muscles that stirred beneath his hands.

Her mouth drifted down to his belly, then lower still, to his thick strong thighs. Her tongue trailed its way down first one leg, and then the other, tormentingly until, at last, she kissed the spheres of his manhood and let her lips slide tauntingly, languidly, up the bold shaft, then down, then up once more, her tongue flicking quickly along his flesh. When she sensed he could endure no more, she poured what remained of the wine upon him. Then her mouth closed around him, sucking at him, taking him deep into her throat before her tongue swirled about him deliciously, fluttering here and there like a hummingbird until he strained against her and gave a low cry.

She raised her head at the sound; her fondling hands moved to his waist, where they tightened upon him as deliberately she pulled herself up and poised herself above him briefly, then lowered herself upon him, engulfing his fiery sword with her velvet sheath. Again and again, she enveloped him, riding him faster and faster until she could feel the tension in her womanhood building, heightening, and then erupting in a blaze of glory. She clutched him tightly with her dark, molten core as her climax came and, with it, his own, his hands gripping her hips as he thrust into her wildly, crushing her to him, impaling her upon his blade until, at last, they were still.

Warrick's heart pounded crazily in his breast, for he had seldom made love, in the past, in the manner he had just experienced with Isabella. For an instant, he understood what it meant to be taken, for there was no other way in which to describe what his wife had just done to him. Still panting for breath, he stared up at her wonderingly. Her head was flung back; her shimmering mane of hair was wet and clinging to her wantonly; her lips were parted as she too rasped for air. Her skin glistened like satin with a fine, dewy sheen and was flushed with the rosy afterglow of their violent lovemaking. He had never seen her look more exciting, more beautiful, like some savage pagan goddess in her naked splendor. He reached up to cup her breasts with his hands as she bent to kiss him one last time before easing herself from him, then curling up next to him, her head on his shoulder.

What had she done to him, his witch of a wife? For somehow, Warrick felt different, changed. Briefly, the alteration puzzled him; then suddenly, he recognized what it was. Brangwen's bitter ghost had ceased to haunt him. To his surprise, he found he could not even recall her face. How could that be when he had loved her so, hated her so? He did not know. He knew only that it was Isabella who now filled his thoughts, Isabella's lovely countenance that shone clear and pure in his mind. Without his even realizing it, a deep sense of peace invaded his soul as, link by link, the chains of his past fell away; and he was free.

"Oh, 'Sabelle," he said. "Oh, 'Sabelle, what magic have ye wrought upon me?"

But the sorceress who had so enchanted him did not answer. She was fast asleep, a soft smile of triumph curved upon her mouth.

Chapter Twenty-three

ISABELLA AWAKENED IN THE MORNING TO A CHAMBER FULL of roses, white roses. Slowly, she sat up and stared with amazement at the room, thinking, for an instant, that she had somehow wandered into the royal gardens. Then the chamber door was flung open wide, and old Alice bustled in, carrying yet another large bouquet.

"Oh, good morning, my lady," the nanna greeted her. "So, you're awake at last, and high time too, for 'tis nearly noon. Still, the Lord said ye were to sleep as long as ye wished, so we didn't disturb ye," Alice rattled on as she set the basket of long-stemmed blossoms down and began rearranging them. "I'll have your breakfast in just a minute, my lady."

"Alice."

"Aye, my lady?"

"Where—where did all these flowers come from?"

"Why, from the courtiers, my lady, all, that is, except for that single bloom lying there on the table. That one came from the Lord. Oh, isn't it exciting, my lady? They've been arriving all morn. Goodness knows where we're going to put them all—"

"Take them away," Isabella directed softly as she reached out and picked up the solitary rose that lay beside her bed, for to her, it was the most perfect blossom in the room.

She buried her face in its velvet petals, her fingers trailing caressingly down the gay riband of white silk that had been tied around the stem in a bow.

"I—I beg your pardon, my lady." The nurse, thinking her ears had deceived her, gazed aghast at her mistress. "But did ye say—did ye say—"

"Take them away, all of them, save for this one." Isabella indicated the flower she held in her hand.

"But—but, my lady!" Alice sputtered, stunned. "What—what will I possibly do with them all?"

"Give them to the Church or the poor. I do care not. This single bloom is the only one I desire."

"Aye, my lady."

The nanna shook her head and sighed, believing her mistress had surely lost her mind. Nevertheless, Alice gathered up the basket she had just brought in and carried it from the chamber, calling to Jocelyn and the others to come and help her. Isabella smiled to herself as she heard the maids' small cries of dismay and bewilderment at the news that all the roses except for one must be removed at once, followed by their grumbling under their breath as they entered the room and began the arduous task.

Again, the girl inhaled deeply of the fragrant blossom she had pressed to her nostrils, then touched the petals wonderingly before tossing back the covers of the bed and rising. It was then that she saw the note that lay upon the table where the lone flower had been. With trembling fingers, she broke the wax that sealed it. The single word, written with a commanding flourish upon the page, leaped out at her, black and bold: *Warrick*. She smiled once more, her heart beating with joy in her breast. Warrick. Her hus-

band. The bloom and note clutched to her chest, Isabella
danced a few lightly skipping steps across the room, much
to the surprise of Alice and the maids, who looked askance
at the girl, as though fearing she'd gone quite mad. At the
sight of their stupefied faces, Isabella whirled to a stop and
broke into peals of laughter.

"My lady. Are—are ye all right?" Jocelyn asked.

"Aye, oh, aye, Jocelyn. Did my lord say when he would
return?"

"Sometime this morn, my lady."

"And 'tis nearly noon now! Oh, we must hurry. Quickly,
Mathilde, Edith, take away the roses. Alice, Jocelyn, come,
and help me get dressed at once."

At last, Isabella was clothed in a most becoming gown
of brown satin and a gold surcoat, Warrick's colors.

She blushed with shame and yet delight as she thought
of her husband and how wantonly she had made love to
him last night. Aye, there was no other way to describe it.
She had been the aggressor. *She* had made love to him.
What had he thought, she wondered. That she was bold,
brazen? Yet, she must have pleased him, for he had given
her the rose. . . .

The girl fidgeted impatiently as Alice and Jocelyn plaited
her long thick hair into two braids, then deftly coiled the
plaits about her ears. As a finishing touch, Isabella tucked
Warrick's blossom into the left braid. Left. For taken. She
was determined that after this morn, there would be no doubt
in the courtiers' minds that she belonged to her husband—
and to him alone.

Singing softly to herself, she then moved to the bird
perch that Rhys had managed to obtain yestereve from the
mews and where Ragnor now sat, waiting. Talking quietly
to the hawk all the while, Isabella slowly removed the hood
she had covered him with last night. He stirred and peered
about fiercely, blinking his yellow eyes rapidly a few times
to accustom them to the sudden light. Finally, he seemed
to recognize the girl. He squawked and attempted to flap
his wings, nearly falling off the bird perch and scaring poor
Alice half out of her wits.

The nurse screamed and dropped the vase she was holding. One hand fluttered to her ample, heaving bosom, where her heart was now thudding much too quickly.

"Oh, my lady!" she gasped. "I'm sorry, but such a fright the creature didst give me. In all the excitement, I'd quite forgotten about it."

"'Tis all right, Alice," Isabella assured the flustered nanna, who had stooped to retrieve the scattered flowers and shattered glass. "There is naught to fear. Ragnor will not harm ye. He cannot fly."

"So I see, my lady. What a pity the poor thing's wing is broken," Alice clucked.

"Aye, but I have set it, and 'twill mend with time."

As will Warrick's heart and soul, I hope, Isabella added earnestly to herself.

After the nurse had left the chamber, the girl plucked a dish of beef, left over from her breakfast, from the hunting table that ran along one wall. Carefully avoiding his sharp beak and talons, she started to feed the chunks of meat to Ragnor, certain he was hungry. But despite her attempts to encourage him, he ate little, for the beef had been cooked. Isabella made a mental note to tell Rhys the hawk must have raw meat in the future. Once Ragnor had ended the small meal, she caught hold of his jesses and, after setting him on her wrist, succeeded in coaxing him up to her shoulder. There, he appeared content to perch quietly, surveying his surroundings.

"Oh, my lady. Surely, ye don't intend to take that bird with ye to Westminster Palace," Alice chided as she bustled back in to carry out yet another large bouquet.

"Is that where my lord means to escort me today?" Isabella inquired curiously. "But of course, Ragnor shall go with me. He's quite famous, ye know, and now a part of me besides."

As Warrick is now a part of me, and I of him, she thought.

Almost as though he had sensed her musing about him, her husband strode into the room at last. He paused, studying the girl intently for a moment as she turned to him, waiting breathlessly for his approval. His half-closed eyes raked her, casually, it seemed; but Isabella, who had lain with him yestereve, knew better. He was observing the colors she wore, the rose intertwined in her hair, and the hawk upon her shoulder. She wished desperately she might guess what he was thinking, for no trace of emotion showed upon his face, although his amber orbs were glowing with desire—and something more.

"Good morning, my lady," Warrick said.

"Good morning, my lord."

"I trust ye slept well."

Was there just a hint of a smile about his lips? The girl blushed.

"Very well, my lord."

"I see the courtiers have lost no time in making their admiration of ye known." Warrick spoke dryly as he glanced about the chamber, which was still half-full of blooms.

"Aye, still, there was only one blossom that interested me, my lord. I have told my maids to send the rest to the Church or distribute them among the poor."

Warrick's eyes gleamed speculatively at that.

"How disappointed your cavaliers will be, madam," he drawled.

"All but the one whose rose I kept, I hope."

"Oh, he is pleased, my lady, very well pleased indeed. Come, 'Sabelle. Westminster Palace awaits us."

Westminster Palace was very old, for the building of the original structure had been initiated by Edward the Confessor. It stood between the Benedictine abbey located on the Isle of Thorns, a low, marshy area on the shore of the River Thames, which was overgrown with hawthorn bushes and brambles, and the river itself. Over the centuries, the monastery had been sacked and burned many times by marauding Danes, but the palace itself had managed to hold fast against attack. Following Edward the Confessor's death, subsequent rulers had taken up residence in the palace and had continued the construction that Edward had begun. William the Conqueror had finished much of the edifice, and his son, William Rufus, had raised the huge Westminster Hall, where King Henry III had once entertained over six thousand guests on New Year's Day. Henry himself had redone the old wooden hall in stone and transformed the royal bedroom, where Edward the Confessor had died, by having artists paint the ceiling with angels and the walls with rich blue, gold, and red representations of divine favors being bestowed upon kings.

In 1236, because the River Thames had no embankments, the great hall had been flooded, and men had actually rowed their boats into it to reach their chambers. In a later year, the waters had just as suddenly receded, leaving behind a vast sea of mud in which large quantities of fish had been stranded. In 1267, a mob had forced its way into the palace and had drunk up the King's wine and defaced and broken the glass windows.

By the time that Richard II had become King, Westminster Palace had been in sore need of repair. In 1394, Richard had commissioned his architect, Henry Yevele, to start the work of restoration on the palace. They had heightened the old walls and fortified them with buttresses. Then they had knocked down the pillars that had supported the roof and, in a brilliant feat of medieval engineering, had replaced the entire structure with a magnificent hammerbeam roof made of oak and ornamented with carved angels.

Warrick told Isabella that just one of the timbers in the elaborate, soaring canopy weighed almost one hundred and forty-three stones.

The arched roof was truly beautiful. The great hall itself was lined with curved apertures, and, at one end, there was a huge cathedral window. Tiers of stone steps led up to the dais where the King and Queen sat to hold Court. The entryway on one wall was flanked by tall, heavy brass candelabra; a small staircase, adorned by intricately worked statues, led down to the great hall from another portal. It was through this door that Isabella and Warrick made their appearance, causing a stir among the courtiers gathered at the palace.

The newlyweds moved slowly through the throng, pausing, now and then, to chat with those whom the Earl deemed worthy of notice. Several gay cavaliers flocked to Isabella's side to inquire whether or not she had received their bouquets; and much to her admirers' disappointment, with a light, lilting laugh, she confessed she had given all the flowers away, except for the precious, solitary bloom from her husband.

"If the King's gardens have a single white rose left, I shall be much surprised," she quipped, "for my chamber was filled to overflowing with blossoms no doubt stolen from His Grace. There was but one, however, that found favor in my eyes."

She laid her hand upon Warrick's arm and smiled up at him sweetly. Someone remarked that the Earl was indeed a lucky devil, and after acknowledging the comment, Warrick led Isabella away, leaving those behind cursing his jealous nature under their breath.

The Countess of Hawkhurst, it seemed, was one flower they would not be picking.

After the newlyweds had paid their respects to the King and Queen, Warrick took Isabella shopping in the market-place, where he bought her a filigreed silver bracelet. Then they returned to the Tower. There, Warrick said he must leave her in order to take care of some business, and instead of going back to their chamber, Isabella decided to visit Lion Tower and view again the royal menagerie. There were many wild beasts in the care of the Master of the King's Bears and Apes. There were lions, tigers, leopards, lynxes, and bears. There was an elephant kept in a great house that had been especially built for such and a polar bear that was trained to catch fish from the Thames. There was a wolf that was most highly prized, for the animals were scarce in England. There were even an eagle and a porcupine.

Most of the creatures were housed in cages with wooden lattices; and the cost of their upkeep was considerable, much to the sheriffs of London's dismay, for they were required to bear part of the expense of maintaining the menagerie. Each lion daily consumed a quarter of a sheep; for purchase of their food, the leopards were allotted sixpence a day, the bears, four.

In light of this, Isabella was outraged that the human prisoners in the Tower dungeons were allowed daily but a penny apiece for their rations.

Even the ravens that flew freely about the palace were given a weekly ration of three shillings' worth of horsemeat:

for there was an ancient legend that said if the ravens ever left the Tower, the palace was doomed to fall and, with it, all of England.

As Isabella neared Lion Tower, she saw a crowd had gathered around the barricade that encircled a deep pit below. Curious, she moved toward the mingling mass, wondering what was going on. After a time, she managed to edge her way up to the stone wall and peer down into the pit. She gasped with horror as she saw it was an animal baiting that drew the onlookers, but still, she could not seem to tear her eyes away. Below, three powerful lions were pacing restlessly back and forth, occasionally snarling and swiping at each other with their deadly claws. Fresh blood stained the stone floor of the pit, and a scattering of feathers drifted here and there. After several minutes, a door was opened, and another live cock was thrown to the cats, who instantly ripped the hapless rooster to shreds.

Sickened unto death by the gruesome sight, Isabella turned away, pressing her handkerchief to her mouth to keep from vomiting. Hot, angry tears stung her eyes, and she sobbed, stricken by the cruelty of the spectacle. Blindly, she tried to push her way through the now-cheering throng. But the crowd, still eagerly lusting for blood, refused to fall back so a path might be cleared for her. Almost panicking now, the girl glanced about wildly, seeking somebody to aid her in escaping from the mass, but there was no one.

"Not a pretty sight at all, is it, my lady?"

With a sense of relief, Isabella sought out the voice that had spoken to her. It belonged to a strange woman who was garbed in a cheap black gown, which had seen better days, and a steepled hennin, whose wispy, tattered black folds veiled her face.

"Nay. 'Tis horrid, *horrid!*" the girl wept in agreement, glad to have found a friend. "Oh, please, won't ye help me get out of here?"

"Oh, aye, my lady, I'll help ye all right," the harridan cackled slyly, sidling closer. "I'll help ye right over the edge!"

Some primitive instinct warned Isabella at the last mo-

ment as the stranger suddenly lunged at her, attempting to
force her over the stone wall into the pit. The girl screamed,
and screamed again, as frantically she struggled with her
assailant; but no one heard her terrified cries over the raucous revelry of the throng. Even Ragnor's shrill shrieks as
he flapped his wings and dug his sharp talons painfully into
Isabella's shoulder to retain his balance attracted no attention, much less any assistance. Why, the woman was mad!
Horribly deranged. The girl didn't even know her, and yet,
the harridan was trying to kill her!

"Oh, why? Why are ye doing this?" Isabella wailed.

"Ye stupid slut!" the stranger, whom the girl had, at first,
thought her savior, spat as she saw she was not going to be
able to push Isabella over the edge of the barricade. One
hand curled like a claw about Isabella's arm. Terribly frightened by the woman's strength, and fearing the crazed harridan might still succeed with her murderous plan, the girl
tried desperately to yank away; but her assailant refused to
release her. "Ye cast me out to suffer the rest of my life in
poverty, and yet, ye don't even recognize me!" the stranger
sneered accusingly.

"Why should I?" Isabella asked, trying to humor the
madwoman and playing for time, praying someone would
observe her distress and come to her aid. "I'm certain I've
never seen ye before in my life. As for casting ye out—I
wouldst not have been so cruel. I am afraid ye have mistaken
me for someone else, madam."

"Nay, *you're* the one who has made the mistake, my
lady. But I'll have my vengeance on ye yet!" The harridan's
grip on Isabella tightened hurtfully, and her dark orbs, barely
visible behind her veil, narrowed as she slithered even nearer
to hiss evilly in the girl's face. "Ye never guessed 'twas
me, after Percy died, who set the reivers to raiding your
lands, did ye, my lady? Oh, I was clever, so very clever,"
the stranger chortled. "I knew the boy, Ham, held a grudge
against Sir John—for Percy and I had made it our business
to know all there was to know about Rushden—and 'twas
easy enough to assemble a group of rough men without
scruples and instruct them to approach the lad for infor-

mation. I didn't even have to tell the reivers what to do afterward. They would have destroyed ye, in time, ye know, had it not been for Lord Hawkhurst and his brother."

"Lady—Lady Shrewton!" Isabella gasped, recognizing the woman at last.

"Aye, 'tis I all right. I'll warrant ye thought you'd seen the last of the likes of me, eh, my lady? As I believed I'd seen the last of ye, ye bitch! I thought for certain that old dog would kill ye."

"Dog? What dog?"

"Why, the mad dog, my lady, the one ye found that day upon the road. It belonged to my husband. I went back to him, ye know, after ye cast me out to starve. I had nowhere else to go. He set me to work in the kitchen like some common churl, the bastard, as punishment for my leaving him. But I fixed him right enough. He was like ye, a soft spot for animals but none for me.

"One day, he came home from hunting, with that sorry old hound cradled in his arms. The beast had been bitten by a mad fox, he said: and though he knew the dog would most likely go mad too and die, my husband couldn't bear to slay it, for 'twas his favorite hound. He told his squire to tie it up in the stables instead and keep a close watch on it. Only if the madness had possessed the animal would they kill it. Ha!" the insane Countess jeered. "He should have slain the beast immediately, the fool! But thanks to his kind heart, he didn't. I saw my chance, and I took it.

"That night, I poisoned the whoreson's stew; a most fitting end, I told him before he died, for 'twas a dish I'd cooked myself in the kitchen where he'd sent me. After he was dead, I crept down to the stables and coaxed the hound into a cage. Then I stole a drunken tinker's cart and, disguised as a peddler, hied myself to Rushden Castle, where I intended to leave the dog outside the keep for ye to find. But the crofters told me their lady had gone to her manor house, Grasmere; curse my luck. I was halfway there when I saw Lord Hawkhurst's banners and realized he was escorting ye home. Quickly, I drove the cart off the road and turned the hound loose. I knew it wouldn't get far, for I'd never fed it, and 'twas weak with famine. Then I hid in some bushes and watched to be sure ye discovered it. When ye bent down and touched it, I believed 'twas the end of ye, and good riddance!

"Thinking my revenge complete, I made my way to London, hoping to find some sort of employment, me, Lady Shrewton!" The Countess gnashed her teeth with rage as the girl listened in growing horror. "I'd squandered all the gold and jewels that Percy had given me, and my husband had left me nothing, the son of a bitch! And though I'd tried to find a new protector, no one would have me. I was too old and used up, they said, me, who'd been such a beauty once—before ye turned me out to grow haggard and aged! I couldn't believe my eyes when I saw ye today in the marketplace. That stupid dog must not have been possessed by the madness after all, eh, my lady?"

Isabella shivered uncontrollably as she recalled the terrible sickness she'd somehow managed to survive.

"Oh, my God," she breathed, attempting once more to escape from her captor; but still, Lady Shrewton held her fast. "Oh, my God."

"I followed ye back here, to the palace," the Countess went on ruthlessly. "When I realized ye were heading toward Lion Tower, I bought a ticket to view the royal menagerie. Now, ye whore, you're going to pay for what ye did to me—and Percy too, for I always suspected ye had something to do with his death, ye know, though I could never prove it."

"You're mad!" Isabella exclaimed. "You'll never get away with this!"

"Oh, aye, I will," Lady Shrewton wickedly assured the girl. "'Twill seem a most unfortunate accident, your falling into the pit, just as Percy fell. What a heyday the lions will have with ye, my lady. 'Twill indeed be a most fitting end for ye, just as my husband's demise was. You'll be torn to shreds by three of the beasts ye love so well, and I—I shall be standing up here watching—and laughing."

Again, Isabella gasped. Then, her terror spurring her on, giving her a strength she hadn't known she possessed, she wrenched herself free of the Countess's viselike grasp, at last, and ran, pushing her way wildly through the crowd, not caring that she actually struck people in order to get by.

So desperate was she to get away, the girl never saw the tall dark man who had overheard the entire exchange, who now bent to speak to Lady Shrewton, then took the Countess's arm and steered her deftly through the milling mass until they were lost, swallowed up by the throng. The man smiled wolfishly as he glanced back to be certain they had been unobserved. He had no use for Lady Shrewton at the moment, but he was a master of intrigue and deception, and he never passed up an opportunity to acquire something that might prove of valuable benefit to him in the future. As long as she obeyed him, he would find a place for the Countess in his household until he had need of her. If she gave him any trouble, he would kill her, as he had slain countless others in the past.

As though the devil himself pursued her, Isabella fled blindly through the long, twisting corridors of the palace, not caring that the courtiers stared, open-mouthed with curiosity and amazement, at the sight of her. Lord Thomas Grey, Marquis of Dorset, remarked loudly that his uncle Anthony, Earl Rivers, must be chasing the girl, for surely that was enough to make any maiden flee. And although this was not the case, Lord Anthony Woodville, Earl Rivers, the Queen's brother, being extremely handsome and very much admired, still, the cavaliers tittered with amusement and called to Isabella to come hide in their chambers.

Heedless of their laughter, she ran on.

By the time she had reached her own room, the girl had a stitch in her side and was gasping for air. Briefly, she leaned against a wall for support while she caught her breath; then she burst into the antechamber of her room.

Upon spying her highly distraught state, Caerllywel, who had been serenading Jocelyn with his lute (and quite badly, although she was pleased just the same), instantly sprang to his feet in alarm.

"'Sabelle! What's wrong?" he demanded to know as her maids scurried forth to attend her.

Clucking and fluttering about her like a brood of hens,

they inspected her for damage to her person, gasping with shock as they viewed her gown, which Ragnor had torn with his sharp talons, and the blood seeping slowly down her breast from the wounds made by the hawk's claws. Until now, Isabella had not even been aware of the painful gashes. Dazedly, she glanced down at herself as old Alice shrieked.

"Oh, my lady! Just look what that wicked bird has done!"

"Nay. Nay, 'twas not Ragnor's fault," Isabella protested and frantically waved away the nanna's ministrations. "Caerllywel, where is Warrick?"

"Here, my lady," her husband answered, to her relief, himself, appearing from their bedchamber in response to the clamor that filled the room. Upon seeing she had been hurt, he strode immediately to her side. "What is it, sweetheart? What has happened? By God, if one of the courtiers has laid a hand on ye—"

"Nay, 'tis not that. No man has touched me," the girl assured him. "Oh, my lord, something dreadful has happened! I must speak to ye at once in privacy."

"Of course, sweetheart," Warrick said, concerned and not in the least discomfitted by his brother's raised eyebrow upon hearing the endearment for a second time. "Come."

He led her to their bedroom and, much to the disappointment of Caerllywel and the maids, firmly closed the door.

"Now"—the Earl spoke, turning to his wife and gently taking her hands in his—"tell me what is wrong, 'Sabelle."

"Oh, Warrick! 'Tis so dreadful, so incredible, that even now, I can scarcely believe it," the girl cried, then proceeded to inform her husband of what had occurred. "Oh, Warrick, 'twas horrible, so horrible," she reiterated once she had finished her tale. "And there's—there's something more I must tell ye besides, my lord." Isabella bit her lip, knowing it would be foolish now to withhold the truth of her previous warden's death. "'Tis—'tis about Lord Oadby. . . ."

"What about him, my lady?"

"He—he didn't really lose his life in a hunting accident," the girl blurted out in a rush, fearing her courage to speak would otherwise desert her.

Warrick inhaled sharply, as though he had suspected as much.

"How did he die then, 'Sabelle?" he questioned. "Did ye set your brother's men on him?"

"Nay, oh, nay!" the girl denied this fervently.

"Tell me the truth, sweetheart," her husband ordered. "I cannot help ye if I don't know precisely what I'm dealing with."

"Oh, Warrick, 'twas indeed an accident. Truly, 'twas. It happened in the stables, at Rushden, where I keep my menagerie. Lord Oadby discovered me there one night, and he—he tried to—to—"

"Rape ye, 'Sabelle?" Warrick's mouth tightened whitely with anger at the thought.

"Aye. I was in the loft, and I couldn't escape from him. I fought him, and—and during the struggle, he lost his balance and fell over the edge of the loft. He—he struck his head on one of the stall doors below. It broke his neck; he was killed instantly. Hysterical, I went to the keep and wakened my brother; and together, with Lionel, we made it seem as though Lord Oadby had suffered a hunting accident."

Isabella was so upset, she didn't even notice how easily, naturally, Lionel's name had come to her lips. But Warrick did and was momentarily pleased she had not faltered over her previous lover's name. Then he turned his attention back to his wife as breathlessly she went on.

"Lord Oadby had—had badly mistreated Giles and me, ye see, and we despised him for it. He had forced his whore's presence upon us, had fed and clothed us as though we were common paupers, and had lined his purse with much of Rushden's gold. For all this, Giles and I had—had sworn to have our vengeance upon him; and we—we were afraid the Earl had friends at Court who would blame me for his death and bring the King's wrath down upon us."

"No one would have done so, 'Sabelle," Warrick told her, setting her mind at ease. "But I can well understand your actions. Ye were young and frightened. Well, there's naught for ye to fear now, sweetheart. I'm here, and I'll protect ye. I shall set about at once to discover Lady Shrewton's whereabouts and see she is brought to justice for her crimes. And if she accuses ye of murdering Lord Oadby, ye need but repeat the story ye have just told me. The Earl was well known at Court and little liked. None will doubt your tale of his demise, I assure ye. In fact, I doubt that Edward will even care what really happened. Now. Give me a smile and a kiss, my lady, then let me call Alice and the others to treat these gashes." He examined the tiny wounds made earlier by Ragnor.

Glad, truly glad, for the first time, that Warrick was her husband, Isabella complied easily with his request, smiling as she moved gratefully into the warm, protective circle of his arms and lifted her lips to his. He kissed her deeply, lingeringly, forever, it seemed, before slowly drawing away, his golden eyes dark with desire. For a moment, he studied her intently, as though he meant to take her to bed; at last, sighing slightly with disappointment at the thought that her hurts must be tended first, he turned and shouted for her maids.

For many weeks afterward, following that dreadful day, Warrick searched diligently for Lady Shrewton; but finally, grim with worry, he was forced to tell Isabella the evil Countess had mysteriously disappeared.

Chapter Twenty-four

Isabella had been at Court for over two months when Giles, at last, arrived. The King's sister Margaret, Duchess of Burgundy, had come home to England for the first time in twelve long years; and her family, including Richard, Duke of Gloucester, had gathered at Edward's palace in Greenwich to welcome her home. Instead of taking up residence there, with his liege, Giles had begged Richard's leave to stay at the Tower with Isabella. Kind, as always, the Duke had given his permission.

Upon discovering which chamber Isabella and Warrick were lodged in, Giles, knowing she was not aware he was in the city, had decided to surprise his sister by showing up unannounced to visit her. Now, as he entered the room's antechamber, he laid one finger to his lips to silence the delighted cries of the maids who flocked around him in greeting. Instantly, guessing his intent, they fell still. His eyes dancing, Giles tiptoed across the room and knocked softly on the door to Isabella's bedchamber.

"Aye, come," she said, and as he opened the door a crack and peeked in, she cried, "Giles! Oh, Giles!"

Laughing now, he strode inside as Isabella flung herself across the room and into his outstretched arms.

"Oh, Giles!" she said again as she embraced and kissed him. "I did not know ye were here. Why didn't ye write to me, and tell me ye were coming?"

"I wanted to surprise ye."

"Dear brother, 'tis so good to see ye. And ye look so well," she noted, observing that the shadows that had haunted his eyes over Catriona's death and his slaying of her clansmen were gone. "But how came ye here? I thought ye were in Scotland. Is Gloucester with ye? Come. Sit down, and tell me everything that has happened since last I saw ye. Have ye bathed and eaten? Mathilde, Edith," the girl called to the smiling maids hovering just outside the door, "prepare a bath for my brother, please. Alice, Jocelyn, fetch some ale and a light repast for us. So"—Isabella turned back to her brother—"what are ye doing in London?"

"Her Grace the Duchess of Burgundy has come home to England to visit. Naturally, Richard wanted to see her. He is with her now at Edward's palace in Greenwich," Giles explained. "I begged my lord Duke's permission to lodge with ye in the Tower, and of course, he gave it."

"Oh, Giles, how wonderful!" the girl exclaimed. "Then ye will be with me for some time. How glad I am of that and that ye must not leave right away. So tell me. Didst speak with Gloucester of your fears that ye wouldst be unable to serve him with your whole heart and soul?"

"Aye, 'Sabelle."

"And 'tis all right, then?"

"Oh, aye, dear sister. Ye were so right about him. He was so kind to me. Though he had many more important things to do, he gave orders that he was not to be disturbed, and he listened to me well into the wee hours of the morn as I poured out my story to him. Then he laid his hand upon my shoulder and told me that no man with compassion ever joyed in war, though he did his duty and well: for battle did naught but bring suffering and death, even to those who triumphed in the end. Richard said he often lay awake at night, thinking of those whom he had slain. He told me 'twas natural to feel remorse at the taking of a life, that only a monster wouldst be unmoved by the deed. Then my lord Duke ordered me to put my mind at rest, saying I was the best of squires and soldiers; and then, oh, 'Sabelle! He bade me kneel, and he *knighted* me!"

"Oh, Giles, I am so happy for ye." Isabella's eyes shone with joy for her brother. "How I wish I had been there to see it."

"Aye, Lionel was most put out when he discovered I had beaten him in the race for our spurs." Giles laughed, then sobered as he realized what he had said. He was silent for a moment, then went on softly. "I'm sorry, 'Sabelle, so very sorry. I know—" He broke off abruptly and ran one hand raggedly through his hair. "I know ye loved him, that ye had hoped to wed him—"

"Aye, but that is all in the past now, Giles. Do not think ye have wounded me by speaking of him, for I have done my best to put him from my heart and mind; and each day, the hurt he did me grows less painful, though still, sometimes, I do ache inside," the girl confessed.

"To his credit, Lionel—Lionel told me what he'd done, 'Sabelle; and though I cannot forgive him for it, I understand what drove him to deceive ye. He—he wanted ye so desperately, and he thought he could find some way out of his betrothal to Gilliane Beaumaris; but he could not. God only knows why he didn't tell ye the truth when he learned he could not free himself. I guess he loved ye so much, he couldn't bear your scorn and so continued the charade, still hoping to discover some means of making ye his. . . ." Once more, Giles was still, then suddenly he swore under his breath and slammed his fist into his open palm. "God's wounds! I should never have brought him to Rushden. I'm sorry, dear sister, so very sorry," her brother apologized again, "for Lionel did not play the gentleman with ye, and I know he hurt ye deeply."

"Aye." Once more, Isabella acknowledged the truth of this. "Still, I try not to mind it, for I would not have been able to marry him in any event. The King had already betrothed me to Warrick."

"And is he good to ye, 'Sabelle? Warrick, I mean. Has he made ye happy?"

"He is a hard man, but no husband could be kinder, Giles. Though he had no wish to wed me, he is attempting to make our marriage work. I have no cause for complaint. He sees to my every want and need."

"But does he love ye, 'Sabelle? Are ye *happy* with him, dear sister?" Giles asked again, wanting to be certain that Isabella was not, in truth, miserable and trying to hide the fact from him.

She answered slowly, considering.

"Warrick—Warrick does not love me, Giles, not yet, though I have set about to win his heart. Like me, he was terribly hurt in the past by the betrayal of his love; and the wound has yet to heal. But still, he desires me," the girl told her brother frankly, "and methinks he has come to care for me a little. 'Tis a beginning at least. And he does give thought to my happiness, which is more than many men would do. I know he would fight like an animal to protect me, even as he did that day at Oakengates. Aye, I am content."

Giles seemed relieved by this.

"Then I am glad for ye, 'Sabelle."

"Then come, dear brother." Isabella smiled and held out her hand. "I wouldst like for ye to know my husband better, for if he is to love me, he must also love ye, who are so much a part of me."

* * *

It was nearly three days later when Lord Lionel Valeureux made his appearance at Court. With him was his wife, the Lady Gilliane. Despite the fact that he despised her, Lionel had realized it was only proper she be presented at Court, and so he had sent for her to join him in London.

Isabella's fingers tightened whitely on Warrick's arm as she spied Lionel across the great hall, for though she had guessed he too, like Giles, had come to London, she had not realized how the sight of her former lover would affect her. Warrick glanced down at her stricken face, then searched the chamber rapidly for the cause of her distress. His jaw set in a hard line.

"So ye do yet have some tender feelings for Lord Lionel after all, madam," the Earl growled accusingly.

"Ye of all people must know that a wound such as I suffered at his hands takes time to heal, my lord," Isabella reminded her husband quietly. "His appearance took me by surprise. I am sorry I was not better at masking my emotions at his presence, but do not think I love him still, Warrick, for I do not. 'Tis but a wistful sadness for what might have been that pierces my heart a little. I pray ye do not judge me too harshly for that."

"Nay, I do not, my lady. I do but warn ye to remember ye are my wife and that I demand your loyalty to me—in both body and mind."

"I do not forget, my lord. My loyalty is yours and has been since the day we were wed. I wouldst not be so foolish or cruel as to deceive ye—in any manner. May we—may we retire now, Warrick?"

"Nay, 'Sabelle. I'll have no coward as my wife. Ye shall not hide from him but stay, and let him see ye do not wear your heart upon your sleeve for him."

"As—as ye wish then, my lord. Tell me: Is—is that his wife?" the girl asked, gazing at the woman who accompanied Lionel.

"I believe so."

"She—she doesn't look very happy, does she?"

"Nay, madam, she does not. Rhys told me 'twas well known the Lady Gilliane had no desire to marry the heir of

St. Saviour—or any other man, for that matter. She is very religious and wished to enter a convent."

"Then I am sorry for her," Isabella said as she studied the Lady Gilliane covertly. "For I do not think that Lionel has treated her as kindly as ye have me, Warrick."

And indeed, this was the truth. Lady Gilliane Valeureux, née Beaumaris, was absolutely terrified of her husband. Small, brown, and plain, she reminded one of a shy, frightened mouse and looked just as scared as she stared about the great hall, thoroughly miserable and ashamed.

Earlier, though she and her maids had tried their best to win his approval, Lionel had been, as usual, highly displeased by her appearance. Angered, as always, by just the mere sight of her, he had shouted at her meanly and, after dealing her several sharp slaps for being so stupid and unattractive, had curtly ordered her to change into a decent gown. But Gilliane had had nothing more appropriate. Upon being informed of this, Lionel had ripped open the lids of her coffers and yanked out every one of her dresses, wrathfully flinging them about and trampling on them in disgust when he saw she had spoken the truth. He had then alternately raged at and abused her for over an hour for not having had sense enough to purchase some garments suitable for Court; and Gilliane had been too intimidated by him to point out that he had given her no money with which to do so. Now, she was even more dejectedly aware that her dull drab attire, which resembled a nun's habit, was hopelessly out of place among the stylish, brilliantly colored clothes worn by the rest of the Court ladies; and though she was trying very hard not to cry, she was petrified she would burst into tears at any minute. That would be disastrous, for Lionel would surely beat her again without mercy once they had reached the privacy of their chamber. She yearned fervently to slip away unnoticed, but she knew her husband would refuse his permission for her to leave the great hall, and so she said nothing of her desire. Instead, she attempted to concentrate on the conversations going on about her and wished desperately that she were not so ugly and slow-witted.

In truth, Gilliane's plainness stemmed far more from her natural timidity than anything else, for her countenance was not disagreeable. She had a pair of fine, soft brown eyes that could glow quite beautifully upon occasion (though she seldom raised them long enough for anyone to discover this fact), and her upturned nose was set above a gently curving mouth that gave evidence of her sweet nature. Her round cheeks were fair and dusky-pink in hue, and her brown hair curled about her face in a touchingly childlike manner that was really most fetching, had Lionel but taken the time to observe it.

She was not at all stupid. On the contrary, she was, in reality, very intelligent and highly learned, for she had spent most of her life studying diligently in preparation for the day when she hoped to seek her vocation at the cloister near her father's keep. Gilliane had not believed that Lord St. Saviour, upon being told of her religious aspirations, would still insist on her betrothal to his son, or that her father, Lord Devizes, would actually force her to wed Lionel Valeureux. She knew it had been only to join their lands: for though Lionel was his father's heir, Gilliane's father had none. The Devizes charter prohibited women from inheriting. Unless Gilliane were to bear a son, her father's estate, upon his death, would be forfeit to the Crown, leaving her virtually penniless. But the girl had not cared. Had she entered a nunnery, she would have had no need of riches. The small income she would have received would have sufficed.

"Look!" Gilliane was startled out of her reverie by Sir André Montague's cry. "'Tis the Rose of Rapture. Come, Edmund. We must discover whether or not she is wearing Geoffrey's bouquet. If she is not, then we have won our wager!"

Feeling more conspicuously malapropos than ever, Gilliane gazed after the hurriedly departing courtiers, who were jesting and laughing as they made their way toward one of the loveliest women she had ever seen in her life. Hesitantly, Gilliane laid her hand on her husband's arm, then ventured tentatively to ask, "My—my lord, who is that lady there? The one to whom Sir André is speaking?"

Lionel felt as though someone had hit him hard in the stomach when, frowning, he glanced impatiently at the woman his wife had been curious enough to dare to question him about.

Isabella. Oh, God, Isabella!

His heart caught in his throat, for she seemed even more beautiful than he had remembered. For just an instant, his golden visage was naked with pain and hunger; and Gilliane, by his side, gave a soft little cry of pity.

"Why, ye love her, my lord," she breathed in sudden understanding. "That is why ye despise me so."

"Aye, ye simpleminded strumpet," Lionel snarled down at her, his hand tightening on the chalice of wine he was holding. "For once, ye got something right."

Gilliane cringed at her husband's hateful words, but still, she dared to inquire again after the woman's identity.

"But who—who is she, my lord?"

"Lady Isabella Tremayne, Countess of Hawkhurst," Lionel replied tersely, a muscle working in his jaw. He took a large draught of the liquor, then wiped his mouth on his sleeve. "And the whoreson son of a bitch with her is her husband, Warrick, a half-Welsh bastard," he sneered, then gave a short, ugly laugh, his blue eyes narrowing dangerously. "I wonder how she likes his bed, the witch!"

Sir André Montague, returning in time to overhear this last remark, spoke.

"If ye are referring to the Rose of Rapture, the answer to your question is, apparently, quite well indeed. Lady Hawkhurst has eyes for no one but her husband, much to her would-be cavaliers' dismay. Though the courtiers have wooed her most relentlessly, she has scorned all their attempts to win her favor. Even so, they still persist in their attentions to her and have even begun wagering amongst themselves as to who will be the man fortunate—or foolish—enough to cuckold Lord Hawkhurst."

"Why, that's terrible!" Gilliane uttered, shocked.

"One of the Court's favorite pastimes, Lady Gilliane, I'm afraid," Sir André stated somewhat dryly.

Well, I'm no fool, Lionel thought as he took another

long swig of wine from his cup. *But if I'm clever, I might get lucky.*

Isabella, standing by her husband's side and talking to her brother and Lord Montecatini, shivered suddenly as she saw the way in which Lionel's eyes were raking her body— and before his wife too, the poor girl.

"Is something amiss, Lady Hawkhurst?" the Count queried, raising one dark brow curiously.

"Nay, 'twas naught," she assured him quickly, knowing both Warrick and Giles had guessed the cause of her distress but were too protective of her to comment upon it before the Italian. She gave a little laugh. "For a moment, I thought I spied Sir Geoffrey Twyford coming this way, and I feared he meant to reproach me for not wearing his bouquet, thereby causing him to lose his wager with Sirs André Montague and Edmund Lacey."

Briefly, Lord Montecatini studied Isabella thoughtfully, aware she had not given him the real reason behind her sudden discomposure. Then, from beneath half-closed lids, he gazed surreptitiously about the room to ferret out the true cause of her unease. Neither Lord Lionel Valeureux's glittering blue eyes hungrily devouring Isabella, nor the Lady Gilliane's misery escaped the Count's detection. He perceived too that neither Lord Hawkhurst nor Lord Rushden had favored Lord Lionel with more than a curt nod of recognition, indicating that they were *not* on the best terms with the heir of St. Saviour. Inwardly, the Italian smiled. The Fates had indeed been most kind to him of late.

"'Twas most foolish of Sir Geoffrey to have made such a wager in the first place," Lord Montecatini continued smoothly. "He has no one to blame but himself for the losing of it, for any fool can see ye have eyes for no one but your husband." He turned to the Earl. "Ye are indeed a most fortunate man, Lord Hawkhurst."

"I have always thought so," Warrick agreed somewhat coolly, for there was something about the Count that disturbed him, although he couldn't quite put his finger on what it was.

He had heard certain rumors about the Italian, but that

was all they were, for Lord Montecatini was a most secretive man and jealously guarded his privacy. There was no actual proof the Count had ever been involved in anything unsavory, although, of course, all Italians were always suspected of dealing in poisons, fatal potions being, apparently, a favorite method of eliminating one's rivals at the Roman Court. Even in England, there were those lords and ladies who so feared being murdered in such a fashion that they would drink from nothing but cups of the finest hand-blown crystal, the glass being thought to render poisons harmless. And there were others who were always careful to pass a shark's tooth over a chalice before sipping from it (it was believed the tooth would turn colors if poison were present in the contents of the cup).

Still, although gossips speculated on Lord Montecatini's knowledge of this murderous art, it was not these rumors the Earl found distasteful. Though poison was not a means that Warrick would have chosen to rid himself of his enemies, it was certainly no more dishonorable than sneaking down a shadowed corridor to knife someone in the back, the method preferred by the English.

The dark hints that the vain, handsome Count favored young men rather than young maids were what gave the Earl a slight sense of disgust and unease whenever he encountered the Italian.

Warrick scrutinized Lord Montecatini carefully, certain the Count had guessed the true cause of Isabella's momentary anguish. For some strange reason, the Earl found the thought vaguely discomforting; and he did not like, besides, the manner in which the Italian was staring at Giles. For one unguarded instant, Warrick could have sworn he saw a blaze of lust in Lord Montecatini's black eyes when they looked at Isabella's brother. Without warning, the Earl realized that as his wife was beautiful, so Giles was handsome. The idea that the Count might seek to seduce Giles alarmed Warrick. His brother-in-law was young and relatively inexperienced. He would be at the mercy of a clever, determined man like the Italian. The Earl must take immediate steps to prevent Giles from falling into the Italian's clutches.

To do that, Warrick must find some way to be rid of Lord Montecatini and whatever schemes he might be plotting.

"Come 'Sabelle. Giles," Warrick ordered abruptly. "The hour grows late, and as Giles and I have both entered our names on the lists for the King's tourney tomorrow, we should no doubt seek our beds. Do ye tilt, my lord?" the Earl asked of the Count.

"Alas, nay. I have no taste for jousting, I'm afraid."

"But of course. Your . . . *preferences* are well known, Lord Montecatini," Warrick drawled, deliberately provocative and insulting. "What a pity. Methinks 'twould be most interesting to cross steel with ye."

The Italian did not miss the double meaning of—or warning in—the Earl's words. One eyebrow lifted.

"Indeed? Then, of course, ye must allow me the honor of granting ye that privilege, my lord," the Count stated politely.

"Until tomorrow then," Warrick said. "Come, 'Sabelle. Giles."

Isabella's brother was surprised and slightly offended at being commanded by his sister's husband to leave the great hall, especially as the Earl's rank was no higher than his own. Then Giles recalled how desperately Isabella longed to make her marriage work and how difficult this would be if there were to be trouble between Warrick and him, so he made his adieus politely and followed the newlyweds from the chamber.

Not a one of the three looked back, thereby missing the faintly twisted sneer of amusement that Lord Montecatini wore upon his shuttered face and the sudden flame of anger that lit his black eyes.

Chapter Twenty-five

THE DAY OF THE KING'S TOURNEY DAWNED BRIGHT AND clear that warm summer day of July. Above, the yellow sun shone down mellowly this early morn, although it promised to grow hotter the higher it rose in the brilliant azure sky. Huge, white cotton-candy clouds floated serenely in the firmament, little wisps drifting away, now and then, with the breeze. Below, Tower Green was like a sea of emerald, the trees wafting gently with the wind, their verdant branches rustling. The River Thames sparkled blue beneath the sun, its rippling waters lapping softly at the hulls of the boats and barges that filled the harbor.

All along the shore, merchants hawked their wares, and crowds thronged, hoping to catch a glimpse of some of the more famous personages who were making their way toward the river. Isabella fairly skipped along on her husband's arm; she was so excited. When they had gone to Westminster Palace, they had ridden by horse, taking King's Road, on which only persons of blood or rank were allowed to travel. To reach Edward's residence at Greenwich, where the tourney was to be held, they were journeying by barge. As Isabella had never been aboard any type of water-going vessel before, she was naturally quite thrilled by the prospect. Even the slight rocking of the barge as Warrick handed her into it did not dim her anticipation, though Jocelyn grew quite pale and begged her mistress to sit down immediately. Caerllywel laughed as he sprawled down beside the maid, encircling her waist with his arm and vowing cheerfully, at the cost of his own life, to prevent her from drowning, should the vessel sink.

"Oh, sir," Jocelyn breathed with dismay, gazing down at the river that now seemed too close for comfort. "Do ye think there's a chance that might happen?"

"Of course not, Jocelyn!" Isabella asserted, frowning sternly at her brother-in-law. "Caerllywel was jesting, as usual."

"What makes ye so certain of that, my lady?" he asked, his eyes dancing.

"Because ye wouldst say anything in order to gain the opportunity of consoling a pretty maid," the girl responded tartly, though she was not at all displeased by the romance that appeared to be budding between her maid and Caerllywel. "Pay no heed to the rogue, Jocelyn," she commanded firmly. "And tell him he must mend his wayward manners before you'll have aught to do with him."

"Aye," Warrick said with a grin as he took his place beside Isabella under the striped canopy that protected them from the sun's rays. "The devil could well do with some lessons on that score."

Caerllywel's answer to this was to snatch off the Earl's plumed hat and toss it overboard.

"Oh," Isabella gasped as the two brothers proceeded to scuffle good-naturedly, and the barge tilted alarmingly.

"Oh, my lord and sir, I beg ye to stop at once," Jocelyn pleaded, clutching one side of the vessel frantically.

Even Ragnor, perched firmly upon Isabella's shoulder (for the hawk now accompanied her wherever she went), squawked with annoyance.

"Here, here, Warrick. Caerllywel," Giles put in as he retrieved the now-sodden hat before it floated away. "You're frightening Jocelyn, and Isabella is looking none too well either. Remember—neither of them has ever been aboard a barge before."

Upon being reminded of this and seeing that the two girls really did look a trifle green about the gills, the brothers ceased their mock battle and settled down in their seats once more. As best he could, Giles wrung Warrick's hat out and, trying hard not to laugh at its shameful condition, handed it back to the Earl. Warrick glanced ruefully at its sadly dripping feather while Caerllywel shook with silent merriment.

"Ye *know* I always repay ye for these childish pranks of yours, brother," the Earl said somewhat crossly, "so I do not understand why ye persist in them."

"And *I* do not understand why ye don't develop a sense of humor, Waerwic. Really, Isabella, how do ye stand the arrogant churl?"

She was saved from replying to this question by Warrick asking whether or not he was to consider the damage done to his hat diverting.

"I found it most diverting indeed," Caerllywel assured his brother, thereby earning another box to his ears.

This would have set the brothers off once more, had not

Isabella protested that others were now getting into the barge, among them Lord and Lady Stanley, who would not look leniently on being overturned into the Thames. Warrick and Caerllywel sobered quickly enough upon having their attention drawn to this fact, although the Earl had the temerity to grab off his brother's hat and exchange it with his own. Caerllywel tried to smile nonchalantly as he was forced to doff the wet hat to Lady Stanley, who eyed him reprovingly before taking her seat.

Shortly thereafter, the barge began to move slowly down the river until it had reached the Royal palace at Greenwich.

The Palace of Placentia, as it was now called, was extremely old. It had come to the Crown through King Henry V in 1414; but for over five centuries before that, it had belonged to the Abbey of St. Peter of Ghent. His Grace the Duke of Gloucester, Humphrey, Henry's youngest brother, had been made a grant of the manor and there had built himself a large keep, complete with battlements, towers, and a moat. He had named it Bella Court. A smaller, outlying fortress, which was now known as Duke Humphrey's Tower, guarded the strategic road from Dover to London.

After the Duke had been arrested for high treason and had died in prison, Bella Court had passed into the hands of Queen Marguerite of Anjou, who had changed its name to the Palace of Placentia. The vain Queen had taken great pains to leave her mark upon the castle, fitting the windows with the costliest of glass and paving the floors with terracotta tiles that were engraved with her monogram. In addition, she had commanded sculptors to ornament the pillars and arcades of the residence with her emblem, the ox-eyed daisy that bore her name. To house her many jewels, she had ordered a vestry constructed; and west of the keep, in the Thames, she had had a pier erected so royal barges might land without mishap there, no matter the state of the tide.

It was this wharf that the vessel containing Isabella and the rest of her companions now approached. Once they had reached the dock, several able-handed men ran forward to catch the lines cast to them by the numerous oarsmen who had rowed the barge, and the vessel was safely moored until such time as it would be needed again. Warrick, Caerllywel, and Giles leaped lightly ashore, then turned to assist the girls as they disembarked.

After that, they made their way to the palace greens, where the tourney was to be held. Although the keep did not boast a formal tiltyard, Isabella saw, as they neared the fortress, that great pains had been taken to prepare the lawns for the coming joust. Tiered benches, set beneath canopies, lined one complete side of the arena and were already starting to be filled with the spectators who were making their ways from the barges. On the opposite side of the stadium stood the brightly colored pavilions of the lords and knights who had entered the lists. The gay tents, with their banners rippling gently in the slight breeze, had been erected earlier that morn by each participant's men-at-arms and squires, who had been entrusted with the bringing of destriers and armor as well.

"My Lady Hawkhurst?" A small page ran forward upon spying the girl.

"Aye."

The boy bowed respectfully, then, his young face puckered up with concentration, breathlessly rattled off the message he bore for her.

"Her Grace the Duchess of Gloucester humbly begs the presence of ye and your companions in her box and would be most pleased if ye would join her."

"Oh," Isabella gasped with surprise, startled and much touched. "How kind of her grace. Do go, and inform my lady Duchess that we are most honored by her request and would be very happy to join her," the girl said, handing the lad a silver coin from her purse.

The boy's face beamed as gladly he accepted the half crown she offered him. Then, after being certain he had committed her reply, word for word, to memory, he raced off to deliver it.

Warrick, Caerllywel, and Giles escorted Isabella and Jocelyn to Anne's box, then, after paying their respects to the Duchess, departed for their pavilions to ready themselves for the tilting. Isabella, although she had corresponded with Anne over the years, had never met the Duchess and sat down a trifle shyly beside her.

Like Isabella, Anne was very small and slender, even more so: for the Duchess seemed almost too thin and wan, too frail to endure the rigors of the world. Her delicate, exquisitely drawn face was heart-shaped and her skin, almost translucent; it was so pure and pale. Her hair was a bright, lustrous shade of chestnut streaked with gold that matched the amber flecks of her warm, dark brown eyes. Her cheekbones were fine and high; her nose was straight and narrow; her mouth was full and soft. Arrestingly beautiful, her whole appearance was such that Isabella found no difficulty in perceiving why Richard loved his wife so and fought so fiercely to protect her; and the girl knew at once that she too would love Anne.

"Your grace," Isabella murmured, "how kind of ye to invite us to join ye."

"My lady"—Anne's voice was low and gentle—"'twas the least I could do for Giles's dear sister and one whose letters have oft brightened my days. I hope I didst not upset any other arrangements ye might have made, but I found I couldst not forego the opportunity to meet ye at last."

"I had no other plans, your grace," Isabella assured her, "and I also am glad of the chance to meet ye and to thank ye, in person, for your many past kindnesses to me and my brother. Ye cannot guess what I, especially, would have suffered in my childhood, had it not been for ye and your husband. 'Twas indeed most generous and thoughtful of ye to take an interest in a young maid who had no claim upon ye."

"I fear ye are too kind, my lady, for it cost me little enough to befriend ye. A few letters written to a frightened child—what is that?" the Duchess asked.

"Yet, there are those who would not have done as much," Isabella remarked.

"Then I pity them," Anne stated simply, "for they are without compassion and doubtless find little love or joy in their lives. How could I have done less when I learned of your plight, my lady? Indeed, I wish only that I had been able to do more. It must have been horrid to have been raised by such persons as Lord Oadby and Lady Shrewton," the Duchess went on softly, her dark eyes flashing a little with anger. "I guessed immediately, from Dickon's letter to me, explaining the matter, how things stood at Rushden. My heart ached for ye, my lady, for I too was once in the clutches of those who would have used me ill; and I know how bereft one feels at knowing one is helpless to defend oneself."

Isabella knew that Anne was referring to her late brother-in-law George, Duke of Clarence, who, in order to retain control of her vast lands and wealth, had held her prisoner and attempted to prevent her marriage to Richard. Only by disguising herself and fleeing, with the aid of friends, to work as a scullery maid in a tavern, had the Duchess been able to escape from George and remain in hiding long enough for Richard to find and save her.

"'Twas indeed a sore trial to me, your grace," Isabella confided. "I only hope I faced it as bravely as ye didst your own difficulties."

"I have no doubt ye did, 'Sabelle," Anne told her, smiling. "I hope I may call ye that . . . 'Sabelle, I mean. I have grown so accustomed to hearing Giles refer to ye so."

"But of course, your grace."

"Nay." Impulsively, the Duchess took the girl's hand. "Ye must call me Anne, for in my heart, I know we are going to be the best of friends, dear 'Sabelle."

And so did the relationship between the two women, begun so long ago that day in the courtyard at Rushden when Richard had handed a frightened child a single gold sovereign, deepen into a friendship that was to last until Anne died, with Isabella, heartbroken, at her beloved lady's side.

Still, the two women had no knowledge then of the tragic illness that was to claim the kind young Duchess's life, and so they laughed gaily together as they turned to view the sights, the coronet of Anne's russet hair glowing like a halo beneath the golden sun.

The Duchess's face softened tenderly as her eyes found

Richard, her husband. Mounted upon a chestnut steed with four white stockings, he slowly approached their box, leaning from his saddle to kiss his wife's outstretched hand. Briefly, they caressed each other with their eyes, as though they were alone; and Isabella saw the two were indeed deeply in love. For one painful instant, the girl felt an empty, aching sense of longing in her heart. If only she and Warrick loved so! Then Richard smiled at her, and the moment passed.

"My Lady Hawkhurst," he greeted her.

"Your grace. I have been thanking your wife for her many kindnesses to me. Now I must thank ye too, your grace, for what ye did for my brother."

With one gauntleted hand the Duke waved away her gratitude.

"'Twas naught, my lady. I didst but listen and offer a few words of comfort to Giles."

"Aye, perhaps, but they cheered him beyond measure, your grace. We are both deeply indebted to ye and her grace. I do not know how we shall ever repay ye."

"Remember us in your prayers, my lady," Gloucester reminded her gently. "We ask for no more than that."

"Then know that as long as I live, ye shall never be forgotten, your grace," Isabella vowed fervently, "for I do pray for ye both each night and ask God's blessing to be upon ye."

"'Tis payment enough then," Richard said, then teased, "but I wouldst not cast aside a small favor for luck this day, my lady."

Both Isabella and Anne unwound a riband from their braids and, with much laughter, wrapped the trailing silk about the Duke's arm. He glanced down at the favors that had been bestowed upon him and once more smiled.

"I cannot fail to win the honors," he announced, "for I have been doubly blessed."

"Ye shall not be the only man here so favored, however, your grace," Giles declared as he rode up, armored now, "for I too must claim ribands from these ladies."

"And I," Warrick and Caerllywel, also now ready for battle, echoed as one.

By the time the men had departed (Caerllywel considering himself the luckiest of the four, having garnered a favor from a blushing Jocelyn as well), neither Isabella nor Anne had a single riband left. They gazed at one another ruefully, then burst into laughter, for the intricately woven plaits their maids had arranged so skillfully this morn now seemed woefully bereft.

"Well, if one of our men at least does not win here today, Jocelyn will have my head," Isabella jested, her eyes twinkling as she glanced at the maid, who had braided her mistress's hair earlier.

"Oh, my lady," Jocelyn said, "ye know full well there were so many ribands precisely so ye *couldst* give them away. All the ladies have done as much. Only think how unhappy ye wouldst be if your plaits were still adorned like that poor woman's there." Jocelyn pointed surreptitiously.

"Aye, how sad," Anne exclaimed while Isabella's mouth twisted with pity and anger upon spying Lionel's wife, the Lady Gilliane. "Who is she?" the Duchess inquired, her dark eyes filled with sympathy for the obviously miserable girl's plight.

"The Lady Gilliane, Lord Lionel Valeureux's wife, your grace," Isabella informed her friend, still wroth over Lionel not begging a favor from the girl, even for appearance's sake.

He might as well have publicly slapped her, for it was clear he had no interest in his bride. Even now, Isabella could see the girl was trying hard not to cry; she was so crushed by her husband's open repudiation of her.

"Lionel's wife?" Anne's brown orbs widened with surprise. "But I did not know she was at Court. I must ask her join us at once."

"Aye, please do, Anne," Isabella urged, "for I believe she has made few, if any, friends here; and I know that Lionel is—is not kind to her."

"Oh, 'Sabelle," the Duchess sighed sorrowfully, her face downcast. "'Tis true, then. I—I had heard that Lionel was most displeased with his bride, but I had hoped 'twas not true—" She broke off and bit her lip. "Does he—does he treat her so badly, then?"

"Ye have only to look at her to guess the answer to that, your grace."

Anne's lips compressed together sternly.

"Tim. Tim," she called to her page; then, when the boy had bowed before her, she directed, "Go, and tell the Lady Gilliane that I wouldst be most pleased if she wouldst join me in my box."

"Aye, your grace." The lad bobbed again, then scampered off.

Presently, timidly, as though she feared she were the butt of someone's nasty jest, Lionel's wife approached them.

"Your—your grace," she stammered painfully. "I'm so sorry to disturb ye, but I—I received a message..."

"Aye, my lady. Ye didst indeed. Please, join us. I'm so glad you've come," the Duchess stated graciously with a smile, then bade her women make room for Gilliane and her maid.

Relieved to find it had not all been just a prank, Gilliane sat down gingerly on the edge of one of the terraced benches and had nothing further to say, beyond thanking Anne for her invitation, until the Duchess began kindly to draw the girl out. Before long, much of Gilliane's fear had receded, and Anne had obtained a riband from the girl, explaining that she wished to send it to Richard in order that the number of his favors might equal Caerllywel's. Secretly, the Duchess intended to ask the Duke to mention the matter to Lionel in hopes that the heir of St. Saviour would be pleased that Gilliane's gesture had won Gloucester's regard. In addition, Anne was determined to inform Richard of Lionel's mistreatment of his wife (for she was, by now, indignantly certain the girl *had* been terribly abused), and she meant to beg the Duke to strongly reprimand his knight.

This decided, the Duchess lifted her chin a little, then turned her flashing eyes toward the field as the herald announced, at last, the start of the tourney.

"Lord Thomas Grey, Marquis of Dorset, and Lord William Hastings," the herald bawled over the din.

The opening bout was merely a formality. Neither lord was expected to be unhorsed, and, after making three relatively tame passes at each other along the wooden barrier that separated them, the two men retired from the arena amid a scattering of polite applause. The crowd was somewhat disappointed, for the rivalry between these two favorites of the King was well known; and the audience had secretly hoped for a more stimulating battle, despite it being the ceremonial tilt of the tourney.

"Lord Anthony Woodville, Earl Rivers, and Sir Edmund Lacey," the herald announced.

"I do not know why Ned persists in holding these jousts," Anne leaned over to whisper of the King. "Anthony, who is Ned's champion, is the best tilter in all of England. Doubtless, he will win again today and crown the Queen, his sister, queen of the tourney, as usual."

"Is he so very good then?" Isabella inquired.

"Aye, ye wouldst not think it, because of his scholarly disposition—ye know he aided William Caxton in publishing the first bound book in England—but Anthony knows full well how to handle his lance," the Duchess claimed. "That is why so many young knights like Sir Edmund choose to joust against him. 'Twould indeed be quite a feather in their caps if they were to unhorse Earl Rivers."

Unfortunately, this glorious fate was not to be Sir Edmund's that day. On the first pass, he was ignominiously unseated and left to sprawl in the dust amid the laughter of the spectators. Hurriedly, his squires ran forward to assist him to his feet (for he could not rise unaided; his armor was so heavy). Then, not to be undone, he took off his helmet and, with a flourish, bowed gallantly to the crowd, who shouted its approval.

The day wore on, growing hotter with the sun's ascent, as Isabella had earlier perceived it would. Though the canopy above provided a welcome shade, the girl fluttered her fan languidly now and then, glad she had had the foresight to bring it. Other ladies, less thoughtful, were having to purchase the devices from the vendors who, hawking their wares in loud voices, strode among the audience. One merchant, seeing that Gilliane's hands were empty, approached her and held up a pretty fan for her inspection. But though she eyed the device longingly, Lionel's bride shook her head reluctantly and waved the man away. Isabella, who had noticed the exchange, rightly guessed that Gilliane had no money.

"Oh, look, Jocelyn!" Isabella exclaimed, nudging her maid covertly. "Do ye not think that fan would go well with my powder-blue gown?"

"Aye, my lady." Jocelyn, an astute young maid, correctly interpreted her mistress's intent and called the vendor to their side.

Isabella paid for the device, then, after studying it closely for some moments, sighed as though highly aggrieved.

Somewhat crossly, she said, "Jocelyn, I am persuaded this is not the right blue after all. In fact, I am certain 'tis much too dark. I cannot think what possessed me to believe 'twas otherwise and to buy this fan for which I am now sure I have no use. What is to be done? I fear my lord will be most angry upon learning how foolishly I have wasted his coin. Indeed, he is so jealous, I doubt he will even believe I purchased the device at all. I'll warrant he will think 'tis a gift from one of the courtiers. Oh, Gilliane, I wish ye had bought the accursed fan yourself, for it matches your dress perfectly!"

"Why, there is your answer, my lady," Jocelyn declared. "Ye have only to give the fan to the Lady Gilliane, and say naught to Lord Hawkhurst at all. Then he will know nothing of the matter."

"Oh, how clever of ye, Jocelyn!" Isabella turned back to Lionel's wife. "My dear Lady Gilliane, do be kind enough to assist me out of this sad tangle. I am newly wed, ye know, and 'twould be most distressing to me to incur my husband's wrath; I have tried so hard to win his favor."

"'Twould then be most churlish of me to refuse your request, my lady," Gilliane answered softly.

"I am most grateful to ye," Isabella told Lionel's wife, handing her the device.

"And I to ye," Gilliane murmured. "'Tis ye who are most kind."

"Not at all," Isabella disclaimed, then added excitedly, "Oh, look, Anne! My brother has bested his man!"

"That was well done of ye, 'Sabelle," the Duchess observed under her breath as they enthusiastically applauded Giles's victory on the field. Then, more loudly, she queried, "'Tis his first tournament too, is it not?"

"Aye, oh, how proud I am of him!" Isabella's eyes shone for her brother.

"And I of ye," Anne said quietly. "How glad I am that Dickon bade ye write to me that day. Oh, here are two of Dickon's dearest friends, Lord Francis Lovell and Sir Richard Ratcliffe. I must make ye known to them. Why, they have brought us some wine. How thoughtful."

The women spent some time conversing and laughing with these two gentlemen, both of whom proved most amiable; then Isabella's attention was drawn once more to the stadium as the herald called two more names.

"Lord Warrick ap Tremayne, Earl of Hawkhurst, and Lord Dante da Forenza, *Conte di Montecatini*."

"How odd of the Italian," a woman in the next box remarked curiously. "He is not usually given to entering the lists. 'Tis said he is too vain to risk injury to his handsome face, the arrogant devil."

"That is so, Agatha," another woman uttered in response. "But my husband, Cedric, who happened to overhear their conversation, tells me the challenge was issued by Lord Hawkhurst; and of course, the Count could not possibly refuse it."

"Well, naturally, a man must defend his honor. Still, it does seem rather peculiar. I wonder: Did they quarrel, Juliet? Oh, surely not," the Lady Agatha mused. "For doubtless, Lord Montecatini would not be so foolish as to allow himself to be drawn into an argument. After all, he is one of Italy's ambassadors to England and must refrain from becoming embroiled in our affairs."

"Hmph!" the Lady Juliet snorted. "Ye cannot tell me consideration of his position would weigh with the Italian if it interfered with any of his own schemes. If ye ask me, the man's a master of intrigue and meddles far more in England's business than we know. However, that's neither here nor there, as I doubt seriously that politics was the reason behind the challenge. Cedric did not say so, but I cannot help but think 'tis the attention the Count has paid to Lady Hawkhurst that made Lord Hawkhurst wroth, for ye know that Lord Montecatini has singled her out most markedly."

"Oh, that is nothing, Juliet; I'm sure," the Lady Agatha sniffed. "The Rose of Rapture has been the bane of us all since her arrival at Court. I vow there's not a cavalier left whose heart remains uncaptivated by her. Even dear Rufus, whom I always believed to be a most estimable husband, has fallen for her charms."

"Perhaps," the Lady Juliet conceded, "but I'm certain I do not need to tell ye the gossip about the Count's preferences, Agatha. One cannot help but think 'tis strange of him to be wooing Lady Hawkhurst—if rumor is to be believed. And I, for one, did not notice he paid her any more heed than was courteous until her brother, Lord Rushden, arrived. 'Tis well known the Ashleys are extremely close. To befriend one is to become the other's companion as well. I'll wager that Lord Hawkhurst has no intention of seeing his young brother-in-law fall prey to the Italian's clutches."

"*Juliet!*" the Lady Agatha gasped, horrified.

The Lady Juliet merely shrugged, having lost interest in the subject.

"'Tis merely my own conjecture, of course," she said, "but I wouldst not be surprised to learn 'twas true. However, ye may believe what ye choose, Agatha."

The matter thus disposed of, the Lady Juliet turned to view the two combatants on the field.

Had Isabella overheard the two women's conversation, she would have been beset with anxiety for her brother. But her ears had discerned nothing of the exchange, and so she knew no fear for Giles. Only worry for Warrick filled her mind, for despite the jousts being but games, accidents *did* happen, and she had no wish for her husband to be injured or killed.

She was unaware her face softened as she caught sight of him, looking like some dark and pagan god upon his mighty brown destrier with its golden-cream mane and tale. His armor glinted silver where the sun's rays struck it, enveloping him in a blaze of flame as he saluted the King and Queen, then wheeled his steed to pace slowly down the stadium. His gold-lined, brown satin cloak swirled down in shining folds from his broad shoulders; the hawk embroidered on its back proudly proclaimed his heritage for all to see. His tobacco-brown hair, streaked with gold and shagged back in wings on either side, and his aquiline nose reminded all uncannily of the bird whose badge he wore—as the bend sinister on his shield reminded them of his bastardy. In battle or game, he would be a deadly opponent.

When he had reached the end of the field, Warrick turned and dipped his lance toward Isabella in acknowledgment of his lady. She was touched by the unexpected gesture, and as the audience roared its approval, she caught Ragnor upon her wrist and raised him high, as though in victory. The hawk, somehow sensing all eyes upon him, flung back his head and gave a shrill wild cry that echoed sweetly across the arena. His fierce amber eyes pierced the Earl's own, and for a moment, it seemed almost as though Warrick and Ragnor were one and the same. Then the Earl broke the spell, donning his helmet, fewtering his weapon, and charging down the field toward his opponent.

Lord Montecatini, at the opposite end of the stadium, spurred his own horse forward, meeting the onslaught grimly: for briefly, the bird's sharp scream had disturbed him. Superstitious, he had thought it an ill omen and had shivered with a sudden, strange premonition, as though someone had walked over his grave. Deliberately now, he forced the unnerving notion from his mind and tried to concentrate on the bout. Though he had no taste for tilting, he was far from being a novice at the sport. Having regained his composure, he studied Warrick with cool assessment as the Earl galloped toward him. Perceiving Warrick's line of attack, the Count shifted his shield accordingly and aimed his own lance expertly. The hooves of his ebony stallion thundered over the turf along the wooden barrier that separated him from his foe. His red-and-gold satin cloak, with its rosettes bearing the badges of griffins, shimmered down from his shoulders like molten fire in the sunlight. His black eyes narrowed, watching Warrick closely for any perceptible movement.

There. Now!

Violently, the two men engaged arms, lances shattering viciously against shields. The Italian rocked in his saddle from the impact, even as the Earl did, for Warrick had not guessed the strength concealed by Lord Montecatini's slender figure.

"God's blood, brother! That was close." Caerllywel whistled as he caught the bridle of the Earl's prancing destrier while Warrick's squire Rhys ran forward with a new weapon. "I thought ye said the Count did not fancy jousting."

"Aye." The Earl nodded tersely. "Still, I should have suspected the whoreson was no fool at the game. Christ's son, but the Italian cavalier is no Court card after all."

"For God's sake, keep your guard up!" Caerllywel warned. "I mislike the look of him, and that was a bad blow ye took. If ye had not switched your shield in time..."

"Do not fear, brother," Warrick said. "I am never twice a fool. I shall be ready for him this time, and then we will see whether or not he persists in his attentions to my wife and her brother."

Caerllywel's eyebrows lifted.

"Though ye paid her a signal honor this day, I did not know ye cared so deeply for 'Sabelle—or for Giles," he commented.

"What is mine, I hold, brother, as well ye know," the Earl told him fiercely before spurring Gwalchmai into the second run.

Again, lances splintered sickeningly upon shields. Isabella half-rose from her bench, one hand going to her throat as a startled cry of anticipation and bloodlust, somehow different from its previous cheering, suddenly rose from the crowd. The King leaned forth in his chair, snapping to attention. That the bout was the most exciting one of the day could not be denied; but without warning, it seemed to have taken on a serious—almost macabre—note that did not belong to the sport.

Elizabeth, the Queen, glanced coolly at her husband,

whose hand had tightened upon the chalice of wine he was holding.

"Methinks this joust is no longer a mere game, Ned," she stated, her icy blue eyes glittering. "It appears that Lord Hawkhurst is even more jealous of his bride than Court gossip has rumored. I do believe he intends to kill the Italian. What will Rome say to that, I wonder?"

"Hawkhurst is not such a fool, Bess," Edward replied curtly. "He means only to humble the Count; I am certain."

"And what of Lord Montecatini? Dost think he intends but to 'humble' Lord Hawkhurst?"

"I do not know. Who can guess what goes on in the minds of foreigners?"

Elizabeth smiled with cruel amusement.

"If he slays your favorite, Ned, do not say I didn't warn ye."

As the audience waited tensely, the two men prepared for the final charge of the bout. Isabella's hand gripped her maid's arm so fervently that her nails dug into Jocelyn's flesh.

"Oh, Anne. I don't understand why, but I—I think they mean to kill each other," Isabella breathed, then wailed, "oh, why doesn't the King put a stop to it?"

"I do not know, 'Sabelle"—the Duchess spoke thoughtfully. "Ned must not feel there is any danger, or I'm certain he wouldst call a halt to the proceedings. After all, the Count is a guest in our country, and Lord Hawkhurst is one of Ned's favorites. He cannot mean to let them battle to the death."

But Isabella was yet afraid as the two men set their gilded spurs to their horses' sides, and the pounding of hooves once more rang out over the field.

Warrick's eyes, like slits behind the visor of his helmet, met Lord Montecatini's ominous gaze unflinchingly. The hawk, with its talons poised to strike, embroidered upon the back of the Earl's cloak seemed to take flight as the breeze caught the material, sending it rippling. The golden griffin that emblazoned the back of the Count's cloak stalked its prey across a sea of red. The beasts clashed, snarled with fury, clawed wickedly at one another until, at last, as though in slow motion, Isabella saw the eagle-headed lion fall, a bright splash of liquid crimson gushing from the wound her husband's lance had made.

An eager, almost unnatural yell came from the throats of the spectators as they leaped to their feet, thirsting for more. Even the King and Queen were standing, watching, waiting.

"My God!" someone shouted. "The Italian's dead!"

"Nay," Isabella whimpered. "Nay."

Warrick had already dismounted and run to his opponent's aid. Quickly, he ripped off Lord Montecatini's helmet, pushed back his mesh hood, and tore away those pieces of armor that had not been broken during the joust.

The Count groaned and smiled faintly as the Earl exposed the gash in the Italian's shoulder and moved to staunch the flow of blood.

"I congratulate ye, my lord," Lord Montecatini said dryly. "The taste of victory is always sweet. Shall I survive, do ye think?"

"Aye." Warrick nodded. "'Tis only a flesh wound and clean. Methinks 'twill not prove mortal."

"And my face, my lord?"

"Your face? Christ's son, Montecatini! Ye might have been slain!"

"Aye, but I am yet alive and wouldst know of my dark beauty. 'Tis my one overwhelming vanity, ye apprehend, this face of mine."

"A few scratches only. 'Twill not be scarred."

The Count sighed with relief.

"Thank God for that. Ye are a worthy foe, Hawkhurst. Methinks we will meet again."

"Be warned: Next time, I mean to kill ye," the Earl threatened through clenched teeth.

The Italian laughed shortly.

"Aye, I suspected as much."

"Keep away from my wife—and her brother," Warrick ordered grimly.

"I have but befriended them, my lord."

"Do not seek to play me for a fool, Montecatini. I know what ye intend."

"Do ye? I wonder. There is only one thing sweeter than victory, Hawkhurst—revenge. I shall have it, I promise ye."

"The boy will scorn ye," the Earl hissed.

"Dost truly believe so, *signore*? I fear ye must enlighten me, then. Why, then didst ye challenge me?"

"Had I thought your victims were all willing ones, I should not have done so. But a man who dabbles in potions—and no doubt the Black Arts as well—is without morals or scruples. I have some slight knowledge of the drugs ye Italians employ, Montecatini. I wouldst not see young Giles made your slave by a craving for the poppy's nectar. I trust, after today, ye will perceive the wisdom of leaving England—before ye are forced to do so. I do not think that Rome will look lightly upon this affair, and I don't believe ye wish to be recalled home in disgrace."

The Count shrugged, his black eyes unfathomable.

"A minor nuisance only, my lord, I assure ye. My family stands high at the Italian Court, very high indeed. Methinks they will manage to salvage my position. Ye have played your hand and lost, Hawkhurst."

"Have I? Giles is one of Gloucester's favorites, Montecatini, and a staunch Yorkist as well. If ye trifle with him, ye will have to answer to the Duke—and the King."

"But then, I am not subject to the whims of the Plantagenets—or to the laws of England, am I, my lord? Besides, 'tis no longer just a matter of the boy. Ye have humbled my pride, *signore*. That I shall not easily forget or forgive."

"Methinks I am well able to defend myself," Warrick rejoined inscrutably. "After all, *I* was the victor here today, was I not?"

"Aye, ye have that satisfaction, Hawkhurst." The Italian's teeth flashed whitely as he smiled again. "Let us hope ye are equally adept at guarding your wife." The Earl inhaled sharply. "Ah, that strikes home, does it not?" Lord Montecatini continued. "I thought perhaps 'twould."

"If ye touch my bride, ye will die most unpleasantly; I swear it," Warrick vowed.

"Dost think so? In Italy, they say I lead a charmed life."

"Even so, Montecatini, I wonder how ye wouldst like living it if something were to happen to your face."

With that parting shot, the Earl walked away, having derived considerable pleasure from seeing the Count blanch momentarily with fear.

Sighing with relief, Isabella settled back upon her bench as she watched her husband leave the arena. The Italian was wounded but not dead, and Warrick was alive and unhurt. That was all that mattered.

"Lord Montecatini will live to fight another day, it seems," Anne observed as the Count's squires pulled him to his feet and helped him off the field.

"Aye," Isabella agreed. "Thank God for it. For a minute, I feared that Warrick had slain him."

The remaining bouts, which included Caerllywel's, were uneventful. Though a relief to Isabella, the rest of the audience soon grew bored and were glad to see the judges begin to compare notes.

"My Lady Hawkhurst?" A small page tentatively approached the box.

"Aye."

"My Lord Hawkhurst wouldst have a word with ye, if ye please."

"But of course." Isabella rose hurriedly to her feet, wondering what her husband wanted. "Oh, I do hope nothing is wrong. Anne, ye will excuse me, won't ye?"

"Of course." The Duchess smiled. "The tourney is almost over anyway. Already, I see the judges conferring among themselves as to which contestant garnered the most points this day."

"Well, if 'tis Earl Rivers, then there's no chance of my being crowned queen, so I won't miss anything. Nay, Jocelyn," Isabella protested as the maid stood. "Ye stay, and see the end, so I will know who won the honors. I will be safe enough with my husband to protect me. In fact, after today, I seriously doubt any courtier will be foolish enough to speak to me."

This soon proved to be the case, for although many admiring glances were cast in Isabella's direction as she followed the page through the crowd, her previously gay cavaliers were noticeably reluctant to attract her attention. Only the most brazen and high-ranking of courtiers, such as Lord Thomas Grey, Marquis of Dorset, dared to accost her and tease her about her husband's now-infamous jealousy. Blushing, the girl scurried on, wishing that Warrick had not made his possessive nature toward her so public and through such means, particularly as Lord Montecatini had pursued her almost indifferently, without the fervent ardor that had characterized many of her cavaliers. Indeed, now that she thought about it, Isabella believed the Count had joined the chase only because it had been the fashion to do so. Certainly, he had been much more talkative to Giles than to her. She wondered curiously why, then, Warrick had singled out the Italian for punishment. Somehow, it seemed rather odd.

"Through there, my lady." The page, as they reached their destination, indicated the open flap of a pavilion, drawing the girl back, with a start, to the present.

"But—but this is not my husband's tent," she stuttered, confused, for Warrick had pointed out his pavilion to her that morning, and as she now attempted to recall it, she did not think it had resembled at all the one she now stood before, nor did she spy any banner to tell her to whom this tent belonged.

The boy shrugged.

"I don't know about that, my lady. This is where my lord said I was to bring ye...."

"Do not fear, lad," Isabella reassured the youth, who was gazing up at her somewhat anxiously. "I have not accused ye of any wrongdoing. 'Tis merely that this is *not* my husband's pavilion. However, perhaps he has some reason for wishing to meet me here. Here." She handed the page a silver coin. "Please go, and tell my maid ye have seen me safely delivered to my husband."

The boy scampered off, as though glad to escape from her presence, causing Isabella to smile a trifle ruefully to herself and to shake her head slightly with amusement.

Children! Briefly, she wondered idly when she might have one, then, mortified, hastily pushed the notion from her head as she remembered how such an event would be brought about. Marry-go-up! Warrick would know instantly that she had been standing outside, daydreaming about their love-making. What on earth would he think? Still a little flushed and flustered by the unbidden pattern of her thoughts, the girl took a deep breath to calm herself and entered the tent.

"Lionel!" Isabella was so stunned, the word burst from her lips involuntarily.

"Aye, 'tis I." The heir of St. Saviour stepped from the shadows, where he had been waiting. "Nay, 'Sabelle, don't go. Please. I'm sorry to have misled ye, but I simply *had* to see ye."

"I'm sure I don't know why. We have nothing to say to each other."

"Don't we?" he asked, his voice low and throbbing with passion. "Oh, 'Sabelle," he whispered feverishly, catching her hands before she realized what he was about. "Ye cannot tell me ye have not hungered for me, as I have hungered for ye since our parting."

"I can and will. What was between us is past. Now let me go. Ye have a wife, and I have a husband who is notorious for his jealousy."

The girl glanced about anxiously for someone who might come to her aid, but she and Lionel were quite alone in the pavilion; he had seen to that, of course.

"Dost think I care for my wife—or your husband?" the heir of St. Saviour snapped. "Oh, God, 'Sabelle. When I think of what I have lost in ye, I damn Gilliane Beaumaris to hell and back! What is she, compared to ye? And what is Hawkhurst? He does not love ye as I do; I swear it!"

"Gilliane is your wife," Isabella repeated coldly, trying to pull her hands from his tight grip. "And ye have shame-fully abused her. Why, do ye know she did not even have money today to buy a fan—the most meager of devices—that she might keep cool beneath the sun's rays? And her garments are pathetic, fit only for the lowliest of scullery maids! I have no doubt that ye beat her besides, for she is terrified of ye, my lord; and I—I am disgusted by your treatment of her, Lionel! I knew ye for a cheat, but until now, I had not thought ye cruel. Now take your hands off me! Warrick is my husband, and I wouldst not play him false, especially for ye."

The harsh words stung, as they were meant to. Snarling under his breath, Lionel yanked her into his arms, causing Ragnor to squawk loudly. Wrathfully, the heir of St. Saviour knocked the hawk from Isabella's shoulder.

"Ragnor!" she wept, horrified, and tried to reach the bird, who was fluttering helplessly upon the ground; but Lionel restrained her.

"That is what I think of your husband, my lady!" the heir of St. Saviour growled, his blue eyes glittering with rage and raking her lustfully. "Your husband! What does he know of ye? *I* know ye. I know ye as he never will. Oh, 'Sabelle, 'Sabelle."

He pressed his lips hotly against her throat, as though he would devour her with his mouth.

"Nay, ye do not," Isabella retorted, seeking once more to escape from him, "else ye wouldst not be attempting to woo me in this fashion. 'Tis crude and deceitful, but I guess I should not have expected any better from ye. For the last time, my lord, I am warning ye: Release me, or I shall scream this tent down about your ears!"

"Nay, 'Sabelle, ye will not, for what would your husband say if he found ye here . . . in my pavilion . . . in my arms?"

"Against my will, Lionel!" the girl reminded him sharply.

"Dost truly think that Hawkhurst would believe that? Nay." Lionel gave a small, nasty laugh. "I thought not. Come, dearest heart. Ye are a maid no longer. I ask only that ye give to me what that whoreson Welsh bastard has had of ye."

Isabelle gasped with shock at his crudity. Managing to free one hand, at last, she brought her palm up and boxed his ears smartly, struggling furiously in his grasp all the while.

"Let me go, ye contemptible scoundrel!" she raged. "How dare ye insult me in such a manner? God's wounds, but

Warrick shall kill ye for this! Let me go! God damn ye! *Let me go!*"

But Lionel only laughed again, tearing at her bodice as he flung her to the earth and fell upon her. And in that moment, Isabella knew, without a doubt, that she did not love him, had never loved him. How could she have? She had not known him. He had been but some romantic figure born of a childhood promise and sought to fulfill a dream. Why, he wasn't fit to wipe Warrick's boots! Warrick, who had mocked her, married her, made love to her. . . .

"God damn ye!" she cried once more. "Ye are no better than Lord Oadby!"

Without warning, the heir of St. Saviour abruptly ceased his assault, for her last accusation battered his senses as none of her previous words had done; and in the sudden lull that had fallen between them, Isabella was somehow able to break loose of his hold and flee. Staggering to her feet, grabbing up Ragnor and clutching him and the torn remnants of her gown to her breast, she ran.

Once outside the tent, she paused a minute to catch her breath, then looked about apprehensively to be certain no one had observed her flight from Lionel's pavilion. She inhaled sharply, the fresh air she'd taken in seeming to choke in her throat as her grey-green eyes met her husband's golden ones. For only an instant, she was frightened; then joy filled her heart until she thought she would burst from it. How he had found her, she did not know or care. He was there, as he had always been there. It was enough.

"Warrick. Warrick!" the girl sobbed with relief, throwing herself into his arms.

But there was no welcome in his strong embrace, and his dark visage, when she gazed at him again, was as hard as stone. Slowly, in sudden understanding, she drew away from him, all her earlier dread returning.

"Warrick, please. *Please*. 'Tis—'tis not what you're thinking. Oh, God. 'Tis not what you're thinking! I—I can explain."

"I am quite certain ye can, madam," the Earl said, his voice as cold as ice and chilling her to the bone. "However,

I do not choose to be made a fool of again. Sweet *Jesù*," he suddenly swore bitterly and thrust her from him. "To think I had begun to care for ye."

Then he turned and walked away.

BOOK THREE

The Windswept Moors

Chapter Twenty-six

Hawkhurst Castle, England, 1480

TO THINK I HAD BEGUN TO CARE FOR YE.

Warrick's word's hammered like a death knell in Isabella's brain. Oh, God damn Lionel Valeureux to hell and back! 'Twas he who had caused her husband to turn against her. Her husband, whom she had just begun to heal, whom she had just begun to love. Aye, love. Isabella knew, with certainty now, that it was so. She had fallen in love with her husband, Lord Warrick ap Tremayne, Earl of Hawkhurst. Now—now, when it was too late, she dared to face what was in her heart.

Oh, God, oh, God!

How she longed to bury her face in her hands and weep bitterly for what she had lost. But she did not. To do so would be to disgrace herself before Warrick and his men. Once they had reached the sanctuary of Hawkhurst Castle, the girl would find a quiet place in which to lick her wounds. Until then, she must remain strong so none would guess how her heart was dying inside of her.

Only Giles and Caerllywel suspected her pain, for they alone knew what had happened that day of the King's tourney. And though together, valiantly, they had accosted Warrick and forced him to listen to the truth of the matter, he had not believed them.

"Ye love her," he had snarled. "Both of ye! Ye wouldst say anything to protect her. Well, I am not such a fool as to believe ye. Now get out. Get out of my sight! And take that cheating witch I married with ye!"

That had hurt worst of all—the fact that Warrick had no longer even wanted her. Quietly, Isabella had moved her possessions into the antechamber of their room and there had shared a pallet upon the floor with Jocelyn until they had left the Tower and London behind. How endless the nights had seemed as Isabella had lain huddled next to her maid and pressed her face into her pillow to muffle her racking sobs so none would hear her weeping. How filled with agony the long hours had been as she had waited restlessly, sleeplessly, for Warrick to return to their chamber. Sometimes, it had been almost morning before he had come in, more often than not inebriated, though he had held his liquor well. Isabella had not known where he'd spent his nights and had not asked. That he'd sought out arms other than her own, she'd had no doubt. She would have been greatly surprised, though highly gratified, to learn he had but sat in his horse's stall in the stables and drunk himself into a stupor while pouring out his heart and soul to his much-bemused destrier.

Then, one morn (having grown weary of passing his evenings upon a pile of hay), the Earl had ordered his wife to pack her coffers. They were leaving London, he had told her curtly. He was taking her home to Hawkhurst Castle. Isabella had not wished to go, but still, she had made no protest against him. A devil had taken hold of Warrick, and she was not the only one who'd been more than a little frightened of him those days.

Now, as her husband's fortress came into view at last, the girl's heart sank with despair: for she had no doubt that Warrick intended to shut her away here, alone, and return to Court without her. Aye, this would be her prison, perhaps for life. She had sinned against her husband (or so he thought); and he had tried and condemned her without mercy, sentencing her to Hawkhurst Castle for her crime. He might as well have delivered her to that infamous dungeon known as Little Hell in the Tower, Isabella thought, for such a prospect could not have been bleaker or more daunting than the one she now faced.

The Yorkshire moors, to which the girl was accustomed, were wild and often rocky, but their gently swelling crests did not jar the eye as the land here did, for the hills of

Devon were steep and savage. Rugged granite and sandstone promontories dropped sharply into wooded plains, desolate heaths, and marshy valleys, which were a legacy of centuries past, when the sea had swept in to drown the lower terrain. Even now, in the distance, Isabella could hear the roar of the ocean above the drizzle of the depressing rain and taste the cool, salty spindrift that swirled in a blanket of mist upon the wings of the wind.

High above, upon a cliff that ascended stonily before her and fell away starkly on the other side in a sheer drop to the sea below, Hawkhurst Castle loomed over the girl, as dark and forbidding as the rocky crags among which it was set. Its tall, powerful towers gleamed ominously against the horizon, its machicolated battlements cutting a cruel, jagged scar across the firmament as a sudden flash of lightning lit the sky. The massive grey fortress had no moat, for there was no need of one. There was no way to gain access to the keep other than by the single road that wound almost dangerously up to the ridge upon which the castle perched like a brooding hawk and whence it had drawn its name.

Isabella's breath caught in her throat as she eyed the fortress despondently, for there was nothing welcoming about those stern, gloomy walls, which seemed so different from Rushden's protective barriers. No wonder Warrick had spent so little time here in the past. Besides having crumbled, in places, to wrack and ruin, there was an air of disquiet about the keep that even the bravest of souls must have found unnerving.

The girl swallowed hard as the stout iron portcullis was lowered on rusty, creaking chains behind her to clang shut with a sudden, eerie bang. They were passed through the inner gatehouse, then Giles and Caerllywel were lifting her down from her mare to follow Warrick into the castle.

"Do not look so terrified, 'Sabelle," Caerllywel whispered encouragingly, giving her hand a gentle squeeze. "For all its strange appearance, I assure ye that Hawkhurst has no ghosts. 'Tis merely that the fortress is very old—'twas built during the time of William the Conqueror—and the Tremaynes have been notoriously careless about its upkeep. Waerwic, I'm afraid, has proven no better than the rest at maintaining his inheritance. Like his ancestors before him, he has preferred life at Court and in battle to Hawkhurst."

"'Tis no wonder," Isabella said with a little shiver as she glanced about somewhat apprehensively.

The great hall in which they now stood was huge and might have been overwhelming in its magnificence, had any effort been made to care for it. As it was, smoke from the torches had stained the walls with black blotches of grimy soot; the sconces themselves looked as though they had not been cleaned in decades. The once-beautiful tapestries had faded with time; many were moth-eaten, rotten, and hanging in tattered shreds. The trestle tables, which no one had bothered to dismantle after the midday meal, were badly scarred and were layers deep in dust besides, as were the benches ranged haphazardly alongside them. The floor was almost knee-deep in filthy rushes, new reeds having been laid down without first removing the old ones. The musty air stank with the foul odor of the decaying straw, which was made even ranker by the scraps of molded food and other offal that had infiltrated the rushes over a period of time. Isabella was certain the putrid reeds hid virtual armies of roaches, maggots, lice, and bedbugs, as well as the rats her ears discerned rustling through straw.

"Marry-go-up," she breathed with dismay.

Warrick, who had overheard the remark, had the grace to flush slightly with shame at the condition in which his bride found his home—now her home too. For the first time in his life, it dawned on the Earl just how dirty and sorely in need of repair Hawkhurst really was, especially when one compared it to Rusden, as Isabella and her brother must be doing. Isabella was plainly horrified by the keep; and though less shocked than his sister (for he had sojourned at bachelor households in the past and often found them less than clean), Giles was startled as well. Even Caerllywel was too embarrassed to meet his brother's eyes. Really! the younger man thought. The least that Warrick could have done was to have sent word of their coming so his servants might have prepared for their arrival. After all, it was not as though the Earl were still a bachelor. He had a wife to think of now.

Warrick realized this also, but he told himself he did not care what they thought. Isabella's feelings, especially, were not important to him. But nevertheless, in a sudden fit of anger at his lack of foresight, his hand swept out to knock several silver chalices from one of the tables. The cups clattered to the floor, stirring up a cloud of dust.

"Christ's son!" he swore wrathfully, then shouted for his steward. "Farrell! Farrell, where are ye?"

"Coming, my lord. Welcome home, my lord. Sir Caerllywel, how good to see ye again." Master Farrell bowed and smiled, apparently unafraid of the Earl's temper. "I trust ye had a pleasant journey, my lord; but then, of course, ye did not. How could ye have done so in this rain? So tiresome. Perth, Anson. Light the hearths—and quickly— so his lordship and guests may dry themselves. Mary, Leah. Bring food and drink," the steward directed, then turned back to Warrick. "Not knowing how many guests, if any, to expect when the sentries announced your arrival, my lord, I had only your chamber prepared. If ye will excuse me now, I will go and have Sir Caerllywel's room made up, as well as chambers for the Lord and Lady." He indicated Giles and Isabella respectfully, waiting expectantly to be presented.

Abruptly, Warrick recalled his manners.

"I'm sorry, Farrell," the Earl stated stiffly. "Isabella, Giles, this is my steward, Master Farrell. Farrell, this is my wife, Lady Hawkhurst, and her brother, Lord Rushden."

If the steward was surprised by this announcement, he did not show it, though Isabella was certain he could not help but think that Ragnor, ruffling his damp feathers upon her shoulder, and her own wet, bedraggled appearance combined to present a very strange picture indeed. Farrell merely bowed once more and politely welcomed both her and Giles to Hawkhurst.

"I'm afraid ye find us in a sad state, my lady," the steward apologized somewhat anxiously. "Had we but known ye were coming . . . His lordship is so seldom in residence, ye see, we do not maintain very many servants here. However, no doubt that will be changed now, and we shall be able to set matters to rights."

"I'm sure we shall, Master Farrell"—Isabella spoke warmly, for though she had, at first, suspected the steward of gross neglect and incompetence, she recognized now that his hands had been tied by her husband's total lack of interest in the estate.

"Are my brothers here, Farrell?" Warrick inquired abruptly, tersely changing the subject.

"Nay, my lord. Lord Madog returned to Gwendraeth some time ago, taking Sir Emrys with him."

"And my mother?"

"She is not in residence either, my lord."

"Thank ye, Farrell. That will be all for now."

By now, the men-at-arms who had escorted them on their journey had joined them in the great hall, and the huge, central stone hearths had been lit and a plain but hearty meal brought. Isabella was glad to see the food at least was decent. Before sitting down to dine, she moved gratefully to one of the fires that now burned cheerfully, dispelling some of the fortress's dank and dreary atmosphere. The autumn wind and rain had chilled her more than she'd realized. As she stretched her hands out to the blaze, Giles came to stand beside her.

"Sweet *Jesù*, 'Sabelle." His voice was low. "I do not know how Warrick came to let his keep fall into such a shambles. It certainly looks as though ye have your work cut out for ye. I almost wish I had not asked Gloucester's permission to accompany ye here. Methinks I would as lief be battling the Scots as trying to help ye set this place to rights, especially when Warrick is so wroth with ye."

"Oh, Giles. Ye know 'tis not my fault."

"Aye, I know. God damn Lionel! I could kill him! If only Warrick would listen to reason."

"Ye and Caerllywel both attempted to persuade him of my innocence in the matter and failed. 'Tis hopeless, Giles. Warrick will never believe I didst not betray him. Oh, Giles. What am I to do? I tried so hard to win his favor, and he *had* begun to care for me a little; he said so. Now everything is ruined. He will never trust me again; and where there is no trust, there can be no love."

"I know, 'Sabelle. I'm sorry. Do ye wish me to take ye

away from here? Ye have your manor house, Grasmere, and ye know ye will always be welcome at Rushden."

"Nay, dear brother, though I thank ye for your offer. My place is with my husband, no matter what. I have made my bed; now I must lie in it. Only . . . do not leave me so very soon. Stay with me . . . for just a little while."

"I shall, dear sister. Do not think otherwise; and remember, when I go, that Caerllywel is also your friend."

"Aye, but I must not impose on him, Giles. He wouldst be so torn between Warrick and me. I could not bring such pain upon him."

"Ye are so kind and good, 'Sabelle. I do not understand how Warrick can believe ill of ye."

"He was hurt, Giles, and the wound went deep. I can understand that. I am only sorry I couldst not heal him."

That night, Isabella lay alone in her chamber, waiting. But Warrick did not come to her. She heard him pacing restlessly in the room next to hers, but though he paused several times before the door that lay between them, he did not open it. Finally, toward dawn, he sought his bed. Still, he did not sleep and, at last, at sunrise, rose and ordered his horse to be saddled.

Isabella's heart sank as she heard him give the command to his squire Rhys. Then she realized, from his conversation with his other squires, that he was but going hunting; and her spirits lifted a little. At least he was not returning to Court—not yet.

Hurriedly, after she was certain he had gone, she summoned her maids and bathed and dressed, for there was much to be done at Hawkhurst. As she ate her breakfast, the girl pondered the matter thoughtfully, writing down a list of those things she had already observed were needed. Then she went downstairs and called all the servants into the great hall.

"I am your new mistress, Lady Hawkhurst," she informed them for the benefit of those who had not met her yesterday and who were eying her curiously. "And this is now my home." She paused to let this sink in, then continued. "I know that, for many years, ye have been without

a chatelaine, so I will make no comment on the condition
in which I discovered Hawkhurst Castle yesterday upon my
arrival. But I *will* say that I do not ever expect to find it in
such a state again. So if ye wish to remain here—and I
hope ye do—ye must accustom yourselves to several
changes. I plan to start immediately to set this keep in order.
It has been sorely neglected, so there is a great deal of hard
work to be done. I shall expect ye all to do your fair share
of chores. If ye perform your tasks well, ye will be rewarded. If ye do not, ye will be dismissed. Now—I want
ye each to step forward, one at a time, and tell me your
name and position. After that, I will give ye your instructions."

But though she waited expectantly, no one moved forth.
Instead, they stood silently, staring at her.

"Come. Why do ye delay?" the girl asked impatiently.
"Ye will not find me a cruel mistress, I promise ye."

"Begging your pardon, my lady." Farrell cleared his throat
hesitantly. "But—but the servants—they—they are
afraid. . . ."

"Afraid of what, Master Farrell?"

"The—the hawk, my lady."

"Why, that's ridiculous! Surely, they have seen hawks
before. Why, I know for a fact that my lord owns several."

"Hunting hawks, my lady, to be sure," the steward agreed
somewhat nervously. "However, that bird doesn't appear
to be—to be tame, my lady," Farrell observed, then took
a hasty step backward as Ragnor suddenly flapped his wings
and let out a shrill cry, his round yellow eyes gazing fiercely
at the steward.

Isabella suppressed her desire to laugh and stroked the
hawk's head gently to soothe it. Then she coaxed the bird
upon her wrist and held him up high for all to see.

"This is Ragnor," she said. "He was given to me as a
wedding present by His Grace Edward, the King." Noting
that this announcement was received with appropriate awe
and respect, Isabella went on. "Ragnor's wing was broken,
and though I set it, and it has now mended, for some reason
unknown to me, he is still unable to fly. I assure ye he will
not hurt ye. Now—let us get on with our work."

It was not to be expected, of course, that the keep could be set to rights in a single day, for centuries of neglect had taken their toll. But Master Farrell, a good man who had long despaired of his master's inattention to Hawkhurst, saw Isabella as a godsend; and the girl was able to make a tolerable start. In addition, Sir Bevan, the master-at-arms, was only too eager to describe the "shocking" state of the armory and the "well nigh indefensible" condition of the castle walls and to take Giles, when he rose, on a guided tour of the fortress to point out these "unpardonable" deficiencies. No sooner had they departed than the chief bailiff, Master Isham, appeared with a long list of grievances about the keep's farmlands, herds, and tenants.

"I do not scruple to tell ye, my lady, that if there is a single bushel of grain to be discovered in the storehouses, 'twill be a miracle," he sniffed. "And if there is a cow or sheep to be found, God will indeed have smiled on us. Most of the villeins have run off, and indeed, one can hardly blame them, for I would not house so much as a goat or a pig in one of their cottages!"

Though she sympathized with him, Isabella, with a stern eye, silenced the bailiff: for despite Warrick's appalling mismanagement of his inheritance, it was not Master Isham's place to criticize the Earl.

"Bring me the account books and a list of the keep's inventory this afternoon, Master Isham," the girl directed. "If the ledgers have been maintained as badly as the rest of the fortress, I have no doubt 'twill take ye and your clerk that long to put them into some semblance of order."

The bailiff drew himself up stiffly at this, but as he flushed a dull red, Isabella knew her accusation had hit home and was able to dismiss him without further qualm for her rudeness.

There then came, somewhat shyly, the castle priest, Father Francis. Wisely, he spoke no word against his master but instead quietly lamented the fact that Mass had been reduced to a Sunday morning service (when it ought to have been said daily), because the stained glass windows of the chapel were broken, permitting the most fearsome draughts to enter, and the pews were so badly splintered, it was actually dangerous to sit on them.

"And ye know, my lady, that one does not kneel through the entire Mass," the priest sighed, "else we would not need the benches at all."

Isabella promised him the matter would be taken care of, then, having disposed of the four chief personages with regard to the keep's affairs, rolled up the sleeves of her gown and set to work.

Already, in the great hall, stout men armed with rush-rakes had succeeded in removing much of the filthy straw that had covered the floor, and maids with buckets of water and bars of strong lye soap were scrubbing that portion of stone now laid bare. Hastily, Isabella instructed the women to begin with the walls instead, pointing out that the grimy residue from the torches would otherwise run down onto the clean floor, which would then have to be washed all over again. She also directed them to lace their pails of water with turpentine in order to kill the crawling creatures that had infested the reeds, then sent two pages to the stables to fetch a basket of cats she intended to loose upon the rats.

Then, seeing everything in the great hall was progressing smoothly and adjuring her maids Mathilde and Edith to ensure it continued to do so, the girl set about to inspect the rest of the fortress. Seldom in use, the upstairs chambers of the castle were not nearly as dirty as the rooms below and needed primarily to be swept, dusted, and aired. Nevertheless, Isabella decided to scrub them down thoroughly as well, a few chambers at a time. All the tapestries and rugs, she determined, would have to be replaced; and all the mattresses would have to be thrown out and new ones sewn and stuffed with fresh ticking. She told the women who had accompanied her upstairs to begin in Warrick's room—that it alone, complete with new mattress, must be finished before nightfall. Only the tapestries and rugs could wait, the former taking many weeks to embroider, and the latter having to be purchased from the weavers. The maids eyed her askance, as though they thought her crazed, and began to wail about the impossibility of the task, but Isabella remained adamant, leaving Alice in charge of them to be certain there was none who shirked her duties.

After that, Isabella sought out the larder, wine cellar, storeroom, and storehouses. Only the second of these was sufficiently well stocked, Warrick, it seemed, having a care for his liquor—if nothing else. Much to the women's amazement, the girl wrote an extensive list of produce that would have to be planted in the vegetable gardens, come spring, and remarked somewhat wryly that with Cheddar Gorge, in Somerset, being relatively near, 'twas unbelievable the larder contained no cheese. They would cure some of their own cheeses later, of course, from cow, goat, and sheep milk, and there would be headcheese, a cooked and jellied meat loaf made from boars' or hogs' heads; but the delicious cheddar they would obtain from Somerset. This copiously noted, Isabella sent pages for the head huntsman and head fisherman and instructed them to hunt fresh game and to catch fresh fish to fill the larder.

In the storeroom, she was irritated but not surprised to discover the keep was low on tallows and torches. She put several maids to work making new ones at once.

But there was nothing she could do to fill the nearly empty storehouses, which ought to have been fairly overflowing with grain, the harvest being just past. What little of wheat, oats, and barley there was, she allotted carefully for the baking of bread and cakes and the cooking of soups and porridge; and she entered, on her list, the urgent need for seed for the spring planting. Her pen scratched away so furiously, due to her anger, that it sputtered and left a large blot upon the page.

In the kitchen, the chief cook was strictly informed that from now on, she was to consult Isabella, the first thing every morning, about the day's meals; and she was to start preparing immediately a thick stew to be fed to the toiling servants. And lest she had any intention of dishing up less than the poor best that was available (in order to peddle the castle's staples on the side, as Isabella was certain the cook had been doing for some time), Jocelyn would remain to supervise the kitchen and to whip it into satisfactory shape.

The girl then visited both the inner and outer wards of the fortress and, with the grim assistance of her trusted knights, Sirs Eadric, Thegn, and Beowulf, hounded Warrick's own men-at-arms into hard and unaccustomed labor.

Her tour complete, she then returned to the keep to go over the account books with Master Isham and to consult with Giles and Sir Bevan about what was necessary to shore up the castle's defenses.

Needless to say, when Warrick arrived home that evening, he was utterly stupefied by the changes that had been wrought. The fortress, normally eerily quiet, was now a buzzing hive of activity; and for one astounding moment, he could almost believe he had somehow entered the wrong keep by mistake. Had he not been so amazed, he would have laughed at the sight of his proud knights mucking out the stables and hauling cartloads of manure outside for dumping beyond the fortress walls. Caerllywel, who strode up to meet his brother, did laugh, but his mirth rose primarily from the stunned look on the Earl's face.

"You'd best hide yourself—and quickly—Waerwic," Caerllywel urged as he caught the bridle of the Earl's steed, "for if I'm not mistaken, your men-at-arms plan to murder ye this eve."

"Christ's son, Caerllywel!" Warrick swore as he dismounted. "What in the hell is going on here? Nay, do not bother to reply, for I already know the answer. 'Tis that witch I wed. She has overturned the place in my absence."

"Well, I do not know about that, Waerwic," Caerllywel rejoined coolly, "but she has certainly made an effort to start setting it to rights; and I, for one, am most grateful to her. I confess that, until now, I had grown so accustomed to the disorder here that I scarcely realized we lived like pigs."

"I don't recall that I forced ye at sword point to stay, brother," the Earl pointed out dryly. I am sure that Madog would welcome ye at Gwendraeth, or, failing that, ye might seek employment with some other lord who has need of that battle-ax ye wield so well."

Caerllywel raised one eyebrow frostily.

"Do not take that tone with me, Waerwic," he warned. "On more than one occasion, ye have been glad I fought at your side."

The Earl had the grace to flush guiltily.

"I'm sorry, brother," he apologized. "'Tis 'Sabelle with whom I am wroth, not ye. I should not have spoken so to ye."

"Waerwic," Caerllywel uttered slowly, "methinks ye are a very great fool indeed. I say again: Ye have no cause to despise your bride. She was but a victim of Lord Lionel's deceit. Had ye not been so wounded by Brangwen, ye would have realized as much. 'Sabelle has been and always will be the most honorable and faithful of wives."

"Oh?" Warrick drawled sarcastically. "And what makes ye say that?"

"She loves ye—although why, I'm sure I don't know."

With that parting shot, Caerllywel turned on his heel and walked away.

She loves ye. She loves ye.

Over and over, the words rang in Warrick's mind as he stared silently at the door that stood between him and Isabella. Caerllywel had said he was a very great fool. Was he? Was he so blinded by bitterness that he had judged his wife wrongfully? Had she, in truth, been tricked into entering Lionel's tent that day of the tourney?

For the hundredth time, Warrick tried to think back, to remember how she had looked when she had come out of the heir of St. Saviour's pavilion. She had been panting hard, he recalled, as though she had been making love; and the bodice of her gown had been torn open, as though by hands too impatient to wait to undress her properly. But . . . would not a struggle have caused her to be gasping for breath? Would not Lionel, attempting to take her by force, have ripped open her garments?

The Earl inhaled sharply.

Aye, it could have happened like that, he concluded, as usual. Why, then, did he continue to doubt his wife? Oh, if only he could be certain of what had really occurred!

She loves ye—although why, I'm sure I don't know.

Warrick gazed thoughtfully about his chamber, noting how clean and fresh it now was. Even a soft new mattress lay upon his bed. Would Isabella have worked so hard to please him if she did not care for him? Another woman would have seen to her own comfort first, but Isabella had thought only of him. Even Giles's room, the Earl knew, she had left undone so his own chamber might be finished by nightfall. Would she have placed him above her brother if she did not love him? He did not know,

Again, Warrick glanced at the door that barred him from Isabella. It had been many nights since he had held her in his arms; and though he might have slaked his lust on another woman, he had not. The Earl did not ask of others what he could not give in return. When he had wed her, he had demanded his wife's loyalty and pledged her his own. He was not a man to break his vows.

They had been lonely, those evenings he had spent in the King's stables at the Tower, pouring out his heart and soul to Gwalchmi. Now that he recalled them, Warrick decided even his cherished destrier had looked at him as though he'd been a fool.

Was I? he wondered. Am I? Aye, for I have let the witch enchant me, and now I cannot break free of her spell. How many nights did I waste drinking and dreaming of her, wanting her? Had she been a man, I would have challenged her, dueled with her, triumphed over her. But because she's a woman, I let her go without a battle. Fool? Aye. I should have fought to win her, conquered her heart and soul, driven Lionel Valeureux from her mind. More fool I. I thought 'twould be enough to gain her loyalty. How could I have guessed I would want her love? Aye, love. I love her. I have loved her all along and would not face it. Damn my pride. Curse my arrogance. 'Twas not until that day at Lionel's tent that I knew, and then ... then ... *Jesù*! To find she had betrayed me was too much to bear. I wanted to kill her, to hurt her, as she had me. And yet ... and yet ... Did I not also long to take her into my arms and make love to her until she cried out her surrender, vowed that Lionel was

nothing to her? *Nothing!* Hear her swear 'twas me she loved?
Me—and me alone. She tried so hard to explain what had
happened. Was I wrong not to listen, to believe she had
played me false? If I had it all to do over again, would I
still walk away? I don't know. I don't know. Oh, God. Oh,
God. What a mess I have made of things! Caerllywel told
me she loved me, but I know he is mistaken. How could
she, now, after I have been so cold and cruel to her? Still,
she's my wife! 'Tis my right to have her, no matter what
is wrong in our marriage, no matter if she no longer wants
me. I will take her and *make* her want me. Even if she
scorns me, laughs at me, I shall win her love if 'tis the last
thing I ever do! She is mine. Mine! I'll not walk away
again.

His mind made up, Warrick strode to the door—and
opened it.

"Come," he said to his much-startled wife. "I have need
of ye."

Slowly, not knowing what to think, Isabella rose and
followed him to his room. Was he angry? She did not know.
Earlier that evening, he had not said one word to her about
the changes she had wrought in Hawkhurst. Perhaps he had
only waited until now to vent his wrath upon her for her
upheaval of his home. The girl shivered. Warrick could be
so cruel at times.

"What is amiss, my lord?" she asked quietly. "Is there
aught here that has not been done to your liking?"

He looked at her with surprise.

"Nay, of course not."

"Then what is it ye wish of me, my lord?"

He indicated, with a sweep of his hand, the massive
canopy bed that dominated the chamber.

"I know, from the grumbling of the maids, that mine is,
as yet, the only new mattress in the keep. I thought ye
wouldst like to share its comfort with me"—he spoke casually.

At first, when she understood what he desired, Isabella's
face grew pale; and the Earl's heart sank. It was as he had
surmised. She no longer wanted him and intended to deny
him. If he meant to have her, he would have to take her by

force, and there would be no joy in the act for either of them. Then she blushed and turned away, trembling a little; and Warrick knew he was wrong. He watched her silently from beneath half-closed lids as awkwardly, with quivering fingers, she began to unlace her robe and shift. Why, she was frightened, as frightened as she had been the first time of their mating. Then the Earl realized that for her, this night *was* like that first one, for she did not know what to expect from him.

Suddenly, it occurred to him how very strong and masculine he was, how very fragile and feminine Isabella was. For a moment, Warrick wondered how he would have felt, had he been in the girl's place; and he truly understood, for the first time, how very small and helpless a woman was against a man. Oh, a maid might struggle, even wield a dagger against him, but a powerful and determined man could easily overcome these obstacles to his desire. A man who was not the woman's husband might be punished for the deed—provided she had other powerful and determined men to defend her—but against her husband, she had no recourse. She was his chattel, to do with as he pleased. No wonder so many maids went terrified to their wedding beds— as Isabella had come to Warrick's.

Then, he had brushed aside her fears, dismissing them without a second thought. It was natural to be scared of the unknown; once he had taken her, she would no longer be afraid. Now, the Earl recognized it was more than just that. It was the surrender of her body and soul, her very *life*, into a man's hands that so frightened a woman.

Yet, here was Isabella, bravely, if a trifle shyly, slipping from her nightclothes without protest, trusting him to use her kindly, though she knew he had wanted to slay her that day of the tourney, though she believed now that he despised her. He wondered, had he been in her place, if he would have been so valiant; and he was touched by her courage.

"'Sabelle," he breathed, the word as soft as a caress.

She turned, letting her garments float gently, like a whisper, to the floor.

"Aye, my lord?"

She made no effort to shield herself from his hungrily

raking gaze, merely stood there, quietly, her eyes falling before his. In two long strides, he had reached her.

"'Sabelle." Once more he spoke the endearing nickname she had not heard upon his lips since that awful day of the tourney.

Curiously then, almost pleadingly, yet strangely defiant too, she looked up at him.

"Aye, my lord?" she said again.

But somehow, Warrick could not find the words he longed to say; for the first time in his life, he felt as confused and oddly lost as a person in a daze. He must go slowly, carefully, give her time. If he suddenly told her he loved her, she would not believe him, would think it was some sort of jest to hurt her further. He must wait and woo her if he wished to win her heart.

"Naught. 'Twas naught," he told her.

He cupped her face with his hands, entwining his fingers in her hair, his eyes darkening suddenly before his mouth closed over hers. He kissed her forever, it seemed, scarcely feeling her hands, which shook slightly against his chest, for they neither encouraged nor restrained him, just pressed there, clutching a little at his shirt, as though she might fall otherwise. But he could not mistake the vulnerable trembling of her lips beneath his own, and for an instant, he wished he knew whether they quivered still with fright—or now with passion. Slowly, he released her, his hands sliding down her shoulders to her breasts.

How beautiful they are, he thought. So very pale, like marble, for I can see the blue of her life's blood within.

He brushed her nipples with his thumbs, delighting in the manner in which the rosy crests stiffened, puckering with excitement at his touch. He laid his mouth upon that soft place at Isabella's nape, where it curved down so gracefully to her shoulder. Tingles of pleasure radiated from the spot as he kissed it, teased it with his tongue, and traced his way to the hollow of her throat, where her pulse was fluttering jerkily. His lips traveled up the slender white column, then down, found her breasts, first one, and then the other. He did not know how the rigid little buds could be so hard and yet so soft, and he marveled that it was so as his mouth closed over them, sucked them, teased them. His teeth grazed them lightly, caught hold of them as his tongue darted out to titillate the pink tips until they grew even firmer with excitement and passion.

At last, he drew away, pushing Isabella gently toward the bed. She slipped into the massive, canopied four-poster, looking very small among all the pillows as she settled against them and drew up the sheet and ermine-furred coverlet to hide her nakedness.

Her wide, fathomless eyes watched him in the candlelight as languidly he pulled his shirt over his head to reveal his broad chest with its mat of dark hair, then shed his hose. Without a word, he slid in beside her, encircling her in his embrace, kissing her deeply, lingeringly, again. Impatiently, one hand encroached upon the soft folds of her womanhood. Finding that secret place wet and warm, and unable to wait any longer—he had been so long without her—Warrick rolled atop her and spread her thighs. The tip of his maleness pressed against her, penetrated her, then suddenly thrust into her with a single swift, savage motion that left her breathless with desire as just as rapidly he withdrew, then entered her once more.

Wantonly, Isabella locked her legs around his back and arched her hips to receive him, again and again, until her loins quickened, and suddenly, it felt as though the earth had dropped out from beneath her. The sensation burst through her like an explosion, shock waves rippling through her entire body, sending her reeling. Never had she reached her pinnacle so quickly. It was only dimly that she felt the long, sighing shudder that undulated through Warrick before he too was still.

Yet, though sated, he made no move to leave her, remained a part of her still; and after a time, she could feel him growing hard inside of her once more. Her eyes, drowsy with his lovemaking, flew open in surprise to see him gazing down at her curiously, searchingly. A tiny hope that all was not yet lost flickered in her bosom, a little flame of yearning that he might yet forgive her, come to trust her once more, care for her a little, though he would never love her now; she was sure.

How she longed to brush his hair back from his face, caress his cheek, cradle him against her breast, and tell him she loved him. But she did none of these things, knowing instinctively that it was too soon after that dreadful day of the tourney, that he would not believe her, that she must tread slowly and carefully if she were to win back that small, precious measure of caring he had had for her.

The candles had long since guttered in their sockets, but the autumn moon streamed in through the windows, casting a veil of shimmering silver over the chamber. Again, Isabella had the impression that Warrick was some dark pagan god from the past, some ancient demon of the night come to steal away her heart and soul. She could see his amber eyes glittering in the half-light, like two twin coals as they burned down into her own, blazing their way through the caverns of her mind, as though to ferret out her innermost secrets. She shivered slightly. In the past, her husband had called her a witch; and she thought if it were true, she was indeed a fit mate for him, for he was surely a devil.

Twice, she could have sworn there had been magic in their lovemaking; and now, once more, she felt that same incantation of enchantment begin to take hold of her, haunt her, envelop her in its veil of sorcery. She couldn't tear her eyes away from him. His rich tobacco-brown mane streaked with gold beckoned her fingers to entwine themselves among its silky strands. His yellow eyes hypnotized her with their passion-darkened depths. The curve of his carnal mouth held her spellbound as his lips possessed hers, devoured her mouth, so their breathing became as one.

His palms cupped her breasts, squeezed them gently but firmly. His thumbs stimulated her nipples, making them grow hard and rigid, even as Warrick's manhood stiffened inside of her, filling the innermost depths of her.

Isabella found she couldn't move, didn't want to move, as he drove strongly between her thighs, bewitching her, taking her to the heights of rapture with his wizardry.

She moaned deep in her throat, a low, rippling noise like the purring of a cat that made him laugh softly in her ear before he bit her lobe gently and muttered fiercely, "Witch.

Witch! I'll make ye forget him if I have to slay ye to do it!"

The girl wanted to speak, to protest, to tell him she had never loved Lionel Valeureux, that she never would love him, for she had given her heart to her husband. But Warrick's mouth claimed hers once more, silencing that which she would have said. She didn't care. For some strange reason, the Earl had decided to fight for her, to win the love he would not believe was already his.

The ember of hope in her breast blazed like wildfire at the thought. She would yet heal him; she *would* yet have his heart. She wrapped her arms about him tightly.

"I have forgotten him," she whispered. "I have forgotten him, my love."

With a savage snarl of triumph, Warrick arched her hips to meet his wicked thrusts, spiraling down into the hot moist core of her until she cried out her surrender and let the waves of volcanic lava engulf her.

Chapter Twenty-seven

"Dio mio!"

With an evil hiss of anger, Lord Dante da Forenza, *Conte di Montecatini,* crushed viciously the scroll he held, then cruelly knocked the messenger, who had delivered the writ, in the head, sending the boy sprawling across the floor.

"God damn that whoreson half-Welsh bastard!" the Count spat.

The woman sitting anxiously by the fire raised one trembling hand to her throat, for there was nothing she feared more than the Italian's murderous temper. Sometimes, she wished she had never taken up with him.

"What—what is it, my lord?" she asked nervously, her dark eyes filled with apprehension.

"La vita è piena di guai. Life is full of troubles!" he translated for the woman's benefit. "I have been recalled to Rome—recalled in disgrace. Me! Montecatini! Repri-

manded for a joust that was forced on me by that whoreson half-Welsh bastard! God damn Hawkhurst! He shall pay for this, I promise ye!"

"But—but I thought ... Ye said your family wouldst smooth things over," the woman stammered, distraught. Now, what would become of her? Where would she go? What would she do? "Ye said naught wouldst come of the matter," she whined accusingly, feeling very sorry for herself.

Lord Montecatini gave her a look that withered the hard heart in her bosom.

"Well, I was mistaken then, wasn't I?" he drawled with a sarcasm that pierced her like a sharp knife. *"Sangue di Cristo!* To be called home, *in disgrace*, over a damned bout instigated through no fault of my own and in which *I* was the wounded party. Hawkhurst must stand even higher in King Edward's favor than I had realized. God damn that whoreson half-Welsh bastard! He shall pay for this!" the Count reiterated, gnashing his teeth with rage. "I shall make him pay if 'tis the last thing I ever do!"

Once more, his gaze stabbed the woman by the fire. She cowered on her stool, more afraid and upset than ever. Tears filled her eyes. Perhaps he intended to beat her, as he had done in the past when displeased.

"Well, what are ye waiting for?" the Italian inquired wrathfully. *"Che idiota! Si alzi!* Get up! Do not sit there shrinking and blubbering like a fool. Go, and pack your things at once."

"Do ye—do ye mean I am to go with ye, my lord?" the woman stuttered, some of her fright and agitation receding and hope rising in her breast.

"Ye stupid slut!" Lord Montecatini growled. "Did I not just say as much? What a simpleton ye are! Truly, I do not know why I continue to allow ye to live. Dost really believe I wouldst leave ye here to meddle in my affairs during my absence—especially when ye have no more brain than a half-wit?"

The woman stiffened slightly at this. After all, one must have *some* pride.

"I will remind ye, my lord, that—" she began, then broke

off abruptly as he suddenly leaped to his feet, towering over her.

"Silenzio!" the Count ordered. "Ye will remind me of nothing, do ye hear?" He shook his fist at her threateningly. "Ye played your hand and botched it! The game is mine now. *Mi comprendi?* And I will not be hindered in it by any of your idiotic schemes. Christ's son! When I think of your appalling lack of finesse, *signora,* I confess I am sore tempted to kill ye." The Italian gave a short, ugly laugh. *"Non saresti davvero una grande perdita."*

The woman cringed again, for she had heard him say this often enough to understand what it meant. He had told her she really wouldn't be a very great loss.

"Ferite di Dio!" he went on jeeringly. "Reivers, a mad dog, and a lion baiting!" he snorted with contempt. "Was that the best ye could do, *signora?"*

"'Tis more than ye have done, my lord," Lady Shrewton returned, trying indignantly to defend herself, despite her fear of him.

After all, her plans *had* been good ones, no matter what he thought. 'Twas not her fault they had all failed.

"They were the plots of a bumbling *sciocco,*" Lord Montecatini sneered, disgusted. "Ye left too much to chance, ye silly bitch, always the mark of an amateur. Now I, on the other hand, shall leave nothing to the Fates, for *I* am a professional!"

"Ye forget, my lord, that *ye* are being forced to go home to Italy," Lady Shrewton pointed out, garnering a small mean satisfaction from the knowledge that he was not as clever as he thought.

"È vero. Still, eventually, I shall return to England, I assure ye; and then I shall have my revenge. Do ye doubt me, *signora?"*

"Nay. Nay, my lord," she answered at last.

She did not doubt him in the least. She had come to know the Italian Count far too well for that.

"God damn him!"

Lord Lionel Valeureux stared down at the scroll in his hands and swore yet again as he reread its contents.

"God damn him!"

The heir of St. Saviour was its heir no longer. His father was dead, accidentally drowned in a boating accident off the Isle of Wight. Lionel was now the Earl of St. Saviour-on-the-Lake. Bitterly, he wadded up the message telling him the news and tossed the crumpled parchment angrily into one corner of his tent. Just a few more months! If Lionel had been able to wait just a few more months, he need never have wed Gilliane Beaumaris. As the Earl of St. Saviour-on-the-Lake, he could have broken the marriage contracts himself. At the realization, he cursed his father even more vehemently. How dare Lord St. Saviour die after ruining his son's life? It just wasn't fair! It just wasn't fair at all!

Well, there was no help for it. What was done, was done. Still, Lionel was certain of one thing: Sooner or later, some way, somehow, he was going to get rid of Gilliane and make Lady Isabella Tremayne, Countess of Hawkhurst, his if it killed him.

Throwing on his cloak, he left his pavilion to seek out Richard, Duke of Gloucester. Lionel must gain his liege's permission to return home at once.

Far away, Lady Isabella Tremayne, Countess of Hawkhurst, sang softly to herself as she left the new cottage of one of her tenants.

"My knight knelt and bowed his head, asked me to wed.
I had but riddles four to guess, then happiness.
Oh, listen all ye maidens fair; come—have a care,
So ye may know the love I won when I was done.

"What is paler than white milk, yet rose as silk?
What is brighter than star clear, shines with a tear?
What is sweeter than red wine, grapes on a vine?
What is higher than a tree, deeper than the sea?

"My skin so pale yet rosy when touched by thee.
My eyes so bright with joyous tear when thou art near.
My lips so sweet, like grapes' red wine, when kissed by thine.
My love so high and deep, for e'er, 'twill keep."

* * *

There was joy in her heart, for slowly but surely, Warrick had set about to woo his wife, and she once more shared his bed. Sometimes, perceiving how cautiously he handled her, Isabella had to bite her tongue to keep from blurting out her love for her husband. How she wanted to tell him he need not court her—that he already held her heart—but she knew he would not believe her. So she kept silent and watched and waited to see what he would do next; and the seed of hope for her marriage that had withered in her breast that day of the King's tourney was born again and began to flourish.

The work at Hawkhurst was progressing well too. The inside of the castle was now complete, and the shoring up of the defenses was coming along nicely under Sir Bevan's watchful eye. The chapel had been restored, much to Father Francis's delight, and Mass was now said daily. By Christmas, all the villeins would have new huts and, come spring, vegetable patches as well, Warrick having given his permission for the planting of these. At first, Isabella had feared he might refuse to allow this, but upon her asking him about it, he had merely raised one eyebrow and smiled wryly.

"This is your home now, 'Sabelle," he had told her. "Ye are free to do whatever ye please with regard to managing the estate. As ye are aware, I have paid scant attention to my keep. In fact, I am surprised ye even consulted me at all, knowing what a shambles I have made of my inheritance."

"Ye have spent most of your time at Court and in battle, Warrick," the girl had said quickly, "and have had no wife to serve as chatelaine here at Hawkhurst. Ye are not to blame for that."

"Aye, I am, and well I know it. 'Twas just that I became accustomed to a different way of life and scarcely thought of Hawkhurst as my home. I did not intend to marry, and so there seemed to be little point in pouring my hard-earned gold into the fortress."

"I have kept a careful accounting of my expenditures, my lord," Isabella had reassured him hastily. "Though many of the repairs have been costly, your purse has not been cheated, I promise ye." Then she had blurted out in a rush, "And I—I shall pay for the cinnamon sticks I ordered for the larder, if ye wish, for I—I confess they were a trifle dear."

How he had laughed at that, laughed until she had grown almost angry and asked him what was so funny.

"I'm sorry, sweetheart. 'Tis just—just that ye looked so—so *guilty*, like a child caught stealing cookies from a jar. Keep your money, 'Sabelle. I have not accused ye of trying to impoverish me, and I am hardly a pauper besides. And even if I were," he had gone on casually, his eyes half-closed, "dost think I am such an ogre, I wouldst deny ye your favorite treat?"

"Nay, of course not!" Isabella had retorted indignantly. "Indeed, Giles says ye are overly generous, my lord!"

He had merely smiled strangely at that.

Thinking of that grin now, the girl frowned. Warrick was up to something, but what, she had no idea. At last, she shrugged, dismissing the matter. Whatever it was, she had no cause for complaint. She had gotten her way about nearly everything concerning Hawkhurst—with two exceptions. Her husband had forbidden her to enter the stables, saying his men-at-arms would be shocked; and despite all her pleading, he had sent Sirs Eadric, Thegn, and Beowulf back to Rushden, telling her they were Giles's knights, not his.

"But they're *mine*," she had protested, tears in her eyes. "They've been with me since childhood. Giles has given them permission to serve me as long as they wish. Oh, Warrick, please," she had begged, "don't send them away!"

"I'm sorry, sweetheart," he had apologized but had remained firm in his decision just the same.

And Isabella, not wishing to destroy the progress of her marriage, had bit her lip and quietly turned away. Still, she'd found the loss of her trusted men-at-arms difficult to accept and had been deeply hurt when Giles, upon learning of the matter, had refused to sympathize with her. It had been the first serious disagreement of their lives.

Now, as the girl spied her brother, she called out to him warmly, sorry for their quarrel.

"Giles!"

"Good afternoon, dear sister," he greeted her, sweeping off his hat and bowing. "Making your rounds, I see."

"Aye. I want to be certain the crofters are happy with their new cottages."

"How could they not be? The huts you're having them build are probably the finest houses they've ever owned."

"I hope so. At any rate, they do seem to be pleased. Some of the tenants who left Hawkhurst are even returning now. Oh, Giles, I'm so glad. Everything is going well, isn't it?"

"Aye. Ye should be proud of yourself, 'Sabelle. Hawkhurst looks like a different keep now."

"Do ye—do ye think that Warrick is pleased?"

"Of course. How could he not be? Which reminds me: He and Caerllywel have fetched the Yule tree from the forest. Warrick said ye must come, and tell them where to put it, lest the servants think he is attempting to take over your management of the fortress."

"Oh, Giles." Isabella smiled. "He is taking an interest in things at last, isn't he? Sir Bevan told me that Warrick had made all kinds of improvements on the ideas we had for the restoration of the castle's defenses."

"Aye. I'm going to instigate some of them at Rushden when I return. Thank God, I decided to stay at Hawkhurst until spring. When I think of how cold Scotland must be right now, it gives me the shivers! I'll warrant that Richard and his men are a foot deep in snow."

Isabella sighed.

"Dear brother, I know ye miss Rushden and Gloucester even more, but do not talk of our parting, Giles. It saddens me so. Doubtless, Warrick and Caerllywel will go back to Court when ye leave, and I will be left here all alone."

"I would not be too sure of that, 'Sabelle, if I were ye. Warrick appears to have every intention of remaining."

"Oh, I hope ye are right."

"Wait and see." Giles grinned. Now, come. The Yule tree awaits us."

It was with much difficulty and shouts of laughter and encouragement that the enormous pine tree, which Warrick

and Caerllywel had felled in the woods and brought home
in a cart, was finally erected in the great hall. But at last,
it stood proud and tall before them, and they all gathered
around to trim its branches. There were garlands of paper
chains; strings of raisins and cranberries; delicious candy
canes and fat gingerbread men (which Caerllywel said looked
just like Warrick's roly-poly bailiff, for which Isabella reprimanded him sternly, saying that Master Isham couldn't
help his looks, to which Caerllywel replied he had no doubt
the bailiff had been gorging himself on all the missing live-
stock, and he certainly *could* help that!); a hundred candles
at least; and a shining silver star for the top. When that was
done, they hung their smaller presents on the bedecked pine
boughs and stacked the larger ones underneath. Then the
Yule log was lit in one of the hearths, where it would burn
till Christmas Day was over. All the while, they sang carols,
Warrick and Caerllywel teaching Isabella and Giles several
old, traditional Welsh melodies. Isabella especially liked
the gaiety of one in particular.

> *Deck the hall with boughs of holly,*
> *Fa la la la la, la la la la.*
> *'Tis the season to be jolly,*
> *Fa la la la la, la la la la.*
> *Don we now our gay apparel,*
> *Fa la la, la la la, la la la.*
> *Troll the ancient Yuletide carol,*
> *Fa la la la la, la la la la.*
>
> *See the blazing Yule before us,*
> *Fa la la la la, la la la la.*
> *Strike the harp, and join the chorus,*
> *Fa la la la la, la la la la.*
> *Follow me in merry measure,*
> *Fa la la, la la la, la la la.*
> *While I tell of Yuletide treasure,*
> *Fa la la la la, la la la la.*

Warrick said *he* would have liked the tune a lot better,

had Caerllywel not been inspired, by the second verse, to grab up his lute and accompany them, making a most fearful din.

"If ye insist on playing that instrument, brother"—the Earl spoke dryly—"I wish you'd learn how."

Before Caerllywel could retort to this remark, Jocelyn stunned everyone into silence by declaring *she* had thought Caerllywel's playing superior. Isabella and Giles choked with amusement on their wassail punch, and Warrick rolled his eyes with disbelief, claiming only a woman in love could have been deaf to all the discordant, jarring notes struck by his brother upon the strings.

To this, Jocelyn blushed and artlessly rejoined, "Well, I'll warrant he might have done better if he hadn't danced while he played," sending them all off into peals of mirth again.

Christmas came at last, so different from the year before, when the dark cloud of Isabella's sickness had hovered over them. This season, they were filled with laughter as they sang and danced and played games. The men chased the women around and caught them several times under the mistletoe (as they did not try too hard to escape). Then all ate the Yule feast and opened their gifts. Finally, the boughs of the tree were bare, and nothing remained on the floor beneath its branches.

From where she knelt amid the scattered ribands and wrappings, Isabella glanced up questioningly at Warrick, for her husband alone had given her no present. He leaped to his feet and held out one hand to her.

"Come," he said.

Slowly, puzzled, she followed him from the keep, Giles, Caerllywel, and Jocelyn trailing behind them.

Outside, the night was a grey haze of shimmering moonbeams and flurrying white snowflakes. Isabella gasped, for the fortress appeared almost like some enchanted, magic castle in the darkness. All around the battlements, hundreds of torches had been lit and gleamed in the mist, casting a glowing halo about the keep, making it seem as though it were ringed in gold. Warrick's men-at-arms, dressed in shining armor, stood to attention on the ramparts, and the villeins had gathered in the courtyard, many with their heads bowed.

Isabella was awed by the sight and would have addressed them all, for she was certain that never before had they known a night such as this; but Warrick restrained her, saying, "Not yet, sweetheart."

It was not until she realized he was leading her to the stables that she thought she understood. The Earl had arranged a living nativity to be performed, she guessed. But she was wrong. Smiling, yet curiously anxious for her approval, Warrick flung open the door at one end, and Isabella stepped inside. Her hands flew to her face, and tears filled her eyes.

"Oh, Warrick," she breathed, stunned. "Oh, *Warrick*!"

The entire section of the stables had been painstakingly turned into a menagerie for her; and there stood Sirs Eadric, Thegn, and Beowulf, grinning broadly, with Isabella's animals from Rushden all about them. Tinker, her goat, was there; Matey, her raven; and Jasper, her squirrel; and all the rest, looking as at home as though they had lived there all their lives. Eagerly, the girl embraced them, bubbling over with joy as she talked to, petted, and examined them all to be sure they were truly real. Then, recalling her manners, she hugged her faithful knights, who had transported the creatures to Hawkhurst.

"Oh, Warrick," she sighed once more with happiness as she turned back to her husband. "'Tis the best Christmas of my life. However did ye manage to keep all this a secret?"

"Well, 'twasn't easy, sweetheart," he told her, "what with ye turning the whole place upside down. But everyone helped: Caerllywel, Giles, Jocelyn, all the knights and servants and crofters. 'Twas the devil of a conspiracy, but somehow, we managed it. Didst not think it strange how *all* the tenants insisted ye visit their new cottages?"

"Aye, but I thought 'twas merely because they were so proud of them."

"Well, they were, but also, we had to get ye out of the

castle and yet keep ye from the road as well so ye would
not see the beasts arriving. Each time ye would go to a new
hut, the villeins would give a signal, and the knights would
bring yet another cartload of animals up the hill. Why, it
took one whole trip just to get that stubborn goat up here.
He refused to get in the cart and finally had to be led up.
We were frantic ye would see."

"Why, that must have been the day that old Berta insisted
I stay to tea and positively talked my ear off!" the girl
accused.

"Aye." Warrick grinned. "'Twas. She told me she had
no doubt ye thought her the village idiot; she babbled so,
scarcely even knowing what she was saying; she was so
afraid you'd leave at the wrong time. She said 'twas only
the fact that ye were too polite to interrupt and take your
departure that saved us from discovery. She vowed she was
never so relieved in her life as to see, from her window,
the knights' signal that the course was clear."

"Well, I wondered"—Isabella spoke, laughing. "For there
she was, just chatting away; then suddenly, she jumped up
and told me she had to fix supper and practically thrust me
out of her cottage!" The girl giggled again, then sobered.
"And Giles, dear brother." She turned to her brother. "How
wroth with ye I was at your letting Warrick send my knights
away. However did ye stand me?"

"Well, 'twasn't easy, 'Sabelle," Giles confessed. "In
fact, I was so upset, I almost spoilt everything by telling
ye the truth. But as Warrick and Caerllywel threatened to
throw me off a cliff if I did, I managed to keep my mouth
shut."

"I thank ye, Warrick." The girl's voice was earnest as
she gazed once more at her husband. "I thank ye more than
I can ever say for the gift ye have given me this eve."

Then she hugged him tightly and kissed him until Sirs
Eadric, Thegn, and Beowulf cleared their throats and shuffled their feet awkwardly at being present at such an intimate
moment.

After that, they went outside to join the others, who broke
into song at the sight of them. As the last notes of the carol

died away, all knelt to receive Father Francis's blessing; and Isabella wept silently with joy, knowing this special night would live in her heart forever.

Chapter Twenty-eight

SPRING TURNED SLOWLY TO SUMMER THAT YEAR OF 1481, as gradually the buds that earlier had been only a promise blossomed into reality. Upon the mountains, alongside the rivers and rills that crept through rocky passages, fir club moss lay like a soft, green velvet carpet, innocently but deceptively hiding the sharp, dangerous crags. Upon the wild, windswept moors below, bracken as gold as the sun bowed and rippled gently with the breeze like a vast, shifting sea. In the marshy valleys, the decaying scent of peat that filled the deep stretches of mire mingled pungently with the fragrant white flowers and aromatic berries of the bog-myrtle that bloomed there also. In the wooded plains, the branches of the old oaks, tall ashes, and slender poplars came to life again, throwing once more into the shade the feathery pines that had reigned supreme in the forest all winter. All about Hawkhurst, the barren fields that had lain fallow were now bursting with acres and acres of ripening grain. Upon the hillsides, small but sturdy herds of cattle, sheep, and goats grazed contentedly, the tinkling chime of bellwethers, answered by gentle bleating, the only sounds that disturbed the peaceful, sweeping terrain.

Yet, for all this, Isabella was frowning slightly as she walked upon the moors toward the sea; and there were more than a few of the crofters who, upon spying her, secretly made the sign of the cross and murmured a quiet prayer for her soul. It was not that they despised the girl; indeed, they loved her dearly. But she was as fey as the wounded creatures she wondrously healed; and there was something about her solitary figure—and, perched upon her shoulder, that hawk, a wild and wicked bird, they thought—that gave the tenants pause.

Still, the Lord loved her; that much was plain to see. After all, had he, who had never cared about his inheritance, not allowed his wife a free hand and purse to restore it as she had seen fit? Had he, who had never before given a thought as to whether his villeins lived or died, not given his permission and supplies for them to build new cottages and plant vegetable patches for themselves? Had he, who so joyed in the hunt, not torn up one end of his stables and remodeled it so it might serve as a menagerie for wounded beasts? Had he, who had once had a never-ending string of mistresses, not become so fiercely faithful to his wife that his yeomen were afraid to cheat on their own women, fearing to incur the Earl's disapproval and displeasure?

If that was not love, what was it? the villeins marveled. Aye, the Lady Isabella had bewitched him right enough, and they were glad of it, for their own lots had improved considerably because of it. But still, sometimes, she frightened them a little just the same.

A gregarious, happy people, they did not understand her need for solitude or the fact that despite her joy and contentment, a small cloud of shadow had settled on her horizon. There was no reason for her disquiet, yet the girl was uneasy all the same; and she bit her lip thoughtfully as she recalled, with distress, the letter that had come this morn.

Once more, Lady Stanley's fine neat script leaped out at Isabella, as though it lay before her even now. The Baroness had written that one of her husband's favorite falcons was ill, and the falconers had been unable to cure it. It seemed the bird must die. Lord Stanley was heartsick. Was there nothing to be done, he had asked, and Lady Stanley had remembered Isabella's way with sick and injured animals. Would the girl be so kind as to advise the Baroness in the matter? The bird was suffering from such and such symptoms.

The letter had then chatted on politely about life at Court during the Tremaynes' absence. Lord Dante da Forenza, *Conte di Montecatini*, had been recalled home to Italy. Lord St. Saviour had drowned in a boating accident; his son, Lord Lionel, was now the Earl of St. Saviour-on-the-Lake (Isabella scarcely even noticed this piece of gossip). The

King's excesses were growing steadily worse, and he did not look well. Edward's eldest daughter, the Princess Elizabeth, was fair to rivaling the Queen in beauty. Lady Stanley had had a letter from her son, Harry. How kind and thoughtful he was in his love and duty to his mother; she was surely most blessed in her child.

They had been the sort of newsy remarks anyone might have written in a letter. But still, Isabella found herself remembering that first night, at supper, in the great hall at the Tower, when images of the Duke of Buckingham, Lord and Lady Stanley, Harry Tewdwr, and Warrick as conspirators against the throne had filled her mind; and now, she shivered a little.

The pretext on which the Baroness had written the girl might be legitimate enough; it was true her special way with beasts had been much noted at Court. But still, Isabella found herself wondering. Hawkhurst lay just across the Bristol Channel from Wales, Harry Tewdwr's—and Warrick's—homeland. What dark Lancastrian schemes might, even now, be plotted there? What plans against the Crown and Edward and Richard Plantagenet might be discussed late into the wee hours of the morning? Isabella could not guess or even know if such were happening. She had only her suspicions, roused by Lady Stanley's seemingly innocent letter.

The girl sighed. There was nothing for her to do, she supposed, but reply. But perhaps she could manage to word her answer in such a way that the Baroness would be discouraged from writing again. Isabella knew she would be forced to show her husband Lady Stanley's letter, whether she wished to or not. After all, someone at the castle was bound to mention that a message from the Baroness had come to Hawkhurst, and Warrick would think it strange if Isabella did not share its contents with him. She had no reasonable excuse for not doing so; and if she chanced keeping quiet about the letter, hoping no one would say anything to the Earl about the messenger's arrival, and then someone did, Warrick was bound to believe his wife was deliberately hiding something from him.

Isabella would have done almost anything to keep from

losing her husband's trust again. How she wished Giles
were here, so she might consult him, but he had returned
to Rushden and, from there, journeyed on to Scotland to
rejoin Gloucester. The girl sighed. She might have to show
Warrick the letter, but she would never, ever—not as long
as she lived or as much as she loved him—aid him in any
Lancastrian schemes to wrest the throne from her beloved
Yorkists' grasp.

Though she did not care for him, Edward Plantagenet
would be her king until he died; and Richard, his brother,
would be her savior forever. They were York—and all it
stood for and everything that Isabella had ever believed in—
through and through. She would not let that go without a
fight.

She squared her small shoulders determinedly and walked
on across the windswept moors to the sea, where, in the
distance, she could see the savage hills of Wales rising up
before her, like far ships, come to conquer England's shores.

"Christ's son! What's this?"

Isabella turned, startled, at the sound of the voice behind
her: for it was still her practice to bar all but those closest
to her from her menagerie, and all of Warrick's knights
knew and obeyed this. Slowly, puzzled, she rose from where
she knelt, wondering what was going on. There must be
something wrong that one of her husband's men-at-arms
had dared to enter; but as she approached the doorway, the
girl saw two strange yet oddly familiar men and their squires
standing there in some confusion, their horses half-in, half-
out, of the stables. Somehow, she knew one man was a
lord, the other, a knight, though there was little difference
in their garments. They both wore cloaks of green lined
with gold and bearing rosettes upon which were the badges
of cockatrices; green doublets slashed with gold; and green
hose and high, black leather boots. Across their chests were
the same sort of savage breastplates that Isabella had seen
upon Warrick and Caerllywel the first time they had come
to Rushden. And just as she had instinctively known Warrick
to be a lord and Caerllywel, a knight, so she recognized the
same of the two strangers.

Why, they must be guests, she realized at last, then wondered curiously why the servants had not taken care of them.

"Pardon me, my lord," she said courteously, "but ye must take your men and horses to the other end of the stables. As ye can see, this section now serves a different purpose, and few besides myself are allowed in here. But ye are strangers, of course, and could not have known that. I do not understand why the grooms have not come forth to assist ye. Perhaps they did not hear your arrival. Let me call them for ye, my lord."

The lord, who was obviously in charge, appraised her body crudely with his pale blue eyes, causing her to blush and think she looked little better than she had the first time that Warrick had ever seen her. She had tied a kerchief on her head, as was her custom when visiting her menagerie, and her gown was a little mussed from kneeling in the straw. Nevertheless, her hair was hanging freely about her ripe, slender figure, and the lord, an astute man, saw at a glance the haunting beauty that was Isabella's.

"Well, well," he drawled, grinning. "Whom do ye belong to, I wonder? And why is he so foolish as to keep a tempting morsel like ye hidden away here in this—this place?"— this with some disgust.

Before Isabella, surprised and slightly offended by his lack of respect, could answer, the knight, with a quiet smile, spoke up.

"Perhaps she is as wild as these creatures, brother, and in sore need of taming."

The men all laughed at this, but still, the lord's eyes glimmered with curiosity and speculation.

"Methinks mayhap you're right, brother," he agreed. "There is indeed something wanton about her. You've only to look into her eyes to know. Still, her master is a fool to believe keeping her in such a place as this will achieve his ends. I'll warrant she wouldst find my method of breaking her to the bit much more . . . enjoyable. Who is your master, wench?" he questioned abruptly, then made an impatient movement with his hand, cutting off her response. "Nay, do not bother to reply," he told her curtly, "for it matters

not. I've a fancy for ye; I have. Consider yourself mine
from now on," he instructed arrogantly, reaching out to
tease one lock of her hair. "You'll like my manner with
women far better than your master's, I assure ye."

Outraged, Isabella gasped with shock and yanked the
tress from his fingers. Why, how dare the lord indulge in
such a brazen piece of impertinence toward her? Even the
courtiers had never been so bold.

"How dare ye, my lord? Your manners are not fit to woo
a sow!"

The girl's voice shook with wrath, and her body trembled. She was Lady Isabella Tremayne, Countess of Hawkhurst, not some maid who must cower before the lord's
insults and advances.

"Brother, don't," the knight pleaded, all trace of his
previous, gentle merriment now gone from his face.

The lord only laughed and strode toward Isabella deliberately, his intent plain and alarming. The girl was horrified.
Why, he meant to rape her—and before the amused eyes
of his men as well! She couldn't believe it. She had heard
of men who engaged in such sport, but never before had
she been exposed to such. But then, what did she know of
a man's behavior toward a maid who was not noble born
(for by now, the girl was certain the lord thought her some
yeoman's daughter)? Perhaps all women of common birth
were subjected to such treatment at the hands of men. Terrified, Isabella pivoted to flee, but the lord caught her cascading mane once more and, with a single jerk of his hand,
sent her sprawling in a pile of hay. Almost immediately,
he fell upon her and pinned her furiously fighting body to
the earth. His hands tore at her clothes; his carnal lips sought
hers.

"Let me go!" she cried desperately, mortified, twisting
her head this way and that to avoid his searching mouth.
"Damn ye! *Let me go!* I'm—I'm—"

"Come," he interrupted before she could inform him of
her identity. "There is no need for ye to play coy with me,
wench," the lord coaxed smoothly. "I'll be generous enough
with ye."

"The maid has said she does not want your generosity,

brother," the knight observed. "Release her now. Ye have
teased her long enough."

"Nay, I mean to have her," the lord vowed, "whether
she wants me or not. But if you've no stomach for the sport,
brother, then leave us. And take the squires with ye!"

Isabella gasped again and renewed her struggles frantically as roughly the lord attempted to shove her skirts up
about her thighs. Finally, managing to free one hand, she
smartly boxed his ears.

"You'll pay for this," she warned, rasping for air as he
growled and caught easily her fist. "I promise ye, you'll
pay if ye don't release me, and now!"

"Oh? And just who's going to make me, wench?" the
lord inquired, lifting one eyebrow as though he found her
threat diverting.

"My husband, my lord," Isabella retorted proudly. If the
lord thought her without protection, he would soon learn
otherwise. "He'll slay ye for this, I promise ye. Now—
let—me—go! I'm—I'm—"

"Ye have promised me much, wench," the lord broke in
again before she could tell him who she was, "but naught
yet that which I desire. Come. What say ye? I assure ye
your husband will not mind parting with ye. In fact, I'll
warrant he's tired of ye by now anyway."

"I doubt that!" Isabella snapped, infuriated. "Since we
are but newly wed."

"What a pity. Still, I shall compensate him most handsomely for his loss, I assure ye," the lord uttered, caressing,
with his fingers, the hollow between her heaving breasts
that swelled with rage above her bodice.

"Then prepare to do so with your life, my lord!" the girl
spat. "For if I'm not mistaken, 'tis his steel ye now feel at
your neck!"

The lord stiffened, for he did indeed feel the prick of a
blade upon his flesh. He tried to crane his head around to
see who held the weapon so threateningly against him, but
the sword jabbed him warningly, cautioning him to be still.

"Emrys!" the lord called to his knight. "Why dost thou
stand there, doing naught?"

"Perhaps because Caerllywel has a dagger at his throat

to ensure just that," Warrick answered grimly in response. "Though I'm certain the sport ye had planned was not to his liking, Emrys *is* your brother and would no doubt make some foolish attempt to save ye if he could."

"Sweet *Jesù*! Waer—Waerwic?" the lord queried hesitantly, startling Isabella now more than ever.

"Aye, 'tis I, " her husband purred silkily, his voice now having taken on a dangerous, deadly edge. "Now get up, Madog, slowly, and tell me what ye mean by trying to rape my wife."

"*Your* wife! God's wounds, Waerwic! I did not know she was so; I swear it! Ye know I wouldst never have touched her otherwise! For God's sake, brother! 'Tis the truth; ye have my oath on it!"

Isabella did not know whether she was more surprised to learn the lord was her husband's brother Madog—although as he now rose, she saw the resemblance at once—or to find that Warrick blamed her not at all for what had happened.

"My Lady Hawkhurst"—Madog turned to her, his hands spread apologetically—"I am indeed sorry. Had I realized—"

"Ye wouldst not have touched me, of course," Isabella finished tartly, still frightened and upset and now more angry than ever. "A fine attitude, my lord. Ye take only those maids who are lowborn and helpless against ye! Well, I warn ye right now that should I discover ye attempting to force yourself on *any* woman here, regardless of her rank, ye shall still feel the bite of my husband's steel. I do not know how things were before I came to Hawkhurst, but ye will find now that they are greatly changed!"

"*Brava!*" a woman's voice exclaimed as she clapped her hands with approval. "A woman's body should be given freely, with joy, not taken, as though she were but chattel."

A sudden silence fell as the men looked guiltily at the woman and flushed. For a moment, they seemed like nothing more than young boys caught in some forbidden act, and had Isabella not been so wroth, she would have laughed at the expressions on their faces.

"A notion far too advanced for your time, Mother, surely,"

Warrick rejoined, at last, as he strode forward, bowed low, and kissed the woman's hand.

Caerllywel, hastily releasing his hold on his brother Emrys (a hot-tempered lot, these Welsh, it appeared), quickly followed suit as Isabella stared in amazement at Warrick's mother, Lady Hwyelis uerch Owein.

Although the girl guessed the woman must be in her forties, the years had been kind to the Lady Hwyelis. She was tall and slender, with a grace that Isabella knew belonged only to those who were a part of the moors and forests, as the girl herself was. Hywelis's rich brown mane hung freely to her waist, indicating that she thought of Hawkhurst as home, for no woman wore her hair unbound outside of a family keep. Her honey-gold skin was as smooth as a young maid's, marred only by a few fine lines around her startlingly pale blue eyes, which gleamed with mystery. She had the same handsome facial structure, aquiline nose, and sensuous mouth that marked all her sons; but she was not truly beautiful. Still, one never realized that: for when she smiled, as she did now, Hwyelis's entire countenance lit up, glowed with that rare, deep, inner light born of the joyous, earthy knowledge that one has lived—and loved— to the fullest.

She stretched out her hands to Warrick's wife; and as Isabella grasped them, the girl knew, somehow, some way, that she had found in the Earl's mother a strange peace she hadn't even recognized she'd been searching for.

"My lady," she whispered and knelt, pressing her forehead to Hywelis's knuckles. "My lady."

If Warrick and the others thought this greeting odd, Hywelis did not. She gripped Isabella's palms tightly in her own for an instant, waiting for the tears she knew had started in the girl's eyes to pass. Then, gently, the Earl's mother raised Isabella to her feet and kissed her.

"So ye are Waerwic's wife," Hwyelis breathed. "I was afraid, so afraid, but now I see there is nothing at all to fear."

And if Hwyelis's sons thought this even stranger still, Isabella did not.

"Nay, my lady," she answered softly.

Warrick sensed that something of greatest importance had passed between his mother and his wife, but he could not guess what it had been. It was not until years later that he learned that in that first moment of their meeting, Hwyelis had known instantly that Isabella loved him truly, with all her heart.

The hush was broken finally by the sound of Isabella's animals recalling their mistress and the rest to the present. Warrick presented his brother Emrys to the girl, then she explained to them all about the menagerie. Hwyelis, especially, took a genuine interest in the beasts and bent to pet each one while Isabella stood by quietly, knowing instinctively that the creatures would accept Warrick's mother as easily as they did their mistress.

"And this one?" Hwyelis asked as she moved toward Ragnor, sitting upon one of the bird perches. "Who is this?"

"That is Ragnor, my lady," the girl replied as she hoisted the hawk onto her shoulder, "my special love. He was a gift from the King."

"And what is the matter with him?"

"I do not know, my lady. His wing was broken, and although I set it, and it has mended, still, he cannot fly."

Hwyelis studied the bird thoughtfully for a minute, then turned her pale blue eyes to gaze at Warrick. Then she looked back at Isabella, and once more, something passed between them.

"Do not fear, child," Hwyelis told the girl. "'Tis only that he is not yet ready. When the time is right, Ragnor will fly, I promise ye."

Chapter Twenty-nine

ISABELLA HAD NEVER KNOWN WHAT IT MEANT TO BE A part of a large family before, but with the arrival of Hwyelis, Madog, and Emrys, she soon learned. Somehow, even more than it had done at Christmas, the keep seemed to come alive, to be filled with an electric anticipation. The girl never knew what might happen. One moment, the four half brothers might be laughing together like the best of friends, and in the next, they might have drawn steel against each other like the worst of enemies. Yet, somehow, their fierce quarrels, born of hot tempers, always came to naught, for the blood bond between them was as strong as that between Isabella and Giles. It was just that it was different, as the brothers themselves were different. They were all tall and broad-shouldered and bore similar facial features; but there, the resemblance ended.

Madog, the oldest, had his father Bryn-Dyfed's coal-black hair, which contrasted strikingly with the pale blue eyes he had inherited from his mother. The most militarily inclined of the four, he had a mind that (when not bent on ravishing a pretty maid) coldly and calculatingly pored over strategies in battle and ferreted out his opponents' most vulnerable weaknesses. He was accounted a brilliant war commander and a dangerous foe; and those who had once sought to wrest his inheritance, Gwendraeth, from his grasp had discovered, much to their misfortune, that, at fifteen, Madog had needed no one's protection. He had soundly defeated his enemies (without the aid his grandfather had so obligingly offered) and had sent them scurrying, tails between their legs, back to their own fortresses. Now, at thirty, there were few men in Wales who dared to cross him. He was indeed a lord worthy of the cockatrice badge he wore.

With his brown hair streaked with the gold of his father's and his father's amber eyes, Warrick was the most moody and mysterious of the four. In battle, he did his duty and did it better than most, but he was not obsessed with war like Madog. He was certainly a great deal more sensitive, but this was tempered with a hard edge—those walls that made him so difficult to know and grow close to. Ofttimes, he was darkly brooding and withdrawn, almost indifferent to those around him, even those he cared for; and they would know they had trespassed on his privacy, his need for solitude that only Isabella and Hwyelis fully understood. Because he hid behind a mask, he was, at twenty-seven, the most dangerous of the brothers, for the simple reason that one never knew what he was likely to do.

There was little of his father, Powys, in Caerllywel. With his mother's rich, dark brown hair and pale blue eyes, he was the court jester with a heart of gold. In battle or game, he was a worthy opponent, for they were good sports, both. Still, all things considered, he loved nothing so much as gaiety. Wooing pretty maids, playing at pranks, drinking, dicing—he joyed in all these and went through life light-heartedly pursuing its pleasures. Yet, he had a serious side as well, one that enabled him to sense unhappiness in others; and he did his best to ease the burdens of those he cared for. He was as gallant to a common wench as he was to a queen, as friendly to a simple yeoman as he was to a lord. Unlike Madog and Warrick, he was not feared, perhaps; but at twenty-four, he *was* loved and usually managed to charm his way through most of the crises in his life.

Emrys had his father Newyddllyn's chestnut hair and green eyes and thus least resembled his mother in physical appearance. He was, however, the most closely aligned to her in temperament, for he joyed in life and the living of it. He was not very adept at battle, knowing just enough to defend himself; and inwardly, he hated war, though he knew men must defend their homes and honor. If it were necessary for him to ride into battle, he would frequently be found upon the field, tending the wounded and dying, desperately fighting off his enemies only if attacked. Of a scholarly bent, he had studied medicine and was well versed in the arts of healing. He loved Madog dearly (as he did his other brothers as well) but disapproved of him and, at twenty-one, had chosen to serve him in the as-yet-unfulfilled hope of teaching him a better way.

But it was Hwyelis whom Isabella truly loved, and the two women soon became the closest of friends. It was almost as though Hwyelis had taken the place of Isabella's own dead mother, Lady Rushden; and now, more than ever, the girl often felt a pang of regret that she had not known her mother well before Lady Rushden had died. For the first time since Lady Rushden's death, the girl understood what she had subconsciously missed and longed for all those years: for only now did she feel she had an older and wiser head to guide her, someone to turn to, to lean on, a shoulder to cry on, someone with whom she could share all those little things that women share.

Often, as Isabella went about her daily chores, she would consult Hwyelis about various matters, glad of the older woman's advice.

"What do ye think, Mother Hwyelis?" the girl would inquire.

And Hwyelis, her pale blue eyes twinkling, would smile and respond, then hug Isabella affectionately.

The older woman seemed to understand, without being told, what the girl had suffered in her past. But then, because Hwyelis was a child of nature, like Isabella, she sensed a great deal that went unspoken, even though the girl, usually so shy, easily poured out much of her heart and soul to the older woman. In return, Hwyelis told Isabella the story of her own life and talked of her sons, especially Warrick, about whom the girl never tired of hearing.

Poor, lonely boy! The more that Isabella learned of her husband, the more she loved him. He had suffered, even as she had. No wonder his courtship of her was so slow and careful. Warrick was like Ragnor, not yet ready to fly, to speak of the love for her she knew now was in his heart. Yet, he showed his caring in so many other ways that the girl was content.

Often, at night, when she lay in the circle of his warm embrace, basking in the afterglow of his lovemaking, she wondered how she had ever thought she loved Lionel, now Earl of St. Saviour-on-the-Lake. When Isabella recalled those days long past, it seemed almost as though she had lived them in a dream instead of reality. She realized now that she had been too young and naive, her childish mind filled with too many foolish, romantic dreams, to understand that love—true love—never comes in a blinding flash of glory as she had thought it had come to her. Instead, it grows slowly, like a rose, from a seed that gradually sprouts, buds, and unfurls its petals beneath the sun—and the rain. Aye, that was the true measure of love, surviving the hard times, as well as the good, perceiving the faults of one's beloved—and loving him still.

Isabella had seen Lionel as some young golden god, and she had worshiped him as such, scarcely daring to breathe at knowing he was hers. But Warrick . . . ah, Warrick was indeed a man. For though he too often reminded the girl of some ancient pagan god, she knew he was not. She had seen his feet of clay, had touched them, had kissed them, and had been glad to find them flawed. Now, more than ever, did she recognize that Lionel had been but a dream, and Warrick was reality.

She smiled to herself in the darkness as her husband stirred, reached out his arms to her, and drew her near, knowing instinctively that she did not sleep.

"Sweetheart," he murmured drowsily against her ear, his breath warm upon her face. "Is something troubling ye?"

"Nay, my lord," she rejoined softly.

"Yet, ye are still awake"—he spoke half-questioningly, slowly raising himself on one elbow to study her.

"Aye. But there is naught amiss, Warrick. I was but thinking."

"About what?" he asked, his fingers beginning to slide caressingly over her flesh, reawakening her desire for him, which he had sated earlier.

"About ye," she said, sighing with pleasure as she snuggled closer to him, her heart swelling with joy and contentment at the now-dear, familiar touch of his hands.

"Ah," he breathed, somewhat teasingly, as though to hide his true thoughts. "A serious matter indeed to hold slumber at bay. I had not realized I weighed so heavily on your mind. What is it about me that keeps ye awake, 'Sabelle?"

"Right now, 'tis your hands, my lord," she jested lightly.

He laughed lowly for a moment, then sobered.

"Come sweetheart. Tell the truth now. Ye must never lie to your lord."

"I wouldst not; but even so, ye wouldst not believe me if I told ye what was in my thoughts."

"How do ye know?" he inquired. "Did I not tell ye once 'twas unwise to be so sure of things?"

"Aye."

"Then answer the question, 'Sabelle," he coaxed gently, kissing the corner of her mouth. "I am your husband. 'Tis my right to know what ye think of me."

Isabella wondered what was in his mind at that, but Warrick had his eyes half-closed against her, so she could not guess. Still, it seemed to her there was more than just curiosity behind his probing. His demeanor, as he waited for her response, was a shade too casual for the matter to be unimportant to him. Somehow, she sensed he cared desperately what she thought of him; and now, tonight, the girl decided she would tell him. She took a deep breath.

"I—I was thinking about how much I love ye, Warrick," she said.

She felt him stiffen beside her, and his hands tightened on her body.

"God's blood!" he swore quietly, fiercely. "Do not lie to me, 'Sabelle. Never lie to me about a thing like that."

She swallowed hard, her heart jerking queerly in her breast; but still, she managed to say, "I told ye, ye wouldst not believe me, my lord."

He released her so suddenly, she was startled, and flung himself, with a growl, from their bed. Frightened, Isabella sat up, drawing the sheet up to hide her nakedness as he fumbled around momentarily in the darkness, then lit a candle, which he set upon the table next to the massive four-poster. The light shone in the girl's face, but she did not turn away from it as Warrick sat down on the bed and laid his hands on her shoulders, his eyes staring at her searchingly.

"Now," he uttered. "Say again what ye told me when 'twas dark, and I could not see your face."

"I love ye, Warrick."

He inhaled sharply, and for a moment, as the girl gazed at him, she feared she'd lost him for all time.

Then he queried, "'Tis true then? Ye do not lie?"

"Nay, my lord."

"And that day at Lionel's tent?"

"He had deceived me into coming; and when I told him I wouldst have none of him, because I wouldst not betray ye, my husband, he grabbed me like a madman and attempted to force himself upon me. I was so angry, I accused him of being no better than Lord Oadby. He—he seemed to regain his senses at my words, and I was able to escape from him. That is all, my lord. Lionel did kiss me, aye, and tear my gown, but there was no more to it than that, I swear: for I knew then, that day, that I did not love him, had never loved him. 'Tis ye who have my heart."

"Oh, 'Sabelle, sweetheart," Warrick muttered as he suddenly crushed her to him. "Ye do not know how long I have waited to hear ye say those words."

Then he ground his mouth down on hers hard, kissing her forever, entwining his fingers in her mass of silvery-blond hair, as though he feared he might somehow lose her. Feverishly, he rained searing kisses on her temples, her eyelids, the tip of her nose, and then her lips once more. He could not seem to get enough of her, and Isabella gloried in the notion.

"Oh, my love, my love!" she cried, clutching him to her. "I've wanted for so long to tell ye what was in my heart, but I was afraid, so afraid ye wouldst not believe me. After that day at the tourney, I feared ye would never speak to me again. And when it seemed as though ye no longer even wanted me..."

"Oh, 'Sabelle, I did, sweetheart. I did. 'Twas just that I couldn't bear the thought of being hurt again. I had begun to care for ye, ye see; and when I believed ye had played me false, I attempted to put ye from my heart and mind so ye couldst not wound me further. But I could not dispel your image, no matter how hard I tried. All those nights without ye, I did but dream of ye."

"Yet, ye didst not come to me."

"Nay, like a fool, I sat in the King's stables and cursed ye to my horse!"

"Oh, Warrick, nay." Isabella stifled a small giggle of relief at knowing he had not deceived her after all. "Did ye really?"

"Aye."

"And I thought—I thought..."

"That I had sought another's arms?" he inquired gently.

"Aye."

"I do not ask of ye what I do not offer in return, 'Sabelle. Come. Let me show ye."

As long as she lived, Isabella would never forget this night: the touch of Warrick's hands as he drew away the sheet to bare her nakedness to his passion-darkened eyes; the heat of his lips upon her mouth, her breasts, her belly, as he kissed every part of her tingling body; the feel of his weight as he lay atop her, driving into her, filling up her senses with all that he was—and more. With a thousand shooting stars, the galaxy swirled up to engulf her, so she knew not where her burning flesh ended and Warrick's began. They were as one as they spiraled down into the all-enveloping blackness at the center of the blinding conflagration. Flames of fire blazed wildly through Isabella's veins, roaring in her ears as she cried out sweetly her surrender; and Warrick whispered huskily, "*Cariad*, my love, my Rose of Rapture," before he wrapped her long blond hair around his throat and told her he loved her.

Chapter Thirty

ISABELLA'S FACE, WHICH OUGHT TO HAVE BEEN FILLED with joy, was instead marred by a troubled frown as she stared down at the letter she held in her hands. The message was from Lady Stanley, Harry Tewdwr's mother, who had continued to correspond, despite the girl's attempts to discourage this; and now, more than ever, Isabella was certain the Baroness had an ulterior motive in writing to her. Lady Stanley's true messages, the girl was sure, were directed to Warrick. He read the letters without any apparent interest, but later, Isabella would often find him closeted with his brothers, deep in discussion. And although the men spoke in low-voiced Welsh, which, despite Warrick's instruction, she still had difficulty understanding, conversation nevertheless broke off abruptly if she chanced to enter the room.

Sometimes, she wished that Madog, especially, had never

come to Hawkhurst, for she felt certain he was the fuel that fanned the flames of rebellion she believed were smoldering at the keep. Madog, who so joyed in war, would think nothing of enlisting his brothers' aid in his battles. Isabella's heart leaped to her throat at the idea. She loved Warrick, her husband. She did not want him to be killed, either in war—or at the hands of an executioner for treason. Aye, treason, that ugly word that had sent so many to their deaths.

She closed her eyes and gave a small cry of agony at the thought, crushing Lady Stanley's letter. Fervently, Isabella prayed the Baroness would cease writing to her, though this seemed unlikely. Lady Stanley was clever, very clever. Her messages to the girl were innocent enough except to those who, like Warrick, knew how to read between the lines. Should the correspondence ever fall into the wrong hands, nothing could ever be proven against the Baroness. After all, what harm could there be in her letters to Isabella, who was known to be a staunch Yorkist who supported the Crown?

The girl longed to throw the message down a garderobe, as she had the straw baby that Lady Shrewton had given her long ago, but she dared not. Warrick would definitely be suspicious of such behavior, and she would do nothing to ruin his newfound love for or trust in her. Besides, if she kept quiet, Isabella might conceivably learn something of importance and somehow, some way, prevent from taking place whatever was being plotted against the throne.

Oh, if only Madog would go home to Gwendraeth! Perhaps then, Warrick would not be drawn into whatever was being planned. Her hopes were in vain, however, the girl knew. Caerllywel and Jocelyn were to be married at harvest; and of course, Madog, Emrys, and Hwyelis wished to attend the ceremony. Even now, they had not quite forgiven Warrick for wedding Isabella without their being present at the rite. The Welsh, like the Scots, were a very clannish race, it appeared.

Even after the harvest, there was to be no escaping from Madog, for he himself was to be married; and all were to journey to Gwendraeth for the nuptials. As Warrick was Madog's heir, Madog's first wife having died in childbirth and his only child having been stillborn, Madog had (or so

he'd said) wanted to tell his brother the news of his forthcoming wedding in person. Naturally, Madog hoped, this
time, to get a son of the marriage, who would then be his
heir. Besides, they had all wanted to meet Warrick's bride
as well, so they had come to Hawkhurst.

Isabella sighed as she glanced down once more at Lady
Stanley's letter and tried to smooth out the crumpled parchment so that Warrick would not know how distraught she'd
been at its receipt. Bitterly, she cursed the Baroness and
Margaret's son, the Lancastrian heir, Harry Tewdwr, under
her breath. If not for them, Isabella would have been happier
than she'd ever been in her life.

Wales, or *Cymru*, as the Welsh called it, was a wild, savage
land; and, following their sojourn at Gwendraeth for Madog's wedding, as they traversed the terrain's steep, rocky
hills to the Bristol Channel, Isabella was glad to be going
home. It was not that she disliked Wales—indeed, she had
found its untamed beauty breathtaking—but the Welsh were,
to her, a strange, barbaric race; and she had known little
ease at Gwendraeth. The castle, although well guarded and
heavily fortified, had been most primitive in condition; and
she had understood, for the first time, how, before her
arrival, Warrick and Caerllywel had lived at Hawkhurst
without truly realizing the many comforts the keep had
lacked.

Further, the talk at Gwendraeth had proven most unset-
tling to Isabella: for much of Wales, it seemed, bore little
love for England, its long-time foe. Isabella was certain the
Welsh would not hesitate to support the Lancastrian heir,
Harry Tewdwr, who was one of their own, should he be so
bold as to attempt to wrest the Crown from the Yorkists.

Inside her ermine-furred cloak, the girl shivered; but it
was not the cold of the dying winter that chilled her.

That night, at the inn in which they stayed, Isabella had
become so anxious about the matter that she finally dared
to broach her fears to Warrick. But her husband said nothing
to put her mind at ease.

"A man must do what he thinks is right, sweetheart,"
Warrick told her.

"But what ye intend is treason, Warrick!" she cried. "I know, in my heart, 'tis! As long as he lives, Edward Plantagenet is the rightful King of England."

"Aye, and as long as he lives, he will be my liege, for there is no man who will succeed in wresting the throne from Edward's grasp, 'Sabelle. But even a king does not live forever, *cariad*, and methinks that Edward's endless nights of carousing have taken their toll on him. He has grown slack and soft, and his power and the people's respect for him have lessened. I tell ye this, 'Sabelle: If he dies, England will not accept his son young Ned as her ruler. She has suffered before under the reign of boy kings, and she will not endure such again."

Isabella bit her lip at the thought. King Richard II had been only ten when he'd ascended to the throne; the real power of the Crown had lain in the hands of his uncle John of Gaunt and a regency council chosen specifically so that no one could gain complete control of policy. Naturally, England had not prospered under this weak government, and in 1381, the peasants had revolted. Even after Richard had attained his majority, England had continued to suffer under his reign; and when John of Gaunt had died in 1399, his son, Henry Bolingbroke, had forced Richard to abdicate and had proclaimed himself King Henry IV of England. Richard had retired to Pontefract Castle, where, it was rumored, he had been murdered.

Then, in 1422, Henry IV's grandson, less than a year old, had inherited the throne. Isabella knew what England had endured under the saintly but simpleminded King Henry VI's reign. She had lived through the last few years of it.

Young Ned Plantagenet, Edward's son, was only twelve.

"'Sabelle," Warrick continued seriously, "ye do see that if Edward were to die, the power of the Crown would fall into the hands of the Woodvilles, don't ye?"

"There is my lord Duke of Gloucester," she suggested.

"Young Ned scarcely knows Gloucester," her husband replied. "'Tis Lord Anthony Woodville, Earl Rivers, who has reared the boy at Ludlow."

"Nevertheless, Warrick, young Ned is the rightful heir

to the throne; and even if he were not, there are others with claims far more legitimate than Harry Tewdwr's."

"Perhaps," her husband conceded. "But legitimate or not, the fact remains: He is the sole, surviving Lancastrian heir. If we are not to have the Yorkist Woodvilles, we must have the Lancastrian Tewdwr."

"I am a Yorkist, my lord, as is my brother," Isabella reminded him quietly, "as our father was before us and his father before him. We will never change our allegiance. Wouldst ye meet Giles upon a battlefield somewhere and slay him?"

"I hope not, 'Sabelle." Warrick's voice was earnest. "But if it comes to war, I shall do my duty against my enemies like any man of honor."

"If it comes to war, *I* will be your enemy, Warrick," the girl pointed out, with a small sob of despair, before she turned and ran from the room.

Blinded by tears, she sought out Hwyelis, who was accompanying them back to England. Falling to her knees and laying her head in the older woman's lap for comfort, Isabella poured out her grief and fears to Warrick's mother. Hwyelis listened until the girl was finished, stroking Isabella's hair soothingly all the while.

Then the older woman sighed and said, "I do not know what my sons are planning, child, and I do not want to know. War is a man's business, after all, and not a very pleasant one at that. But I *do* know this: Ye love Warrick, and he loves ye, something that has given me much joy. No matter what happens, your place is by his side."

"And—and what of my allegiance to the King, my lady?" Isabella wept.

"My dear 'Sabelle, His Grace is not yet in his grave. Doubtless, he will live for many years still; and in that time, much may change."

"Oh, Mother Hwyelis, I hope so," the girl whispered fervently. "I hope so with all my heart."

But Isabella hoped in vain. A year later, at age forty, His Grace Edward IV, King of England, was dead.

* * *

His Grace the Duke of Gloucester, Richard Plantagenet, stared silently at Lord Hasting's travel-stained messenger, who knelt before him. That the youth had ridden long and hard was evident from the grime that covered his clothing, as though he had not bothered to change the garments for days. The contents of the scroll, which he held out to Richard with one hand, were urgent then; the Duke knew without asking. Still, Gloucester did not reach for the letter. Motionless, he stood, gripped by the same terrible premonition that had seemed to strangle him that day at the Battle of Barnet when he had asked after the fate of his cousin Richard Neville, Earl of Warwick, the Kingmaker.

Dead. Dead. *Dead*...

Never again would Richard laugh with Neville, the cousin who had reared him here at Middleham Castle and whom he had loved. Neville, who had put Ned on the throne, then betrayed him and tried to wrest the Crown from his grasp, was dead.

Strange that the Duke should think of Neville now. Neville—and Ned. It was a bad sign, Gloucester thought. Slowly, he took the letter the messenger handed him and broke its seal. For a moment, after reading the scroll's contents, Richard feared he would be ill, would swoon; and briefly, he laid his hand upon the messenger's shoulder to steady himself. He gazed blindly at the great hall of Middleham, which suddenly appeared to have frozen before him as, one by one, his guests began to realize how still and silent he had fallen. They were frightened by the whiteness of his face, the blank opaqueness of his slate-blue eyes. Hesitantly, they stirred and looked to him for reassurance, but the Duke had none to offer.

Dear God. Ned was dead. Had been dead for days.

Nay! *Nay!* 'Twas not possible! Edward of the three suns was not just a king; he was the sun itself in splendor, a golden god at whose feet all of England had knelt.

Dead. Dead. *Dead*...

Gloucester turned and staggered unseeingly from the great hall. He never even heard his beloved wife, Anne, crying his name.

* * *

Her Grace the Duchess of Gloucester, Anne, was frightened,
more frightened than she had ever been in her life. She had
never before seen Richard like this. Cold. Silent. Withdrawn. He was devastated by grief yet drawn with grim
determination too as he prepared for the worst battle of his
life; and she did not know how to help him. That was what
hurt the worst of all. She, whom her husband had never
failed, was failing him now, in his greatest hour of need;
and because of her helplessness, Anne was afraid, so desperately afraid, for the man she loved more than life itself.
If only she could find some way to comfort him, lessen his
sorrow, ease the terrible burden that had fallen upon his
shoulders; but she could not. She was but a woman; Edward
Plantagenet had been a king. Anne alone could not lighten
the heavy responsibility with which His Grace had charged
his brother.

In his will, Edward had named Richard, Duke of
Gloucester, Lord Protector of young Ned, now Edward V,
boy King of England.

It was an awesome position, and the man who wielded
it must tread carefully—or lose his very life.

Much as Anne tried to forget the history of her country,
she could not. Thomas of Woodstock had been an uncle of
the boy King Richard II. When Richard had reached his
majority, he'd had Thomas arrested and murdered. Humphrey, Thomas's son, had been named Lord Protector of
the boy King Henry VI. Like his father, Humphrey had
been arrested; a day later, he'd been dead. This in itself
was enough to alarm Anne. What absolutely terrified her
was that both Thomas and Humphrey had held the title that
was now her husband's: Duke of Gloucester.

It seemed an ill omen.

Richard was weary, so very weary. He closed his dark slate-
blue eyes and laid his head on his arms on the table before
him.

All his life, he had been Ned's right arm. Richard had
sailed with his brother on the flight into Burgundy when
Neville had betrayed them. Richard had ridden at Ned's

side in the Battles of Barnet and Tewkesbury. Richard had
been there in France when his brother had bargained with
King Louis XI and signed the Treaty of Picquigny. Richard
had marched into Scotland, when Ned had been too ill to
do so, and had recaptured Berwick and entered Edinburgh
unopposed after soundly defeating King James III and his
army of marauding Highlanders and Border Lords.

And though Ned was gone now—dead—still, he reached
out to Richard from the grave.

Richard had written to Lord Anthony Woodville, Earl
Rivers, at Ludlow, requesting him to bring young Ned to
a rendezvous point somewhere on the journey south to London so they might enter the city together. Anthony had
cordially agreed to the meeting, which was to take place in
Northampton; but still, Richard's mind was uneasy. Lord
Hastings had sent a second messenger to Middleham, informing Richard that the Queen and her Woodville kin meant
to overthrow his protectorship of young Ned. They had
already won England's Chancellor, Archbishop Thomas
Rotherham, to their cause and were wooing Lord Thomas
Stanley, the Fox. Richard knew the forthcoming battle with
the Woodvilles for control of the throne would be the fight
of his life. He wondered how many would side with the
Queen against him. So far, the only bright note he had
received had come from his cousin Henry Stafford, Duke
of Buckingham, who had offered to accompany him on his
journey south and to place a thousand men at his disposal.

Sighing, Richard picked up his pen to reply to his cousin's message. Buckingham's offer of assistance was indeed
heartening, for he had long borne a grudge against the
Woodvilles, who had forced him to marry the Queen's sister
Katherine. But still, Richard could not forget that his cousin
was Lady Stanley's nephew by marriage as well. As he
accepted Buckingham's offer, Richard prayed that blood
was thicker than water, though he knew that when it came
to winning a throne, nothing was sacred.

On Tuesday, April 29, 1483, Richard rode into Northampton, only to discover that Lord Anthony Woodville, Earl
Rivers, had already come and gone—taking young Ned

with him. Richard, angered by this deceit, was waiting
impatiently for Buckingham's arrival when Anthony returned, accompanied only by a small party of men. He
apologized for his earlier absence and explained that young
Ned had wished to press on to Stony Stratford. The excuse
was a lame one, and Anthony flushed slightly, guiltily, upon
delivering it. The truth was that his nephew Sir Richard
Grey had reached him with a message from the Queen, in
London, ordering him to cancel his rendezvous with
Gloucester. Under no circumstances—Elizabeth had under-
lined these words twice—was Gloucester to be permitted
to get his hands on young Ned. Possession of the boy King
was the key to gaining control of the Crown. The Queen
had commanded Anthony to bring young Ned to London
posthaste and assassinate Gloucester. This last, however,
Anthony knew he could not undertake. He would move
heaven and earth for his sister Elizabeth; but murder he
would not do. A man had his conscience after all, and God
was an entity with whom even the Queen could not intervene.

Still somewhat flustered, Anthony took his departure,
and Buckingham rode in, full of news—most of it unpleasant.

Edward had been properly laid to rest at Windsor a week
ago Sunday. Richard need not worry that the ceremony had
not been fitting. The Queen, in her own cold way, had loved
Ned; and though she had not attended the funeral rites, she
had made certain he was buried with all honors and glory.
Elizabeth herself had been busy at Westminster, persuading
the council to outfit a fleet of ships, whose command had
been given to her brother Sir Edward Woodville. Her eldest
son, Lord Thomas Grey, Marquis of Dorset and, since March,
Deputy Constable of the Tower, had seized possession of
the treasury. In addition, the Queen had succeeded in prevailing upon the council to disregard Edward's Will naming
Richard Lord Protector of the boy King and had gained its
consent, as well, to her demand that young Ned be crowned
at once. The coronation was set for May the fourth, this
coming Sunday.

Richard inhaled sharply at that. Once young Ned was

crowned, Richard's protectorship would come to an end. By God! How did she dare—that common-born bitch from Grafton Regis, who had kept her thighs closed until Ned had married her? By what right did she countermand Richard's authority—that cunning, coldhearted whore, who had hounded Ned into executing his brother George, Duke of Clarence, and who would have gotten rid of Richard too, had she been able.

Abruptly, Richard stood and banged his fist down on the table. By God! It was not to be borne, and he would not bear it!

"Francis"—he turned to Lord Lovell—"rouse the men. We ride for Stony Stratford immediately."

They reached the town at dawn's first light. There, Richard arrested, among others, both Lord Anthony Woodville, Earl Rivers, and Sir Richard Grey and ordered them imprisoned in Pontefract Castle.

Chapter Thirty-one

Hawkhurst Castle, England, 1483

THE MEN CAME SUDDENLY, WITHOUT WARNING; BUT AT first, Isabella was not alarmed. Since the King's death, numerous large parties had passed by Hawkhurst on their ways to London. Had Isabella not been with child, she and Warrick would have been among those making the journey. As it was, the Earl had said his wife's health and well-being were far more important to him than politics; and he would not make the trip to London with her in her present condition, nor would he go without her.

Now, Isabella smiled softly to herself at the thought, childishly pleased, for she had not wished to be parted from her husband. Then, shaking her head a little over her selfish delight, she eased the small Welsh pony and cart that Warrick insisted on her driving now (horseback riding was too dangerous for her, he claimed) over to the side of the road to allow the rapidly oncoming troop of men room to pass. A tiny frown knit her brow. There was something vaguely disturbing about the entourage, but Isabella couldn't quite put her finger on what it was. Briefly, she was puzzled by the matter; then shrugging, she turned her thoughts to a subject she preferred—Warrick.

How kind and considerate he was, even if Isabella did think him a trifle overzealous in his protection of her. After all, it wasn't as though she were ill. Except for the usual bouts with morning sickness, her pregnancy was progressing smoothly. Still, Warrick persisted in treating her as delicately as though she were a fragile china doll. Ofttimes, the girl was tempted to laugh at what she considered her husband's foolishness; and sometimes, she did, gaily, until Warrick joined in sheepishly, understanding she was but teasing him. Still, it was nice to be pampered, and Isabella was glad to know her husband looked forward to the babe's arrival with as much joy and excitement as she did. She patted her rounding belly gently, filled with love and anticipation. She couldn't wait to hold Warrick's child in her arms!

The thundering hooves of the nearing cavalcade brought her back, with a start, to the present. The men seemed to be bearing down on her at a frightening pace. Did they intend to ride her down? Surely, she had given them ample room in which to pass. Suddenly apprehensive, the girl clucked to the pony, maneuvering even farther to the side of the path, so that they were almost in danger of toppling into the ditch that ran alongside the rough road.

All her concentration riveted on getting out of the way, it was not until Isabella once more looked up that she finally recognized what it was that had nagged her earlier about the men. They were garbed completely in black livery, which bore no identifying arms.

A little shiver of fear chased up her spine at the realization, for it could mean only one thing: The men were either disguised knights of some lord, or bandits, and either boded ill for whomever crossed their path.

Thoroughly scared now, Isabella grasped the pony's reins

more tightly, urging the animal into a gallop as she turned the vehicle around.

She was not totally alone. There were crofters working in the fields, but still, the villeins would be of small use against the armed troop on horseback.

Fool! Fool! Isabella chided herself mentally, recalling how she had laughed at Warrick's suggestion that her three faithful knights accompany her on her outing today.

Why, she was only going to old Berta's cottage, she had said, well within sight of Hawkhurst's walls. Warrick must stop suffocating her with attention! She was only pregnant, not helpless!

Now, chagrined, the girl gazed longingly at the keep in the distance, wishing she had paid more heed to her husband. Oh, surely, the Earl's sentries had spied her distress and were, even now, sending men to her aid!

The crofters, who had observed her plight, were shouting and running toward the road, their hoes and scythes in hand. But as Isabella had surmised, they were defenseless against the entourage in pursuit of her, and she screamed at them to fall back, lest they be killed.

The pony was racing along furiously now, and the wheels of the cart rattled and bounced precariously over the path. Once, after a particularly nasty jolt, the girl was nearly thrown from her seat and narrowly missed being toppled into the ditch. Her heart leaped to her throat at the thought of being overturned, but she dared not slow the beast. The animal's short, stocky legs could not outrun those of the destriers pounding after her. Even now, the cavalcade was quickly gaining on her.

To her horror, Isabella saw a large rock protruding from the road ahead. Frantically, she swerved to avoid it, but one of her wheels struck the stone sharply anyway, and the front axle shattered at the impact. The cart veered dangerously, wood splintering along the ground, until, at last, the pony broke free of its harness, and the vehicle plunged into the ditch.

Fueled by the power of terror, Isabella righted herself and managed to climb down awkwardly from the cart; then she began to run. But it was no use. In moments, she was the prisoner of the unknown men in black livery.

Desperately, she struggled against them, but they easily subdued her, then tossed her upon a horse they had apparently brought along with them for just this purpose.

At least, Isabella realized dimly through her fright, they were not bandits. They had planned and come prepared to kidnap her deliberately—but why? Did they mean only to hold her for ransom—or worse?

She did not know. She did not recognize any of the brutal men who had taken her captive; and when, tremulously but indignantly, she dared to question their identities and motive in abducting her, they stonily refused to answer.

Finally, utterly petrified, discouraged, and bereft, the girl ceased her queries and, tears stinging her eyes, rode on in silence.

Isabella did not know how long or far they had galloped before the violent, unremitting jolting started to take its toll on her. She ground her teeth together to keep from crying out in sheer anguish as, at first, tiny twinges of pain, and then shards of shooting agony, began to rip through her belly.

Oh, God, not the babe, she prayed fervently. Please, God, not the child!

Until this moment, all her mind-numbing fear had been for herself. Now, her heart was wrenched by a new and even more panicking terror. What if she lost her babe?

"Please, please, slow down," she begged. "I am with child."

But her desperate cries went unheeded. In fact, when they heard the sounds of pursuit and realized that Warrick and his men had given chase, the kidnappers sped on in frenzied haste.

Hurry, Warrick! Oh, please, God, hurry! Isabella screamed silently.

And far away, as though he could hear her, the Earl, like a man driven by the devil, grimly pushed his knights harder and harder. Several of his men's less-able destriers actually staggered and went down; but still, Warrick pressed on determinedly, praying that Gwalchmai would not falter beneath him.

By nightfall, the Earl had caught up with his wife's abductors.

The ensuing battle was short and swift, for Warrick fought like a madman, as did Madog and Caerllywel, who accompanied him. Even gentle Emrys wielded his sword with a fury previously unknown to him. Again and again, viciously, steel struck steel, until, at last, the earth was littered with decapitated bodies and stained bright red with blood. When the horrible melee was finished, only one of Isabella's captors, barely standing, remained alive.

Though Warrick, Madog, and Caerllywel tortured the captive unmercifully, he doggedly refused to name his lord; and finally, Madog, angered, slit the man's throat. The knight gagged as blood, punctuated by an odd whistling sound, spewed from the mortal wound; then slowly, he sank to his knees and crumpled into a heap upon the ground.

Moments later, Isabella fainted into her husband's strong arms, a sudden, thick warm moisture seeping between her thighs.

Isabella was not well. All of a sudden, the world she knew seemed to have gone quite mad; and to one only recently recovered from a miscarriage and still suffering from depression because of it, the thought was even more disturbing than it would have been under normal circumstances. Her head pounded horribly as she lay down upon the massive canopy bed in her chamber at the Tower. Old Alice placed a wet cloth on the girl's forehead, and, with relief, she closed her eyes at the cool, comforting touch. She wished desperately that Jocelyn would return with one of the Court physicians.

But the Tower was in an uproar over the King's death and the Queen's subsequent machinations to seize control of the Crown. There was no telling how long Jocelyn would be. No one with any sense showed his face at Court these days, lest he be drawn into the struggle for power being waged between Elizabeth and Richard.

Richard would win, of course. Unlike the rest of the Court, Isabella had no doubt of this. She need have no fear for her savior, only for Warrick, who had come to the Tower to plot and plan now that his liege was dead.

Oh, if only she had not lost the child! she thought for the hundredth time.

She might have kept her husband at home, at Hawkhurst, where they both belonged. But she had miscarried the babe, and she cursed bitterly the unknown person responsible for the shock that had caused her loss. Isabella was certain the evil, deranged Lady Shrewton was the culprit; Warrick was not so sure. In any event, it was unlikely they would ever know the truth of the matter.

Physically, Isabella had recovered from the terrifying ordeal of her abduction, but mentally, she was still dazed and depressed over the loss of her child. She wished that Warrick had not insisted on traveling to London, but he had remained adamant about his decision.

"'Tis true I did not carry the babe in my body, sweetheart," he had said, "but my grief at its loss is no less than yours. I know 'tis little comfort, but ye are young, just seventeen. In time, there will be another child. Meanwhile, life must go on, and we must look to our future—and that of the babes we will have, *cariad*. 'Tis necessary we go to Court, 'Sabelle; otherwise, I would not ask it of ye. Ye know I would not. 'Tis that I cannot know fully what is happening there if I remain here at Hawkhurst. Besides, the doctor suggested a change of scenery might do ye good."

Though he had not pressed her further, Warrick had been deeply upset and anxious about his wife. Hawkhurst was a remote and isolated castle, and Isabella would not be happy confined behind its walls for safety. Though he had not told her of his fears, Warrick had felt certain her abduction had been instigated by Lord Montecatini. The Count had not, to Warrick's knowledge, returned to England, but the Earl knew the Italian was a dangerous man who would stop at nothing to gain the revenge he had sworn to have. Warrick had said naught to Isabella about Lord Montecatini's vow, however, or the Count's unnatural interest in Giles. The girl would have been worried sick about her brother. It had been better for her to assume that Warrick's jealousy had been the cause of his joust with the Italian; and Giles, with whom Warrick had privately discussed the matter afterward, had agreed. As long as her husband and her brother were on their guards, Isabella need not be troubled. But now, Warrick must take his wife to Court, where there would be safety in numbers and where he could attempt to ascertain precisely who had been behind the wicked scheme to kidnap her.

Hwyelis had agreed with her son, and finally, Isabella had been persuaded to undertake the journey.

"I could not find a physician, my lady"—Jocelyn spoke as she entered the chamber, recalling the girl, with a start, to the present. "But Lord Montecatini has rejoined us here at Court and was considerate enough to mix a draught he told me will ease the pain in your head and help ye to sleep."

"How kind of him," Isabella stated, "especially after Warrick jealously wounded him in that joust because of his attentions to me. Please, Jocelyn. Say nothing to my husband about the Count giving me the potion. I'm sure that Lord Montecatini has no special interest in me, and I do not want any more trouble."

"Of course, my lady."

Isabella drank the sweetly flavored draught and drifted into blessed slumber at last.

On Sunday, May 4, 1483, the day that young Ned was to have been crowned King, he rode into London, with his uncle Richard, Duke of Gloucester, and his uncle by marriage Henry, Duke of Buckingham, at his sides. The older men wore mourning black, but the boy King was garbed in blue velvet. Ned was just twelve years of age, and the sudden turmoil in his life had made it difficult for him to grieve for his dead father, whom he had seldom seen. He was more concerned for his uncle Anthony Woodville, Earl Rivers, who had reared him at Ludlow, where he'd lived most of his life, and his older half brother Sir Richard Grey, both of whom had been arrested by the man that Ned had begun to think of as "my wicked uncle," Richard, Duke of Gloucester. Over the years, Ned had heard terrible stories

from his mother and the rest of his Woodville kin about his
uncle Richard and had instinctively shrunk from him that
dawn at Stony Stratford. When the boy had learned that his
uncle Anthony and brother Dickon had been arrested, his
worst fears about his uncle Richard had been confirmed.

Still, Ned was somewhat cheered at the sight of the crowd
that had turned out to greet his arrival in London. Surely,
no harm could come to him when so many people obviously
loved and welcomed him as their king. King. The word had
a glorious ring. Aye, he was, in truth, King of England.
After his coronation, he would free his uncle Anthony and
brother Dickon and have his wicked uncle Richard put to
death.

In the Jerusalem Chamber of the Abbot's lodgings at Westminster Abbey, Her Grace Elizabeth, Queen of England,
cowered with her sons and daughters, whom she had taken
with her into sanctuary. This was the fourth day of their
self-imposed exile, and already, their taut nerves had worn
thin.

"God's wounds, Thomas!" the Queen snapped to her
eldest son. "Will ye stop that endless pacing. Ye remind
me of one of the beasts in Lion Tower. I must think what
is to be done. All is not yet lost. . . ."

"Oh, Mama, how can ye say such a thing?" Bess, the
Queen's oldest daughter, asked with despair. "Just look at
what all your wicked scheming has brought us to!" she cried,
gesturing about her at the huge piles of tapestries, paintings,
plate, jewels, and bolts of cloth-of-gold they had managed
to strip from the palace. The coffers surrounding them were
filled to overflowing with the stolen treasure. So greedy had
the Queen been that when the Abbot had suggested that one
chest, too large to fit through the doorway of the abbey, be
left behind, Elizabeth had commanded that a hole be broken
in the wall of the sanctuary in order that the trunk might be
carried in. Bess was appalled by her mother's thievery. "And
I know that Uncle Dickon never meant us any harm," Bess
continued defiantly, despite her mother's threatening ad-
vance. "Father would never have left Ned in Uncle Dickon's
care otherwise. 'Tis only that ye hate Uncle Dickon and

always have. Had it not been for ye, we might have remained at the palace—"

"Shut up, Bess!" the Queen hissed, her pale blue eyes narrowed and glittering like ice as she shook her daughter viciously and smartly boxed her ears. "Ye know nothing of your father's treachery toward us! *Nothing!*"

Elizabeth's cold hard heart froze with terror at just the thought of what Ned had done, the lie they had lived all these years, the secret that would be the undoing of her, Elizabeth, the Queen.

Oh, God damn ye, Ned, she swore silently. God damn ye for your sins. I hope ye rot in hell. . . .

Oh, if only she could lay her hands on Bishop Stillington. She would tear out his cowardly heart, as Ned had foolishly refused to do, even when his brother George, Duke of Clarence, had learned the fatally damning truth. Aye, she would be safe then. Bishop Stillington was the only one left who knew. . . .

"Uncle Dickon, Uncle Dickon," the Queen went on sarcastically, feverishly mimicking her daughter's voice. "Is his arrest of my brother Anthony and my son Dickon and their imprisonment at Pontefract not proof enough for ye of his evil intentions toward us?"

Elizabeth's wildly blazing eyes burned like hot coals into Bess's own.

"He would never have arrested them if *ye* had not sent them to wrest Ned's protectorship from Uncle Dickon's grasp," Bess shot back with a strangled sob, her hands pressed to her still-ringing ears.

"Oh, be quiet, Bess," Lord Thomas Grey, Marquis of Dorset, ordered curtly. "Ye know nothing of politics. Do not despair, Mama"—he turned to the Queen. "Uncle Ned's fleet is still anchored in the Channel, with the rest of the treasure, and we have the Great Seal in our possession."

"Aye, thanks to Thomas Rotherham, the fool," Elizabeth sneered. "He hied himself to Crosby Place fast enough to beg Richard's pardon when he discovered how our plot had gone awry. Well, he'll find no mercy there, I'll warrant."

"It doesn't matter, Mama," Thomas reassured her soothingly. "We'll make other plans."

"Aye." The queen nodded, then reiterated, "I must think what is to be done."

At Crosby Place, wherein Richard was lodged, a dead silence had fallen over the great hall. For a moment, no one present even dared to breathe, for only twice before had the men gathered there ever seen that sick, stunned look on Richard's face: once when he'd been told of Neville's murder and once when he'd learned of Ned's death. Briefly, Lord Francis Lovell wondered worriedly how many more shocks Richard's psyche would be able to sustain. Concerned, Francis moved to fetch his beloved liege a chalice of wine but was halted abruptly when Richard suddenly leaped to his feet and said quietly, fiercely, "Nay, 'tis a lie."

Robert Stillington, Bishop of Bath and Wells, flushed and shuffled his feet nervously beneath the Duke's steady, piercing gaze.

"Your—your grace, I swear upon my—my soul that 'tis not," the Bishop stammered, his hands trembling upon the rosary beads he fingered anxiously with fear. "Why, I performed the ceremony myself!"

Nay, it could not be. Godamercy! Surely, *surely*, Ned would never have done such a terrible thing! Built his kingdom on a lie so dreadful that its consequences would affect the fate of all of England. Richard's mind reeled at the horrible thought. Elizabeth was not Ned's widow, for she had never been his lawful wife. At the time of their marriage, Ned had not been free to wed. More than two years previously, he'd been secretly troth-plighted to Lady Eleanor Butler, widow of Sir Thomas Butler of Sudley and daughter of Lord John Talbot, Earl of Shrewsbury. Nay, sweet *Jesù*. It could not be. In the eyes of the Church and the Law, all of Ned's children were bastards. Young Ned was not his father's heir and had never been his father's heir. The right of inheritance had belonged to George, Duke of Clarence. George, whom Elizabeth had hated, whom Ned had so suddenly, inexplicably, executed for treason. . . .

Oh, God. 'Twas true. Richard knew now, in his heart, that it was. Ned would never have ordered George's death otherwise; George had plotted against the throne often enough before and been pardoned. Only that last time, somehow, some way, George had stumbled onto the truth about Ned's marriage and had become too dangerous to live.

"The boy cannot be crowned King, your grace," Bishop Stillington declared more firmly now, bringing Richard, with a start, back to the present. "He is not the rightful heir to the throne."

"My God! Don't ye see what this means, Dickon?" Buckingham cried when still Richard remained silent. "The Crown is yours. My God! The Crown is yours! Ye need only to take it—"

"Nay!" Richard burst out. "I cannot!"

"Christ's son, Dickon! What do ye mean ye cannot?" Buckingham chided, his voice filled with eager encouragement. "'Tis a damnable choice, I'll admit. We all know how much ye loved Ned, and no one expects ye to enjoy proclaiming his children bastards; but 'twould indeed solve all our problems."

"Nay, Harry." Richard shook his head. "Ye are forgetting George's son, Edward, Earl of Warwick. If Bishop Stillington's words be true, then 'tis Warwick who is Ned's rightful heir, not I."

"For God's sake, Dickon!" Buckingham swore again. "He's only a boy and somewhat simpleminded, as well. God knows, England doesn't want or need another King Henry VI on the throne! Besides, the Bill of Attainder against Clarence for treason bars Warwick from the succession. I tell ye the Crown is yours if ye want it! 'Twas written in the stars all along. Dost not recall what that astrologer told Ned so long ago—that the name of the next King of England would begin with the letter *G*? Everyone thought 'twas *G* for George, but I tell ye 'twas *G* for Gloucester!"

Richard's face went white once more at Buckingham's words.

Oh, Ned, oh, Ned. I loved ye so, and what a mess ye made of it all. Why didst thou not tell me the truth?

"I must think," Richard said slowly, unknowingly echoing Elizabeth's words. "I must think what is to be done."

* * *

It was Friday the thirteenth, said to be an evil day. Isabella was certain now that it was so. Lord Thomas Grey, Marquis of Dorset, had managed to escape from the sanctuary of Westminster Abbey and flee the country; but others had not been so fortunate. That morning, when the council had met in the Council Chamber in White Tower, another plot by the Queen against Richard's life had been exposed.

After Edward's death, his raucous mistress Jane Shore had taken up with Lord Dorset and, ludicrously disguised as a nun, had been meeting him secretly at Westminster Abbey. Through her, Lord Dorset had managed to persuade Lord William Hastings, who was besotted with the harlot, to Elizabeth's cause. Together, with Archbishop Thomas Rotherham (who had again switched sides); John Morton, Bishop of Ely; and Lord Thomas Stanley (whose piously clever wife, Lady Stanley, had made several visits recently to Westminster Abbey, ostensibly to offer the Queen comfort), they had conspired to murder Richard and crown young Ned King at once.

At the council meeting, Richard had accused the men pointblank of treason. There had ensued some sort of a scuffle, during which Lord Stanley had been slightly injured; and Richard had ordered Lord Hastings to be dragged out to Tower Green and executed immediately.

Isabella was appalled by Richard's uncharacteristically brutal act and, following the dreadful execution, had gone at once to Crosby Place to comfort her beloved Anne, who had come to London and who was now deeply distressed.

"Your grace, Anne, please lie down," the girl begged. "Ye have always been frail, and I fear ye will make yourself ill with this fretting. Please lie down, and rest. I'll have a draught brought to soothe your nerves."

"Oh, 'Sabelle, 'tis no use," the Duchess wept. "Not even that would help me sleep, I fear. I cannot believe that Richard has done this mad thing. Will Hastings was one of Ned's closest friends! To have ordered him executed without even a trial—"

Anne broke off abruptly, biting her lip, tears streaming silently down her pale cheeks.

"Richard *must* have a good reason for acting as he did,

Anne. My lord Duke is not unkind. No one knows that better than ye and I. . . ."

Isabella's voice trailed off, for she could not bring herself to tell her stunned and disbelieving friend the awful remainder of the tale: That Archbishop Rotherham and Lord Stanley had been arrested and imprisoned in the Tower. That Bishop Morton, far more dangerous, had been arrested and given into Buckingham's custody at Brecknock, in Wales, as far away as possible from London. That Lord Anthony Woodville, Earl Rivers, and Sir Richard Grey had been condemned to death at Pontefract Castle. That Jane Shore had been arrested and thrown into Ludgate Prison. That Lady Stanley had again been stripped of her possessions by the Yorkists, who would murder her son, Harry Tewdwr—if only they could get their hands on him.

So swiftly had the terrible blows fallen that the royal heralds were, just now, at Paul's Cross, announcing Lord Hastings's death.

Isabella shuddered and closed her eyes as she thought once more of the blood that had gushed from Lord Hastings's severed neck, spewing out, like water from a fountain, staining the hastily erected block and soaking the grass of Tower Green bright red.

"Do ye see now what I meant when I told ye that England would not again suffer a boy king, 'Sabelle?" Warrick had asked grimly as they'd turned away from the sickening sight. "Ye mark my words: This is only the beginning."

How right he had been.

Archbishop Rotherham and Bishop Morton were sentenced to remain imprisoned, the council being reluctant to shed the blood of priests, especially after Richard's shocking execution of Lord Hastings. Lord Stanley, the wily Fox, was able, however, to get himself released, since the evidence against him was largely circumstantial. The Baron had either cleverly shielded—behind his wife's skirts—his involvement in the ill-fated affair, or he had been her unwitting dupe. Either way, as usual, nothing could be proven against him. Jane Shore was spared a trial for treason but was forced to do public penance, for whoring, by walking barefoot through the city streets, garbed only in her shift and holding aloft a candle. London was much amused by the sight.

Only Lord Thomas Grey, Marquis of Dorset, escaped punishment. He had managed to reach Brittany, where he joined Harry Tewdwr in exile—an ominous portent, Isabella thought.

Shortly thereafter, Cardinal Bourchier, Archbishop of Canterbury, entered Westminster Abbey and demanded the Queen yield up her last and youngest son, Richard, Duke of York. The boy was subsequently taken from sanctuary and lodged in Garden Tower with his brother young Ned.

Following this, in an act known as the *Titulus Regius*, Richard declared King Edward IV's marriage to Elizabeth Woodville (hereafter to be referred to as Lady Grey) null and void, because he had been troth-plighted to Lady Eleanor Butler at the time, and proclaimed all of Edward's children bastards.

On June 22, 1483, Friar Ralph Shaa, at Paul's Cross, delivered his sermon to the people of London, quoting from the biblical text, "Bastard slips shall not take root."

Four days later, at Baynard's Castle, England offered her crown to Richard, Duke of Gloucester.

BOOK FOUR

Tears

Chapter Thirty-two

ISABELLA'S HEART WAS FILLED WITH JOY AND ACHING AT
the same time. Her beloved Richard was to be crowned
King—and already, ugly rumors about him were being
spread. He was a hunchback, gossip whispered, a deformed
monster who had denounced his royal nephews as bastards,
had imprisoned the boy Princes in the Tower, and usurped
young Ned's throne for himself. The scandalmongers had
even dredged up the old slander that had claimed that King
Edward IV had been a bastard himself, born of his mother's
affair with an archer in Rouen. None of the vicious hearsay
was true; Isabella knew, in her heart, that it was not, that
Richard had done only what he'd believed to be right and
for the good of England. But still, the spiteful, malicious
slurs hurt.

"Are ye ready, sweetheart?" Warrick inquired as he buckled on his dress sword.

"Aye."

"Then we'd best go. The pages say the procession is
forming."

Today, July 6, 1483, was Richard's coronation. Isabella
was to be one of Anne's attendants at the ceremony. What
Warrick thought of all that had occurred and his wife's close
association with the new King and Queen, the girl did not
know. Richard treated Warrick courteously when they
chanced to meet, but after the trouble with Lords Dorset
and Hastings, all who had been Edward's favorites were
now suspect. It was only because of Isabella that Warrick
held his place at Court.

They left the palace, chancing, as they passed Garden Tower, to see the two Princes playing on the lawn. Isabella bit her lip at the sight.

"Young Ned does not look happy, does he, Warrick?" she asked.

"Nay, but then, under the circumstances, I'd say that was understandable. He has ever been a petulant, whining lad. Earl Rivers spoilt the boy, I do believe, and indulged his every whim. Doubtless, his changed status in life has been a severe blow."

"It does not seem to have affected Dickon," Isabella observed as she watched the two brothers.

"Nay, but then, Dickon was not reared to think he would someday be King. I wonder how long 'twill be before Gloucester puts them to death."

"*Warrick!*" Isabella cried with horror. "Do not tell me ye believe those awful speculations! Richard loved Edward, and he loves Edward's children. He would never murder two innocent lads, especially his nephews."

"He can't afford not to, 'Sabelle," Warrick rejoined dryly. "Not now. As long as they live, those two boys are a threat to Gloucester's crown."

"Then 'tis a threat that Richard will live with," the girl stated firmly. "Anne told me he is planning to take the lads north, to his castle at Sheriff Hutton, in Yorkshire."

"That's a fool's notion," Warrick said, "and I do not believe that Gloucester is a fool."

"Ye forget yourself, my lord!" Isabella uttered more sharply than she'd intended. "Richard is no longer Duke of Gloucester but King of England and your liege. 'Tis not for ye to doubt the word of honor of one whose motto is *Loyaulté Me Lie*—Loyalty Binds Me. Even setting aside his love for and loyalty to Edward—and to Edward's children—Richard knows full well that England would not countenance the murder of his nephews. 'Twould sound the death knell for his crown if he were to be implicated in such a plot. Now, speak no more to me of this, Warrick. Richard is the King and your liege," she reiterated.

"He is King of England, aye," Warrick agreed, "but not my liege, 'Sabelle, never that. I am sworn to Harry Tewdwr now, as well ye know; and in Wales, we too have a motto: A man who underestimates his enemies is a man on his way to a grave."

The girl gasped at hearing her worst fears confirmed.

"Warrick," she pleaded, "ye must give up this mad plan to put the Lancastrian on the throne. His claim is illegitimate, and the Stanleys are in disgrace besides."

"Are they?" Warrick queried, lifting one eyebrow with amusement. "They do not call Tom Stanley the Fox for naught, sweetheart; and Margaret Beaufort hides a shrewd brain behind that pious face of hers. Methinks ye will be surprised to learn the extent of her intelligence."

"Oh, she is clever; I'll grant ye that, Warrick. Still, methinks she has meddled once too often to be forgiven yet again. The next time, she might just lose that scheming head of hers; and I do not believe, for all her piety, that Margaret is that eager to meet her Maker. Besides, Richard said one could be certain of only one thing about the Stanleys: Only a fool ever trusts them. And ye said yourself, my lord, that Richard is no fool."

Warrick shrugged noncommittally.

"As ye wish, 'Sabelle"—he spoke. "I only hope our love is strong enough to survive whatever the future holds."

"Oh, Warrick"—the girl looked up at him earnestly—"never say 'tis not. I—I could not bear if ye no longer loved me, and I—I would not even have a babe of your making to comfort me for your loss."

"I shall always love ye, *cariad*," he vowed softly, taking her face between his hands and kissing her tenderly. "Whatever comes, never doubt that. Ye are mine, forever mine; and I promise, someday, ye shall have the child ye so desire, a dozen if ye like." He smiled. "We have the rest of our lives to see to that. 'Twas not your fault the first babe was lost, 'Sabelle; ye must stop blaming yourself for that."

"But ye wed me to get an heir. That was the whole purpose behind Edward's commanding our marriage."

"But I keep ye because I love ye, sweetheart; and if we never have a child, I shall not love ye any less. Now come, or we will be late for Glou—the King's coronation."

Hastily, they joined Giles and made their way to Baynard's Castle, the home of Richard's mother, Proud Cis, as she was known, Duchess of York. Isabella was slightly in awe of Richard's mother, Cecily Plantagenet, née Neville, for she had been a flower who'd bloomed at Court long before Isabella's coming. The courtiers had called Cis the Rose of Raby, and the girl knew the Duchess was somewhat amused by the fact that they had named Isabella the Rose of Rapture.

The girl swept the Duchess a low curtsy, then turned to greet Richard and Anne. How magnificent they both looked. Richard was garbed in a blue doublet slashed with gold and wrought with nets and pineapples. Over this, he wore a long, ermine-furred robe of purple velvet adorned with over three thousand powderings of bogy shanks. Anne too was clothed in blue and gold, the train of her gown sweeping out gracefully behind her.

After all were assembled for the procession, Warrick helped Isabella mount the white mare she was to ride, then kissed her and left to take his own place with the other nobles of the realm. Slowly, the parade began to move through the streets of London toward Westminster Abbey where, in the Chapel of St. Edward the Confessor, Richard was to be crowned King.

First came the nobles, decked out in their finest splendor. Following them was England's new Chancellor, John Russell, Bishop of Lincoln. Then, a little apart, rode Henry Stafford, Duke of Buckingham, recently named Chief Justice and Lord Constable for North and South Wales, an appointment that had greatly disturbed Isabella. He was in a blue velvet robe embroidered with golden cartwheels, and his golden-green eyes glittered as they raked the crowd that thronged the streetsides. After him came Lord Francis Lovell, England's new Lord Chamberlain. Behind him were Queen Anne's attendants: five pages in blue velvet and seven ladies-in-waiting in crimson (Isabella was one of these), all on white horses. Anne herself was borne in an ornate litter. There then followed Richard's attendants: seven knights (of whom Giles was one) dressed in crimson doublets and cloaks of white cloth-of-gold. Lastly, alone, came Richard himself, riding his destrier White Surrey, who had been a gift from his brother Ned.

Once they had reached the Westminster Abbey, all dismounted and followed Richard and Anne inside to the chapel; and the lengthy ceremony began. At last, now naked to the waist, the royal couple knelt upon the altar and were anointed with the sacred chrism. Isabella was glad to hear the murmur of surprise that rippled through the abbey, for she knew, from Anne, that Richard had insisted on this part of the rite so all might see he was *not* the deformed hunchback rumor whispered. Finally, the King's and Queen's bare torsos were clothed in cloth-of-gold; and they were crowned by Cardinal Bourchier, Archbishop of Canterbury.

The coronation was ended. It was not until they were outside, descending the steps, that a deeply shocked Isabella realized it was Lady Stanley who carried the Queen's train.

They met just southwest of Birmingham, on the road from London to Shrewsbury—a chance encounter, it seemed: for Henry Stafford, Duke of Buckingham, was bound for Wales, and Lady Stanley was en route from Worcester to Bridgenorth.

"'Tis your nephew, His Grace the Duke of Buckingham, my lady," a man-at-arms told the Baroness, who had drawn her mare to a halt at the sight of the approaching party.

"Aye." Margaret nodded, for she too had recognized Harry's banner fluttering in the wind. "We will wait."

The knight delivered the order to the rest of Lady Stanley's escort, and presently, Buckingham was upon them.

"Good day to ye, my lady aunt," he greeted her and smiled. With a flourish, he swept off his cap and bowed low in his saddle. "What a pleasant surprise. Dare I hope ye be going my way to Wales?"

"Nay, Harry." Margaret smiled back, but the warmth of her curved lips did not quite reach her dark eyes, which were assessing him with cool detachment. "I am but bound for Bridgenorth."

Harry Stafford was her nephew; his family had fought for the Lancastrians; and he despised the Woodvilles, who had forced him to marry the Queen's sister Katherine, then relegated him to the position of a nonentity at Court. Because of this last—and because he'd seen a chance at seizing some of the power and glory he had so desperately craved— Harry had come forward, after King Edward IV's death, to support Richard, Duke of Gloucester. Harry had been largely instrumental in putting Richard on the throne and had been well rewarded for his services. But still, it had not been enough. Harry had the same obsessive ambition and weakness of character that had tainted George, Duke of Clarence—and George's fatal charm as well. Second best had never been good enough for George, and it wasn't good enough for Harry. He would have it all—if he could. Margaret, a keen judge of character, had read him like a book, just as she had read Richard.

It was simple to understand why Richard, who had loved George, despite his failings, so favored Harry. Harry was George made over, and Richard would not see through his cousin any more than he had seen through his brother.

Margaret had counted on this when, some time ago, she'd bought Harry's soul. That he would seek to dupe her and had meant to do so from the start, she'd had no doubt. He had, after all, his own legitimate claim to the throne through Thomas of Woodstock, while her son's claim descended through the illegitimate line of John of Gaunt through his mistress Katherine Swynford. Nevertheless, Margaret had known she could manage Harry. She had outwitted men far more intelligent than he was. In the end, it would be Harry who was deceived; but by then, he would have served his purpose, and his usefulness to her would be over. If he lost his head to the executioner's ax, so much the better. Alive, he would be a liability she and her son could not afford. But first things first. There were two in Garden Tower to be disposed of. Had Harry done the deed? Had his hunger for the Crown been great enough to outweigh the mortal damnation of his soul? He had stayed behind in London, had let Richard begin the royal progress without him, as they had planned. But had Harry done it? Had he?

Margaret smiled again, and this time, the warmth reached her eyes.

"I do spy an inn yonder, Harry," she said. "Do ye dismount, and join me in a light repast."

"My lady aunt"—Buckingham grinned—"I would be delighted."

And she knew the deed was done.

"Oh, Warrick, hold me. Hold me!" Isabella cried as she stumbled into their chamber at the Tower, hot tears stinging her eyes.

"What is it, sweetheart?" he asked as he leaped to his feet in concern and clutched her trembling body to his chest. "What is it? Has someone accosted ye? Was it—was it that damned Italian—"

"Nay, nay. 'Tis nothing like that and has naught to do with him besides. Ye know he has scarcely so much as bowed to me in passing. 'Tis something much worse that a moonstruck courtier. Oh, Warrick, I cannot believe it. It simply can't be true!"

"What, 'Sabelle?" her husband inquired gently, trying to make some sense of her nearly hysterical babble. "What can't be true?"

"What people are saying. Oh, 'tis wicked. *Wicked!* I heard it in the marketplace."

"Heard what, *cariad?*" Warrick queried again.

"Oh, Warrick. People are saying that—that Richard has—has *murdered* the Princes!"

"Aye, I know, but I hoped ye wouldst not learn of it."

"Oh, Warrick, 'tis cruel, so cruel of them. How can they slander him so? Have they not cast enough stones at him? Must they besmirch his name and honor with so foul and despicable a crime, 'tis not to be borne? 'Tisn't true, I tell ye! Richard loved those boys. He would have cut off his right arm before he would have allowed any harm to come to them. I know it!"

"Hush, 'Sabelle, hush. You'll make yourself ill."

"I don't care. I don't care," she wept. "That he, who is so kind and good, should have so foul a deed imputed to him . . ."

"I know 'tis difficult for ye to accept, sweetheart. But

the fact remains: The lads have not been seen since Richard departed London nearly three months ago for the royal progress—"

"He took them north with him to Sheriff Hutton. He *must* have."

Warrick was silent for a moment at this, then he asked softly, carefully, "Even if he did, 'Sabelle—and I do not believe he did so—why have they not been seen?"

"I don't know. I don't know. But I'll tell ye this, Warrick: If aught has truly happened to those boys, 'twas none of Richard's doing. I wouldst stake my life on it! Besides, it doesn't make sense for Richard to have slain the lads and then kept their deaths a secret. He'd have wanted it known, so there'd be no uprising on their behalf. Nay, he did not do it, I tell ye."

"Then whom would ye accuse?"

Isabella inhaled sharply, and her eyes narrowed.

"There was only one man here in London, in Richard's absence, with enough power and ambition to have carried out such a dastardly crime: the Lord Constable, His Grace the Duke of Buckingham, Henry Stafford. *Lady Stanley's nephew*. Of course, Harry Tewdwr would want the Princes out of his way, wouldn't he, since he means to seize the throne?"

"I would think that an accurate assumption, aye," Warrick replied evenly. "Their existence would certainly pose difficulties to any would-be claimant. However, that still does not explain why Buckingham would have done the deed. What could *he* possibly hope to gain by it?"

"The Crown, of course, as well ye know. He wants it himself, and he has a legitimate claim to it. Lord Hastings did try to warn Richard as much, but Richard wouldn't listen to him. Buckingham was there when Richard needed him, and naturally, Richard trusted him because of it. But I never thought he was to be trusted, and neither did Anne. She said he reminded her of George, Duke of Clarence, and that Richard always had a blind spot where his traitorous brother was concerned. Aye, if those boys are dead, I'll wager that Buckingham is to blame. Mayhap Harry Tewdwr had naught to do with it at all, though I doubt it. After all, he's promised to wed young Bess Woodville if he wins the throne, hasn't he?

"Mother of God, what an alliance! Another one of Elizabeth Woodville's wicked schemes, I'll warrant, aided and abetted by Lady Stanley. Aye, I'll wager the Baroness is in it up to her pious, clever brain! 'Twas doubtless she who hatched the entire plot. Her son, together with the Woodvilles and Buckingham, would be strong enough to unseat Richard from the throne. Naturally, once Richard was dead, Buckingham would try to seize the Crown for himself, but then, Lady Stanley would have guessed that, wouldn't she? So they'd prepared, she and Harry Tewdwr. And once Buckingham was dead, who would be left? George's young son, Edward, Earl of Warrick, a simpleminded boy? No one would want him on the throne, of course. That would leave only Jack de la Pole, Richard's nephew by his sister Elizabeth, a minor nuisance, I would imagine.

"Aye, I see it all now. I'll tell ye this, my lord: If the Princes are dead, 'tis Lady Stanley's doing. Buckingham's not smart enough to have carried out such a crime all on his own."

"Nay, I would think not," Warrick conceded. "However, this is all sheer speculation on your part, 'Sabelle. There is no real proof the boys are dead. They may indeed be at Sheriff Hutton as first ye surmised."

But the Princes were never seen again; and in October, Henry Stafford, Duke of Buckingham, allied with John Morton, Bishop of Ely, who had been remanded into Buckingham's care at Brecknock, in Wales; Harry Tewdwr, and the Woodvilles marched against Richard, the King.

Nothing went right with the uprising from the start. At the beginning of the rebellion, a terrible storm blew up that lasted for days, bringing with it sheets of such blinding rain that people were calling it The Great Water. Numerous persons drowned as the rivers of England overflowed their banks, flooding the terrain beyond. Lakes stood where once fields had lain, and the dirt roads were quagmires of mud. Most of the Welshmen who would have joined Buckingham in support of their countryman, the Lancastrian, Harry

Tewdwr, were cut off from the Duke's forces by the Vaughns, who were Yorkists and who had a grudge against Buckingham anyway. No sooner had the Duke left Brecknock than his enemies torched his lands as well.

In Herefordshire, Buckingham's own cousins Humphrey and Thomas Stafford opposed him, and the people whom the Duke had thought would rally to his cause had had enough of civil war. The accursed rain had so swollen the River Severn that Buckingham and his rapidly dwindling forces were unable to cross it and thus were cut off from the Woodvilles, who would not, by now, have helped them anyway. Lord Dorset's part of the uprising, in the south, had already been contained; and Bishop Morton had fled. Harry Tewdwr's ships were driven back twice by the storm; and by the time he reached the Dorset coast, a trap was laid and waiting for him. Fortunately, having lived in exile nearly all his life had sharpened Harry's wits, and, suspicious of the soldiers who lined the shore, claiming to be Buckingham's men, he refused to land. He sailed on up to Plymouth, in Devon, where, by now, Lord Warrick ap Tremayne, Earl of Hawkhurst, was waiting to inform him that Buckingham was a fool, and the rebellion was a failure.

The rain was still falling heavily as Harry's mercenary soldiers rowed Warrick out to one of the ships, anchored in the Channel, where Harry waited. The day was grey and bleak, and the sharp, tangy scent of autumn mingled with the damp and the sea. Warrick was chilled to the bone as the treacherous waves swept over the small boat. By the time he had boarded the larger vessel, he was numb with cold and soaked to the skin. Thank God, there was a fire burning in the brazier in Harry's cabin. Warrick stretched his hands out gratefully to the blaze as several squires toweled dry his drenched body, then gave him some food and brandy. When finally he was warm, he turned and studied Harry assessingly in the flickering candlelight.

The two men had been children together in Wales. In the past, before Harry's exile, Warrick and his brothers had often been visitors at Pembroke Castle, and later Harlech Castle, where Harry had lived with first his mother and his uncle Jasper Tewdwr; then, after his family had been named

traitors, with his warden, Lord Herbert. Warrick's grandfather, Lord Owein of Pencarreg, was one of Jasper Tewdwr's
staunchest friends. Still, Warrick had not seen Harry in
several years.

Harry Tewdwr, at twenty-six, was three years younger
than Warrick but looked older for the simple reason that his
face was generally an emotionless, wary mask. Of medium
height, he was slender in build, almost too thin; and his
pale blond hair and icy grey eyes made him seem somewhat
washed of color. His features, however, had the classically
chiseled elegance of his mother, Lady Stanley; and his voice,
when he spoke, was low and pleasantly modulated.

"So, Waerwic," Harry said tiredly once the amenities
had been gotten out of the way. "I am not yet then to be
King of England."

"Nay, Harry, not this time anyway."

Briefly, the two men were silent, each thinking his own
thoughts, remembering the past. They had gone separate
ways then—of necessity; they had understood that. Now,
the paths of their lives had come together once more. They
shared a common goal: to put Harry on England's throne.
Warrick was sure now that he'd made the right decision.
Harry would marry young Bess Woodville, Edward's
daughter, and unite the Houses of Lancaster and York once
and for all.

"Tell me what happened, Waerwic"—Harry spoke again
at last.

"Buckingham botched it, of course," Warrick stated
wryly, swirling the brandy in his chalice a little. "He
tried to deceive ye, as we knew he would, but the people
refused to rally to his cause. Even his own cousins would
not come to his aid but opposed him in battle instead. Richard's men took Buckingham prisoner and marched him to
Salisbury, where Richard is camped. There, they brought
Buckingham up before Sir Ralph Assheton, the Vice-
Constable, and charged him with treason. Buckingham
was found guilty and executed the next day. He died badly,
I'm told, a coward to the end."

"And the Woodvilles?" Harry inquired.

"Hiding in sanctuary or fled."

"I see." Harry paused, considering. "Well, then," he continued, "there's no need for me to linger here. I do but endanger ye, as well as myself, Waerwic, especially as my mother has informed me your wife is a devout Yorkist."

"Aye, my lord," Warrick answered smoothly the question in Harry's eyes. "Our political differences be a source of pain to us both. She loves Richard, for he and his wife, Anne, were most kind to her when she was a child."

"Richard is indeed fortunate to have so loyal a subject," Harry remarked somewhat dryly.

"Aye, my lord," Warrick noted frankly, then went on somewhat defiantly, "but I wouldst not part with my 'Sabelle all the same, Harry, for I do love her dearly. 'Twas she who healed the bitter wound that Brangwen's betrayal of me left. If you'd rather I were not your man—"

"Nay, nay," Harry interrupted. "I'm glad of the happiness ye have found with your wife, Waerwic, no matter her loyalties; and I do apologize if I sounded harsh. 'Tis merely that I am weary of this waiting and do long for Wales, for home. I wouldst not ask ye to give up your wife for me, and I was not questioning your loyalty to me. I know ye have served me faithfully."

"Then there is something else, Harry, that methinks ye should know before returning to Brittany."

"Aye, what is it?"

Warrick took a long draught of his brandy, then uttered slowly, "I do believe the Princes are dead."

Harry inhaled sharply at this. For a moment, his heart raced as he considered how the demise of the Princes would place him that much closer to the Crown he so desired. Then finally, he shook his head, his pale visage tinged slightly with regret.

"Nay, Waerwic. It must be vicious rumor only. From what I have learned of him, I do not think that Richard Plantagenet would have murdered his brother's children. He stands to lose much by their deaths, and there are too many others who stand to gain if such were to happen. I do not believe that Richard would make such a mistake."

"Nor do I, my lord. Methinks 'twas Buckingham who did the deed, probably during Richard's absence from London."

"Buckingham was a fool, Waerwic. Ye said so yourself," Harry pointed out. "I doubt if he was bright enough to have carried out such a plan on his own. He would have to have had someone more clever than he was behind him, a puppeteer who pulled his strings. Who would have aided him in such a plot?"

Warrick's lids lowered warily over his amber eyes, for there were limits to a man's friendship after all.

"I do not know, my lord," he responded, in a voice he hoped was even, as he stared down into his chalice, unable to meet Harry's eyes.

"Come. Out with it, Waerwic!" Harry ordered, sensing there was more to it than Warrick was telling. "Ye have your suspicions, surely, if ye truly believe the Princes are dead and that Buckingham murdered them."

"Aye." Warrick nodded, confirming this, then paused deliberately. "But I do hesitate to speak of them to ye, Harry. Methinks ye wouldst rather not know whom I suspect."

There were only two people so close to Harry that Warrick would have refused to name them; and of those two, one had been in Brittany with Harry, too far away to have planned the murderous scheme with the meticulous attention to timing and detail necessary for success.

Without warning, the cabin grew suddenly still. Inside, a coal sparked and snapped upon the brazier, and the flames of the candles wavered with a gusty draft of air. Outside, the rain still poured down, beating, without mercy, upon the roof of the cabin and the deck of the tossing ship. The wind whined and howled ominously, tearing at the trailing canvas of the furled sails and causing the vessel's masts and timbers to creak and groan as they strained against the gale. The waves of the Channel roared and slapped against the hull of the ship as though to batter it to pieces.

Harry's countenance was white, his breathing so shallow, he seemed scarcely to breathe at all. His heart, in his chest, felt as though it were constricting into a tight hard knot, squeezing the air from his body.

How could his mother have committed such a foul deed? Harry had wanted the Crown, aye—but at any price? Aye, perhaps 'twas so. If he was honest, he knew he must share the guilt of his mother's crime—the murder of two innocent boys.

"I do hope she prays for all our souls," he muttered quietly at last, then buried his head in his hands, like a man bereft.

Like a shadow, Warrick slipped softly from the cabin and gently closed the door.

Isabella sighed and stirred faintly as she felt the bed sink with the weight of the warm body that slid in next to hers. Though the chamber was in darkness, and she was still drowsy with sleep, she would have known that familiar scent anywhere; and eagerly, she stretched out her arms to her husband.

"Warrick," she breathed, snuggling closer to his naked flesh. "Oh, how I have missed ye!"

He gave a low laugh.

"And I, ye, sweetheart. But what makes ye so certain 'tis I, 'Sabelle?" he asked. "Have I not told ye before 'tis unwise to be so sure of things?"

"Hmmm. But even were I blind, I wouldst know ye anywhere, my lord, my love. Besides," she teased, "ye are the only man who could have gotten past Caerllywel into my room."

"Aye," Warrick agreed. "He was like to slit my throat until he realized 'twas I who sought entrance to your chamber. Thank God, 'twas not Madog I did leave behind to guard ye. Doubtless, ye would have awakened to find yourself a widow."

"A dreadful thought, Warrick." Isabella shuddered involuntarily. "Do not speak of such things to me. How was our home? Still standing?"

"Aye, there has been much damage done by the storm, but already, the crofters have set about to repair it. I cannot tell ye how my heart swelled with pride, 'Sabelle, when I saw what they had already accomplished on their own. Before I married ye, most of the villeins would doubtless simply have left after such a catastrophe. I have much to love ye for, *cariad*."

"Then do love me, my lord, for it has been more than a month since ye have lain with me, and I have hungered for ye these many nights past."

"And I, ye," he murmured before his mouth found hers in the blackness.

The earth seemed to fall away beneath her, as that swoon that always swept through her body at his touch jolted her now and left her trembling with quickly wakened passion in his arms. Her lips quivered vulnerably beneath his, stirring in Warrick an odd thrill of desire as he kissed them, tasted them, parted them with his tongue. Almost fiercely, he explored the inner sweetness of her mouth, ravished it, savored it, growing more demanding with each lingering moment. Isabella's tongue entwined with Warrick's own, touching, swirling, filling him with delight. It had indeed been too long since they had lain together.

As they kissed, they caressed each other lovingly, their hands moving slowly over bare, tingling flesh, exciting it to even greater heights of sensation. Warrick's fingers cupped Isabella's breasts; his thumbs brushed her nipples lightly, making her shiver with pleasure as the rosy tips stiffened to taut little peaks. And though she could trace only the outline of his face in the shadows, she knew his golden eyes were dark with passion. She reveled in the thought that he desired her, that she had managed to tame—if only for a little while—this powerful man who wore the hawk's badge.

His lips melted across her face to her temple, the silky strands of her hair. His breath was warm upon her ear, and the words he whispered there made her heart beat fast with joy.

"*Cariad,*" he sighed, his voice low and husky. "My beloved Rose of Rapture. How I want ye. I will never get enough of ye. Ye have bewitched me, sweetheart."

"If so, 'tis but the spell of love that binds ye, Warrick: for I am no sorceress, though ofttimes, like now, I have thought there was magic in our nights."

"Aye, I too have felt it. We were meant for each other,

'Sabelle, belong together, now and for always. Naught will ever part us; I swear it!"

He buried his face in her silvery mane, which cascaded out, like a glorious waterfall, over the pillows. So soft, it was, like strands of silk. He kissed the tangled tresses and slowly wrapped them about his throat, drawing them, like trailing ribands, across his skin.

"Sweet, sweet," he muttered.

Isabella's arms tightened about him and slipped down his body to his hips to caress the strong thick muscles that rippled in his back as he moved against her, pressing his flesh to hers so closely that she could feel the ridges of the white scars from battle that marred his chest, his belly, his thighs. Another woman might have thought the rough old wounds were ugly, but to Isabella, each one was a chapter in Warrick's life, a test of courage he had passed with flying colors.

His mouth covered one breast while his hand crept down to fondle the warm, moist, secret place between her flanks, even as Isabella's fingers found his manhood and urged him to enter her, for she was eager for him and as ready as he.

Soon, he was driving down into her, filling her to overflowing with his maleness. Wantonly, she arched her hips to receive him, wanting him, aching for him. Hot wild desire coiled itself within her, like a taut drum being drawn even tighter before suddenly it burst to reverberate through her body in roll after roll of ecstasy.

And then they were on their sides, the rhythm of their lovemaking adjusting smoothly to this new beat, throbbing in perfect synchronization as Warrick thrust into her faster and faster, his face now buried in that soft place upon her shoulder, his teeth nipping lightly there, sending tiny electric shock waves through her blood to mingle with its feverish pounding.

Isabella cried out, gasping, as again the sweet, torrid tremors of delight shook her; and Warrick suddenly crushed her to him, shuddering with pleasure against the length of her body.

Quietly, they lay together, the stillness broken only by

the sounds of their breathing as slowly the primitive, tempestuous force that had held them in its wake subsided. Warrick cradled Isabella tenderly against his chest, one hand ensnarled in her damp hair as he pressed her head to his shoulder and kissed her.

"I love ye," he said.

"And I, ye," Isabella responded softly before closing her eyes and drifting into slumber, secure in the knowledge that she was safe in her husband's protective arms.

Chapter Thirty-three

Sheriff Hutton Castle, England, 1484

IT HAD BEEN A LONG TIME SINCE ISABELLA HAD COME home, to the wild moors of Yorkshire, and her return was not a happy one. She stared out blindly over the gently rolling terrain, not seeing, at all, the hills covered with a riotous cascade of heather and bracken, trailing broom and gorse, ferns and gillyflowers. The sunlight spilled over the land like melting butter, and the clear rills that wound their ways through the stony knolls shone blue and dappled beneath the branches of the ashes and pines, the poplars and oaks, and the spreading yews.

"They do say . . ." Anne took a deep breath, then sighed heavily. "They do say 'tis—'tis God's judgment upon Dickon, ye know, for—for murdering his nephews," she said painfully, startling Isabella back to the present.

The girl turned, noting how thin and frail the Queen looked. Anne's pale face was drawn with grief; her dark, haunted eyes were red-rimmed from weeping and ringed with mauve shadows from lack of sleep. Her trembling fingers kept clutching and tearing at her handkerchief nervously; and every so often, her body was racked by a hacking cough that was alarming. The Queen was ill, Isabella knew.

"Ye know that is a lie, Anne," the girl stated flatly. "'Twas Buckingham who slew them."

"But no one will ever believe that, 'Sabelle, especially now." The Queen's tone was bitter. "Dickon will go down in history as the man responsible for the murder of two innocent boys. Oh, God, 'Sabelle. Young Ned was only twelve and—and little Dickon but ten. Ned—" Her voice broke, but she mastered it and went on. "*My* Ned was ten too, almost eleven. He—he would have had a—a birthday soon. He was—was so excited about it. . . ."

Isabella bit her lip with anguish for the Queen as once more Anne's eyes filled with tears. They had buried Richard's and Anne's only child, Edward, in the church of St. Helen and the Holy Cross just that day. Without warning, the boy had suffered some sort of internal rupture. Nothing could be done. In minutes, he'd been dead.

The girl closed her eyes tiredly. *Was* it God's judgment on Richard? His was not the hand that had killed his nephews; but had he not proclaimed them bastards, taken the Crown for himself, might they be alive today? No one would ever know, and 'twas useless to ponder the question. What was done, was done.

Suddenly, Anne was seized by another fit of coughing that shook Isabella from her reverie. Concerned, she hurried to the Queen's side, supporting her fragile body until she could reach a chair and sit down. Still, the spasms racked her as she held her handkerchief to her mouth in an attempt to stifle the horrible rasps.

"Your Grace, Anne, let me send for the physicians, please," Isabella begged, but the Queen refused.

"Nay," she gasped. *"Nay!* I'll be all right in a minute."

But when the fit had finally passed, the girl knew, suddenly, terribly, that the Queen had lied to spare her. Isabella's heart turned cold in her breast, shriveling up into a hard little ball of fear and agony, for she knew there was no hope to be had. She felt as though, without warning, an iron band had enclasped her lungs, growing tighter and tighter until she could not breathe. Tears stung her horror-stricken eyes as she pressed her quivering hands to her mouth and shook her head with shock and grief and, most of all, an overwhelming pity.

"Oh, Anne," she wept softly, the sobs choking in her throat. "Oh, Anne!"

Isabella knelt and grasped the Queen's hands, slowly opening them to reveal the handkerchief that Anne had held to her lips earlier. Flecks of blood, a dark, ugly red, stained the fine, white linen square. It was the lung tisick, Isabella knew, and it was mortal. Anne's sister, Isabel, had died of it.

"Oh, Anne. I'm sorry, so very sorry."

"Don't, 'Sabelle. Please, don't. I don't think I—I can bear it if—if ye cry." The Queen's face was pinched with agony.

Isabella turned away, unable to bear the dark, pleading eyes that gazed at her so helplessly, filled with fear and the knowledge of death. Fiercely, the girl brushed away the hot, blinding tears of sorrow and anger that were now streaming down her cheeks. Oh, God. It just wasn't fair. It just wasn't fair! How could God be so cruel as to take from Richard his child and now the shadow at his side that was his beloved wife, Anne? Anne, sweet Anne, cut off in the bloom of her youth. . . .

"Does—does Richard know?" Isabella asked haltingly.

"Nay, and I don't want him to . . . not yet. I want to keep it from him as long as—as long as possible."

"Oh, Anne. 'Twill kill him; he loves ye so. Is there . . . nothing to be done?"

"Nay. 'Twas the same with Bella."

"How long—how long before—" Isabella broke off abruptly, unable to continue.

"I have a little time left to me yet, 'Sabelle. A few months, or more, if I'm—if I'm lucky. Oh, help me, 'Sabelle; please, help me! Ye alone know my secret. If the others find out, they'll summon the physicians; they'll tell Dickon; and I cannot burden him now . . . not now. Surely, ye see that! Oh, 'Sabelle. I helped ye all those years ago; do not turn away from me now; I beg of ye!"

"Of course, I won't. How couldst ye even think such a

thing? 'Tis only that . . . the physicians might know something, anything. . . ."

"Nay. Do ye not think we did all we could for Bella? I
tell ye there is naught to be done. I'm going to—to die,
and soon. Until then, I've got to be strong, 'Sabelle; I've
just got to! For Dickon's sake. Oh, if only we could have
stayed at Middleham, lived out our lives in peace and quiet
there. I would have been so happy. We never wanted any
more than that, Dickon and I, not then, not now, not ever.
We never wanted the Crown."

"I know," Isabella rejoined softly. "I know."

Almost desperately, Anne clasped Isabella's hand tightly.
The Queen's eyes were bright, feverish; her skin, nearly
translucent beneath its pallor, was stretched too tautly over
her bones. Her breathing was shallow, ragged, as though
she could not get enough air.

"Promise me—promise me you'll look after Dickon,"
she rasped as yet another fit of coughing seized her.

"Ye know I will," Isabella whispered, sobs choking her
throat once more as she hugged Anne's frail body in an
attempt to prevent her from being racked painfully by the
spasms. Then suddenly the girl cried, "Oh, Anne. *Anne!*
Ye are so young, too young to die! Whatever will we do
without ye, we, who have loved ye so?"

"Ye will go on, dear 'Sabelle. Ye must. Ye must not
fail me, do ye hear? Dickon will need ye more than ever
when I'm—when I'm gone, for I—I do fear the worst is
yet to come. Pray for me, 'Sabelle. Pray for us all. And—
and think of me sometimes. . . ."

"As long as I live, Anne, I promise ye! I'll not forget
ye . . . ever! As long as I live, ye shall be always in my
thoughts and prayers; I swear it!"

On March 16, 1485, after returning to London, Anne
died. Isabella was with her beloved friend until the heart-
wrenching last, clasping the Queen's pale thin hand in
her own, feeling Anne's flesh growing colder and colder
until, at last, Isabella realized the Queen was dead.

Still, the girl did not let go, vainly trying to keep Anne

with her for just a little while longer. Through the blur of her tears, Isabella saw those who hovered in the Queen's chamber moving to carry out the necessary funeral arrangements; dimly, the girl heard the muffled sobs of Anne's women and, in the distance, the tolling of the church bells that marked the Queen's passing. Isabella knew she should release Anne's hand and go to comfort the sorrowing maids. The Queen would have wanted her to do that, the girl knew. But it was not until she looked up and saw Richard's face, from across the bed where Anne lay, that Isabella rose.

In a quiet voice of command, which brooked no disobedience, the girl ordered everyone from the room, even Lord Francis Lovell, England's Lord Chamberlain; and strangely enough, no one questioned her authority. One by one, they took their departures until only Isabella and Richard remained. Slowly, the girl made her way to the King's side and laid one hand upon his shoulder.

"Your Grace," she began tentatively, and then, when he did not answer, she said, "Richard."

He glanced up at her then but with no recognition in his slate-blue eyes.

"Dickon," she murmured gently, calling him by the loving name she would never have presumed to use before. "Dickon. 'Tis I, 'Sabelle."

With an effort, the King seemed to rouse himself, to know her. He blinked once or twice, then spoke haltingly, as though it were almost too much for him.

"'Sabelle," he whispered brokenly, his voice a strangled sob of despair. "Dear 'Sabelle, how she loved ye."

"And ye, Your Grace."

For a moment, there was silence in the empty chamber, that odd, uneasy hush that death brings to the living. Outside, Isabella could still hear the church bells ringing out their mournful knell, the dirge echoing through the city streets. Though it was yet day and nearly spring, the grey sky was dark—and growing oddly darker. Through the window, the girl could see the queer, ominous blackness that had begun to settle over London as slowly, forbiddingly, the sun was snuffed out, like a candle, in the firmament, leaving a strange ebony void in the heavens, where the yellow ball had been. In moments, the sky was as though it were night.

"Dear God," Isabella breathed involuntarily, one hand going to her throat as, on the streets, the people of London started to cry out with fear, some falling to their knees and praying, believing it was the end of the world. "Dear God."

At the girl's words, the King turned. Briefly, he stared out the window in horror at the unholy sight.

Then, stricken, he uttered lowly, "'Tis a sign, an ill omen. I have sinned against God, and now he is punishing me."

"Nay, Your Grace! 'Tis not so! Never think it!" Isabella cried.

"Oh, 'Sabelle!" Richard's dark visage was a twisted, tortured mask of agony when he looked at her. "'Tis true. 'Tis true! God has taken away the very light of my life!"

Then, Richard, King of England, flung himself to his knees before Isabella and, burying his face in her lap as she sank to a chair, wept with grief.

Chapter Thirty-four

London, England, 1485

ISABELLA WAS SICK WITH DESPAIR: FOR EACH DAY, THE rumors about her beloved Richard, the King, grew; and as they waxed, so did Richard himself seem to wane. He had always been quiet and somber, of course; but now, his soberness was somehow ominous, foreboding. He did not seem to care whether he lived or died. He had spoken the truth that day of Anne's death. The light in his life had gone out, just as surely as the strange solar eclipse that had marked the Queen's passing had blotted out the sun that day.

In the eyes of the people—and perhaps Richard's too— God had judged the King and condemned him. Gossips whispered that Richard had murdered his nephews and had poisoned his wife to hasten her end, knowing she was too frail to bear him the heir he desired. And, most horrifying of all, the rumors spread that he intended to marry his niece young Bess.

Isabella was stunned to discover the monstrous proportions to which the scandalmongering had grown. She did what she could to stop it, but it was like trying to put a lid on a pot that was boiling over; the contents bubbled and hissed and seeped out to scald and hurt. Over and over, she damned Lady Stanley and the Duke of Buckingham for the heinous crime they had committed and for which they would never be blamed. Over and over, the girl wept and raged that Richard, who had loved Anne more than life itself, was accused of murdering the Queen. Isabella swore that he would sooner have plunged a dagger into his heart, but few believed her. Most painful of all was the idea that he meant to marry young Bess. Richard's morals were unimpeachable. He had been the most faithful of husbands to Anne— even those who spread the hateful gossip knew better than to charge the King with infidelity. That he would contemplate an incestuous relationship with his niece was ludicrous in the extreme. Every fiber of Richard's being would have been revolted by such a match. Isabella was certain the evil idea sprang from young Bess's mother, Elizabeth, who would stop at nothing to regain the power she had lost. If Elizabeth could not gain influence through young Bess and Harry Tewdwr, she would do it through young Bess and Richard: for Elizabeth did not care what wickedness she wrought as long as the throne was hers once more, and young Bess was like a leaf upon the wind in her mother's path.

Surely, Isabella thought, people could see that!

But still, the malicious whispers persisted, poisoning the King's subjects against him.

Richard could not bear it. The girl knew, when she looked into his eyes, that he could not.

At last, driven beyond endurance, he stood up in the great hall of the Priory of the Knights of St. John of Jerusalem and denied the slanderous accusations. Then he sent young Bess, who had left sanctuary and come to Court, away, away from those who would use her and hurt her, as they had wounded him.

Every eve, Isabella went to the chapel at Westminster to

pray for the King and Anne, sweet Anne; to light candles for them both, and to leave a single gold sovereign in the alms box.

Tonight, as she dropped the coin into the receptacle, Isabella hesitated, her attention caught by the wraithlike figure who slipped from the shadows and knelt to pray. It was Gilliane, Lionel's wife, now Lady St. Saviour. As usual, she looked as though she had been crying. Isabella's heart went out to the girl. After all, it was not Gilliane's fault that Lionel had not wished to wed her; and despite Gilliane's attempts to please him, Isabella had heard that his treatment continued to be most cruel. Even in the distance, she could see an ugly bruise upon Gilliane's face. Lionel must have struck her! Isabella's mouth tightened whitely with rage at the thought; and emboldened by her anger, she started forward, intending to offer what comfort she could to the lonely, miserable girl.

"So this is where ye hide to escape from my attentions, madam," a voice sneered, causing Isabella to pause and instinctively secrete herself behind a pillar. "God's blood!" Lord Lionel Valeureux, Earl of St. Saviour, swore with disgust. "Prayer! I should have respected ye more if I'd discovered 'twas a lover ye didst seek here."

Gilliane cowered upon her knees before her husband, her head bowed, as though expecting a blow. Her voice, when she spoke, was soft and trembled a little.

"Ye are my husband, my lord," she said. "For me to take a lover would be to sin against God's Commandments and damn my mortal soul."

"Christ's son, ye stupid slut!" Lionel gave a short, ugly laugh. "If that is the case, then nearly all at Court are destined to burn in hell, myself included."

Gilliane quivered with hurt at the knowledge of her husband's adultery. Though he had flaunted his mistresses before her often enough in the past, the reminder of his many betrayals still brought pain, for she had tried hard to make their marriage work. She bit her lip, and tears sparkled upon her eyelashes.

"I shall pray for ye then, my lord," she told her husband quietly.

"Aye, you'd best pray all right," he growled, suddenly grabbing her hair and twisting her bowed head up roughly. "But it had better be for yourself if ye don't give me an heir—and soon. I'm sick of bedding ye, ye frigid, barren bitch."

"Then set me aside, my lord!" Gilliane cried pleadingly. "Keep that of mine that our marriage brought ye, and allow me to enter a convent, as ye know I so long to do. I shall cause no trouble for ye; I swear it."

"Nay, madam, what ye desire cannot be. Your father would not consent to the dissolution of our marriage; and even if he did, he would, of course, insist upon the return of your property. I am very much afraid, madam, that ye and I are bound together for life, however much we may despise the matter. Now get up, ye little brown mouse, and scurry away to our chamber. Though I've no stomach for ye, I mean to get an heir on ye yet!"

"Nay, my lord, please," Gilliane begged, beginning to weep. "Ye—ye hurt me, and I—I cannot bear it...."

"Then that is your misfortune. I warned ye how 'twould be, did I not? Now get up. Get up, ye simpleminded strumpet!" Lionel ordered curtly.

When Gilliane did not obey, cringing in fear instead, he shook her unmercifully, then slapped her viciously, sending her sprawling upon the floor. Isabella, watching from the shadows, gasped, numb with shock at Lionel's brutality. To the girl's horror, Gilliane, as she fell, struck her head on one of the pews and suddenly lay very still, her face as white as death.

My God! Isabella thought. He's killed her. Lionel has murdered poor Gilliane, and I did nothing to stop him. *Nothing!* Oh, dear God, forgive me.

Lionel, bent over his wife's body, glanced up sharply at the small, horrified sound that Isabella had made. His cold, glittering blue eyes narrowed as they searched the chapel suspiciously, probing the shadows intently.

Trembling uncontrollably, sick to her stomach with terror and shame, Isabella shrank back behind the pillar, suddenly realizing that if Lionel saw her, he would slay her also. She was a witness to his crime—the only witness. He would have to kill her too, no matter how much he wanted her. Oh, God. If only she could escape, could somehow reach the door. But Isabella knew it was fruitless. If she attempted to creep from the chapel, Lionel would surely spy her. Her only hope was to remain still and in hiding. Petrified, tears streaming silently down her cheeks, she flattened herself against the cold marble of the pillar and waited, scarcely daring to breathe.

After what seemed like an eternity, she, at last, heard the sounds of Lionel dragging his wife's body across the floor. Cautiously, Isabella peeped around the edge of the pillar. Aye, he was carrying poor Gilliane away. Doubtless, he meant to bury her somewhere so she wouldn't be discovered. . . . Nay! He was but merely shifting her position, placing her at the foot of a small staircase that led down from a door to the chapel. An accident! He was making Gilliane's death appear like an accident. Of course. How well Isabella remembered how quick and clever Lionel had been, years ago, in making Lord Oadby's demise seem so. Her heart pounding in her breast, she waited for Lionel to leave. But he didn't. Instead, he walked over to the altar and picked up one of the heavy gold candlesticks that sat upon the dais. For a moment, Isabella was puzzled, and then; horribly, she understood.

Dear God. Gilliane was still alive. The blow from the pew had only stunned her, knocked her unconscious. Lionel meant to finish her off with the candelabrum.

"Nay!" Isabella screamed, shocked from her dazed and frightened state at last. "Nay, Lionel! Nay!"

Still crying out, she ran up the aisle of the chapel, shoving aside her fear for her own safety in light of Gilliane's dire plight. Stricken, Lionel stared at Isabella uncomprehendingly for an instant, giving her the time she needed to tear the sconce from his grasp.

"Ye can't! Ye can't do it, Lionel! I won't let ye! I won't let ye, do ye hear?"

"'Sabelle," he breathed. "'Sabelle." And then, "God's wounds, ye little fool. Don't ye see? 'Tis our chance—our chance to be rid of her once and for all! Give me the candlestick, dearest heart. There has never been a woman for me but ye."

"Dear God. Art mad? Even were ye free, *I* am not—"

"Why, we'll kill him too, that half-Welsh bastard," Lionel stated, his eyes filled with a strange and terrifying light. "Aye, 'tis the only way, 'Sabelle. I see that now. Now come, dearest heart, and give me the candlestick," he coaxed slyly. "We must hurry if we're not to be discovered."

"Dear God," Isabella repeated like a mindless puppet. "Ye *are* mad. I love my husband! I love him, do ye hear? I'd not marry ye if ye were the last man on Earth!"

"Oh, come, 'Sabelle. This is no time for ye to tease me. I've always been the man who held your heart; ye cannot deny that."

"I can. I do!"

Briefly, Lionel made no response to her outburst, merely looked at her, considering. Then he began to walk toward her purposefully.

"I'm sorry to hear ye say that, 'Sabelle," he told her ominously. "Very sorry indeed. I would have done anything for ye, ye know."

Slowly, understanding her danger, Isabella backed away from him, petrified but unwilling to leave the still-unconscious Gilliane to his savage mercy. If only she could run for help! But Lionel stalked her every step. One sudden move would provoke him into making a lunge for her. As it was, he kept his careful distance only because of the candelabrum she held threateningly in her hands. The girl bit her lip, wondering how long she had been in the chapel, how long it would be before she was missed, and Warrick or Jocelyn would come searching for her. If only she could stave off Lionel's attack until then. She could feel the beginnings of hysteria rising in her throat, and with difficulty, she choked the ragged sobs down. She could not afford to give way to her emotions—not now, not with death staring her in the face.

How strange it was that Lionel, a man she'd once believed she loved, meant to kill her. Almost detachedly, she wondered what it would feel like to have those hands, which had once caressed her so tenderly, strangling the very life from her body. She inhaled sharply at the thought and shook herself mentally, forcing the morbid speculation from her mind.

"My lord ... Lionel ... ye are not yourself. Of course, ye are distraught. Your wife has suffered an accident. I know ye did not intend to hurt her," Isabella lied. "'Twas not your fault she struck the pew. 'Twas an accident," the girl reiterated slowly. "Go, and fetch one of the Court physicians. I will stay with Gilliane until ye return."

"It won't work, dearest heart," Lionel purred, "much as it grieves me to admit it. I saw your face, just now, and there was no love in it for me, only for *him*, that half-Welsh bastard!" Lionel spat. "Oh, 'Sabelle, 'Sabelle. We could have been so happy, ye and I. We *were* happy ... once. Where did it all go wrong, I wonder?"

To the girl's surprise, Lionel truly sounded sad; for a moment, she almost pitied him. She steeled herself against the emotion. He was like one of the Scottish wildcats about which Giles had told her. If she showed one sign of weakness, one hint of fear, Lionel would turn on her in a minute, tearing her to shreds. And it would do no good to scream. She had screamed earlier, and no one had come to her aid. The chapel was deserted at this late hour.

"We were never happy, ye and I," she said, "for our love was built on lies, *your* lies, my lord, lies that I, young and trusting fool that I was, believed."

"Sweet *Jesù*," he groaned. "I loved ye, 'Sabelle; I did!"

"Nay, Lionel. Had ye loved me, ye wouldst never have lied to me. Ye only wanted me, as ye want me now—now more than ever, perhaps, for I am not yours and never will be."

"Because of *him*, that—"

"'Half-Welsh bastard,'" Isabella finished wryly. "Aye. Warrick is that—and more. But ye will never understand that, my lord. Ye scorn him because of the blood that runs in his veins, a circumstance of birth in which he had no choice; and ye hate him because 'tis he who holds my heart. Yet, I love him for those very same reasons. Warrick's birth has made him vulnerable, and he holds my heart because he has been man enough to admit to that vulnerability, to let me inside the walls that protect him from those like ye. He needs me, and in a strange way, I need him too. We are alike, Warrick and I, as ye and I never could be."

"Aye, I see that now ... when 'tis too late—too late for both of us," Lionel said. "I cannot let ye go, 'Sabelle. I meant to murder my wife, and ye know it. Ye will tell Richard, and then I will have nothing: for somehow, that stupid slut I wed managed to win Anne's heart, and the King does love those whom the Queen held dear."

This is the end, Isabella thought. Lionel is going to slay me. Oh, Warrick, Warrick, my lord, my love....

"Run, my lady! Run!"

Both Isabella and Lionel turned, startled, at the command. The girl's heart thudded wildly in her breast with relief. It was Jocelyn—Jocelyn, heavy with Caerllywel's child but, even so, prepared to defend her mistress. Even now, she was advancing toward them, the torch she held in her hands thrust out threateningly.

"Jocelyn! Get Warrick. Lady St. Saviour is here. She's had an accident, and I dare not leave her," Isabella called as she continued to watch Lionel warily, trying to guess his next move.

She could almost see the wheels clicking furiously in his brain as he studied the three women: Isabella, slight but determined; Jocelyn, pregnant but valiant and now hesitant, not knowing whether to stay and fight or to run for aid; and Gilliane, helpless and unaware. With a sudden, swift movement, Lionel lunged at Isabella, wresting the sconce from her grasp and swinging at her wildly. Just in time, she managed to avoid the fatal blow. The candlestick came crashing down upon a pew, splintering the top of the wooden bench. Hurriedly gathering up her skirts, the girl raced toward the altar, intending to use one of the remaining candelabra there as a weapon to replace the one that Lionel had wrenched from her hold. But he stopped her with one awful sentence.

"Don't move, dearest heart," he instructed, "or I'll kill her."

She turned and saw he was standing over Gilliane's inert body, his sconce poised to strike. Isabella gasped.

"Nay!"

"Oh, aye, 'Sabelle," Lionel jeered. "Now get over here, and tell your maid to do likewise, or I swear I'll slay this frigid, barren bitch I married."

"I think not, my lord."

The voice that had spoken was cold and hard and deadly, but Isabella had never loved it more than she did in that moment when she looked up to see Warrick standing on the small staircase above them. His dark visage was a murderous mask of rage, and a muscle was working in his tightened jaw. Quickly, before the much-surprised Lionel could gather his wits, Warrick leaped to the floor and kicked the candlestick from Lionel's hands. It smashed against a wall and then fell upon the floor, cracking the inlaid marble.

"Ye didst promise we would meet again, my lord," Warrick growled. "And so we have. Draw your sword, ye whoreson coward, for I mean to kill ye."

For an instant, Lionel's face was white with fear, then deliberately, he grinned, tossing his mane of blond hair like a strutting cock, its comb.

"With pleasure, my lord. I have waited a long time for this," he declared.

Steel scraped upon steel as blades were yanked from scabbards. Curtly, the two men saluted, then started to circle slowly, intently, not even glancing around as Caerllywel and Giles burst into the chapel, drawing up short at the sight that met their eyes.

Upon spying her brother and Caerllywel and realizing they would intervene if Lionel attempted any treachery, Isabella, recovering her senses, made her way to the font at the main door of the chapel. There, she dipped her handkerchief into the holy water, then moved, with Jocelyn, to care for Gilliane. To her relief, Isabella saw the girl was, at last, beginning to stir. Isabella pressed the wet cloth to Gilliane's forehead and felt gingerly for any injuries the girl might have sustained, but there appeared to be nothing other than the cut, swollen bruise that had formed where her head had struck the pew.

Scarcely six feet from where Isabella and Jocelyn knelt by Gilliane's form, the duel between Warrick and Lionel had been engaged. The deadly broadswords of the two men clashed with a resounding ring that echoed ominously to the rafters of the deserted chapel and seemed to jar every bone in Isabella's body. She gritted her teeth to keep from screaming out in protest against the battle and forced herself to concentrate on Gilliane. Still, it required all of Isabella's effort not to watch the two men, especially when, out of the corner of one eye, she saw Lionel make a wild lunge at Warrick and her husband barely manage to parry the wicked thrust. She gasped, trembling with fear for the man she loved, and turned away, swallowing hard to choke down the sudden lump that had risen in her throat. Isabella was thankful when Jocelyn, sensing her distress, moved to shield her from the sight.

"Take heart, my lady," the maid encouraged her with a small smile. "My Lord Hawkhurst knows what he is about."

"Aye." Isabella nodded. "But Lionel has become a madman. There is no telling what treachery he may attempt."

"Caerllywel and my Lord Rushden will guard my Lord Hawkhurst against any evil, my lady."

"Aye. Ye are right, of course; I know. Come, Jocelyn. Help me shift Lady St. Saviour to a more comfortable position. Nay, Gilliane. Do not try to rise just yet. You've had a nasty fall."

The fight continued, blades clattering against each other with a grating scrape that seemed to crawl along Isabella's tortured nerves. She dabbed at the wound on Gilliane's head. From habit, Isabella crooned softly to the girl, as she would have done an aching beast, although she could not have said what she told the injured Gilliane to comfort her. Isabella was only dimly aware the girl had ceased her tiny moans of pain, was content to lie quietly in the arms that cradled her so tenderly.

"What is happening, Jocelyn?" Isabella asked at last, unable to bear the awful sounds of the duel any longer.

Jocelyn turned, glancing over her shoulder, then just as soberly gazed back at her mistress.

"My Lord St. Saviour is faltering. 'Twill not be long

now, my lady. Nay, do not look, my lady. Ye will only distress yourself further. I assure ye my Lord Hawkhurst has suffered no mortal wound."

Once more, Isabella gasped.

"Then he is hurt!" she cried, realizing, without warning, the implications of her maid's statement.

"A cut on the arm—no more, my lady."

"Care for Lady St. Saviour. I must see to my husband."

"Nay, my lady, please. Ye are too gentle to witness what must occur. . . ."

Isabella paid no heed to Jocelyn's pleading, quickly shifting Gilliane's body so the girl now lay in the maid's lap, then springing to her feet, one hand held to her mouth to stifle her whimpers of fear as she saw the blood that dripped slowly down her husband's arm.

"'Sabelle."

Giles was there, supporting her, as her knees buckled, and she almost swooned.

"Oh, Giles, he is losing too much blood!" Isabella wailed softly as she clung to her brother for comfort.

"Nay, dear sister. 'Tis but a scratch, I promise ye. Many times have I seen men lose far more and survive. 'Tis Lionel who is done for, I'm afraid."

Isabella looked at the man she'd once thought she loved and recognized that Giles has spoken the truth. Lionel was breathing heavily, rasping horribly for air as he staggered upon his booted feet, wielding his weapon more and more haphazardly, as though it had somehow grown too heavy for him to lift. His golden hair was sopping wet. An almost feverish sweat beaded his brow, ran down into his eyes, momentarily blinding him, and soaked his dark blue doublet, mingling with the blood that stained the coat as well. His left arm dangled uselessly, nearly severed from its socket, where his shoulder had been deeply gashed by Warrick's sword. There was a gaping wound in Lionel's belly too— a fatal injury; Isabella knew. But still, he fought on. Even the Earl was slightly appalled.

"Give it up, man!" Warrick snapped tersely. "Ye are as good as dead now."

"Nay . . . ye . . . half-Welsh . . . bastard," Lionel responded grimly, shaking his head, then laughed shortly, an eerie, mirthless sound. "I shall . . . have . . . that . . . which is mine, that which . . . ye stole from me!"

"Don't be a fool, St. Saviour! 'Sabelle was never yours and never will be."

"She . . . would have been, had it . . . not been . . . for ye!"

"For God's sake, man—"

Warrick had not time to say anything further, for just then, Lionel lunged at him again with all the desperate strength of a madman. With difficulty, Isabella smothered the screams that rose in her throat as the two men slipped and slid on the blood that lay slick upon the marble floor. Furiously, in a last ditch effort to slay the Earl, Lionel pressed his attack harder, slashing crazily at Warrick but succeeding only in knocking a candlestick from the altar. The heavy gold sconce crashed upon the floor and rolled awkwardly until it was still. Lionel's blade swung on, shattering the devotion candles on their wrought-iron holders to one side of the dais. Glass flew in all directions. Flames sputtered from those wicks that had been lit in prayer. The altar cloth caught fire.

"Caerllywel!" Giles called a warning but unnecessarily. Warrick's brother had already moved to stamp out the small blaze that had started. The acrid smoke stung Isabella's nostrils, mingling with the awful smell of blood and making her long to vomit. Behind her, she could hear Jocelyn quietly retching into her handkerchief; but still, Isabella could not tear her eyes from the scene before her.

Whoosh, whoosh went the deadly weapons, hissing dangerously through the air to clang together with a horrible whack, followed by the awful scraping of steel upon steel. Sparks spat from the metal. Boots thudded upon marble as the two men thrust, parried, the corded muscles in their bodies taut with the strain of the terrible battle.

Then suddenly, it was over. Without warning, Lionel inhaled sharply, as though taken by surprise. He swayed, stumbled, dropping his sword as he clutched his belly, from which blood was now mortally gushing. The blade clattered upon the marble like a death knell before Lionel himself fell, sprawling upon the floor. Blood spurted from his nostrils, trickled down from one corner of his mouth as his head rolled limply, and his arms began to slacken. His lids fluttered once or twice; then, with difficulty, he focused his blue eyes on Isabella.

"'Sa—belle." He tried weakly to hold out one hand to her, but the effort was too much for him. He gave a small moan of anguish. "I—I didst love ... ye, ye know...."

"Lionel! *Lionel!*" Isabella screamed and ran to his side, but she was too late.

Lord Lionel Valeureux, Earl of St. Saviour-on-the-Lake, was dead.

She felt numbed by the realization. Hot, bitter tears stung her eyes—not for Lionel really, but for what he had symbolized—her first love, her youth, all that was past, all that might have been ... but was gone. Gone with the golden god who had proven such a false idol and beside whom she knelt so sorrowfully.

"'Sabelle." Warrick gently touched her shoulder and raised her to her feet. "'Sabelle."

He held her close, tenderly, for a moment, stroking her hair soothingly, whispering words of comfort and understanding, while she clung to him and wept.

But oddly enough, it was Gilliane who dried Isabella's tears.

"Do not weep for Lionel, my lady," the injured girl said, having finally regained consciousness and determined what had happened. "He is not worth your tears. Cry instead for the babe he cost ye, for 'twas Lionel who didst set his men to kidnap ye that day upon the moors, bringing on the miscarriage ye suffered afterward."

"Nay!" Isabella was stricken. "Nay!"

"Aye, my lady. 'Tis the truth," Gilliane insisted softly. "He never meant to harm ye, of course, but when it became known ye had lost your child, Lionel did say he was glad ye were not to bear Lord Hawkhurst's babe."

"Oh, Warrick." Isabella glanced up at her husband, sensing the sudden pain and rage and loss he felt. Lionel had cost them their child, the babe they had so eagerly awaited, had so grievously mourned; and Isabella had yet to conceive again, perhaps would never feel the quickening of Warrick's child in her womb. "Oh, Warrick. I did curse Lady Shrewton for the evil deed, and all this time, 'twas Lionel who was to blame."

"And I thought 'twas Lord Montecatini," he rejoined. "Damn my pride! Had I but believed ye that day at Lionel's tent, I should have been on guard against him and any further treachery on his part."

"Do not blame yourself for that, Warrick. Ye didst not realize how obsessed he had grown in his determination to have me. I don't think any of us did." Isabella's tone was bitter yet oddly confused, for she was hurt and stunned by Gilliane's revelation. "He was like a child crying for the moon simply because he could not have it. Still, strangely enough, methinks, in his own peculiar way, he really did love me after all."

"I'm sure he did, 'Sabelle," Warrick told her. "How could anyone help but love ye?"

Then suddenly, without warning, the Earl sank to his knees, as did Giles and Caerllywel. Jocelyn and Gilliane awkwardly hastened to curtsy. Without even turning to discover the cause of this sudden humility, Isabella too quickly knelt and bowed her head. There could only be one reason for this sudden, wordless obeisance—Richard, the King.

For an instant, the chapel was hushed and breathless as His Grace's dark slate-blue eyes, somber and grieving, surveyed the sight before him. Then he sighed and spoke, his voice low and weary as it broke the stillness.

"This"—his hand swept the chapel—"is God's house, a place where those who seek peace for their souls do come. Why hast thou instead done murder here, Lord Hawkhurst?" Richard's voice rose, shaking slightly with anger. "Tell me: Why hast thou desecrated God's house with your foul deed? Am I so wretched, so accursed, that this is what my kingdom has come to?"

"Nay, Your Grace, nay!" Warrick intoned quietly but with conviction. "Would to God it had been anywhere but here."

"My Lady Hawkhurst, see to your husband's wound, and tell me what has happened here."

Slowly, as Isabella bound up Warrick's arm, she explained what had occurred. At the end of her recital, the King sighed once more, a man bereft.

"'Tis true," he breathed to himself. "I am accursed. I do but taint all those whom I hold dear." Then, recalling himself to the present, Richard said, "My Lady St. Saviour, ye are free of a most unhappy marriage. I do bestow upon ye all your husband's worldly possessions and give ye leave to enter a convent to find the peace ye seek."

"Oh, Your—Your Grace;" Gilliane whispered, tears brimming in her eyes as she kissed the King's hand. "Sire, ye are most kind and good. I shall pray for ye always."

"Aye, do that, my lady," Richard uttered softly. "Perhaps God will listen to ye."

Then soberly, the King turned away, the silence in the chapel echoing painfully through the empty, aching chambers of his heart.

Chapter Thirty-five

IT WAS AUGUST 8, 1485, WHEN HARRY TEWDWR, WITH A force of two thousand French mercenaries, landed in Wales at Milford Haven. Despite those who would have restrained him, Harry was the first ashore. For a minute, he stood silently, surveying the land of his birth and childhood, from which he had been exiled for fourteen long years. His heart swelled in his breast, and for an instant, those who watched could have sworn there were tears in eyes as he knelt and kissed the ground. A great cheer burst forth from the crowd that had gathered there to greet him, but still, Harry did not rise. His uncle Jasper laid one hand upon Harry's shoulder.

"Harry?"—Jasper spoke lowly, somewhat disturbed, for his nephew was not usually wont to give so free a rein to his emotions.

The moment of unguarded expression passed.

Slowly, Harry got to his feet, slightly surprised to discover his men-at-arms, their swords drawn, ranged between him and the spectators.

"Is Richard Plantagenet so near then, uncle?" he queried wryly, indicating his knights.

Jasper flushed a little.

"Nay," the older man replied. "We didst but fear there were others present who might seek to do ye mischief."

"Put up your blades, sirs," Harry told his men. "We are among friends here. This is my home."

Home. How good it was to say the word at last, after all these long years.

Cautiously, the knights began to sheathe their swords. But scarcely had their steel met scabbards than they were drawing the blades again, surrounding Harry protectively from the lone rider who now approached at a rapid pace.

Reining in sharply the snorting destrier before them, the rider dismounted, took off his helmet and gauntlets, and strode toward them, apparently unconcerned that Harry's men had moved to block his path.

"My lord of Richmond," the stranger hailed Harry. "My name is Rhys ap Thomas, and I have a boon to ask of ye." Before Harry could speak, the stranger had thrown himself face-up on the ground before Harry's feet. "Come," Rhys bellowed. "Step over me, Sire."

A much-bemused Harry and his men surveyed the stranger warily yet with some amusement as well. If 'twas a trick to assassinate Harry, 'twas a poor one, for Rhys ap Thomas was a big man, his breastplate, heavy. He would not rise easily without aid, and his current position left him most vulnerable to attack.

Seeing no danger, Harry shrugged and started forward, deciding to honor the peculiar request.

"Hold, Harry," Jasper ordered softly, laying one hand upon his nephew's arm. "The man means to do ye some injury; I'm sure of it!"

"I do not see what harm he can offer me, Uncle, from such a strange vantage point—unless, of course, he intends to cut off my privates."

"Harry!"

Harry grinned like a mischievous lad at the startled expression on his uncle's face, then walked forth to step over Rhys ap Thomas's body.

Rhys roared with laughter and triumph as, seeing naught amiss, Harry's men grudgingly assisted the giant to his feet.

"'Tis done," Rhys crowed. "I have fulfilled my oath."

"Which was?" Harry inquired curiously, eying, with shrewd assessment, the stranger before him.

Rhys ap Thomas, he thought, would be a good man to have at his side in battle.

"I swore to King Richard of England that Harry of Richmond would enter Wales only over my belly," Rhys answered Harry's question. "And so ye have done, Sire. Never let it be said that a Welshman does not keep his vow." Then he drew his sword and offered it, hilt first, to Harry. "Ye will hear rumors, Sire, that I fight for King Richard. Do not believe them. I am *your* man, Sire, now and always. *Fiat!*"

Harry's heart swelled at the words, even though he took them, as he did all things, with a grain of salt. The northern lands of England might belong heart and soul to Richard Plantagenet, but by God, Wales was his—Harry Tewdwr's!

And it was.

That evening, the town of Cardigan opened her gates, without hesitation, to him; and throngs of people flocked to line the streets, their cries of welcome filling the air—and his heart—with joy.

"God save the King!" they shouted in Welsh. "Long live King Harry!"

And in his native tongue, Harry replied. The people of Wales went wild. Not for nearly a thousand years had they heard Welsh spoken by an English king. They surged forward to offer him and his men food and drink. That which was not given freely, Harry paid for and guarded his men like the Cadwallader dragon, which he had taken for his badge, to be certain they committed no outrages upon the town.

Word of his generosity and courtesy spread like wildfire through the countryside of Wales. With joy, Aberayron, Llanrhystyd, Aberystwyth, and Talybont flung open their gates to greet him, and the fierce fighting men of Wales began to swell his ranks. They came from as far away as Merioneth, Caernarvon, and Denbigh as Harry's ever-growing cavalcade passed through Machynlleth, Caerwys, and Newtown on its way to Shrewsbury—to fight against Richard Plantagenet.

On the advice of Sir William Stanley, his uncle by marriage, who had joined him, Harry then proceeded east toward Leicester. From Nottingham, in the north, Richard Plantagenet marched toward the same destination.

It was between Cannock and Lichfield that Harry, much to the frantic horror and confusion of his men, disappeared. Not feeling well, he wished to be alone for a while—something that was nigh impossible among all those who constantly surrounded him—and in addition, he wanted to meet the faithful knights who waited for him at the edge of the woods in Cannock Chase.

However, as dusk fell, elongating eerily the shadows cast by the old, gnarled trees of the forest, he wondered if he had been wise to slip away from his men without telling them. He glanced about warily, cursing himself for his foolishness and realizing suddenly what an easy target he would be for an assassin's blade. Only the soft shrill cry of a hawk relieved his fears. Eagerly, he started forward at the sound.

"Waerwic! Forgive me. For a moment, I didst think ye had deserted me."

"Never that, Your Grace." Lord Warrick ap Tremayne, Earl of Hawkhurst, smiled as he knelt to kiss Harry's hand. "We did but lose our way once in the darkness."

"Madog, Caerllywel, and—nay—it cannot be!" Harry exclaimed. "Emrys?"

"Aye, Sire. 'Tis I."

"But ye were no more than a lad when last I saw ye. Ah, 'tis good to see ye again, all of ye."

"In more ways than one, eh, Your Grace?" Madog questioned with a laugh. "Come. We shan't keep ye in suspense, Sire," he continued as he led the way toward a group of men and wagons waiting for them deeper in the woods. With a wave of his hand, he indicated the contents of the vehicles. "Behold, Your Grace. With York's own guns shall Richard of Gloucester be beaten."

Harry's eyes glittered with anticipation and speculation

as he caught sight of the cold metal bombards gleaming ominously in the moonlight that streamed down in a silver spray between the branches of the trees.

"God's blood, Madog," he swore softly. "Where did ye get them? Do not tell me they came from Waerwic's keep."

"Nay, from Rushden Castle, in York, Sire."

"And I still say 'twas wrong to take them!" Caerllywel spoke for the first time, his voice defiant as he faced his liege and his brothers, then turned, with a muttered oath, to kick viciously at a wheel of one wagon.

"All's fair in love and war, brother," Madog stated coolly, annoyed by his brother's outburst.

"God damn it, Madog! Giles Ashley is Waerwic's brother-in-law—and our friend! Have ye no sense of honor?"

Madog's nostrils flared whitely.

"I honor my king—and my duty to him! Giles did say the fortress was at Waerwic's disposal whenever he wished."

Caerllywel laughed shortly, bitterly.

"That didn't give ye leave to steal three of his cannons!"

"Enough!" Harry commanded. "Right or wrong, the deed has been done, and I confess I am in sore need of the guns— no matter how they were obtained." He turned to Warrick and raised one eyebrow, saying dryly, "I presume, from this little exchange, that the Ashleys are still staunch York-ists."

"Aye, Your Grace."

"And I also presume, Waerwic, that your wife, at this moment, knows nothing of your whereabouts."

"Nay, Sire."

Oh, God, 'Sabelle. *'Sabelle!*

Her hurt, questioning eyes, when he'd left her, had haunted Warrick every step of the way. Like everyone else at the Tower, she had heard the news of Harry Tewdwr's landing at Milford Haven and had guessed what it was to mean to her, to Warrick, and to Giles.

"So," she had said. "I am to be torn, after all, between my love for ye and my love for my brother. Go, then. I shall ask naught of ye, except—except—" She had broken off, inhaling raggedly, tears stinging her eyes, those fathomless twin pools of grey-green. Her hands had fluttered helplessly to her breast, and her voice, when she had spoken again, had trembled a little. "Except that if ye meet Giles upon a battlefield somewhere, do not—do not slay him."

"Nay, 'Sabelle. I give ye my solemn vow that I shall not."

Warrick would not break that oath to her. 'Twas bad enough that he had stolen the bombards from Rushden. He ought not to have done it. He couldn't imagine what had possessed him to let Madog talk him into it. Caerllywel was right. What they had done was wrong. Well, there was no help for it now. And somehow, Warrick thought, had their roles been reversed, Giles would have done the same thing, would, even now, understand, as Isabella never would. War was a man's business after all.

At the early pre-dawn hour, most of the men camped at Sutton Cheney slept; but not King Richard III and not Lord Giles Ashley, Earl of Rushden. The latter studied the King quietly in the greyish light cast by the mist that lay over the countryside and was just now beginning to lift a little.

What was Richard thinking, Giles wondered.

He would have been deeply upset to have learned his liege's thoughts, so it was just as well that Giles did not know them. Richard, King of England, had been wakened by a nightmare, a nightmare in which he had seen himself falling... falling into a sea of red... his golden crown tumbling from his head to float upon the waves. Desperately, he had tried to grasp the glittering circlet, but always, it had bobbed just out of reach.

Now, as Richard stood before his tent, staring unseeingly into the distance, the mist seemed to swirl about him like a shroud; and a sudden, strange premonition of his death struck him.

So, this was it. This was what the mighty Plantagenets had come to: a sodden field outside of Market Bosworth.

Damn ye, Ned! Richard cursed his dead brother silently. Why couldn't ye have taken Bess Woodville at Grafton Regis? Slaked your lust for her and left her? She would not have denied ye. In the end, she would not have denied ye.

But she had. The conniving bitch had kept her thighs

closed tight against Ned, and he had married her to open them. It was *she* who'd brought the mighty House of York down, Bess Woodville, with her greedy, scheming mind and powerful, grasping family. In that moment, Richard hated them all.

He thought of Anne, his wife, and their son, both gone now. What did it matter if he joined them? They were all gone, all those whom he had loved: Edmund, his brother, brutally murdered in his youth. Warwick, the Kingmaker, who had reared Richard at Middleham. George, his brother, weak, unscrupulous George, who had sought to steal Ned's crown. And Ned himself, in all his golden glory. Aye, that was how Richard would remember Ned, as the sun in splendor. He would not think of the sorry, dissipated monarch and the raucously howling Jane Shore at Ned's feet.

Oh, Ned. Richard almost wept at the thought. How could we have come to this?

"Your Grace, are ye ill?"

Richard turned, startled, at the sound of the voice. For a moment, still lost in the past, he did not recognize Giles. Then, slowly, the King returned to the present.

"Nay, Giles." Richard gave a half-smile to comfort his obviously concerned, faithful knight. "I am well."

But 'tis not true, the King thought even as he spoke the words of reassurance. I am sick, sick unto death by the carnage that has been wrought . . . must yet be wrought upon the morrow. How many? he wondered as he gazed at Giles. How many of my friends and followers will die with me?

The faces swam before him: Francis and Phillip Lovell, Richard Ratcliffe, William Catesby, Giles Ashley, Lion— Nay, Lionel Valeureux was already gone, waiting on the other side of the river of death to meet Richard when he came, waiting, with Anne and their son; waiting with Ned, Edmund, and George; waiting with Warwick and Buckingham. Nay, Richard would not think of Harry, gay Harry, Duke of Buckingham, who had betrayed him.

A whisper of wind soughed in Richard's ear, laughing at him, mocking him.

* * *

The Cat, the Rat,
And Lovell, our Dog,
Rulen all England
Under a Hog.

Horrible, hateful words. The people had chanted them in the city streets of London.

Aye, what did it matter if Richard was to die? His shoulders slumped tiredly, like a man defeated, as he glanced off into the distance once more. A trail of sparkling flame in the grey firmament caught his eye.

"There! Did ye not see it, Giles? A shooting star... a dying star," Richard added more softly.

Giles looked at the empty sky and swore silently to himself. If he survived the coming battle, he would surely go and have the physician examine his eyes, for in truth, he had seen nothing save the clouds of mist. Still, somehow sensing Richard's morbid mood, the younger man reassured the King.

"'Tis indeed a good sign, Your Grace. It can but mean that God is on your side. The Tydder will surely lose tomorrow's fight."

"Aye," Richard said, and thought: For he will be King of England, and 'tis a crown that weighs too heavily upon one's head... and heart... and soul.

Dawn broke at last—a grim dawn, despite the fact that the pale pink blush sweeping across the horizon gave promise of a beautiful summer day, rich with golden sunlight—a sun in splendor. Richard's scurryers, being more experienced than Harry Tewdwr's, had scouted the plain and reported to Richard the most promising place from which to conduct the coming battle—Ambien Hill.

Now, from atop the knoll, to which his army had marched earlier, Richard, mounted upon White Surrey, his ghostly destrier, surveyed the scene before him. On his right flank, coming from Nether Cotton, were Sir William Stanley and his men. On his left flank, marching from Dadlington, Richard saw, with a sneer, were Lord Thomas Stanley, the Fox, and his force. Some days past, Richard had sent the Baron a message ordering him to join his king at Leicester at once. To the command, Lord Stanley had replied lamely—and untruthfully—that he could not come, because he was suffering from the sweating sickness.

It appeared the wily Fox had made a remarkable recovery. Richard laughed dryly. He wondered if the Stanleys meant to support him—or turn against him. No doubt they would wait until they saw which way the battle was going before they took any action, despite the fact that Richard held Lord Strange, the Baron's son, hostage to ensure Lord Stanley's loyalty.

Lastly, the King's eyes fell upon his enemy, Harry Tewdwr, whose troops were marching forth from White Moors.

Alone, Richard's men far outnumbered Harry's: for the King's vanguard, directed by the Duke of Norfolk, contained twelve hundred bowmen and two hundred cuirassiers; the main guard, which Richard himself commanded, consisted of one thousand billmen and two thousand pikes; the rear guard, headed by the Earl of Northumberland, had two thousand billmen and pikes and fifteen hundred horsemen.

Still, if the Stanleys cast their lots with the Tydder, Richard knew he was done for.

Slowly, the King donned his helmet, with its golden crown, and lowered his visor. The trumpets sounded, and the battle was engaged.

The fight started off sluggishly, for Harry's inexperienced scurryers had failed to report to him that a marsh lay between him and Ambien Hill, and his army was forced to march around it before reaching Richard's men. Moreover, the sun had now risen and was glaring in the eyes of Harry's vanguard, adding to the difficulties of their progression. Meanwhile, Richard's force wisely waited on the hill, compelling Harry's troops to stagger upward. Arrows were loosed; bombard shots were exchanged. The great stone cannonballs heaved through the air, causing further havoc and confusion as the two armies advanced and finally came to blows hand to hand.

All morning long, the battle raged beneath the hot August sun until the air was thick and putrid with the clouds of dust that mingled with the acrid smoke of black powder and the pungent odor of blood and wounded flesh. Harry's men closed on Richard's own, constraining the King's wings to engage. Richard sent a message to Lord Stanley, ordering the Baron to send reinforcements immediately or sacrifice the life of his son Lord Strange. The King took one look at the face of the squire who had returned with the Fox's answer and knew the fight was lost.

"Your—Your Grace," the squire stammered, awed and afraid. "My—my Lord Stanley refuses your command. He said—he said to tell ye he has other sons."

Bilious gorge born of anger and defeat rose in Richard's throat, choking him.

"God damn him!" the King swore wrathfully. "God damn him!" Then, he commanded, "Behead Lord Strange at once!"

The men in Richard's bodyguard stared at each other with horror, remembering Lord Hastings's brutal execution on Tower Green and shifting uneasily in their saddles as Lord Stanley's unfortunate son was dragged forth and forced to kneel upon the ground. Lord Strange was not very old and was whimpering with fear and pleading frantically for mercy as he groveled upon the earth. Something twisted in Richard's craw at the sight, and he was moved to pity. Had not his brother Edmund been savagely murdered in just such a fashion?

"Wait!" the King cried. Then, swallowing hard at the surprise upon the faces of his men, he muttered, "I—I've changed my mind. Release the boy, and send for Northumberland to join me immediately."

But Northumberland, upon seeing the traitorous Stanleys had swung their troops in to battle on Harry Tewdwr's side, declined to follow Richard's order. Instead, the mighty Lord of the North stood by and did nothing while the King's men were crushed and slaughtered between the three armies that opposed them.

The fight was nearly finished. Hot rage seared through Richard's body. How he would have liked to have slain Lord Stanley! But cool reason prevailed, as it always had in the past. The King was not England's greatest military commander for naught. He had one chance—a slim one—but a chance all the same. If he could somehow cut through the battle lines, reach Harry Tewdwr, and kill him, he, Richard, would win the fight.

"Your Grace, I pray ye: Do not do this mad thing," Lord Francis Lovell begged when the King explained his intent to his bodyguard. "You'll be slain. Let us escape now, while we may yet do so. . . ."

"Like Neville, Francis?" Richard's voice shook a little as he remembered how his cousin Richard Neville, Earl of Warwick, had attempted to flee that day so long ago at Barnet. He, Richard Plantagenet, was a king. He would not be cut down like a coward fleeing the battlefield. "Nay, Francis." He stilled the pleading words that had sprung to his faithful knight's lips. "I am a king. I shall die as one."

Then, with a strange fierce shout of triumph, His Grace Richard Plantagenet, King of England, raised his mighty battle-ax high and charged down the hill. Miraculously, the sea of men parted before him. He did not know they thought him mad; that he and his horse appeared like some blood-covered phantom not of this world but the next; that his deadly blade was severing life and limb without mercy as he plunged through the melee. Richard knew only that his enemies were falling back before his terrible onslaught, that even the Tydder's standard-bearer had gone down. Harry's bright red banner with its golden Cadwallader dragon was trampled into the boggy ground, which was made even more sodden by the crimson blood that seeped into the marsh.

The marsh. Dear God. The marsh. In his ire and haste, Richard had forgotten about the marsh. Even now, he could feel White Surrey slipping, sliding beneath him, plunging into the mire, struggling to break free. . . . With a desperate bound, the King leaped from the saddle of his faithful steed.

"A horse! A horse! My kingdom for a horse!" Richard yelled hoarsely, his screams piercing the air, ringing out over the plain.

Oh, God, to have come this far and to have lost his kingdom for a want of a horse. 'Twas not to be borne! 'Twas not to be borne!

"Your Grace! Your Grace! Take mine, Your Grace!" Giles called as he compelled his snorting, white-eyed mount through the horrible battle. "Take mine!"

He was almost there, had almost reached the King, when suddenly, as though from nowhere, a powerful brown destrier with a golden-cream mane and tail bore down on him.

"Nay, Giles, nay! 'Tis too late! Give it up! The fight is done!" Warrick shouted desperately above the roar of the melee, not wanting to harm his brother-in-law but knowing that Giles must be prevented from reaching Richard.

Through the haze of dust and smoke, Giles recognized Warrick dimly but paid no heed to his cries. Instead, the younger man dug his spurs sharply into his horse's sides and pressed on. Richard would have the steed he so desperately needed—even if it cost Giles his life. He did not think that Warrick would slay him. But even as the thought occurred to him, Giles saw his brother-in-law raise his heavy broadsword and begin the cutting arc that would slice a man—or a destrier—in two. Moments later, the younger man heard his mount's terrible screams of agony as the blade struck, bit deeply, fatally, into the animal's neck, severing its head from its shoulders. The beast staggered, stumbled, and fell, as a fountain of blood spewed from the gaping torso.

"Jump, Giles!" Warrick cried frantically in warning. "Jump! For God's sake, *jump!*"

But Giles, thinking only of Richard, hesitated until it was too late to leap clear. His horse's massive body rolled, blotting out the sun as the steed crushed him, smothering the cries of pain and torment that were wrenched from his throat.

"Richard! *Richard!* RICHARD!"

But the King did not hear. His Grace Richard Plantagenet, King of England, was dead, his corpse lying in a sea of red, his golden crown tangled in the branches of a hawthorn bush, just beyond his reach.

Chapter Thirty-six

OH, GOD. OH, GOD.

Isabella thought she must go mad with grief as they came across Bow Bridge, those bloody, armored men, with Harry Tewdwr at their head and the people of London, who crowded the city streets, straggling alongside and wildly cheering "God save the King! Long live King Henry!" as though he were a savior who had freed them from bondage.

Slowly did they come, shouting and laughing, passing wine flasks among themselves and spraying each other with the rich red liquid that mingled with the blood that spattered and stained their heavy mail. Now and then, they paused to bend down from their saddles to snatch a kiss from a pretty, giggling maid or to take a red rose from a child's outstretched hand.

And so it was that the triumphant, heady glory of victory made that which followed all the more horrible, all the more unreal.

Those of the defeated who could walk—even barely— were in chains that clanked out a knell of failure with each dragging step, pitifully accented by the lumbering clatter, over the cobblestones, of the wheels of the carts that carried the more seriously wounded. With difficulty, Isabella choked down the vomit that rose in her throat at the terrible sight of the men who staggered past her, bleeding, moaning, and weeping.

Behind them rode a horseman, whole in body and grinning with gruesome glee. In one hand, he held the reins of a small bony donkey, across which hung a shapeless thing, dangling like a half-empty sack of meal—lifeless, without form. At first glance, that was what it seemed, a sack of meal—no more. Only its pale white hue, splashed bright with red, belied this: for no farmer had ever marketed his grain in such a sack. Plain brown burlap it ought to have been; and Isabella was puzzled by the pattern of color that dappled the donkey's back. It was only when the beast drew near that she recognized its burden for what it truly was.

"Oh, sweet *Jesù*," she gasped. "Oh, sweet *Jesù*."

Then, before she could help herself, she doubled over in agony, retching upon her gown and the paving blocks of the street. Ragnor, sitting upon her shoulder, nuzzled her cheek gently and gave a soft squawk, sensing her distress, while Jocelyn, who had not yet glimpsed the gory sight, cried out with concern.

"My lady. My lady, let me help ye. Oh, come away. Come away. Ye are ill! Sir Eadric, Sir Thegn, Sir Beowulf. Come. Help my lady."

But Isabella paid no heed to her maid or the faithful knights who started forward at Jocelyn's command. Like a woman crazed, Isabella was already forcing her way wildly through the crowd, toward the sickening thing that, just that morn, had been His Grace Richard Plantagenet, King of England.

Cruelly, humiliatingly, he had been stripped of his clothing to be paraded, naked, through the streets of London for all to gape at and mock. Someone had tossed a tattered remnant of his once-proud banner over his body as a last indignity; and Isabella saw, as she pressed closer, that the lilies dripped with scarlet, and the leopards were mangled beyond all recognition. Oh, the arms of England. Brought down, brought down, as Richard had been . . .

Screaming, weeping hysterically, she rushed forth to touch him, to see if somehow, some way, he did yet live, though she knew her desperate prayers were all in vain. His hands— those tender hands—were white, too white, drained of his life's blood by the thongs with which they'd bound him to the donkey. People laughed and jeered to see her running alongside the beast, clutching frantically at Richard's face, caressing the strands of his black hair, damp and lank with sweat and blood. But Isabella did not care. She fell and scraped her knees, but she didn't feel the pain: for she could see now the felon's rope they'd tied about his neck, as though he'd been a common criminal—Richard, her king. She staggered to her feet and raced on, Ragnor's shrill cries of fear and confusion piercing the air and causing the throng that howled and leered to fall back before her in fear at the spectacle she presented.

"Richard! Richard!" she cried, deranged with shock and grief. *"Richard!"*

But he did not answer; and as the frightened donkey trotted on, prodded savagely forward by the pikes of the Tydder's raucously crowing men, Isabella saw, to her horror, that Bow Bridge was too small, too narrow, for the procession to cross freely. Packed tight the soldiers were, and in the cacophony of their passing, the donkey stumbled, and Richard's dark head was bashed against the stone wall of the bridge. There came the sound of splintering bone as the face that Isabella had loved so dearly was crushed and battered; once more, she fell and retched and forced herself to rise, to run on amid the hateful laughter and insults of the crowd. Chortling, one of the Tydder's men pricked her with his pike, causing her to lurch dazedly upon her feet. She grabbed at his stirrup to keep from falling yet again, but with a sneer, he kicked her away, and she sprawled upon the cobblestones.

"One of the traitor's whores, was ye?" he jibed down at her, then grinned. "Here, take this then. 'Tis more'n ye deserve, but I hates to see a wench cry, even if she be but a whore."

He tossed something at her feet, then rode on.

Dumbly, Isabella reached out for the thing that lay there on the street. Woodenly, her fingers closed about it, and she saw it was a coin—a single gold sovereign. Oh, God. Oh, God. How long ago had another given her such a coin and asked her to pray for him—and Anne?

Oh, Anne. Anne! I'm glad you're dead. For the first time, I'm glad you're dead, that ye didst not live to see what I have seen this day. . . .

Blindly, Isabella clutched the sovereign to her breast—and wept.

She had thought she need bear no more, that God had asked all he could possibly ask of her. But she was wrong. Isabella knew that when they brought Giles's broken body to her and laid it gently on the bed. He lived. Still, he lived, but she did not know how. His legs were mangled beyond repair, and she knew, if by some miracle, they managed to save the twisted, shattered limbs, her brother would never walk again.

Weakly, his eyes fluttered open; he grasped her hand and tried but failed to give it a slight, reassuring squeeze.

"'Sa—belle," he whispered, moaning faintly. "Dear sister. Do not—do not blame . . . Warrick. 'Twas no more— no more than his duty. I would have . . . done the same. . . ."

"Hush. Don't try to talk, Giles," Isabella said even as she wondered what he had meant.

He was feverish and babbling; that was all. Surely, that was all.

"I—I must, in case—in case I . . . die. Warrick—Warrick didn't know . . . the horse would—would crush me. I could have . . . leapt clear, but I—I never was much good at—at that." Giles smiled a little at the poor jest, remembering Scotland. "Then too . . . there was—was Richard. I—I thought only of . . . Richard, until 'twas—'twas too late. . . ."

"Giles, please. Whatever 'tis, 'twill keep. I'm going to get ye something to help ye sleep. Your legs . . ."

"I . . . know. Done for."

"Jocelyn." Isabella glanced up worriedly. "Go, and find Lord Montecatini, for I doubt if any of the physicians are available. Ask the Count to prepare a sleeping draught for my brother. The Italian will know what 'tis. 'Tis the same potion he gave me once."

"Aye, my lady."

Isabella turned back to her brother and saw he had fainted. 'Twas just as well. Grimly, carefully, she began to remove his battered mail so she could tend the pitiful, broken sticks that had once been his legs.

Lord Montecatini smiled superciliously to himself as, choosing his herbs most carefully, he studiously mixed the sleeping draught that Jocelyn had requested. Poor Giles. What a pity, and such a handsome young man too. Well, there was no point in letting him suffer, was there? After all, they put animals out of their misery, didn't they? And if, at the same time, the Count accomplished his revenge as well, then so much the better. He had waited a long time for it—too long.

His dark visage an inscrutable mask, the Italian turned back to Jocelyn, handing her the potion.

"Here is the sleeping draught, mistress," he said. "Lord Rushden will find the taste bitter, but 'tis only because I have added a few herbs that will ease his pain."

"Oh, thank ye, my lord." Jocelyn spoke fervently with appreciation. "My lady will be most grateful. She loves her brother dearly, ye know."

"Aye, 'tis a terrible thing . . . and most . . . awkward for Lord Hawkhurst, most awkward indeed."

"Aye, my lady was well nigh crazed when she learned of it. She'd thought, at first, that Lord Rushden had been rambling, had been delirious with agony. But then, his squire explained what had happened, so there was no mistaking, after all, what Lord Rushden had said."

"Well, surely Lady Hawkhurst will forgive her husband," the Count suggested smoothly. "After all, 'twas an accident, and ye said the injury to her brother is not mortal."

"We pray not, my lord, but we don't know for certain. As to whether or not my lady can find it in her heart to forgive Lord Hawkhurst, I cannot say. He has yet to arrive, but my lady has already said she never wants to see him again as long as she lives. If Lord Rushden dies . . ." Jocelyn's voice trailed off uncertainly.

"Aye, therein lies the difficulty, does it not? What a shame," the Italian remarked.

But inwardly, he was still smiling.

For an eternity, it seemed, Isabella felt nothing. Her heart stopped beating, and her mind was a black, empty cavern, devoid of emotion. Then, without warning, her stomach heaved, as though the earth had suddenly shifted beneath her feet, and great, ragged sobs forced themselves from her throat.

'Tisn't true, she thought dumbly, numb with shock. 'Tisn't true.

But the hand she clasped so tightly in her own was cold,

as cold as Anne's had once been; and Isabella knew that Giles was dead.

Still, she gazed up pleadingly at Jocelyn, silently begging the maid to tell her it wasn't true. But Jocelyn's sober, pitying eyes fell before Isabella's own stricken ones, and the girl knew there was no hope.

"How, Jocelyn?" Isabella asked, stunned and bewildered, crystal tears beginning to stream slowly down her face. "Why? 'Twas but his legs; I know. I didst not think there was any wound inside of him."

"There must have been, my lady. Do ye—do ye not recall how he rose suddenly, as though in agony, and clutched his belly? There must have been some injury inside of him that we couldst not see, couldst not have healed. . . ."

"Nay. He was but bruised. Even his ribs were not shattered, as they would have been, had the horse completely crushed him. I tell ye 'twas only his legs that bore the weight of the steed. Oh, do ye—do ye not think so, Jocelyn?"

"Nay, my lady. Oh, forgive me, my lady," the maid went on in a rush, "but methinks—methinks ye do love your husband and do not, in your heart, wish to blame him for your brother's death."

"But what else can I do?" Isabella queried softly, weeping harder now, trying to force the hollow, sick feeling from her insides. "Giles is dead. My brother is dead." Her voice rose piercingly. "And Warrick *is* to blame. Oh, God. Oh, God. He swore to me . . . Warrick swore to me he wouldst not harm my brother."

"And I didst keep my vow, 'Sabelle," Warrick said quietly, entering the chamber, at last, in time to hear his wife's last words. "'Twas but Giles's horse I slew."

She turned slowly at the sound of his voice and stared up at him uncomprehendingly, her fathomless grey-green eyes wide with confusion, shadowed with accusation, and haunted by pain. It was as though she saw a stranger there, and Warrick's heart was stabbed with sudden apprehension.

"My brother is dead," she told him tonelessly. "The steed didst fall and mortally wound him."

"Nay!" Warrick cried, shocked, disbelieving, his voice

now fervent and pleading as he realized why Giles lay so still upon the bed. Nay. Nay! It could not be true. 'Twas only the boy's legs that had been crushed. Something was wrong. Something was terribly wrong. "'Twas Giles's horse I slew—no more," Warrick reiterated feverishly, understanding now the strange blank light in Isabella's eyes and fearing she would turn against him for all time. "And 'twas but his legs that were caught beneath the animal; I swear it! I thought—I thought he would have time to leap clear. He could have—when the beast staggered to its knees—if only—if only..."

"If only he had not been thinking of Richard," Isabella finished, her voice a small sob of agony that tore at Warrick's insides, twisted them into knots, then ripped them apart.

"Aye," he uttered lamely, knowing the reminder of the King, on top of her brother's death, had wounded her even more deeply.

Even Warrick was sickened by the thought of how disgracefully Harry Tewdwr and his men had treated the body of Richard Plantagenet, the lack of respect they had shown him. Richard had not deserved what they had done. He had been a king. Warrick prayed that Isabella would never discover how they had strung up Richard's corpse in the marketplace, where, even now, the people of London came to jeer and spit upon the naked form of the man who, just that morn, had been their king.

"Oh, God! Oh, God! Get out of my sight!" Isabella wailed suddenly, raggedly, startling Warrick back to the present. "If not for ye, Richard and my brother wouldst still be alive. Alive, do ye hear? Get out! Get out! I never want to see ye again as long as I live!"

"'Sabelle—"

"Nay, don't touch me! I'll kill ye! I'll kill ye—as ye slew my brother! My brother..."

The girl's voice choked off as the sobs in her throat strangled her yet afresh, and she gasped wildly for breath, fearing she would suffocate. She buried her face in her hands, her shoulders shaking with the aftermath of her outburst. Dear God. She loved him still. Whatever her husband had done, she loved him still; and her love for him and Giles was tearing her apart.

"'Sabelle, *cariad*." Warrick tried desperately once more to bridge the awful chasm that had come between them. "Please. I wouldst comfort ye if I could."

"Nay. Ye cannot," Isabella intoned dully, as though she herself were no longer among the living. "Giles is dead, and ye are to blame for it. Oh, God." She looked up at Warrick again, her eyes filled with such torment he could not bear it. "I tried—I tried to save him. I thought—I thought too 'twas only his legs; but there must have been some injury inside of him: for even the Count's sleeping draught did not ease Giles's pain; and suddenly, a little while after I'd given him the potion, he doubled up in agony and he—he died!"

The Count's sleeping draught.

Over and over, the words rang in Warrick's mind, clawed at his brain, spurring him to rage and hunger for revenge for the terrible hurt done to Isabella.

The Count's sleeping draught.

He knew now what had caused Giles's death, for though Giles's legs would have been permanently crippled from the horse's fall, Warrick was positive now that the wound had not been fatal. He'd been too upset, when he'd learned of his brother-in-law's death, to think straight. Now, 'twas all so clear to him what had happened.

Dear God. 'Twas by 'Sabelle's own hand that Giles had died! The realization hit Warrick like a sharp blow, stunning him, sickening him. Dear God. In her blind trust and ignorance of the Italian's true, evil nature, 'Sabelle had unknowing murdered her brother. She must never know, must never find out. 'Twould destroy her if she did. No matter if she hated him forever, Warrick must never tell her 'twas the Count's fatal potion, which she had given her brother, that had killed Giles.

Dear God, Warrick prayed. Make me strong enough to keep silent, strong enough to bear the burden of her blame, though she hardens her heart against me, turns her love for me to hate for all time. . . . Aye, make me strong, God. I love her. I love her more than my life. Better I am destroyed than 'Sabelle . . . dear 'Sabelle . . . my sweet Rose of Rapture.

"Wouldst ye—wouldst ye send Caerllywel to me?" she asked, bringing him back to reality, longing for that cheerful face, for the comfort that Warrick could not give her, and sniffing pitifully in a manner that wrenched his heart yet again.

Oh, sweet *Jesù*. How could he tell her? She had borne so much already. How could he tell her, pierce her with still further sorrow?

"Would that I could, 'Sabelle." Warrick spoke lowly, earnestly. "Oh, God. Would that I could. But I—I cannot. Caerllywel—" His voice broke, but he mastered it and went on. "Caerllywel was—was slain this morn at Market Bosworth."

"Nay! Nay!"

But it was not Isabella who cried out against this new anguish. 'Twas Jocelyn, Jocelyn, whom they, in their torment, had forgotten. Warrick and Isabella were stricken with shame and remorse, even as they mourned Caerllywel. They had loved him, aye; he had been their brother, by blood and by marriage. But they had not lain with him, loved him in that way only a woman loves a man, or felt his child stirring within as Jocelyn had done. No matter how grieved they were by his death, they could not know the horrible sadness, emptiness, sickness, that welled up in Jocelyn as she gazed at Warrick pleadingly, her eyes begging him to say that Caerllywel still lived, that death had not taken the father of her unborn babe. But the pain in Warrick's golden orbs matched Jocelyn's own; and she knew there was no hope that he was mistaken.

"Oh, Jocelyn," Isabella breathed, her own sorrow forgotten in light of the maid's.

Isabella and Warrick still had each other—if they could prevent the shadow of Giles's death from coming between them. But Jocelyn had no one. She could only pray that Caerllywel's laughing image filled her womb, would be safely brought forth into the world so she would yet have some part of her husband.

"Nay!" Jocelyn sobbed brokenly once more and fainted.

Worriedly, Isabella and Warrick knelt over the maid's inert form, their own terrible losses put aside for the moment. Giles and Caerllywel were dead, aye; but there would be time to mourn them later. Jocelyn was alive—and she needed them.

Even as they examined her shallowly breathing body, warm liquid began to gush from between the maid's thighs, soaking her gown.

"'Tis the child," Isabella said. "The shock of—of Caerllywel's death has brought on her labor."

After studying his wife searchingly for an instant and receiving her silent agreement, Warrick gently lifted his brother-in-law's corpse from the bed and, after laying Giles tenderly upon the floor, put Jocelyn in his stead.

It was some hours later when, at last, Isabella placed to her maid's breast the small bundle of joy that was Caerllywel's babe—the son he would never know.

Chapter Thirty-seven

IT WAS THREE DAYS LATER WHEN GILLIANE'S MESSAGE came; and for a moment, as she gazed down at the scroll's contents, Isabella could not bring herself to reply.

Nay. 'Twas too much to ask of her. 'Twas just too much to ask. She had borne enough.

But even as the thought occurred to her, Isabella knew she would go all the same. She owed Richard that.

And so, her heart heavy in her breast, the girl went to the Convent of Grey Friars.

It did not seem possible, she thought as she rode along, that life went on around her, as though death were nothing, had touched none save her. Her eyes bright with unshed tears, Isabella tried desperately to shut out the babble of voices and laughter that surrounded her. Still, the loud, raucous cries of the merchants hawking their wares pierced her ears and made her ache inside. The din somehow seemed so disrespectful, almost mocking. She gazed at the faces about her and wondered how many had, these days past, come to the market not to buy, but to spit upon the man who had been England's king. And Isabella hated them. Hated them as much as she despised Harry Tewdwr, who had taken her beloved Richard's place, and Lord Stanley, the Fox, newly created Earl of Derby, who had plucked Richard's crown from the hawthorn bush and put it upon the Tydder's head.

Oh, God. That she had learned these things. Warrick had sought to prevent her from discovering them, but she had not wanted his protection, did not know if she would ever want it—or him—again. How could she love the man who had slain her brother? How could she not? Sweet *Jesù*. How she wanted to go to her husband, lay her head upon his shoulder, and share her devastating grief with him. But she did not. Alone, she suffered, as Warrick did. For Richard. For Giles. For Caerllywel. And for Madog, whose body they had never found, who lay in a nameless ditch somewhere, leaving behind his childless young bride forever.

So many. Dear God. Why must there be so many? How could the sun go on shining when darkness blinded Isabella's eyes; how could the flowers go on blooming when the scent of death and decay filled her nostrils every hour of every day? How could her heart go on beating when it was broken, when the love that had flamed within it had turned to ashes?

Nay, she would not think of Warrick now—must never think of him again. She must cut him out of her heart and soul, though it killed her to do it. He had slain her brother; and though Giles, on his deathbed, had begged her to forgive her husband for the deed, Isabella would not, *could* not, bring herself to do it. To go on loving Warrick would be to desecrate Giles's memory for all time. Isabella must harden her heart against her husband, no matter the pain.

Already, she had taken the first steps in their estrangement. She had barred Warrick from their chamber at the Tower, and he had not protested her action. Still, it hurt to remember the terrible, empty look upon his face, the quiet dignity with which he'd gone—and not returned.

Oh, Warrick. *Warrick!*

Dumbly, Isabella slid from her horse, approached the gate of Grey Friars, and pulled the bell. Moments later, there was the sound of footsteps, and a young Sister appeared, her eyebrows raised in gentle inquiry.

"I—I've come to see Lady St. Saviour," Isabella said.

Briefly, the nun was puzzled; then she smiled in slow understanding.

"Oh, Sister Anne, ye mean."

"Aye." Isabella nodded, recalling, at last, the name that Gilliane had taken in memory of Anne, dear Anne, whom they had loved.

"Come this way," the nun directed softly, opening the gate.

Oh, what they had done to him. Isabella should have wept, would have wept, but she was all cried out. She had no tears left with which to mourn her beloved Richard.

'Twas in the chapel, upon a catafalque, he lay; and as Isabella drew back the coarse woolen cloth with which they'd covered him, she saw they had not even washed his body. Dried blood and mud and spittle were caked upon his dark flesh; the open wounds, where they'd cut him down in battle, gaped, were foul and putrid with rot. Isabella gagged and grew pale, swayed upon her feet a little so that Gilliane, who stood by her side, put one hand beneath the girl's elbow to steady her.

"'Twas thus they brought him here," Gilliane uttered quietly, ashamed. "The Sisters were afraid to touch him; though our Mother didst give her consent to his burial here, the nuns yet fear the Tydder's wrath."

"They need not," Isabella responded bitterly. "Already, he has turned his mind to other matters." She thought of how quick Harry Tewdwr had been to prohibit the wearing of livery and to confiscate all the black powder in the kingdom, so the powerful lords who had put him on the throne would not seek to wrest it from him—as they had Richard. "The Tydder has no care for Richard. His Grace Richard Plantagenet, King of England, is dead. 'Tis 'His Majesty' Henry Tudor who now wears the Crown."

"Aye." Gilliane spoke. "I had heard that 'His Grace' was

not good enough for the Tydder and that he had Anglicized his name besides."

"Aye," Isabella rejoined. "He calls himself 'His Majesty' Henry Tudor, as though such a grand title and name will pacify England and blot out the stain of what he has done. But 'twill not." Her voice was fierce. "'Twill not! Come. We must do what we can for Richard, our true and rightful king."

Together, they set candles all around him and lit them, so he was bathed in light and reverence. Then tenderly, they washed him, taking care that not a speck of blood or mud or spittle remained to desecrate his corpse. After that, Isabella carefully stitched his wounds until he was as whole as she could make him. Finally, they combed his black hair and dressed him in his garments, which Isabella had stolen from the Tower—the robes he had worn for his coronation.

Gently, Gilliane anointed him and made the sign of the cross upon his forehead while Isabella knelt and wept and prayed.

"Do not mourn him, dear 'Sabelle," Gilliane said, touching the girl upon the shoulder. "He was dead long before this."

"Aye, I know."

"We are not the only ones who loved him, 'Sabelle. In York, they have written it down . . . his death, I mean. 'Twill be there—in the records—for all time: 'Our good King Richard, late mercifully reigning over us. He was piteously slain and murdered, to the great heaviness of this city.'"

"'Tis a fit epitaph," Isabella noted softly, "but 'twill not bring him back."

Then slowly, she rose and pressed a single gold sovereign into the hands clasped peacefully over Richard's breast.

It was done. Now, there was but one thing left: She must take Giles's body to Rushden. Then she could go home, home to Grasmere.

Hawkhurst was hers no longer.

"I have lost her."

How many times had his mind dwelled upon the thought, had he dared to hope it was not true? Warrick did not know.

He knew only that the words, spoken now aloud, rang with a finality that hammered like a nail into his heart.

"I have lost her."

"Nay, Waerwic," Hwyelis said quietly as she studied her son, observing how gaunt he had grown, how weary he looked.

His amber eyes were shadowed by torment, ringed with mauve from lack of sleep. Now, as his shoulders slumped, and he ran one hand raggedly through his unkempt hair, she longed to reach out and touch him; but she did not. Of all her sons, Warrick was the proudest, the one most determined to stand alone against all odds, the one who found it most difficult to ask for help and solace. His silence cried out to her piteously; she knew he had come to her as a small boy does his mother when hurt. Yet, Hwyelis hesitated to offer the physical comfort she realized he so desperately needed; it had been so long since Warrick had done more than kiss her hand in greeting. If she put her arms around him, as she so longed to do, he might withdraw; and not for the world would Hwyelis throw away this chance to heal the scars her leaving of him had made so many years past.

So instead, she used her voice, the sweet, melodious gift that God had bestowed upon her, to soothe this son she so dearly loved—one of two left to her now.

"Ye must give Isabella time, Waerwic. Her brother's passing has grieved her deeply, and at the moment, she blames ye for Giles's death. In time, she will forgive and forget."

"Will she?" Warrick's tone was bitter. "God's blood! If only she knew 'twas the Italian's potion that killed Giles! But then, how could I have told her that, Mother? 'Twould have destroyed her, for 'twas she who gave Giles the draught."

"Aye. Ye didst right to keep it from her. I am proud of ye, my son. Ye have learned to love another more than yourself—something I feared ye wouldst never do after Brangwen's betrayal of ye. Ye had grown hard, Waerwic. Isabella has gentled ye once more."

"And brought me pain. Oh, God! The pain! Would that I had never loved her, could stop loving her now!"

"Ye don't mean that, Waerwic. 'Tis but your wounded heart that speaks so harshly. Nothing worth having ever comes easily, and love is perhaps the most difficult of all to attain: for love—true love—requires that one's body, heart, mind, and soul be given into another's keeping—and given freely, Waerwic, without reservation. That is a commitment most people find too hard to make, and so true love escapes them. Ye are lucky, my son. Ye have discovered it with Isabella, and she with ye. She will return to ye in time, once she has searched her heart and found what it holds."

"Oh, Mother, how I wish I could believe ye are right!" Warrick turned to her pleadingly, the anguish on his dark visage almost unbearable.

"Trust me, my son. I am of the earth and wise in its ways, and in my life, I have seen many things. I am like a wild bird that cannot be caught and caged, for to do so would be to kill it in the end. But Isabella...ah, Isabella is like a fawn that seeks refuge in the forest. Ye are her refuge, Waerwic, her strength, and her solace. All her love and joy are found in sharing, and she has chosen ye with whom to share them. Do not despair, my son. As she is the other half of your soul, so are ye the other half of hers. She loves ye more than life itself. She will be yours yet again, I promise ye."

"Oh, Mother, I pray 'tis so: for if I have lost her, I do not think I can go on!"

Then Warrick, proud Warrick, flung himself to his knees before Hwyelis, laid his head upon her lap, and wept. After a moment, her arms closed about him tightly, and tears glistened on her cheeks for the son who was hers once more.

BOOK FIVE

Lonely Sojourn

Chapter Thirty-eight

London, England, 1487

THE BATTLE OF STOKE WAS ENDED. JACK DE LA POLE, Earl of Lincoln, who had been Richard's heir designate, had been slain; and Lord Francis Lovell, once England's Lord High Chamberlain, had drowned while attempting to escape from the Tydder's army. Lambert Simnel, an unknown lad who had pretended to be young Edward, Earl of Warwick, son of George, Duke of Clarence, and rightful heir to the Crown, had been put to work as a turn-spit in the royal kitchen. Thus, the ill-fated rebellion against King Henry VII had ended.

But for Isabella, the repercussions of the scheme to put a pretender on the throne of England were just beginning.

Though it was July and hot, she shivered slightly as she huddled in the small boat that was taking her to freedom's end. Rowed by the Tydder's men, the craft moved slowly down the Thames, so all those crowded along the banks would have ample opportunity to view the consequences of treason.

Treason. Aye, Isabella was guilty of plotting to wrest the Crown from King Henry's grasp and now, discovered, was to pay the penalty for her crime. This day, she was to be imprisoned in the Tower until such time as the Tydder determined to release her—or execute her.

She shuddered at the thought and trembled yet again as Traitor's Gate loomed before her, was swung open wide, and she was rowed inside. Hands assisted her in climbing the stone stairs up which so many others before her had trodden, but still, she stumbled a little and caught her breath, thinking the misstep an ill omen.

As she stood there, waiting, a herald unrolled a large scroll and delivered tonelessly the charges against her, the accusations she had already heard when they'd arrested and tried her. There was but one crime that stood out in her mind, however. Treason. Like an ink stain, the ugly word seeped through the caverns of her brain, blotting out the rest of the long list that was read.

Once more, she quivered slightly. For all that Isabella knew, she had come here to die, and she did not understand why. Her part in the rebellion had been relatively small; there were others who had been far more involved than she, and they had not been taken into custody. Because of this, the girl was as confused as she was scared, and her bewilderment merely added to her fright.

Impulsively, she glanced back at Traitor's Gate, which was closed now. Through the iron bars, she could see the Thames and London sprawled haphazardly along the river's banks. Swiftly, she imprinted the scene upon her mind. It might be the last time she would ever see it. Then she turned to follow her gaolers to Garden Tower, where she was to be incarcerated. Isabella wished her place of imprisonment had been any tower but that one: for it was there the two boy Princes had been murdered; and instead of Garden Tower, the people of London had taken to calling it Bloody Tower.

That too seemed an evil portent.

Nevertheless, the girl choked down her fear and, head held high, walked bravely toward her fate. Only once did she pause, stricken, when she beheld Warrick standing in the dark dank corridor just beyond. For a minute, she longed desperately to flee, but there was no escaping from her destiny. Isabella swallowed hard as her grey-green eyes met her husband's amber ones and locked, as though they two stood alone there; and suddenly, a hushed little silence fell upon the onlookers, who waited, with bated breath, to see what would happen next.

They were disappointed when nothing untoward occurred: for all knew that, after the Battle of Market Bosworth, the Countess of Hawkhurst had left her husband and had lived alone, in her manor house, Grasmere, for the past two years. What the Earl thought of his wife's desertion was not common knowledge, but it *was* known that he had refused King Henry's suggestion that Warrick set her aside and that he had not displayed one spark of interest in the ladies who had attempted to woo him from his solitary state.

After a moment, Isabella turned away and moved on. The blur that had been, for an instant, the Tydder's men sharpened once more into focus. They eyed her curiously, but from the expressions upon their faces, Isabella knew her own countenance showed none of the emotions that were churning tumultuously inside of her.

Well, thank God for it! She wanted no one to guess how deeply the sight of Warrick had affected her. She had not seen him for nearly a year—since the last time he had come to Grasmere to beg her to return to him. Then, though her heart had yearned fervently to heed his pleas, she had forced herself to remain hard and unyielding; and she had once more denied him admittance to the manor house. Later, after watching him ride away, she had run inside from her balcony to her chamber and wept bitterly until Jocelyn had come and, made bold by Warrick's sorrow and distress, had called Isabella a fool.

Oh, Jocelyn, ye were right! the girl thought as she followed her gaolers through the winding halls of the Tower. I love him still, and he loves me. I can see it in his eyes. Oh, why, oh, why didst I not return to Hawkhurst when Warrick begged me to come? Giles bade me to forgive my husband. 'Twas my brother's dying request, and yet, I didst not honor it . . . could not . . . cannot. Oh, Giles, am I wrong? Am I wrong?

But there was no answer.

Her brother was dead, and Isabella was alone—in Bloody Tower.

Warrick came, as Isabella had known he would; and unlike Grasmere, here, in Bloody Tower, she was not able to refuse him admittance. He was one of the King's favorites and did as he pleased. So though, at first, the girl tried to deny him entrance to her chamber by informing her guards that Warrick was not to be allowed in, he merely overruled her command and came in anyway.

"What do ye want, my lord?" she managed to ask coldly as she turned her back on him.

"Ye know what I want, 'Sabelle." Warrick spoke roughly. "Ye have grieved long enough. 'Tis been nearly two years since ye left me, and I want ye to come home."

She laughed a little, as though she did not care, but was horrified to discover that tears stung her eyes all the same. Hastily, she brushed them away, lest Warrick should see.

"Even if I wished to do so, my lord—which I do not— I could not. I am a prisoner here—or have ye forgotten?"

"Nay, but 'tis an easy enough matter to resolve. I can secure your release from this place any time I choose. After all, your part in the plot to put Lambert Simnel on the throne was so small as to scarcely merit attention."

Her previous puzzlement at an end, in sudden understanding, Isabella whirled angrily at that.

"Sweet _Jesù_," she breathed. "What a fool I was. 'Twas ye! I thought I was to be executed for treason, and all the time, 'twas but _ye_ who wanted me here—here, where I couldn't lock ye out! God damn ye and Harry Tewdwr! Ye let me believe I was to die—"

"As I have been dying these past two years, 'Sabelle," Warrick reminded her grimly, fiercely. Then, more gently, "Sweetheart, 'twas a shameful deception, I know. But I could think of no other way to see ye again. I love ye, and I do not believe ye have hardened your heart against me as strongly as ye would like."

"Ye are wrong, my lord," Isabella declared, though she knew he was not. "And even if ye were not, I would hate ye now for what ye have done."

"Would ye, 'Sabelle? Do ye, _cariad_?" Warrick inquired softly, moving closer.

The tears brimmed from her eyes at the old, familiar Welsh endearment. How many times had she heard him murmur it before—in the heat of passion, in the soft afterglow of a moonlit night, and sometimes, during the day, for no special reason at all? My love. My love. But still, she backed away from him. But the room was small, and there was nowhere she could run to. Soon, she was pressed against a wall, and Warrick had his hands on either side of her so she could not escape.

"Do ye, *cariad*?" Warrick queried again.

"Aye," Isabella whispered, but her eyes belied the word, and he laughed.

"I do not think so," he told her, and bent his head as though to kiss her.

"Nay, don't!" she cried. "Don't touch me!"

To her surprise, he shrugged and turned away, though she did not know what the deed cost him; the very nearness of her, the sweet rose scent of her, had inflamed him so.

"Very well, 'Sabelle. But I warn ye: My patience grows thin. I have waited long enough for ye to get over your grief, for ye to realize that I would never have deliberately harmed your brother, and for ye to return to me. I promise ye, ye will not leave this place until ye are mine once more. I shall come again tomorrow, and the day after that, and the day after that, until 'tis so. And if ye continue to deny me"—his jaw tightened with determination at the stubborn set of her chin—"I shall take ye by force, and there will be none here to gainsay me."

Haughtily, so he wouldn't know how frightened she was, Isabella tossed her head.

"That is rape, my lord," she said.

"Mayhap," he agreed. "But 'tis as I told ye on our wedding night: Willing or nay, have ye I shall."

And he did, though Isabella fought him desperately that night, months later, when his patience finally ended, and as he had warned her, Warrick came to claim, by force, that which was rightfully his.

She was no match for him. She never had been. Her slight, slender body struggling against his was like a willow attempting to stand tall against the wind. She knew she must bend—or he would break her. One look at his anguished, desire-filled face told her that. He wanted her—whatever the cost—and had thrown away his pride to have her.

Still, she resisted him, compelling herself to think of Giles and how he had died, what he suffered at Warrick's hands, those same hands that were, even now, pinning her own behind her back, moving slowly, tantalizingly, over her body, tearing impatiently at the lacings of her gown and the soft material of her undergarments.

"Nay," Isabella whispered. "Nay."

But even to her ears, the words sounded like faint moans of pleasure elicited by her husband's caresses as she writhed against him; and she knew she was lost.

For a timeless moment, he stared down at her, his gaze searching her face, taking in the dishevelment of her silvery tresses that tangled down about her in disarray; the wide, fathomless pools of her grey-green eyes; the dark, crescent smudges her long black lashes made against her pink cheeks when she closed the orbs against his scrutiny; the fine straight nose, its nostrils flaring slightly with anger—and slowly awakening passion; the tremulously parted mouth; the small pulse beating jerkily at the hollow of her throat.

Warrick's yellow eyes swept lower, to the bodice he had torn open just minutes past to reveal the swell of her ripe round breasts that rose and fell rapidly at his nearness. Like a starving man, he feasted on the sight, savoring it, anticipating the banquet yet to come. Then Isabella began to struggle against him once more, bringing him back to the present.

Almost savagely, he caught the shimmering cascade of her hair and twisted her face up to his, his lips closing over her own, so gently, at first, that she was taken by surprise by the tenderness of his kiss. Oh, God. How long had it been since she had tasted his mouth, felt those carnal lips moving sensuously upon her own? Her head spun dazedly, and her belly shuddered, as though the earth had suddenly dropped from beneath her feet. His tongue darted forth, outlining lingeringly the sweetly vulnerable shape of her mouth before parting her lips to explore the softness inside. Her mouth grew hot, tingling with electric sparks of shock as his tongue continued its onslaught against her, searching out every hidden place within, until, at last, she was kissing him back, meeting his tongue swirl for swirl and, with her teeth, nibbling his lips, even as he did her own, making her feel dizzy and faint.

Dimly, she tried again to think of her brother and how he had died, but the memory turned to mist and escaped from her, chased away by her husband's kisses until her mind was but a dark, hungry void, aching to be filled by him. Blindly, she fought against the yearning, attempted once more to free herself from Warrick's grasp; but he only held her more tightly, forcing her to respond to him.

A tide of emotion whirled up to engulf her as roughly now, demandingly, his mouth closed over hers again, and once more, his tongue plunged between her trembling lips, plundering the honey that lay within. Isabella gasped with outrage at his assault—aye, and with desire too; she could not deny that, any more than she could deny Warrick, her husband, her own true love. Even now, her traitorous body was molding itself to his; her very bones were melting inside of her, turning to quicksilver as he continued to stroke and fondle her, touching her in ways and places that no other man had ever touched her, would ever touch her. Her treacherous heart beat fast within her breast; the tiny pulse at the hollow of her throat fluttered like the wings of a butterfly when Warrick kissed it, teased it with his tongue, nipped at it lightly with his teeth. Briefly, half-heartedly, she tried one last time to elude him, but the fight had gone out of her at last. Warrick had claimed her as his, and she was powerless to deny him. Oh, God, what was he doing to her?

Again and again, his lips seared hers until it seemed he meant to go on kissing her forever, drain every last ounce of resistance from her body, leaving her weak and helpless against him. Over and over, feverishly, his mouth slashed like a whip across her face to her cheeks, her temples, her hair, her ears, her throat, then back to her lips, until her mouth was bruised and swollen; her nerves were raw; her thighs were wet; her body was screaming silently for him.

"Cariad," he murmured hoarsely against her ear, making her shiver and whimper a little. *"Cariad."*

There were other words he spoke in Welsh, his breath warm against her face, words that Isabella only half-understood, never having been able to master more than just the basic rudiments of the strange Welsh tongue. But she did not care. She did not need an interpretation; the meaning of Warrick's words was plain, the language of love, universal.

She was drowning, dying; yet, she was so vibrantly alive, she could not believe it. She was a mass of sharp sensation that tingled and throbbed against him in exquisite agony. She could not even think, could only smell and taste and touch and feel. She did not even realize that Warrick's strong, pinioning grip had loosened, allowing her hands the different kind of freedom they now so desperately craved.

Without her recognizing they did so, her fingers crept up to entwine themselves in his rich tobacco-brown mane streaked with gold; her arms fastened around his neck to draw him even nearer as he pressed his mouth once more to her pale throat, that swanlike column flung back now in exultation, laid bare for his taking.

Isabella shuddered with delight and a little fear too as Warrick's lips traveled hotly down the length of that pearly pillar, for his kissing her there made her feel so vulnerable to him. Might not those teeth that nibbled her so gently have just as easily sunk viciously into her throat, torn her silken flesh apart? Might not those hands that lingered there so caressingly have just as easily strangled the very life from her body?

As though Warrick guessed her thoughts, he tightened his fingers there briefly, possessively.

"Mine," he muttered thickly. "Ye are mine, always mine."

Isabella shivered at the words. The power she knew lay coiled within him overwhelmed her, intoxicated her, made her head spin dizzily with passion, that savage, primal emotion that no civilization would ever tame. Her flesh was on fire with it; its heat emanated from her body and engulfed her in a fine, dewy sheen of sweat that smelled of her white rose fragrance, the forest scent that clung to Warrick, and the musk of them both as their mouths met yet again, tasting, devouring, one another. Isabella's knees buckled, and she knew she would have fallen, had she not been enfolded in Warrick's strong embrace.

Little by little, unnoticed, her clothing slipped away, slid as soft as a sigh from her body to fall in a pool of satin at her feet until she stood naked in his arms, a small silvery goddess his hands and lips worshiped without end.

Warrick's loins tightened, racing with excitement as hungrily his eyes raked her, ravished that soft, yielding skin he had gone without for so long. He inhaled sharply, his nostrils flaring slightly, as he sought out every curve, every nuance, that he had ever known so intimately and called his.

His. Only his. Forever his.

He would never let her go. No matter if she hated him for the rest of her life, she would never belong to another—this forest nymph, this water sprite, who had cast her spell upon him, bewitched him with her haunting grey-green eyes, enchanted him with her siren's song. What magic had she woven to bind him so dearly to her? Warrick did not know. He did not care. He loved her, and she was his. That was all that mattered.

Eagerly, he fondled her breasts, those alabaster spheres of perfection that had always so enchanted him. Like marble they were, of so translucent a white, he could trace the blue veins through which Isabella's life's blood flowed. Their pink crests stiffened and blushed even more rosily as his palms cupped the twin globes, gliding sensuously across their tiny buttons in a languid, circular motion that sent waves of pleasure radiating from them in all directions. For an instant, Isabella felt a strange warm fluttering in her belly, then the feeling passed to be replaced by something even more exciting as Warrick's thumbs flicked gently at the rigid buds, taunting them to even greater heights. His mouth covered one flushed tip, sucking, tongue swirling about it deliciously in a manner that made Isabella cradle him even closer and arch her body against his lips, his fingers, hungry for more. She could feel her nipple puckering, growing even harder as, on and on, he tormented it until she thought she could bear no more and was straining feverishly against him, half-mad with wanting. Like wildfire, his mouth scorched its way across her chest, seeking her other breast and setting it ablaze, as he had done its twin, until it too was a smoldering ember; and she was a wild thing with the passion clawing its way through her body.

Deep within the secret place of her womanhood, a small flame flickered and grew until it was a conflagration she longed desperately for him to quench. She ached to have him in her; but still, he went on kissing her, his lips as soft as a wisp of cloud as they floated down her belly, torturing her, making her writhe and seethe with desire. Slowly, he sank to his knees before her, his hands on her slender hips to hold her near. His tongue probed her navel, making her laugh a little, huskily, throatily, for it tickled as well as aroused her; and she found joy in his lovemaking and was glad. It was good to laugh again—if only for this moment— with the man she loved, the man who loved her. She did not realize how much she had missed it until now, when, smiling, he looked up at her, his golden eyes glowing with tenderness. She noted how the fine lines that crinkled the corners had deepened with time and pain; and a shadow haunted her grey-green orbs, recalling them both to the present as the memory stolen from the past was lost.

Warrick's eyes darkened briefly with sorrow—and then something more as his hands tightened for a minute on her hips before deliberately they slid down her legs, following the shape of her calves, then moved back up, and then down yet again, before, at long last, he parted her flanks. Lightly, lazily, over and over, his fingers trailed along the inside of her thighs, making them quiver with a yearning that Isabella could not disguise.

With a little cry of agony, she caught his hands, causing Warrick to laugh low in his throat with exhilaration and triumph.

Slowly, tormentingly, he sought the swollen folds that curved beneath the downy curls, soft as moss, which twined between her legs. Gently, tantalizingly, he stroked rhythmically the warm wet flesh that opened to him of its own accord as he urged it to part. Finally, languidly, his fingers found the dark cavern that beckoned to him so enticingly. His breathing rapid, mingling with her own, he explored the warm moist chasm that grew molten at his touch and trembled with desire, making him long to bury himself within it, plant his seed in its fertile ground. Warrick could feel the tiny tremors of delight that surged within Isabella as he fondled the length of her. With each fluttering movement of his fingers inside of her, each flick of his thumb upon the little bud that flourished upon the valley's knoll without, he knew her excitement was climbing toward its peak. Hotly, his mouth enveloped the small bloom his thumb had teased; tauntingly, his tongue rained upon it sweetly, faster and faster, causing its petals to unfurl and then suddenly close up tightly as Isabella gasped, glorious ecstasy flowering within her, sending blossoms of rapture through her body.

From deep within her throat came a single animalistic cry, a low moan of surrender as she clutched him to her, wanting him, needing him. Convulsively, uncontrollably, she shuddered and arched against him until, at last, she whimpered softly, sighing deeply with the pleasure of her release, and was still.

Without warning, Warrick rose, catching her up in his steely arms and setting her upon the rich velvet cushion of a nearby chair, his lips now upon her own, his tongue probing her mouth so she could taste the honeyed nectar of herself that lingered still upon his lips.

Then, slowly, reluctantly, he drew away to divest himself of his own garments. How quickly he was free of them and standing before her, towering over her like some ancient pagan god. Isabella's heart beat crazily in her breast as her eyes swept the bronzed, muscular length of him; thought about how tightly yet gently those corded arms could wrap themselves around her; how that broad, furry chest felt pressed against her pale silken one; how that flat firm belly and those narrow hips met her own so strongly with each powerful thrust of their mating. . . .

She flung back her head and closed her eyes, running her tongue across her lips to moisten them as she inhaled raggedly, the pulse at the hollow of her throat leaping wildly with excitement and anticipation.

Warrick caught his breath jerkily at the sight; the sinewy muscles in his belly and loins tautened, like a thong, with sharp desire. For an instant, he did not know if he would be able to restrain himself; but he forced himself to breathe deeply, to relax, and the moment passed.

Suddenly, roughly, possessively, his hands tangled themselves in the satin strands of Isabella's long silvery tresses. Her eyes flew open wide at his touch; her mouth parted eagerly as he bent to kiss her yet again, his lips hard and demanding upon her own. Then he straightened, breathless with expectation as her palms reached up to stroke his chest, glide across the dark mat of hair that grew there. Slowly, mesmerizingly, she stood, nuzzling his breast with her cheek before she pressed her mouth to one nipple and sucked it gently until it was as rigid as her own. Her tongue darted out to swirl about the stiff button, lick it, tease it tantalizingly. Her teeth grazed him lightly; and all the while, her hands moved upon his lithe lean body, causing the muscles in his back to bunch and quiver and ripple beneath her kneading fingers. Deftly, her palms slipped down his flesh, tracing the outline of old scars here and there, as her lips traveled across his chest to stimulate his other nipple until it was as stiff with excitement as its mate. She could feel the evidence of his desire hard against her belly; and, firmly grasping his smooth buttocks, she pulled him to her; and her hands found his maleness at last.

Warrick inhaled sharply, then sighed with pleasure as her fingers traced tormentingly the length of him, up, then down, before they closed about him; and she began the slow, sensuous motion that was as old as time. His body jerked and shuddered when her thumb found that soft, sensitive place upon his shaft and flicked it quickly again and again until his flesh was as raw and screaming for release as hers had been earlier. Still, she went on torturing him sweetly, her mouth sliding like a feather down his belly as, little by little, she sank to her knees, lowering her head to kiss the spheres of his manhood that hung just beneath his bold sword. Hotly, her lips and tongue taunted the soft globes until they contracted within the pouch that contained them. Then languidly, almost unbearably, her mouth slid lingeringly up the length of his maleness, then down, over and over, arousing him to a feverish pitch with rapid little kisses and licks of her tongue before finally, slowly, her lips claimed him; and he moaned with delight. Again and again, her mouth engulfed him; her tongue swirled about him teasingly like a moth's wings fluttering against the flame of a candle until Warrick knew he could stand no more.

With a sudden, swift movement, he pulled her to her feet, then pressed her down upon the edge of the rich velvet cushion of the chair, dropped to his knees before her, and parted her thighs. Moments later, the tip of his shaft found her, plunged into the warm wet core of her with a tender fury that made her gasp with keen desire. Then, just as suddenly, his manhood withdrew, only to thrust into her deeply once more. Over and over, his fiery sword pierced her flaming sheath until they were both panting raggedly for breath. Isabella's nails dug into Warrick's shoulders, raking little furrows down his back. Her body stiffened slightly, then melted and quivered with the explosions of ecstasy that shook her. She whimpered a little, tiny moans of rapture that mingled with his own as their passion-darkened eyes suddenly opened and locked. Isabella felt as though she were drowning in those amber depths, so vibrantly intense was the intimacy of that moment. Shyly, yet unable to tear her eyes away, she watched hungrily Warrick's face as his body shuddered with the sweet, savage thrill of his own release, and he spilled his seed within her.

In that precious, primal moment, he offered his soul to her by letting her witness the expression on his dark visage. Always before, he had suddenly crushed her to him, burying her head against his shoulder so she could not see the joy and triumph and sheer sensuality that flitted now across his countenance as his carnal lips parted, and he cried out lowly with exultation, his eyes closing at the last.

Then there was nothing but the sound of their quick breathing, which gradually grew less rapid as the furious pounding of their hearts slowed, and the racing of their pulses gently returned to normal.

Afterward, he kissed her, then, smiling a little as his golden orbs raked her possessively, knowing how victoriously he had conquered her, Warrick withdrew.

And Isabella knew he had taken her heart and soul with him for all time.

Chapter Thirty-nine

London, England, 1489

"DAMN HIM! DAMN HIM TO HELL AND BACK!" LORD MON-tecatini growled as, like a caged tiger, he paced the room restlessly, his wrath and frustration mounting with each rapid step. "Always, he interferes with my plans—the half-Welsh bastard—advising Henry against any scheme I propose. I may as well return to Rome. As long as Lord Hawk-hurst remains a favorite at Court, I am useless here in my position! *Sangue di Cristo,* but I wouldst like to slay that whoreson earl!"

"Ye have wounded him, my lord." Lady Shrewton spoke smoothly, soothingly, fearing the Count would fall into one of his black Italian rages and beat her, as he always did when displeased. Why she stayed with him she couldn't imagine. Still, if she were to leave him, where would she go? How would she live? A few ugly bruises seemed a small price to pay for the security he gave her. "After all, ye murdered Lord Rushden, and his stupid slut of a sister blamed Hawkhurst for the deed. Though the Earl has hidden it well, 'tis said the bitch's abandonment hurt him deeply. And still, he continues to pursue her like a moonstruck fool!"

"Aye." Lord Montecatini nodded. "Still, 'tis poor sat-isfaction for the trouble the bastard has caused me, continues to cause me. I am foiled, made to look a fool at every turn. Even Geoffrey has begun to treat me as though I were naught save a bumbling *sciocco,*" the Count complained, referring to his latest lover. "Well, I shall deal with him soon enough, the ungrateful *idioto! Ferite di Dio!* A mere knight he was when first I took an interest in him. Now that he has attained a barony, he thinks he no longer has any need of me. Well, Geoffrey shall discover his mistake shortly. In the meantime, I must think of a plot for ridding myself of Hawkhurst. For too long, he has been a thorn in my side. But I must take care. No one must know 'twas by my hand the whoreson died, or 'twill certainly be the end of my most lucrative position here in England. Rome will not countenance another disgrace. *Dio!* If only the Earl were not such a favorite of Henry's. If only I could get my hands on Hawkhurst's wife!"

Lady Shrewton's sly, evil eyes widened with surprise at this, for she had never known the Italian to be remiss in learning everything that went on in the Tower—and indeed all of London as well.

"But—but, my lord . . . have ye not heard?" she asked. "The whore is to be released tomorrow from Bloody Tower."

"Nay!" Lord Montecatini's black orbs narrowed with speculation. "*È vero*? Ye do not lie, *signora*?"

"Nay, my lord. Of course not. 'Tis common knowledge. I am surprised ye had not learned of it already."

"That bumbling *sciocco* Florio!" the Count snarled of his squire. "Florio! Florio!" he shouted irately, bringing the terrified young man running. "What is this I hear about Lady Hawkhurst being set free tomorrow? Ye did not inform me of her release."

"N—nay, *signore*," the squire stammered nervously under the Italian's piercing stare. "I—I assumed ye already knew of it, and I—I did not think 'twas necessary to report the matter, *signore*."

"Ye did not think. Ye did not think," Lord Montecatini mocked, then cruelly boxed the young man's ears. "*Idioto! I* am the one who does the thinking around here. *Si alzi!* Get up, ye sniveling fool! Groveling at my feet will not save ye from the punishment ye so richly deserve. Go, and await my displeasure in the schoolroom. I shall join ye presently to teach ye a lesson ye will not soon forget!"

"Oh, nay, *signore*," Florio pleaded desperately. "Please, please do not make me—"

"*Silenzio, sciocco!*" the Count snapped. "Go—before I

decide I have no further use for ye at all and take more . . . permanent measures against ye!"

Petrified, the squire fled; and Lady Shrewton heaved a great sigh of relief that *she* had not been the unfortunate one ordered to the schoolroom for one of the Italian's lessons.

Still, she cowered a little as he turned his glittering black gaze on her, and for a moment, she thought wildly that it was true that Lord Montecatini was in league with the devil.

"Does she go home, then—to Hawkhurst—the bastard's lovely little Rose of Rapture?" the Count inquired with a sardonic curl of his lip.

"Nay, I do not believe so," Lady Shrewton replied, praying she was right. "Methinks the trull will go to Grasmere, her manor house. 'Tis said that for all of the Earl's ardent wooing of her, the slut has yet to forgive him for her brother's death."

"And this . . . Grasmere. What is it like?" the Italian queried.

"'Tis but a manor house, my lord, as I told ye—not built for defense. 'Twould be an easy enough place for several men in disguise to assault, especially now that the King has prohibited the wearing of livery. None will even remark upon the men's appearance. Aye, 'twould be easy enough," she reiterated. "Indeed, I do not know why Hawkhurst did not besiege the place when the bitch refused to admit him."

"Don't be a bigger fool than ye already are, *signora*," Lord Montecatini snorted. "Attack his own wife? Slay his own men in the process? The very idea is ridiculous!"

Hurriedly, Lady Shrewton sought to recover the Count's good will, which she had lost.

"No one need know who took the whore—except Hawkhurst, of course, the fool," she sneered. "Methinks there is very little the Earl would not do to save the trull's life; he is so besotted with her. And if he were to be slain in the process—" Abruptly, she broke off, shrugging noncommittally.

"Beatrice." Lord Montecatini, in one of his rare moods

of pleasure, smiled down wolfishly at her. "For once, ye have been of use to me. Do ye bring me my jewel box, and I shall give ye an onyx bracelet that will go nicely with your gown."

It was snowing hard by the time that Isabella reached Grasmere, but she did not care. She was home—home—after over a year of solitary confinement in Bloody Tower. Henry Tudor had wished to teach her a lesson, and he had. Isabella would not lightly enter into any more plots against the King. The last Lancastrian sat firmly upon the throne of England. He would not see it wrested from his grasp by a mere slip of a Yorkist girl—no matter how high in his favor her husband might stand. Her husband. Warrick. Isabella was certain the length of her imprisonment had been meant also to punish her for deserting her husband and making him unhappy. In fact, the Tydder's last words to her, before she had left Court, had been for her to return to Warrick at once.

"The affairs of Hawkhurst Castle are yours, madam," the King had stated coldly. "Do not seek to meddle in mine again."

And Isabella had known she must once more live as Warrick's wife. Not only had the King commanded her to do so, but before her leaving Bloody Tower, Warrick had wrung from her lips her promise to return to him.

"Swear it," he had ordered grimly, "on your oath, 'Sabelle."

And so she had—not because he had forced her to do so, but because, by then, she had realized the uselessness of fighting him. She loved him still. She had not been able to deny it any longer. The long days and nights that Warrick had spent overwhelming her body and filling up her senses had told her that.

"On my oath, I do swear that I will live again as your wife," she had said softly, "but I need time, my lord... time to adjust. Let me go home to Grasmere for just a little while. Hawkhurst—Hawkhurst will seem so empty without ye and—and Caerllywel and the others."

Warrick was to remain behind at Court for a time to set-

tle some business affairs for the King, and Caerllywel...
Caerllywel was dead, as were Giles and Madog.

At last, Warrick had agreed.

"I shall come for ye in the spring, *cariad*," he had told
her. "For I do love ye."

And Isabella, her heart torn apart inside of her, had
whispered, "And I—I love ye, my lord. But I am ashamed
and sick at heart that I do."

Now, at the thought of him, her grief and sorrow of the
past years suddenly overwhelmed her; and as Grasmere
loomed up before her in the misty twilight, it seemed, to
her fanciful nature, that even here, as never before, ghosts
from the past haunted her. Almost as though they really
stood there before her, Isabella could see her grandmother
beckoning to her from the porch of the manor house, and
her mother and father smiling at her from the shadows of
the trees. Laughing, and whole once more in body, Giles
came running to greet her, and she watched herself, a child,
racing eagerly toward his outstretched arms. Then, as the
snow flurried across the lawn, the image blurred, running
like a watercolor in the rain, and faded into a picture of
Rushden. There, upon the cobblestones of her brother's
courtyard, she knelt before Richard, Duke of Gloucester,
then rose and took the single gold sovereign he held in one
outstretched hand. Isabella closed her eyes in pain at the
memory, and when she opened them again, the vignette
was gone, had been replaced by a swing in a moonlit meadow,
where Lionel knelt upon dew-sheened grass to pledge his
love for her.

Roses—white roses—lay scattered upon the ground, and
as she bent to retrieve them, she heard the laughter of the
gay courtiers who wooed her in vain: for her heart had been
given for all time to Lord Warrick ap Tremayne, Earl of
Hawkhurst. She could almost smell the scent of the newly
mown hay that had filled the stables that summer when first
she had seen him. Even now, he was striding toward her,
as he had then, so dark and handsome. A little behind him
came Caerllywel, laughing Caerllywel, holding a damp-
feathered hat in his hand as he escorted her to her box at
the tourney.

The snowflakes danced and swirled about her, but still, Isabella paid no heed, lost in the past as Grasmere's white-covered lawn became the jousting field at Edward's palace in Greenwich. For a moment, Anne smiled down at her, as soft and lovely as though she truly lived and breathed once more; and tears stung Isabella's eyes, and a ragged little sob choked from her throat.

When Jocelyn and Sirs Eadric, Thegn, and Beowulf spoke to her, Isabella did not hear them, did not see the concern upon their faces as they gazed at her searchingly, puzzled as to why she was not riding on and confused by the odd still expression on her countenance.

They did not know that, in her mind, Madog's eyes were raking her with hot desire, which turned to contrition as he begged forgiveness upon learning she was his brother's wife.

Oh, God, oh, God. She tried to stop the recollections from coming, but still, they haunted her.

It was not until she tasted a single icy crystal droplet, bittersweet upon her lips, that Isabella realized the tears were freezing on her cheeks; and she forced herself to ride on toward Grasmere—and her ghosts.

They came, as Lionel's men had come for her that day upon the moors of Devon so long ago, in plain black livery that bespoke naught of their lord. But Isabella thought nothing of it now, for the Tydder had prohibited the wearing of arms-emblazoned livery. It was only when the troop of men drew near that the first tiny inklings of fear chased up her spine; and, some instinct warning her, she began to run. From the lawn, where they had been building a snowman, she snatched up Caerllywel's young son, Arthwr, who, not understanding their danger, set up a wail. The boy's head cradled tightly against her breast to soothe him, Isabella raced inside the manor house and slammed and bolted the door, crying out frantically for those who would protect her.

Valiantly, her faithful knights did fight to save her life and honor, but Grasmere was not a castle—'twas only a simple manor house, not built for defense—and the men who attacked it were vicious and brutal in their assault.

The battle was short and swift, though it seemed to Isabella it was a nightmare that went on unendingly and from which she could not awaken. Numb with shock and disbelief and horror, she stared at the shattered lead-glass windowpanes that were scattered upon the floor of the great hall, the sharp slivers mingling with the blood of her knights who lay dying—or dead. Her beloved Eadric's eyes gazed up at her sightlessly, and dear Thegn was recognizable only by his blood-bespattered clothes. Gravely wounded, Beowulf limped toward her, frantically urging her to flee.

"Ye—ye must try—try to get to the—the stables, my—my lady. 'Tis—'tis your only chance."

But Isabella knew it was no use. The manor house was surrounded, and already, the black-liveried men were battering down the stout doors, forcing their way inside. There was no place to hide, except in the upstairs chambers, and the savage intruders would find her there quickly enough anyway. Nay, Isabella would not now leave the faithful knights who had tried so courageously to shield her all her life, any more than she had deserted them earlier, during the fight, when they had commanded her to seek a place of safety.

This could not be happening. This could not be real. Who was there who wished harm to her and hers, who had so suddenly, without warning, wrought this evil upon them? And why? Dear God, why?

Isabella was only dimly aware of old Alice and Jocelyn huddled in one corner, attempting to shield young Arthwr's eyes from the dreadful carnage and the men who were, even now, streaming into the great hall. Blindly, Isabella reached for the dagger at her waist, yanked it free, and held it out threateningly. She would not be taken without a fight, and if worst came to worst, she would slay herself before being ravished by these brutal men.

"If ye are reivers, take what ye want, and go," she said. "There is naught here to stop ye now."

But the black-liveried intruders only laughed and strode toward her menacingly, cutting Beowulf down, without mercy, as he made one last brave-hearted but futile effort to defend his mistress.

"Beowulf! Beowulf!" Isabella wailed with anguish, but

she could not help him now. He was dead. Her eyes stinging hotly with tears, she stared in terror at the pitiless men who had murdered her knight. "At least—at least tell me who ye are and why ye have done this wicked thing!" Isabella cried as the intruders closed about her warily, eying the blade she wielded so purposefully. "I—I don't want to die in ignorance."

"Have no fear, *signora*." One of them spoke. "'Tis the Lord's wish ye be not harmed, so put down that knife, and come peaceably. 'Tis our heads if we hurt ye."

Isabella was so stunned and bewildered by the man's words, she only vaguely realized that her title had been spoken in Italian. Somewhere, in the back of her mind, she was faintly alarmed by the fact. But as the only Italian she knew was Lord Montecatini, and he had always been kind to her, she did not make the obvious connection. Instead, she backed even farther away from the men who approached her, until, at last, she was pressed against a wall, and there was nowhere left for her to run to. Unexpectedly, one man braver than the rest made a grab for her dagger and surprised her so that three of the other men were able to wrest the blade from her grasp and take her prisoner, though she struggled furiously against them. Ragnor, so much a part of her now that she had forgotten he sat perched upon her shoulder, squawked wildly and tore at them fiercely with his beak, causing them to fall back, cursing. But finally, the men held her fast, and Isabella closed her eyes tightly as she tried to prepare herself to be raped, for she had not believed the words of reassurance that had been offered her.

But, again to her amazement, no harm was done her. Instead, she was merely yanked from the great hall, thrust out onto the lawn, and propelled roughly toward the stables, whence more black-liveried men were riding, leading her mare, Cendrillon. Only when she was mounted did the Count, who had watched the melee from a distance, at last appear, galloping up on his huge black destrier, which pranced and snorted dangerously under the pressure of his slender iron hands upon the steed's reins.

"Lord—Lord Montecatini!" Isabella gasped as, smiling at her wolfishly, he took the bridle of her horse from one of his men and wrapped it tightly about the pommel of his own saddle.

"Ye are surprised, *signora*, nay?" he asked, lifting one eyebrow demoniacally. "But then, of course, ye do not understand any of this, do ye? No matter." He shrugged. "'Twill all be explained to ye in time."

"My lord—" Isabella began coldly but was stopped abruptly by the terrified screams that suddenly pierced the air.

Dear God. Jocelyn. Jocelyn and Alice. How could Isabella, even in her own paralyzing fear, have forgotten them?

"Jocelyn!" the girl cried. "Alice!" When there was no response save for the hysterical wails of fright that came from the manor house, Isabella turned pleadingly to the Count. "My maid. My nurse. Please," she begged, "make your men let them go."

Once more, the Italian smiled superciliously and shrugged.

"Nay, I shall not. The men must, after all, have their bit of sport; and 'twill, mayhap, ease the lust in their loins and make them less eager to slake their desires upon ye, *signora*. We've a long way to journey, and 'twill be difficult enough to guard ye as 'tis. In fact . . . Florio!"

"Aye, *signore*?"

"The maid, the nurse—how are they?"

"The maid, *signore* . . . she fight like a wild thing, but the men have their way with her. She be young and pretty, after all, and worth the struggle, nay? But the nurse . . . she was too old to bother with. They slit her throat."

"Tell the men to bring the maid along," the Italian ordered. "She will be useful in keeping the men from my prize."

Without warning, incredible grief and rage and hatred welled up in Isabella's throat at Lord Montecatini and his callous, inexplicable assault upon her and hers. She thought of her knights and her old nanna, lying cold and lifeless in the manor house, mercilessly slain at the hands of the Count's men; and of Jocelyn, inside Grasmere, even now being raped repeatedly and not knowing her agony was to continue as long as the Italian saw fit to let it. So great was Isabella's anger that she actually shook with wrath, felt, for the first time in her life, a blinding, overwhelming urge to hurt and maim and kill.

"Ye bastard!" she spat. "Ye despicable bastard!"

Lord Montecatini only laughed; and in that moment, as though sensing her horrible torment and helplessness, as once Isabella had his, Ragnor gave a shrill, wild, murderous cry and flung himself from the girl's shoulder, straight toward the vain dark Count's beautiful, laughing face. As though possessed by some fiend, Ragnor seized that handsome visage, sank his sharp beak and punishing talons deeply into the Italian's flesh. Lord Montecatini screamed and screamed again, a high, inhuman sound that made Isabella's skin crawl even as, in her benighted ire and thirst for revenge, she spurred Ragnor on with a terrible, hoarse, unnatural cry for blood.

The Count's men stared in horror as, frozen with mortification, they watched him struggling convulsively to escape from the bird's torturing grip. In a blind frenzy, he clawed at the hawk, tried to pry it from his face; but still, Ragnor held tight and went on ripping and tearing at the Italian's dark countenance. Lord Montecatini toppled from his destrier, rolled frantically, spastically, upon the snow-covered ground as his hands sought to yank the bird free, until, at last, with another piercing screech of triumph, the hawk flapped its wings and rose.

Against the dying winter sun, into the dusk, Ragnor soared, higher and higher, until suddenly he dropped into a dive, hurtling his body downward like an arrow. Isabella's breath caught in her throat as she gazed upon his beautiful descent, never taking her eyes from the bird, never moving, though he swooped straight toward her. Finally, when it seemed as though he would strike her, Ragnor checked his flight, spreading his wings wide once more. Understanding his intent, Isabella raised her ungloved hand high, and the hawk came proudly to light upon her wrist. Time hung suspended in that moment he perched there, having paid her the ultimate compliment by returning, unrestrained by jesses, to her hand. His talons curved into the softness of Isabella's skin; tiny droplets of blood spurted from the small wounds, but she did not care. As she stared into his fierce yellow eyes, she knew now why he had waited so long to fly. Some primal instinct inside of him had demanded that the debt he owed her be paid.

"Godspeed, Ragnor," the girl whispered. "Fare thee well."

Once more, the bird screamed and rose, soaring into the sky, until finally Isabella could see him no longer. The hawk was gone.

A lump choked in her throat at the thought. Her eyes brimmed with tears at his loss, even though she knew, like Hwyelis, he was a wild thing, not meant to be caught and caged. Isabella loved him. She must not call him back but let him go instead. If Ragnor returned, it must be of his own free will; and somehow, some way, the girl knew, deep down inside, that one day, he would ride again upon her shoulder. They were one—she and Ragnor—bound together by the cruel jest of a drunken king and the vicious revenge of an Italian count.

Even as Isabella thought of Lord Montecatini, he groaned, recalling her, with a start, to the present.

"Beatrice," he rasped, his hands still clasped tightly over his dark visage. "Fetch . . . Beatrice. I—I must have her to . . . tend my—my face."

"*Signora* Shrewton!" Florio cried in response to his master's demand, nearly causing Isabella to fall from her saddle in shock and horror. "*Signora* Shrewton!"

The squire glanced about, frowning, in search of the evil Countess, but she was nowhere to be found. Then suddenly, someone breathed, "*Dio mio*. Look!" and everyone turned to where the man pointed.

There, through the upper story windows of Grasmere, the crazed Countess could be seen moving from chamber to chamber, setting each one afire with the torch she carried in one hand. Even as they watched her, the sound of her strange wild laughter reached their ears, making the napes of their necks crawl.

"Ye deranged bitch!" Florio called, shaking his fist at the manor house, but Lady Shrewton did not hear him. "*Signore*,"—he turned back to his master—"the woman . . . she has gone completely mad. She is burning down the manor house and pays us no heed."

"My face, my face," the Count moaned again, apparently not having heard a word his squire had spoken. "I must have Beatrice to tend my face. Oh, my face, my face. 'Tis ruined, ruined for life."

Poor Florio did not know what to do, but one man, bolder than the rest and finally recovering his senses, stepped forth and, without ceremony, tossed the Italian upon his black destrier.

"Get hold of yourself, *signore*," the man said tersely, "or we're all likely to have our necks stretched at the end of a gallow's rope. Your face will be scarred for life, all right, but you'll live. Angelo, Luigi. Go inside, and get that crazy bitch."

"Forget it, Vincenzo. The place is an inferno, and the bitch is roasting alive. She won't be around to tell any tales. Bring the girl, and let's get going."

"Wait. Here come Davide and Maurizio with the maid. Giorgio, fetch another horse."

Isabella's face blanched with pity and horror, and bilious gorge from her stomach rose sickeningly to her throat as she caught sight of Jocelyn being led forth from the burning manor house. The maid was clad only in a rough cloak that one of the men had thrown about her, and she was shivering uncontrollably with shock and cold as she stumbled unseeingly through the snow, half-dragged along by the men. Of her young son there was no sign.

Sweet *Jesù*. How can ye be so cruel? Isabella asked God silently. The child was but four years old.

And for the first time, the girl was glad she had borne no babe of Warrick's making.

Oh, Warrick, *Warrick!* her heart cried out piteously. Where are ye, my lord, my love?

But naught save the crackling flames that engulfed Grasmere answered.

Warrick was sickened and chilled by the sight of the manor house, burned and blackened to but an empty shell of its former splendor; and inside of his oddly constricted breast, his heart was as desolate as the stark ruin before him.

Isabella. Oh, God. *Isabella!*

If she had died in the fire that had claimed Grasmere, he had no way of knowing it: for though a charred bone here and there gave evidence of a human body that had perished in the blaze, there was no way of telling to whom the bone had belonged.

Not 'Sabelle, Warrick prayed feverishly. Dear God, not my sweet Rose of Rapture.

"My lord! My lord!"

The excited shouts of his men brought him back, with a start, to the present. They were hurrying toward him eagerly, a strange woman, holding the hand of a young boy, in their midst.

Nay, it could not be! It could not be! Was it—was it—

"Uncle Waerwic! Uncle Waerwic!" the child shouted, breaking free of the woman's restraining grip and running forward.

"Arthwr! Thank God! Arthwr!" Warrick cried, hugging the lad close as the boy raced into his outstretched arms. "Arthwr."

Hope surged in the Earl's breast that the child might be able to tell him something, but the small, fervent expectation was quickly dashed as slowly, carefully, so as not to frighten the lad, he questioned the child, only to learn nothing. Still, there remained the woman. Warrick motioned for her to be brought forth and introduced.

"My name be Mary Brown, m'lord, from up Eden's Folly way," she announced and dropped him a shy, awkward curtsy tinged slightly with awe and fear. "But I know no more'n the babe. I found him wandering in the woods, crying out pitifully for his mama, poor mite. But she weren't nowhere to be found, so I took him in, thinking someone would come fer him sooner or later. I—I didn't mean no harm by it. His clothes . . . they was real fine, m'lord, so I knowed he weren't common, and I couldn't jest stand by and let him starve"—this a trifle defiantly.

"Of course not," Warrick agreed warmly. "Ye did the right thing, lass. Do not be thinking otherwise. Ye shall be richly rewarded, I promise ye."

"Well, thank ye, m'lord. I won't say as how a bit of coin wouldn't be welcome; but I ain't greedy, and I hope

I'm a kind woman and know my duty and don't need to be bribed into doing it. Now. Where was I? Oh, aye. But other than saying his house had burnt up, the poor mite knew nothing. Course, we'd all spied the fire and come a'running. It blazed so bright, m'lord; 'twas like a beacon there on the hill. Ye could see it fer miles in all directions; ye could. I'll warrant it frightened the poor mite something terrible, fer he has bad dreams; he does. Wails out something fierce in his sleep at night. Whimpers something awful fer his mama, which is only natural, of course. 'Tis the other thing he says that worries me."

"What other thing?" Warrick asked. "What else does the child say?"

"Well, I can't rightly understand part of it, m'lord, fer it don't make no sense to me; and the rest of it ain't fitting to repeat. My mama done raised me proper; she done."

"Tell me anyway," the Earl urged. "Do the best ye can. Please, Mistress Brown. 'Tis very important."

The woman flushed and bridled with pleasure at his addressing her so. Why, he was a right nice man, was Lord Hawkhurst, not like some of the high and mighty nobles she'd met, who'd treated her like dirt.

"Well, m'lord, it sounds like the lad's saying, 'See Nora—'" Here, she broke off and blushed with embarrassment, biting her lip, but went on at Warrick's prompting. "See Nora . . . slut. See Nora slut. That's what the boy says, m'lord; but as I told ye, it don't make no sense to me. There ain't no Nora hereabouts that I know of, specially a—a woman what ain't proper."

See Nora slut. See Nora slut.

What on earth could the child be saying? And then suddenly, Warrick had it, and his heart turned cold with fear in his breast. Dear God.

Signora slut! *Signora* slut!

That's what the boy was saying. 'Twas the Italian—the Italian had kidnapped Isabella, was holding her prisoner somewhere for his own evil purposes—whatever they might be. Aye, Warrick's wife was alive. Suddenly, the Earl was sure of it.

Dear God. What was his beloved 'Sabelle suffering at

the hands of that treacherous piece of slime—and where had the Italian taken her?

Arising from her stupor, her senses sharply magnified, Isabella stared wildly about her chamber, her nerves taut and screaming silently for the potion that Lord Montecatini had promised her earlier, the sweet poppy's nectar, that pure raw powder, without which she was certain she could not now survive. Her body craved it—desperately—and still, the Count did not come.

God's blood! Where was he? Where was he?

Frantically, she chewed her ragged fingernails—some of which were already bitten down to the quick—in an effort to distract herself. When that proved fruitless, she jumped up from the bed and began to pace the floor restlessly, tearing crazily at the robe she wore, until its silk material hung in tattered shreds about her.

Once or twice, she caught sight of herself in the mirror, but the reflection that gazed back at her meant nothing to her. Isabella did not recognize the gaunt, wild-eyed, hollow-cheeked woman who was herself.

With quick, jerky movements, she fingered the ornate bottles of scent that sat upon her dresser, but the delicate flacons held nothing that interested her; and after a moment, with a little sob of rage and despair, she swept her hand across them, sending them shattering to the floor.

"Temper, temper, *signora*," Lord Montecatini cautioned as finally he entered the room. "A glassblower in Venice spent many long hours creating those crystal treasures, and in a single instant, ye have destroyed all his hard work."

"I don't care!" Isabella spat rebelliously, hating him, despising his maimed, twisted face, which was now crusted over with scabs. "Did ye bring it?"

"Patience, *signora*. Ye must learn to cultivate patience," the Count chided, wishing to prolong her torment as long as possible. "In due time, ye will get that which ye desire."

Slowly, he reached into his doublet and drew forth a small pouch; then he moved to the hunting table along one wall, taking great pains to avoid glancing in the mirror as he passed it. He lived, aye; but his life had been his face, and his face was ruined. He could not bear to look at himself, though he forced everyone else to, beating them savagely if they dared to hide their eyes from his hideous visage. He would never be thought a beauty again, would never again know the glow of envy and adoration his handsomeness had brought when he had preened before a lover. And the Tremaynes were to blame! If not for them, his life would not have been ruined!

To Isabella, each passing second seemed like hours as he poured out a chalice of dark, rich red wine—brandywine. The most potent of all wines made, it was created by boiling down burgundy and lacing it with brandy. After taking a few sips to assure himself the wine had not soured, he opened the pouch and shook its contents into the goblet. The thick powder lay there on the surface of the liquid for a minute before sinking to the bottom of the chalice, where the crystals dissolved as the Italian stirred the draught with a silver spoon.

At last, with the caricature of a smile twisting his distorted face, Lord Montecatini turned and handed the goblet to Isabella. Greedily, she upended the chalice, quenching her thirst with the potion.

Soon, she began to return to the dreamlike existence she lived for nowadays. Slowly, slowly, the feeling of languor crept through her veins, calming her tortured nerves and making her titter slightly at that foolish woman who, just a little while earlier, had paced the chamber floor so restlessly, ridiculously expending all that energy. Now, lying upon her bed, Isabella gazed up dizzily at the cathedral ceiling of the tower in which she was imprisoned. Though it was stained dark and crisscrossed with wooden beams, in her mind, there was no roof at all, just a pattern of brilliant, swirling colors fading up into the sky, pierced by the golden sunlight streaming down from the firmament. She could see herself floating upon the whirl of the flashing, ever-changing kaleidoscope, and she knew she was without substance or form, a goddess who looked down upon her foolish mortal subjects below and laughed. She giggled once more, her head lolling from side to side, her body limp, inert. Drowsily, she yawned, wondering why her eyelids felt so heavy, indeed, why she had any eyelids at all. She was a goddess, wasn't she? She didn't need any eyelids—useless things. Listlessly, she lifted one arm, which felt like lead, and waved it around aimlessly before, at last, she managed to tug at the feathery black fringe of one eye. But the attempt to remove her eyelid was futile, and Isabella soon abandoned it. It seemed like such a waste of energy. It was much more entertaining to study the cherubic angels who had appeared among the colors above and who were serenading her with their harps and horns. Spastically, she applauded, then laughed idiotically; and Lord Montecatini, who was watching her, grimaced.

Disgusting bitch! he thought. I can hardly wait until that half-Welsh bastard gets a look at his Rose of Rapture now!

Aye, he had chosen well, the Count decided. 'Twas the perfect revenge. Truly, none of the other forms of vengeance he had considered and discarded would have served nearly as well. He had thought of turning Isabella over to his men for sport, but what man who loved a woman would cast her out because she had been forced to become a whore? Not the Earl. Proud and jealous, he might be; but he loved his wife, and the fact that other men had known her, against her will, would not diminish that love. The Italian had thought of scarring Isabella's lovely countenance until 'twas unrecognizable—like his own; but that idea he had too abandoned. A man loved a woman—truly loved her—for what she was inside. Marring Isabella's beauty would not have changed that. Lord Montecatini had even contemplated slaying the girl, but this notion also he had dismissed. He meant to kill her, aye, but only when he had the Earl at his mercy to witness Isabella's death and be powerless to prevent it.

Aye, turning her into an addict had been the best means of revenge. What man would love a woman who craved the sweet nectar of a poppy more than she did him, would even slay him to get it and never shed a tear at his demise?

Smiling terribly, the Count looked once more at Isabella. No man could love that disgusting creature.

Satisfied that it was so, the Italian reached for a quill
and ink. It was time to let Lord Hawkhurst know the whereabouts of his wife.

Grimly, Warrick stared at the dark, massive fortress that
rose up forbiddingly before him. Its true name was Boldon-
by-the-Sea Castle, but everyone called it Black Rock. Perched
upon a sheer cliff overlooking the ocean, its towering black
walls were fifty feet high and ten feet thick. It had no moat,
for there was no need for one. There was only one way to
gain access to the keep; that was a steeply graded road that
wound its path precariously up through the jagged rocks to
the fortress. It was one of the most impregnable castles in
all of England; and Warrick's heart sank like a stone in his
breast as he surveyed it. He would never be able to wrest
Isabella by force from the keep.

Oh, God. If only Warrick had the King's men behind
him! But he did not. Lord Montecatini had been far too
clever to allow that. Before leaving London, the Count had
put about the story that he was returning to Rome on a
private family matter; and he had made certain that several
of the courtiers had actually witnessed him boarding the
ship that had sailed slowly down the Thames toward the
open sea.

Warrick, of course, knew the Italian had not returned
home but instead had put to shore somewhere north of
Bridlington, in England, ridden to Grasmere to kidnap Isabella, then reboarded his ship and sailed still farther north
to Boldon-by-the-Sea, which was deep in the mountainous
border lands of England.

Upon realizing that Isabella had been taken captive by
Lord Montecatini, Warrick's first thought had been to de-
nounce the Count at once openly. After further reflection,
however, the Earl had recognized he would only be made
to look foolish. He'd had no tangible proof the Italian had
abducted Isabella, and all of London had believed Lord
Montecatini on the high seas toward Rome, a very unlikely
place from which to have conducted a kidnapping.

So Warrick had remained silent and had set about quietly
to search for his wife, so none would learn of her disap-

pearance and bring the matter to the King's attention. Harry did not like Isabella, and although he might have believed Warrick's tale of her abduction, it had been more than likely the King would have assumed instead that she had disobeyed his command to return to her husband. But although Warrick had sought diligently for Isabella's whereabouts, he had discovered nothing. Only the message he had received from the Count had given him the information he had so desired— and the tangible proof he had needed of the Italian's duplicity. But Warrick had been unable to show Harry the letter from Lord Montecatini, for in it, the Count had warned he would slay Isabella immediately if he learned the Earl had informed the King of the girl's kidnapping and the identity of her captor.

"What do we do now, Waerwic?" Emrys asked, daunted by the sight of the ominous fortress and bringing the Earl back sharply to the present.

"We wait," Warrick said tersely to his brother. "We wait for the Italian's summons. There is nothing more we can do."

Then he buried his head in one hand so his men would not see the despair upon his face. The Earl had never felt so helpless in his life.

"Waerwic, ye cannot go in there!" Emrys pleaded desperately with his brother. "You'll never come out alive—ye know ye won't—and neither will Isabella."

"I know, I know. But what else can I do? God's wounds! What else can I do?"

"Wait the bastard out. Sooner or later, he must make a move."

"And if 'tis to kill 'Sabelle— Sweet *Jesù*!" Warrick groaned, stricken. "I'd never forgive myself."

"He has no reason to slay her yet," Emrys pointed out logically, "not until he can get his hands on ye. 'Tis *ye* he really wants, if what he told ye is true. Christ's son! The man is mad! Ye don't kill someone for opposing ye politically."

"Oh, come, Emrys. 'Tis done all the time."

"A dagger in the back in a shadowed corridor? Aye. But

like this? Nay. The man is mad, I tell ye. Ye *must* wait him out. Let *him* make the next move. 'Tis what Madog would have done; believe me."

"God's blood! Would that our brother were here now to guide me. He would know how to get into that God damned keep!"

"Forget it, Waerwic. 'Tis impregnable. That is why they call it Black Rock."

Once more, Isabella's nerves were raw and screaming silently for the potion that would tame the savage talons that clawed their way through her veins. She did not even care that Lord Montecatini had let her out of her chamber for the first time in three months. She knew only that the warm spring sunlight hurt her eyes and that the Count had yet to give her the draught, though she pleaded with him hysterically to do so.

Instead, he merely dragged her, stumbling, along behind him brutally, dealing her a vicious slap when she fell and groveled at his feet, clinging to his legs to keep him from kicking her as she begged him for the potion.

"Si alzi! Get up!" the Italian growled, yanking her roughly to her feet and boxing her ears. "Your husband dares to defy me, and I must teach him a lesson."

"Warrick?" Isabella asked, dazed, her head ringing from the painful blows. "What is he doing here?"

But she inquired only as a matter of conversation. She did not care if Lord Montecatini answered, did not care what Warrick was doing at Boldon-by-the-Sea. She cared only about the small pouch filled with powder, which the Count carried in his doublet.

"Oh, why won't ye give me my draught?" she cried, trying desperately, dementedly, to wrench it from its place of concealment. "I need it! Oh, why won't ye give it to me?"

"Presently, I shall, *signora*," the Italian responded smoothly. "Ye have but to do one tiny thing for me first."

"Oh, anything. Anything!" Isabella promised rashly, not caring what it was he wished her to do.

She would even kill for the sweet poppy's nectar; she craved it so.

"Good," Lord Montecatini said as, at last, they reached the outer wall of the fortress. "Do ye but climb up on the battlements and walk a little ways so your husband can see ye."

Isabella was not afraid of heights; she had lived around them all her life. And in her hysterical stupor, she gave no thought to the fact that no sane man would have done what the Count now asked of her, that she could easily and probably would lose her balance and fall to be battered upon the rocks fifty feet below.

Instead, she pulled herself up onto one of the embrasures, then clambered up higher still onto the merlon on one side. She swayed precariously for a moment, so the Italian reached out to steady her from behind, but she felt no fear. Not even when Warrick's men, far below, finally spied her and began to shout frantically and point at her did she sense her danger. Thinking it was some sort of game, and remembering the potion that would be her reward for winning, she jumped to the next merlon, teetered there for an instant, then skipped onto the next. And all the while, Warrick watched from below, his heart in his throat.

"My God," he breathed. "Is she mad?"

"Nay." Emrys shook his head. "'Tis my guess the whoreson has drugged her."

"Dear God," Warrick said, and started forward. "I'm going in."

Only the combined strength of his men held him back, for he was like a madman in his fear and rage.

"Don't be a fool, Waerwic!" Emrys exclaimed. "Ye cannot help her, and if ye deliver yourself up to the bastard, you'll be playing right into his hands. Don't ye see? 'Tis what he wants ye to do. 'Tis why Isabella is up there now, risking her life!"

And so Warrick stood and watched helplessly and died a thousand deaths with each little leap his wife made upon the battlements. And when it seemed as though he could stand no more, she fell.

"Si alzi! Get up!" Lord Montecatini snarled as he got to his feet and brushed himself off after being toppled by Isabella's fall. "Disgusting bitch!" he sneered when she continued to lie there upon the walkway, stunned and dazed. "I ought to slay ye as I did your brother!"

It took her a moment, but somehow, some way, through the haze of her drugged state, Isabella grasped his words and was shocked and sickened by their impact.

"Nay! What—what are ye saying?" she questioned, her voice sharp and shrill as she staggered to her feet. "Tell me, ye whoreson bastard!" she cried, grabbing hold of the Count and shaking him wildly. "Tell me! What do ye mean? Ye ought to slay me *as ye did my brother?"*

Irately, the Italian knocked her away, then laughed, a short, ugly sound.

"I mean just what I said, ye stupid slut. 'Twas I who killed your brother. Ye blamed your half-Welsh bastard of a husband for the deed; but 'twas I who killed Giles."

"But—but how? And—and why?"

"I poisoned the sleeping draught ye asked me to prepare for him. 'Twas a kindness, really, to put the lad out of his misery; and I knew you'd blame the Earl for the deed, turn against him, and make his life hell. He'd humiliated me, ye know, that day of the tourney, caused me to be recalled to Rome in disgrace; and I'd sworn to have my revenge upon him—the whoreson."

But Isabella was no longer listening, for only one thing that Lord Montecatini had said had registered on her brain.

I poisoned the sleeping draught ye asked me to prepare for him.

Dear God. 'Twas by her hand that Giles had died. 'Twas *she* who had given him the fatal potion. Dear God.

She went crazy then, running at the Count like a madwoman, clawing at his hideously twisted face, tearing at his doublet, kicking his shins. Viciously, made unnaturally strong by her craving for the sweet poppy's nectar he had yet to give her, she pummeled his torso. Enraged by her assault, the Italian struck out at her savagely, but still, she fought on like a wild thing, forcing him back, until he was pressed up against one of the embrasures.

Then suddenly, the battle was over; and Lord Montecatini was falling . . . falling. . . .

Gasping for breath, Isabella stared down at his broken body, which lay mangled upon the jagged rocks far below. The Count was dead. She had killed him, pushed him over the battlements of Boldon-by-the-Sea; and she was glad she had done it.

Unsteadily, her head spinning, she swayed a little on her feet and realized dimly, in some dark corner of her mind, that she needed help. Like a wounded animal, she wanted the one person who loved her most in all the world, the one person who had always been there for her. She flung back her head and cried out hoarsely, a strange, pitiful little wail.

But even so, he heard it, and his heart leaped with joy in his breast at the sound.

Warrick, she had said. *Warrick*.

Unless defended, no fortress, no matter how strongly built, is impregnable; and upon learning of their Lord's death, the Count's men decided to run, escaping by the postern gate to the ship that waited for them just off the shore.

Warrick let them go. It was enough that he had managed to gain entry to the castle. It was enough that he held Isabella tightly in his arms once more.

Chapter Forty

The Moors, England, 1490

SOME THOUGHT IT WAS THE WIND THAT SOUGHED ACROSS the moors and sent the tall grass rippling, thought too it was the rain that fell from the misty twilight clouds this eve. Only Isabella knew it was not so.

'Twas the plaintive sighs of those she'd known—and loved—whispering faintly in her ear; and the tears of those long dead, who haunted her still, though Warrick had asked her earlier this day to let them go.

Alone, with her ghosts, she walked on past the cemetery, where Caerllywel was buried, and they had erected a stone for Madog, though he lay not there.

She was well now. Warrick and Emrys had made her so, though she did not know how they had lived through the terrible, long months of her gradual withdrawal from the sweet poppy's nectar that had been her bane. Only Warrick's deep love for her had allowed her to survive the horrible ordeal. He had always been her strength and her solace, as Hwyelis had known.

Hwyelis lived with them now, along with Emrys and Jocelyn. Dear Jocelyn, who had survived too, for Arthwr's sake, and was learning to love again, thanks to Sir Bevan's gentle courting of her. Isabella was certain that, in time, Jocelyn would fully recover from her fear of men. Then the maid and Sir Bevan would wed, and children would play in the courtyard of Hawkhurst.

Hawkhurst. Home.

Pausing, Isabella turned to gaze back at the fortress in the distance. There, now, Warrick would be waiting for her, lighting a candle, like a beacon, in their chamber window to guide her home.

Presently, she would go back, would run to his outstretched, loving arms, and tell him of his babe that grew, at last, within her, the first of their children, who would fill up the empty keep and make it ring again with laughter—though they would never take the places of those who had once lingered there, those whom the girl now gently bid farewell. It was time now to let them go. Isabella belonged to the living, to her husband, with whom she would forget the sorrow-filled past and look toward a future bright with the promise of joy.

From the castle ramparts, where Ragnor was now perched, came a shrill cry that sweetly pierced the silent night. The bird had returned to her, as she had somehow known he would. He was hers now, forever, just as Warrick was.

"Hurry," the hawk seemed to be calling. "Hurry home, *cariad*."

Home. Warrick.

Gathering up her skirts, Isabella began to run toward the light from Hawkhurst that shone steadily in the darkness, an unwavering flame of love.

Author's Note

Because this novel deals, in part, with the life of King Richard III of England, and because, in this book, the author has chosen to portray him in a much kinder light than that in which he is traditionally seen, she feels she owes some explanation to her readers for this departure.

Contrary to popular belief, there is no actual *proof* that Richard murdered the two boy Princes; and it is the author's own personal opinion that he did *not* do so. The case that has traditionally been made against him is rife with speculation, riddled with conflict, and, again in the author's own personal opinion, ludicrous in the extreme. She regards it as little more than Tudor propaganda, stemming primarily from the works of Sir Thomas More, based on the recollections of John Morton, Bishop of Ely, one of the men directly responsible for placing Henry Tudor on the throne and hardly an unbiased observer.

Cases equally as persuasive, if no less built on conjecture, can also be made against King Henry VII, and Henry Stafford, Duke of Buckingham, both of whom had as good, if not even better, reasons than Richard for wishing to do away with the Princes. The author personally views Buckingham as the most likely suspect and for that reason has made him the culprit of the crime (in collusion with Lady Margaret Stanley) in this novel. There is some evidence that the meeting, upon the road, between Lady Stanley and Buckingham actually did occur, and there is still much debate about what may have passed between them. Certainly, it is strange that Henry made little effort to determine the culprit(s) responsible for the murders; and if Richard had indeed slain the Princes, it would seem logical that Henry would have widely proclaimed the fact. He did not, suggesting that he either killed the Princes himself or knew who did and did not want the matter delved into too deeply.

For the reader who is interested in learning about the various cases that can be made against all three prime suspects, the author suggests *Richard the Third*, by Paul Murray Kendall (New York: W.W. Norton & Company, Inc., 1956, Appendix I, pp. 465–495), in which an excellent examination of the mystery is discussed.

There is, in addition, no evidence that Richard was a hunchback, as is popularly believed, had a withered arm, walked with a limp, or was in any other way physically deformed. None of the chroniclers of Richard's time make mention of any physical defect, and it was not until after his death that this rumor was given credence. Certainly, it is difficult to believe that in a superstitious age, such as Richard's was, he would have publicly exposed his naked body, as he did at his coronation, if he had suffered any such malformation.

There may be some actual basis for the famous Shakespearean line (in *The Life and Death of King Richard III*): "A horse! a horse! my kingdom for a horse!" Many historians believe there was indeed once a marsh upon the site of Market Bosworth and that Richard's destrier may, in reality, have floundered there during the battle. For this reason, the author included the words.

There are two other points of note that the reader may regard as fiction but that are historically accurate. King Edward IV did, in fact, view three suns in the sky prior to winning the Crown. The peculiar solar effect is known as parhelion and is produced by the formation of ice crystals in the upper atmosphere that causes the sun's halo to reflect bright images. And, strange as it may seem, a solar eclipse actually did occur on the exact day of Queen Anne's death, proof enough for the commonfolk that Richard had sinned against God in taking the Crown.

For the reader who questions why Isabella survived after contracting rabies, a disease generally thought to be fatal, the author can say only that some ancient folklore claims a cure for the illness was known during the time period in which this book is set. Whether or not such was indeed the case has yet to be discovered. However, the author has no doubt that there is much ancient knowledge that has been lost over the centuries; and for this reason, she felt justified in allowing Isabella to survive. The author would also remind her readers that there is, in addition, one rare instance of recovery from rabies on modern medical record (1971).

Lastly, the author would like very much to thank her dear friends Mary Railey, Roberta Gellis, and Janice Young Brooks, who listened to her so patiently during her writing of this novel, mulled over difficulties with her, and gave her such helpful advice. She is especially indebted to Mary for her suggestion that Isabella contract rabies, to Robbie for her suggestion that Lady Margaret Stanley act as the brains behind Buckingham, and to Janice for discussing the details as to how and when Buckingham might have committed the crime. The author would also like to thank her dear friend and editor, Fredda Isaacson, for being so patient, understanding, and encouraging when it sometimes appeared as though this book would never be finished.

REBECCA BRANDEWYNE